BETWEEN WIND AND WAVES

Samuel Harmsworth

Edited By Jessica Tucker

Copyright © 2020 Samuel Harmsworth

All rights reserved

The characters and events portrayed in this book are fictitious. Any similarity to real persons, living or dead, is coincidental and not intended by the author.

No part of this book may be reproduced, or stored in a retrieval system, or transmitted in any form or by any means, electronic, mechanical, photocopying, recording, or otherwise, without express written permission of the publisher.

Cover design by: SelfPubBookCovers.com/RLSather

CONTENTS

Title Page	1
Copyright	2
Prologue	7
Chapter 1: An Inter-dimensional Step	9
Chapter 2: Blind Meddling	20
Chapter 3: The Eldership	33
Chapter 4: Rough Seas	47
Chapter 5: Naufragium's Plight	64
Chapter 6: Limpet's Hideout	80
Chapter 7: Trawl Trauma	93
Chapter 8: Gentle Stuart	110
Chapter 9: No Escape	124
Chapter 10: Solis Occassum	142
Chapter 11: The King's Reckoning	156
Chapter 12: Torture Trouble	173
Chapter 13: Unlikely Alliances	185
Chapter 14: Clover	197
Chapter 15: The Uninhabitable Land	211
Chapter 16: Rodeo Showdown	218
Chapter 17: Sobering News	230

Chapter 18: Bold Beginnings	247
Chapter 19: The Abyssal Plain	267
Chapter 20: Delirium	277
Chapter 21: Colony Crisis	299
Chapter 22: The Jaws Of Death	318
Chapter 23: Misplaced Vengeance	335
Chapter 24: Monsters From The Sea	354
Chapter 25: The Gavoidon	374
Epilogue	387
Acknowledgements	394
About The Author	397

To my parents, Neil and Julie, who gifted me a slice of time in this busy life to indulge in following my dreams, and to my three sisters (Jess, Amy and Megan) who gave me the courage to see it through. I love you all dearly.

PART 1

Lord o' the Sea, cor blimey me,
Mighty in his day, now weak and grey,
Stories of old might warm the cold,
But t' won't put food on my table today.

Lord o' the Sea, you bested the Land,
They say you conquered with a single hand,
With t'other, took Lady Pearl as your lover,
And now the world should be yours to command.

Lord o' the Sea, what happened to thee,
So strong, so powerful and so brave,
Others may be sold on these tales of gold,
But where are the fish we crave?

Lord o' the Sea, woe is me,
My ribs are on show for all,
My baby's cries won't be calmed by these lies,
So give us some fish, you old fool!

- *A Naufragium shanty, popular among meadoweed workers*

PROLOGUE

In some insignificant corner of the universe, an ocean was awaiting death. It stretched as far as the eye could see and was as calm as a lily-pond, disturbed only by a faraway spit of land, a distant and unimportant blight, a relic of a lost battle. The ocean had long since laid claim to the planet, swamping all mainlands and leaving this rebellious mountain for no reason other than there was simply no need to conquer it; the war between sea and land was over.

Although the ocean gave the pretence of tranquillity, it was, in fact, in turmoil. Following its victory against the land, there had been a glorious time of peace where all had thrived and, besides the natural competition for resources between its population, all had been content.

Then, something unexplainable had happened. Forces from beyond had meddled with its fragile ecosystem, shaking the pillar that supported all life and cracking the very foundations of the planet. Why or who was to blame was a complete mystery. Only one thing was certain: in the last few centuries, their actions had upset the balance on the planet to the detriment and slow deterioration of all living beings.

The ocean, from the perspective of the casual observer, would appear to be similar to the ones found on Earth. This could not be further from the truth.

When travelling between dimensions or planets, or - in the most extreme cases - both, the standard advice is to write down the rules of physics at your point of departure and then swiftly throw that information into the nearest waste disposal container. In other words, forget everything you have learnt and start afresh.

Some dimensions are kind, offering no familiarity at all, and therefore the traveller almost expects the unexpected. Others are strikingly similar yet so very different, and each difference comes as a shocking, often deadly surprise. This particular dimension is such a place.

Prior research before making a shift between dimensions is paramount. Unfortunately, such a luxury was not granted to one very confused human. That human was a young, teenage boy called Luke.

CHAPTER 1: AN INTER-DIMENSIONAL STEP

With a terrific flash of blue light, Luke materialised above a seemingly endless ocean.

He hovered ever so briefly and then began to fall. In one hand he clutched a spiralled shell, a whelk, though why or where it had come from was one of the many unknowns in this extraordinary scenario; he appropriately ignored its presence and focussed on the far more immediate danger.

His descent.

He was speeding towards the ocean's surface, picking up velocity, his bright flowery trunks flapping and the wind whistling through his curly, brown hair. The surface was waiting like a pane of blue-tinted glass stretching all the way to the horizon.

As he zoomed downwards, he realised that he was in prime belly-flop position and, with no time to rearrange, all he could do was wince as the inevitable impact drew near.

He *expected* to smack brutally into the sea, submerge briefly, scrabble frantically, and then bob back to the surface. He *expected* the sting of his body colliding with a team of water particles. He *expected* his descent to come to an abrupt, uncomfortable, yet otherwise harmless, end.

That was his first mistake.

Instead, contrary to all his assumptions, he sailed

straight through.

There was no impact, no pain and no slowing of speed. If anything, his velocity simply increased. The only differences were a pleasant drop in temperature and the fact that everything he could see was tinged with blue. Otherwise his ill-fated fall continued.

Despite all this, he still attempted to swim, throwing his arms about and kicking his feet with all his might. He may as well have launched himself off a cliff and flapped in a crazed attempt to fly.

He plummeted through a small scattering of silvery fish and saw his imminent destination: a sandbank. It rose like a desert dune to greet him. A crab, directly in his path, quickened its sideways scuttle to avoid being flattened. Luke hit the ground inches away, throwing up a puff of sediment and tumbling down the hill ungracefully, flopping onto his back when the terrain finally flattened.

All the while, instinct dictated that he held what little oxygen he could within his lungs, and he did so until his body was screaming for more. In these moments, he might have continued struggling for the surface, but the impact had dazed him so much that even a futile attempt to save himself was beyond his capability.

Eventually, there was nothing for it but to open his airways to the mercy of the sea. Once again, he *expected* and, once again, he was mistaken. Instead of flooding his insides and forfeiting his life, he was able to take a shuddering and much needed breath.

As oxygen filled his blood once more, his body felt like it was waking from a coma. After a while, he could feebly move his legs. Given more time, he managed to lift his head ever so slightly and survey the immediate vicinity.

The scenery was out of focus, but he saw something that sent alarms running through his mind. A large shadow approached with the gait of a man. It appeared to walk upright on two legs and, unbelievably, held some kind of balloon. If he was not so scared, he would have laughed at the absurdity of such an idea.

Slowly but surely, the shadow-man walked closer. Eventually, all that Luke could see was a large pair of boots directly in front of his face.

'Help...' he rasped.

'Don't belong,' was what Luke heard moments before he felt a searing pain to his temple and all was lost to darkness.

***

Luke was lying down on an uncomfortable wooden floor. The sound that reached his ears was that of a crowd in the heat of an argument. Pain pounded through his head and his vision blurred sickeningly. Groaning, he attempted to sit up.

'Everyone, shut up. He's waking!' someone ordered.

A curious silence followed. As Luke leant on the curved wall behind, a strong urge to throw up hit him. His brain was trying to tell his eyes to get their act together but to no avail. He cradled his head and grumbled something incoherently.

'Gentle Stuart, my ass,' muttered the man who had quietened the mob. 'How many times did he hit him exactly?'

'The stubborn fool came to before we even reached the outskirts, John,' said a tall, thin youth with a hawk-like nose and a mop of black hair.

'How many times *Brittle*?'

'Twice,' Brittle admitted. 'And hard.'

'Won't be his last if he doesn't cooperate!' growled a new voice, rife with anger.

'Calm down, Con,' the leader warned. 'Where is Stuart anyway?'

'Gone back to his gelata fields,' Brittle answered.

'I see. His presence would have been useful, but never mind. You found him about three miles from Naufragium, you say?'

'Correct, sir. There was a strike of thunder and he fell straight from the surface.'

Luke's eyes finally began to take in the scene before him. He was behind sturdy iron bars and a presumably locked door. A large crowd peered in at his cell. The closest man, the leader, had a great, big, bushy beard and friendly, brown eyes. His face appeared speckled, but with what, Luke could not perceive.

The dingy room beyond appeared to have a familiar layout. All rotting wood and curved edges. His brain had a 'eureka' moment. A ship's hull. He was in some kind of ship.

'Wh-Where am I?' he queried, his voice quiet and feeble.

'We'll be asking the questions, boy,' John asserted, leaving no room for argument. 'What do they call you?'

Luke did not respond. He began to listlessly stare at the floor; there was sand creeping through the cracks.

CLANG!

Someone hit the iron bars with a metal fork.

'I said,' repeated the man haughtily, 'what do they call you?'

Luke pondered this for a while, taking a trip down memory lane to the very beginning. This was not a long trip at all, more like a brief stroll. He last remembered falling. He had fallen from the sky, through water and straight to the seabed. Logically, that meant he was still underwater. Yes, he thought, still underwater. Everything had a clear, blue filter, the entire surface of his skin felt pleasantly cool and his vision wobbled ever so slightly, as if the world was being reflected by a distorted mirror.

'Don't make me ask again,' growled John.

'I'm... underwater.'

'Yes,' John huffed. 'You're underwater. But that's not what I asked. Unless you're trying to tell me that's your name, eh? Mr Underwater?'

Luke shook his head. Try as he might, he just didn't know. He racked his brains, but ended up clueless all the same. There was nothing before 'the fall'. Absolutely *nothing*. His memory was in tatters like pages of a beloved book ripped out by the wind and sent floating out of reach.

'I don't know,' he answered reluctantly.

'You don't know?'

Luke nodded miserably.

'Where are you from?' John persisted, clearly not convinced. 'What are you doing here?'

'I don't know,' Luke replied again.

A man, whose bright ginger hair had been wrapped into a ponytail with a band of seaweed, rushed forward eagerly.

'Are yous saying,' the newcomer said, pointing at Luke, 'that yous don't have a name?'

The whole room seemed to let out a collective groan.

'I might have had one, once.'

The man cricked his joints as if preparing for an almighty feat before declaring proudly 'I'm Whalefin, the town namer, see? So if yous aren't going to give us a name, I'll make one up for you!'

Luke nodded feebly, feeling pretty sorry for himself.

'Hmm, let's see now,' said Whalefin contemplatively. 'What's fitting for you? You're a stranger, most likely from the surface and almost certainly our enemy. And you're new, so in naming terms, you're basically a newborn. Hmmmmm. How about Spongebucket? No that won't do.' He waved dismissively. 'Sanddeck? Shellface?'

The crowd was sniggering now.

'I've got it!' said Whalefin, snapping his fingers and holding his arms aloft. 'You shall hence be known as *Lugworm*!'

This announcement was met with chortles, giggles and general outbursts of that nature.

'Enough!' demanded John. 'Do none of you realise the gravity of this situation?'

There were more than a few shameful faces and Whalefin receded guiltily into the crowd. Luke, however, heard the word *gravity* and suddenly felt very odd indeed. If he were underwater, why was he not floating? Surely he should be swimming, bounding around, or at the very least *drowning*.

The fact that he wasn't was quite frankly extraordinary. He could not remember why it was extraordinary, but in his gut he felt that something was wrong. Very, very wrong.

'We have in our midst,' John continued, 'someone who could be from the surface and yet, they live. In all of our history, this has never happened.'

'Well?' questioned a scarred, bald, beast of a man, who looked like a kettle on the brink of boiling. 'Are you? Are you from the surface?'

Luke must have looked nonplussed because John intervened.

'Con, the boy is clearly still suffering from his knock to the head.'

'You know, the surface?' Con continued, waving his hands about erratically. 'Air? Mountains? Greedy fish-stealing surface-dwellers? Four-legged land creatures with giant udders? Murdering, good-for-nothing men who wreck the seabed and sweep through our lives causing havoc and mayhem without a single thought?'

Luke shuffled away. Something about the man was unnerving.

'Well?'

'I don't...' Luke started, but then decided to change tact. He had no recollection of the surface, but it did seem awfully strange that he was underwater. 'Maybe?'

'*Maybe?* Maybe? MAYBE?' Con ended on a roar, a frown crinkling the vicious scar that crawled down half of his face. Luke started to wish he'd stuck to his standard answer. 'So let me get this straight. You're clearly not one of us; you've not been touched by the sea at all. You arrive here and you claim to know next to nothing. And now, despite hiding ourselves away from the land dwellers for centuries, you've stumbled across our town, the lifeblood of our entire community, right at a time when our competition with the surface for food is at its most fierce?'

There was a pause in which perhaps Luke was supposed

to retort.

'I think,' said Con with a strange half-grin half-grimace, 'we have here a spy!'

This declaration caused chaos.

'Surface scum!' a woman cried out.

'He knows too much!' growled a wizened old man.

'But he's just a boy,' someone said.

'That's just a ploy!' another replied, before realising they'd accidentally rhymed and changing their statement. 'That's just a ruse!'

Con gripped John's shoulder. 'This reeks of a surface scum plot. I say, we end his life here and now!' he roared to the approval of the mob behind.

John slapped off Con's grip, mustered all the leadership skills he'd ever learned since becoming the town mayor, and let out a long, drawn-out 'Siilllenncceeee!'

His experience served him well - the crowd outbreak was abated.

'If he is from the surface,' he said, expertly lowering his voice so that everyone had to strain their ears to hear him, 'does it not strike you as strange that he can breathe down here?' He paused for a half-beat, not actually allowing enough time for anyone to answer his rhetorical question. 'Here's what I think. I think that if he was from the surface, he'd have drowned long before now. I think he's been hit too hard to be of any use to us tonight. I think we should give him time, get to know him, he's not going anywhere after all. I think his arrival here is mysterious indeed. We need to figure it all out *before* we act, not after.'

There was a sea of nods and general agreement all round.

'Look, it's getting late,' John reasoned, relaxing just a little. 'Let us continue this meeting on the morrow. Perhaps Lugworm here will be of more use after some rest.'

'Hear, hear,' Whalefin added.

'He does look awfully dazed,' someone admitted.

And with that, the tide was turned. One by one, people

started making their way towards a rusty ladder at the back of the hull, clambering upwards and disappearing through a trapdoor in the ceiling. John breathed a sigh of relief, spewing a cloud of bubbles, as the crowd slowly dissipated.

'A challenge!' demanded Con, stopping the retreating crowd in their tracks.

John winced.

'A challenge!' Con repeated through gritted teeth. He was rooted to the spot, fists clenched. 'The challenge of the Elder Bell!'

More than a few townsmen had turned back and were viewing the spectacle with curiosity.

'Now, now,' John raised both his hands in what he thought was a calming manner. 'We don't need to -'

'Yes we do,' Con grated. 'That boy invaded our territory - he *needs* to prove himself. Not to mention, we'll finally get some proper answers, one way or another.'

'He's more likely to die,' John retorted. 'Then we will have gained nothing.'

'If he dies,' Con shrugged, 'it'll be case closed and we can get on with our lives.'

'It's never been done. It's impossible!' John said, but it was too late.

'I've never heard the bell ring...' pondered Brittle with wonder while resting one foot on the lowest ladder rung.

'Oh, it was fantastic!' someone gushed, before declaring. 'Weddings haven't been the same without them!'

'You could hear it for miles!' said another.

John gave an almighty sigh, and then accepted defeat.

'Very well,' said John, trying his best not to sound deflated. 'Tomorrow we test Lugworm with the challenge of the Elder Bell! Now, get out of my sight. It's getting late and this meeting has gone on long enough.'

People whooped, eyes were filled with a strange mixture of bloodthirst and hope, and there was a general surge of excitement as this time people left the hull for good.

Eventually the buzz of chatter faded, leaving only Luke, huddled in his cell, and John, pacing up and down with a thoughtful frown.

John paused and inspected his new prisoner. A very strange boy indeed, he thought. Not strange in the obvious sense; from afar he'd look like any other kid. He had a chestnut mess of hair, green eyes and a lack of muscle that could only come from a soft life of luxury.

What disturbed John was twofold. Firstly, the boy was yet to be marked by the sea. Normally, by his age, the sea would have claimed him somehow. A bit of sponge behind the ear, for example, some coral clinging to the arch of his neck, a family of clownfish nestled in his hair.

But this boy had nothing - his skin was smooth and unblemished.

Then there was his otherworldly attire. His shorts were made of some strange material he'd never seen before, decorated with colours so vibrant that they rivalled the town's best coral reefs.

'Are those...' the boy asked, somewhat sheepishly, disrupting John's deep thought, 'barnacles?'

John's naturally reached up to his own speckled face to prod at the rocky pearl-white barnacles that had claimed it as their home when he was merely five years of age.

'You find them strange?' John replied.

'I think so,' said Luke.

'Then you've got a lot to learn, boy. There are many women in town who consider these my best feature,' he chuckled to himself, then turned grave. 'You'd best get some rest, you've got a big day tomorrow.'

Luke could only stare as John pivoted and disappeared up the ladder.

'Tomorrow,' John shouted from a hatch at the ladder's peak. 'You face the challenge of the Elder Bell!'

There was a crash as the hatchway was shut tight and all

light was snuffed out.

***

In the entire extended universe, with all its many parallel dimensions, only one point five beings knew what was going on. The one comprised of a young Gazoid by the name of Garth.

Though roughly humanoid in shape, that is where the similarities ended: his face was a shocking display of red and yellow markings, his feet and hands were webbed and his tongue was thrice as long. He also had a thin stretch of skin that hung down from his wrist and attached to his hip on each side of his body. There was a common misconception that his species could fly, but in reality, these flaps were only suitable for gliding. Unfortunately, Garth had not had the chance to test this out due to one crucial problem – he was a coward. As a result, his gliding flaps had become saggy with disuse.

Aside from Garth, there was another who knew why Luke had suddenly found himself on an alien planet in a collapsing dimension with a severe case of amnesia: The PennDrive2000.

As many intelligent species do, the Gazoids had invented artificial intelligence in a matter of weeks after discovering 'the wheel'. They had quickly learnt an invaluable lesson - as robots become cleverer, they inevitably become more tenacious and rather difficult to put up with. The Gazoids had made the wise choice of dumbing down their computers to a more bearable I.Q., but one company decided to sell cheaper, technically superior but more mischievous, PennDrive2000s, or *Penns* as some hipster Gazoids had come to call them. The running joke was that the term Penn was in fact short for Penn-dragon, owing to the unreliable and dangerous nature lurking within their programming.

'You are in soooo much trouble,' said the PennDrive2000 with undisguised glee. 'Can you even begin to calculate how much they cost?'

Garth was staring, mouth slightly ajar and footlong tongue lolling out uncontrollably, at the molten remains of a precious gem encased in a thick glass cabinet.

Penn was right, of course. He was in *so* much trouble.

CHAPTER 2: BLIND MEDDLING

It had all started, as many adventures do, with a potent mix of curiosity and boredom. The boredom had originated from the strict instructions to tidy his room. These had come from his supervisor - a rather attractive but disappointingly mundane, female Gazoid employed to look after him while his mother glided off to places unknown.

Tidying his room was no easy feat; the 'mess' comprised of a tangled mass of wires from his favourite game consoles, a half-drunk can of Slarg complete with an impressive amount of colourful mould and figurines scattered across the floor from his favourite holofilm series - *Galaxy Battles*. He preferred the term 'organised chaos' to 'mess'. As a result, he had opted for grabbing a mid-morning snack instead. Health fanatics on his planet were known to swoop around feasting on live insects, but Garth had developed the taste for a more available source of nourishment - the fridge.

It was half-way between his room and the kitchen that he had noticed something which made any thoughts of food disappear from his mind. His mother's door was *open*. This astonished Garth for a number of reasons. Firstly, his mother was currently away which meant that the area was *completely* unguarded. Secondly, the expression 'door', though applicable, did not fully portray the nature of its entrance. It was, in fact, similar to one that would be expected to lead to a bank vault and stood out like a sore thumb. Thirdly, and most exciting of all, was the fact that her job was an absolute mystery and took place almost entirely within that room. Garth had finally been given a chance to snoop around and scavenge some answers.

Before his supervisor came along and ruined this golden opportunity, he shot in and heaved the hulk of metal shut. The door whirred and clicked, locking automatically behind him and throwing him into darkness. By scrabbling around, he found a lever-like object and gave it a pull. Ceiling lights had flickered on with a slowness that could only be described as tantalising.

Garth found himself in a fairly cosy area, no bigger than his own bedroom. The contents, however, were wildly different. Wires, some as thick as hose pipes, spilled down each of the four walls and congregated at a curious glass cabinet in the room's centre. As if they were curtains, he curiously parted the wires to find that each of the walls beneath were green and permeated with gold lines. There were purposeful trinkets protruding here and there: heatsinks, fans, chips and graphics cards. Garth, who considered himself a bit of a brainbox, knew that he was standing in the belly of a very powerful computer - *but what was it for?*

Rushing forward, he pressed his face against the glass of the cabinet. Encased within was a diamond-like rock about the size of a clenched fist, as black as space and polished to perfection. It was held in suspension by a silver claw. At each top corner, a gun aimed inwards, seemingly pointing at the pretty gem. Satisfied with his inspection, Garth moved on, leaving behind a misty smudge.

In a nest of wires was unmistakably where his mother carried out her job. There was a large black chair, a panel of buttons and, beyond, an almost comically small screen. Everything appeared to be turned off.

'All these gizmos to power a screen no bigger than a cereal box,' he mumbled to himself.

That was when the room came alive. The screen flickered white, the ceiling lights dimmed, and the aforementioned panel glowed a curious blue.

'My screen may not be big, but you should see what I can do,' replied a voice, caught between feminine and robotic, frightening Garth so much that he almost shed his fourth layer of skin prematurely. 'Come, take a seat.'

Garth shook off his initial fear and bounded onto his mother's chair, wiggling with delight.

'You can talk!'

'Evidently,' came a very dry response.

'What should I call you?'

'Call me...' the voice paused, purely for dramatic affect as this hardly took any processing power at all. 'Penn.'

Had Garth questioned what 'Penn' was short for, he may have stopped the following debacle, but retrospect is a fine thing. Instead, he was distracted by a bulbous, green light on the panel that seemed to lighten and dim with Penn's voice as she spoke.

'Are you bored, Garth?'

'How do you know my name?'

'Oh, your mother did drone on,' Penn replied before quickly returning to her preferred topic of conversation. 'Would you like to play a game?'

This question took Garth completely off guard. He did like games though.

'Ummm,' he said hesitantly. 'Alright.'

'Brilliant!' said Penn eagerly. 'Now put on that helmet.'

Garth looked around nonplussed.

'It's attached to the chair,' Penn directed.

Sure enough, there was a wire which followed out from the left arm of the chair. As he reeled it in, half a metre worth of wire accumulated on his lap. When he came to the end, he found his treasure; the most high-tech piece of headgear he had ever witnessed. It was chalky white and had a symbol on its brow – the letter 'D' with an arrow through it. There were two slits on top for his elf-like ears, a visor and a microphone that, when worn, would descend to about mouth height.

'Well, what are you waiting for?' pushed Penn. 'Put it on.'

His meticulous inspection came to an abrupt end and he carefully placed it on his head. As for the screen in front of him, two pixelated words appeared.

'Penn...What is this?'

'What does it look like?' she replied. 'It's a game, of course.' She let out a strange metallic bubbling noise that was almost, but not quite, entirely unlike a giggle. 'Come on, let's explore. You have to choose a dimension now.'

A simple list appeared on the screen, each bullet point consisted of the word 'dimension' followed by a complex, seemingly random, series of numbers. All in all, it meant absolutely nothing to Garth.

'Which one should I pick?'

'Just choose one,' she replied. 'Live a little.'

There was one list of numbers that seemed to stand out from the rest, in a subtle, nonchalant fashion. Perhaps they were in a slightly larger font, or their colours were more vibrant. Regardless, Garth was drawn to them. 'How about... Dimension 4542?'

'Interesting choice,' said Penn. 'There's only one planet in this one that has any form of life.'

The screen now displayed the name of a planet.

'Eeeee-errr--ffff?' Garth mispronounced.

'Earth,' Penn confirmed.

And with that, the screen flicked to showing a rather attractive little planet; it was a swirling mix of blue and green with a sparse wispy white coating. Around it were twinkling stars and hanging nearby as if enraptured by the scene before it, was a relatively small sphere of grey rock.

'Whoa,' Garth gushed.

'Where shall we go?'

'Anywhere,' Garth said quietly, amazed by the graphics before him.

The screen spun around Earth and then started zooming in on a particular green blob. The stars and the grey rock were quickly engulfed by the planet's vibrant colours. The translucent covering shot by with ease and the visual narrowed in on where the edge of green met the blue.

In moments, Garth watched over a beach from a bird's eye view. It briefly appeared that the scene before him was entirely frozen in time. On closer inspection, the sea was moving, albeit in a lethargic way, flopping clumsily onto the land, the clouds were drifting as if through almost-dry cement and a strange feathered creature was beating its wings with a speed that would have had it plummeting to the ground in real time.

'Why is everything so... slow?' he queried

'Time difference,' said Penn lazily. 'Now, choose your hero.'

For the first time, Garth noticed the specimens that populated the beach. They had the standard features; two eyes, two arms and two legs. However, sprouts of plant grew from their heads, stubby, rounded ears stuck out from either side, and where Garth had webbing, these beings had odd gaps. They also had no wing-flaps; bound to the ground, he reckoned. One of the smaller ones was glaring intensely at the rippling blue blob. Maybe, like Garth, it was baffled by its crazy display.

'That one', Garth commanded, and then wondered how to specify what he meant. Somehow, Penn already knew.

'Really?' she said. 'He doesn't look like much.'

'I like him,' Garth shrugged.

'Oh, very well. One last thing, where shall we transport him?'

The screen flickered and showed another list titled as 'broken dimensions', the beach scene was cruelly snatched away. Once again, one list of numbers seemed to shout out at him, but if anyone had asked him why, he would not have been able to explain.

'Dimension 1303,' said Garth flippantly, desperately wishing the tedious list would go away.

Thankfully the screen snapped back and he could see the beach in all its glory; the speckled sand, the rolling water and a line of jagged cliffs that appeared to be trying to close off the bay in a futile one-armed hug.

'Interesting choice. This might feel a tad on the strange side,' Penn laughed.

'What might feel strange?' mumbled Garth.

'This!'

He felt a tingling sensation and then something awfully bizarre happened.

Suddenly, Garth was floating above the beach. He could feel the strong gust of sea air; hear the crash of water on land. The previous slow motion of events disappeared with a lurch; the sea pounded the beach mercilessly, the winged creature swiftly flew out of sight and even the statue-like two-legged beings started milling around doing nothing in particular.

Garth wasn't actually *there*. The weight of the helmet still strained his neck, the curve of the arms of his mother's chair could still be felt reassuringly under his webbed hands.

'Don't just float, silly,' taunted Penn. Her voice had no direction, as if she was speaking directly into his mind. 'Anchor yourself!'

'And how do I do that?' retorted Garth testily.

'Find something,' she instructed. 'Imagine feeling what it feels, imagine where it came from, imagine *being* it - that is the key to forming a connection.' For a moment, the playfulness was gone from her voice, and then it was back. 'I doubt it'll do anything, it takes years of training, but... entertain me.'

Had she had a physical form, Garth had no doubt that

she'd have been smirking. It only made him more determined to prove her wrong.

He willed himself closer to the ground and slowly, but surely, he crawled through the treacle-like air to where his hero was sitting.

'Oh very good,' encouraged Penn. 'You're exceeding my expectations already.'

Now that he was closer, he could see that Penn was right; his chosen hero was a rather small, pathetic being. Wearing only a pair of brightly coloured, flowery trunks, it was clear that there was nothing special about him: a mass of curls, a small button nose and a sour face that emanated distaste. His slight and weedy figure was planted in the sand, letting the water lap against his pale, unwebbed feet. He was frowning and pouting as if in the midst of a tantrum. His glare passed right through Garth and pierced the distant horizon.

Garth tried to remember what Penn had said.

Find something. Imagine being it.

There was a large, attractive shell half buried in the sand only a couple of steps away from his hero.

'Very good,' Penn approved.

Garth tried to imagine the rough texture of its exterior, the silky sand grains that coated its underside, the slight dampness of the sea yet to dry from the receding tide.

Then it happened.

He suddenly knew the shell had been vacant for a span of weeks, discarded by a hermit crab that had outgrown its home. He knew that it had travelled far and wide, simply by being dragged around by turbulent currents. He knew that its original owner was long gone, but the shell's story had continued. Garth could feel every layer of material that made up its spiral.

'You're glowing,' Penn noted. 'It's a little amateur, but it's a start.'

She was right. The shell, or Garth, or both, had taken on a blue hue and it was only a matter of time before it caught the attention of the curious boy nearby. He scrambled closer and naturally pilfered the shell from the sand's embrace. It was an odd sensation, for Garth, to be lifted from the ground, shaken around and handled.

'You've done it,' gasped Penn incredulously. 'We have direct contact, which means we can transport him!'

It took an awful amount of effort for Garth to remember how to use his own mouth.

'But what are we actually *doing*?'

'Never you mind,' Penn snapped. 'Just press the big red button and let the adventure begin!'

Suddenly, Garth was snapped away from the shell. He was rocketed away from the beach and shoved back into his tired, weary body. The screen was pitch-black and there was a loud whooshing sound. Though he had been playing the game for a matter of minutes, some part of his body clock knew that countless hours had passed. Yawning, he peeled off the helmet in time to see...

A large red button.

It rose tantalizingly from some hidden recess, shining bright, upon a pillar of metal. Protecting it was a hinged half-bubble of glass which swung open. It glowed temptingly in Garth's face.

'What are you waiting for?' prodded Penn.

Garth was hesitant. Something did not seem quite right.

'Don't you want to know what your mother does in this room?' Penn questioned. 'Don't you want *answers*?'

She made a good point. That effect of curiosity, with the looming threat of boredom if he turned back now, allowed him to reach a firm decision.

'Okay, let's do this!' Garth shouted, slapping a webbed hand on to the button and pressing down with all his might.

Penn let out a harsh noise, almost like a cackle.

From directly behind him, Garth heard a loud pulsating drone that shook his nerves. Swivelling around reluctantly, he saw that the glass cage had become a hive of activity. Erratic orange lightning now fired from the guns towards the central chunk of rock. Where these rays made contact, the gem heated to an angry red. Garth frantically moved the chair so that its back was acting as a shield. Scared though he was, he could not resist peeking over the top.

'Turn it off!' Garth cried, already feeling severe regret.

'That is not possible, I'm afraid,' said Penn with undisguised smugness.

She was hardly audible over the increasing noise. The claw that held the rock began to rotate, amplifying the crash of lightning. Occasionally a fiery spark would shoot off, but luckily the turmoil seemed to be contained within the cabinet. This was little reassurance. Garth clutched the back of the chair and gritted his teeth. The rock twirled and the frequency of the drone was boosted to a gratingly high pitch.

'Shut it down!' demanded Garth.

'It's too late.'

'Just make it happen!' he insisted.

'We're past the point of no return,' said Penn gleefully.

Faster and faster the rock span, becoming a molten blur. Garth shoved his hands over his protruding ears, but to no avail. The sparks were so abundant now that he could hardly make out the rock. At the penultimate point, the glass cage looked to be a whirlwind of light with a red glow in the eye of the storm.

'Shut it down, shut it down, shut it down...,' Garth chanted, wild with panic.

Next, a strike of thunder shook the room that made the other sounds seem a mere whisper by comparison. He whimpered with fright and ducked down. Then, without further ado, it stopped. All was quiet except for the background hum of the computer. Gradually, he lifted his head above the back of the chair and saw that the rock had been obliterated. Its smoking remains lay scattered at the base of the cabinet and the claw, now empty, had slowed to a stop. The guns no longer spouted lightning; it was over.

A trap door slid open, removing the majority of the debris had been left behind.

'Dimension Shift successful,' Penn announced happily.

***

Garth stared, speechless at the molten remains of that gem. The dimension shift might be over, but his problems had only just begun.

'You are in sooooo much trouble,' repeated Penn for the thousandth time.

'I know!' snapped Garth, already feeling that sinking regret that only comes post-mischief, but pre-repercussions.

'Do you?' she said. 'Do you actually know just how much trouble you're in?'

Garth did not. And he found he did not have any urge to find out. Right now, he wanted to escape this room and bury his head in the deepest, darkest hole he could find.

'I'll show you,' offered Penn and, uninvited, started to play an instructional video.

The screen changed to a blank white void. He saw a male Gazoid walk across the monitor and stare in his direction. He was well-dressed, handsome and muscular to the point of intimidation. His wing flaps, meanwhile, were taut from regular gliding. Pasted on his face was a welcoming smile, an expression that seemed rusty with disuse. When he spoke, his voice had a gravity which denied anyone to ignore him.

'My name is Colonel Zinc Cougar. Pay attention to what I have to say as it could be the advice that stops you from losing your job. You might as well get comfortable because this is going to take some explanation.

'We face an environmental problem at a multi-universe scale. Entire dimensions are shutting down. Broken dimensions are on a one-way road to destruction and it's your job to prevent this from happening. They are kept open by the amount of life forms within. If this drops dangerously low, dimensions just seem to give up and collapse.

'The grave fact is, we are losing more dimensions and at a faster rate than ever before. Last year, four collapsed and we only managed to save one! This. Is. Not. Good. Enough.

He paused his shouting and the screen zoomed in on his face.

'It is only a matter of time before it is our own dimension at stake,' he continued in a somewhat more quiet voice. 'Clearly we cannot go public with this information. Everything we do is absolutely top secret. Tell nobody. No friends, no colleagues and no family. Nobody is an exception. If this gets out, all hell will break loose.

'If you are listening to this video, you should already know the tasks ahead,' he resumed his bellowing, the screen retreating to a safe distance. 'Our experiments have shown that if the right people are moved from a healthy dimension to a broken one, they can make all the difference. In a nutshell, this is your job.

'Firstly, seek out the right person. This could take days, weeks or years of research. Once you've found someone who could save a dimension, you must establish contact and shift them.

'Your job does not end there. No no, you must guide them and ensure that they carry out whatever they must. When they have saved a dimension, you will be informed and you can start the process again.

'Now some people in the little department of human resources seem to think that this job is too stressful.'

He all but spat with contempt.

'That's why you have something that feels like and looks like a game. It's to stop you getting tense about the magnitude of what you have to do.

'I disagree. This job is *not* to be taken lightly. We can't have you shifting people across dimensions willy nilly. The Quasar Gems that make Dimension Shifts possible are more expensive and rare than you could possibly imagine. We only issue them when they're deserved. Save a dimension and one will be delivered straight to your Dimension Shift cabinet. Shift the wrong person to the wrong dimension and your job will be sacrificed *without* delay.

'One last thing, we can't afford to spend a Quasar Gem shifting someone back to their home dimension. They must understand that it is a journey without return.'

'So that's it,' he said, clapping his hands together to indicate the end of his speech. 'If it sounds simple, it ain't. If you think it will be easy, it won't be. But rest assured, each and every one of you has been chosen for your job. The universe as you know it depends upon you making the right choices. Save enough dimensions and we can ensure our future. It's all down to you, the crummy computer installed on this program, and the poor souls you choose to carry out your master plans.

'We're all counting on you.'

He pointed at where Garth sat and then vanished.

'Not good news, is it?' surmised Penn sweetly.

Garth did not reply. He was dumbstruck by the sheer extent of his troubles. If he did not save this dimension, his mother would lose her job. The alien who was going to help was probably already dead and, on top of all this, by now his supervisor would be wondering where he was. All these problems needed solving.

A surge of annoyance, directed mainly at Penn, rose from within, but then was quenched by an overwhelming tiredness.

'Penn..' Garth yawned.

'Yes my little mischief maker?'

'I don't feel so good.'

'Hardly surprising. Messing with other dimensions is not easy, especially for someone so unpractised. The chances of you being able to do what you did were ridiculously slim. The fact that you are still conscious truly takes the biscuit.'

Her only response was the sound of Garth's loud snores. He was sprawled over his mother's chair with his wing flaps wrapped around himself as a makeshift duvet.

'Honestly,' Penn huffed. 'You try paying someone a compliment and it just falls on deaf ears.'

Garth slept, Penn planned and somewhere far away, in a measurement of distance hardly comprehensible, Luke stirred as light entered his underwater cell.

CHAPTER 3: THE ELDERSHIP

Luke awoke moments before the hatch was swung open. He was a little groggy, and extremely hungry, but his head felt slightly better. There was a shell, a whelk in fact, lying on the sandy floor of his cell that he had not noticed before. Something about it was strangely familiar so he scooped it up and shoved it into his trunk pocket.

'Wake up, Lugworm!' came John's gruff voice.

Luke raised his eyes from the cell floor and saw a pair of sturdy boots making their way down the ladder. Before long, John was standing at the cell bars holding a large, rusty key. He was quickly followed by the scarred, bald man from the night before.

'It's time,' John muttered gravely.

'Can't I have some food first?' Luke asked hopefully. Wherever he had come from, his body was used to regular meals and now he was suffering.

'These are hard times,' John winced. 'You'll be fed after you've finished.'

'Besides,' Con piped up, smiling nastily. 'There's no point feeding a dead man walking.'

'Con,' John growled. 'That's enough already. I think he's spooked enough.'

There was neither agreement nor retaliation from Con, just a hard stare. John blew out a deep breath and started to unlock the cell. 'Lugworm, face us and keep your hands where we can see them.'

Luke did as he was told. He heard the door unlocking followed by a creak as it swung open. 'For this part, your hands will remain free. We need to get you up that ladder which would be tricky without them. There are two of us. I will go first, then you, and then Con will follow. If you try anything funny, Con will be ready with Tooth.'

Con waved about a curved scimitar with a wrap of leather around the handle. Luke flinched as the weapon came uncomfortably close to his face, allowing him to see that it was well-used and freshly sharpened. He gulped.

'Trying to escape will not go well for you,' John reiterated unnecessarily and then turned sharply. 'Let's go!'

Nobody spoke a word as Luke followed John out of the prison cell and to the left. The ladder had a thick coat of orange rust and looked ancient. It was not very tall, but Luke was glad for the use of his hands. All the while, he was painfully aware of Con watching his every move like a hawk.

At the top, he popped his head into a surprisingly cosy room. In the centre, there was a large, oak table surrounded by old chests for seating. Spread out on its surface were a jumble of cutlery and an old-fashioned tankard. The decaying walls were prettily decorated with broken plates painted with simple patterns. Sea life permeated the room, adding to its raw splendour. Anemones flourished in one of the corners like a gathering of cherry tomatoes. Limpets dotted the walls, grazing on green splodges. Beyond the table was half a steering wheel – this ship had not moved for a very long time. Every nook and cranny gave the sense that this was someone's home.

How different it was to the crumbling prison below! As he scrambled off the ladder, Luke's amazement must have shown on his face.

'Like it? This is my humble abode,' John said with pride.

Before he could respond, Con caught up and business resumed.

'We are going to tie your hands now,' the bearded man said gently.

Con grabbed some rope from one of the chests and proceeded to bind Luke's wrists behind his back. It was quickly and professionally done, although he reckoned it was far tighter than needed. Either way, he knew that if he tried to struggle free, it would only be a waste of energy.

'Good. Now we are going to blindfold you.'

On John's instruction, something slimy, presumably seaweed, was wrapped over his eyes, completely obscuring his view. Like a candle blown out, the warm view of John's home was smothered out of existence.

'It's about a mile walk to the eldership. People are gathering there as we speak. I'd advise you to keep quiet until spoken to by either myself or Con. The town people are afraid and you don't want to antagonise them.' He paused to let his words take root. 'Okay, here we go.'

Luke heard a heavy door grinding open and was given a rough shove forward. He stumbled onto groaning floorboards which must have made up the ship's deck. A firm hand on his right shoulder guided him on a windy, disorientating path. Soon he felt that he was going down a steep decline and eventually his feet touched down onto sand. Both of his guides were quiet and, at first, the only sound was the slightest sloshing of the sea surface from far above.

Shortly, however, the hum of a crowd seeped at them from all directions. As they walked, it increased to a buzz of excitement. Underfoot, the soft sand switched abruptly to what could have been a cobblestone street. Even blindfolded, Luke thought that it seemed out of place. As he trudged onwards, the audible footsteps of John's boots were always before him, while Con's iron grip on his person remained sturdy. Before long, individual snippets of dialogue could be extracted from the chaos.

'Surface scum!' a woman jeered.

'Fish sticks! Get your fish sticks here. A fresh snack for the show!' a man bellowed to Luke's right.

'You don't belong here. And now you'll *never* leave!'

someone sneered from somewhat closer.

These comments did not lessen Luke's nerves. He could now hear distorted conversation all around. They must be in a river of people, he thought, all flowing to the same place.

'There's some stairs here,' warned John, perhaps a bit late.

A surprise step tripped Luke to his knees. Con yanked him up by his ear and he let out a yelp of pain. Someone guffawed.

They continued up slowly. Luke tried to count the steps but lost his train of thought beyond twenty-five. By the time the ground levelled out, the noise had increased to an overwhelming volume. A brief slope led him onto the familiar texture of wooden floorboards. Another deck.

'Hurry up!' someone shouted. 'Seaweed grows faster than this!'

There was a ripple of laughter.

'Are you ready, Lugworm?' John asked, ignoring the rabble.

'How can he be?' Con scoffed. 'He has no idea what's coming!'

John removed Luke's blindfold, while Con released his hands.

'Here's what you have to do.'

John looked at him apologetically.

'Take that rope and –'

'Climb the mast and attach the rope to the bell,' Luke finished. It had not taken a second for him to see the coil of rope and a mast the size of a tree trunk, and piece together clues from the night before, allowing him to bluff knowing the entire challenge. By the way that Con's smug grin dropped into a face of astonishment, he knew that his guess had been correct.

'But, how did you know?' the man spluttered.

Luke shrugged nonchalantly.

'Aren't you full of surprises,' said John, eyes twinkling.

'No matter. Do you know any knots?'

Luke thought through his somewhat stunted memory and found that he had a rudimentary knowledge of knots. Enough to get him by anyway. It only made him wonder more about where he'd come from.

Luke nodded slowly.

'Good, I'm going to tie the rope into a loop and put it over your shoulder. That way you'll have both hands free. There's more than enough rope to get you to the bell and back. Luckily, the main mast has metal rungs on so it's not much different than climbing a ladder.'

'A rusty, unstable ladder,' Con added. 'And if you fall, you'll make a mess of our favourite deck.'

It dawned on Luke that, wherever he had found himself, he could not swim or float. In fact, if he slipped from high enough, he would land on the deck with a splat. It would be certain death.

John ignored the interruption and drew near, whispering to Luke confidentially. 'Look Lugworm, the ladder is only half the challenge. When our people settled here, the bell and rope were already in place. Rather convenient, really. Since then, the rope has rotted and fallen away. As our kind cannot breathe above the surface, nobody has managed to replace it. People have tried and failed. If you get as far as the surface and find that, like us, the air above is toxic, then come back down. There's no point you dying pointlessly. Do you understand?'

'Yes.'

'Hold on a second. I'll get the rope.'

While John stooped to gather the equipment, Luke finally had the chance to take stock of his surroundings. They were standing on the deck of a grand tall ship with three masts, each one thick and sturdy. At the bow and stern were large pillars of rock between which the ship was wedged. A spiral of rough steps had been carved into the face of each one and, even now, a trickle of people was making its way up to the peak. The 'Eldership', as John called it, must have been the highest point around town. From here, Luke could look out across Naufragium in its entirety.

Below was a forest of masts that stretched as far as the eye could see. Some were erect, pointing towards the surface, while others were at an angle and gave the appearance of being locked in a sword fight with their neighbour. All of them had been stripped of any sign of a sail, leaving behind a fleshless ship skeleton. Each one led down to a crooked deck in varying states of disrepair. Luke could imagine them on the surface, sails billowing against the blitz of the wind. Now, however, they had become the home of those on the seabed. Naufragium, he realised, was a town of shipwrecks.

In the murky distance, he could see the shadows of lurking fish. They were merely a scattering of shrapnel, their finer details lost to the ocean gloom. Never before had Luke witnessed such a blend of human and sea life. He yearned to walk around, to explore. The whole town was one unique rock pool and his eyes were the net, striving to capture every moment.

'Climb the mast already!' a woman screeched.

Reality came crashing down. He was a freak and a prisoner. The only reason the crowd had come to watch was to see him fail. They thirsted for his blood. For the first time that day, he sized up the mob that surrounded him. A select bunch, maybe thirty, had gathered upon the eldership's deck and formed a ring around the main mast. Beneath its suspended hull, however, was a crowd so numerous that any estimation of their number would have been pointless. Expectant faces spilled out across the sand, filling gaps between the wrecks. The thickest crowd pumped along the broad cobblestone street that meandered through town and snaked to realms unknown.

'Don't forget to scream when you fall!'

Another bout of abuse reached Luke's ears. Attached to the right side of the eldership, he noticed a monstrous jellyfish-like creature. Its body was a translucent purple and it possessed no discernible eyes or mouth. Dark tentacles grew from this beating mass of jelly, drifting threateningly in the ocean blue. Each time the body throbbed, the tentacles followed suit. Had it been free, it would have no doubt bobbed away. Instead, a string extended from its nest of tentacles and anchored the creature to the deck. It was beautiful in an outlandish way.

The privileged people who stood on the eldership were not a pretty sight. Their faces were a mixture of anger, fear and disgust. Luke tried his best to avoid looking at them. They were all scantily clad with most of the men only wearing scruffy shorts. The women, meanwhile, used old clothes, shells, seaweed and string to achieve decent coverage. Every one of them was marked by the sea in some shape or form. A limpet here, coral growing there. He wondered how strange his smooth unblemished skin must seem.

'Here you go, Lugworm.'

John handed over the rope. As if in a daze, Luke looped it over his shoulder and slowly confronted the trial at hand. Of the eldership's three masts, the one he was to climb was by far the tallest. It actually extended beyond the surface, while the other two were entirely submerged.

'It's a long way to go,' John stated.

Luke dealt him a sour look. The bearded man managed to look bashful.

'Good luck,' he huffed.

'Thanks.'

'Don't look down, Wormy,' Con teased. 'That height will flatten you!'

Luke didn't react. His growing anger fuelled his courage. Clenching his fists, he made his way to the mast and inspected the iron rungs. The murmur of the crowd escalated as they realised that he had stepped up to the post and was about to begin his journey. Summoning his bravery, he put his bare feet on the lowest rung and clasped his hands around another rung at chest height.

Slowly, but steadily, he started clambering up. His lack of shoes enabled him to curl his toes around the rungs during his ascent. He did not look down, but always focused on the next step. The sound of the crowd lessened as he made it to the first pair of mast-arms with no issues. He was already about a third of the way up and was feeling confident in his climbing holds. They were rusty but deeply embedded and did not seem to budge beneath his weight. He passed the first section without pausing. The sooner he got to the bell, the sooner he could return to the seabed.

As he neared the second set of mast-arms, he saw something that made his adrenaline begin to pump. Above, there were a substantial number of rungs missing. He stared in disbelief at the wood from which they should have protruded. The next rung was out of reach. A distant roar from the crowd below egged him onwards. Embracing the bare post desperately, he shimmied up until both his feet stood upon the highest available rung. To go further, he would have to leap and grab. A miss at this point would have him plummeting onto the elderships deck. He gulped.

His eyes latched on to his target and he stretched out his dominant hand above his head. The pause was enough for him to recognise the uncomfortable burn of the rope around his shoulder, but right now he had bigger concerns. Crouching ever so slightly, he prepared himself for the leap of faith. Far below him, the circle around the mast widened; they expected the worst. He counted down aloud.

'Three. Two... ONE!'

The final number came out in the form of a battle cry. Legs straining, he launched himself from his post and the rung sailed closer. The next few milliseconds seemed to stretch and drag. He had to make a grab at the very peak of his rise. For the smallest moment, he was suspended in mid water and then he began to fall. It was now or never. He threw his arm out and narrowly caught the hold. Immediately his body slammed against wood almost causing him to lose his grip.

But he held on.

There was an audible gasp from his spectators as he clung by one hand. His arm burned with exertion and he knew he had to move or he'd slip. The second rung waited. He hurled his free hand at it with vigour. Another success. Rung by rung, he dragged his thrashing body towards the surface with the rope trailing limply behind him.

When his feet could finally stand again, the respite was very much appreciated. He took a deserved rest. The hubbub of the audience fell upon deaf ears as he looked upon the view. Naufragium was a large settlement, but not an endless one. He could see stretches of featureless sand beyond its outskirts. Looking even further ahead, he observed that the waters grew shallower and that seaweed fields wafted in the currents. These fields were being attended by yet more townsmen, industriously chopping and snipping; in spite of the mass of spectators below, not *everyone* had come to watch his quarry. His height filled him with fear, but thrilled him in equal measure. His onlookers were now merely an incoherent gathering of ants.

Delightedly, he watched small shoals of fish flitting around like clouds in a harsh summer's breeze. Their ability to swim both confused and intrigued him. Neither he nor any of the people below seemed to be able to float in any shape or form. If he pushed off from his post, he would plummet at a speed that would no doubt be his end. And yet, the fish were there, swimming around, flouting the rules in a carefree way. Luke shrugged. Another question to add to the ever-building unanswered pile.

Luke focused his attention on the task ahead and his destination above. As far as he could see, no surprise gaps awaited him and he continued upwards with apparent ease. He shot clear of the third and final pair of spars without even noticing. Through the surface, the sun shone lazily, an enchanting wobbly beacon of orange. At this depth, its gentle rays caressed the mast. The approaching rungs were plastered with large strands of algae. He increased his grip as he traversed over these slippery characters.

Half a metre from the surface, he stopped.

The surface was somewhat of a mystery. From what he had gathered, the Naufragians could not survive above it. The real question was, was he any different? He could not remember. For all he knew, he could simply be a lost wanderer from another underwater town who had just received a mighty whack to the head. In his bones, he could feel that this was not true.

The answer to his question was within reach and it was time to find out. He filled his lungs with air from beneath the waves and then poked his head effortlessly outside of the sea's domain. Letting go of the oxygen, he drew a hesitant breath. Sheer relief rose intoxicatingly as he felt his body accept this new, yet familiar, source of air.

Luke was beyond the surface and alive. The world above seemed strange by comparison. It felt oddly dry. The wind battered his skin, the sun beat on his back like an old friend and everything just seemed more sharp and harsh than the expanse of dull edges and faded blues below.

An enormous bell glinted elegantly just a stone's throw away. He scrambled closer, removed the rope from his shoulder and untied the loop that John had created. The bell mechanism was more complex than he had expected. There was a metal pole thrust through the mast with a bell attached to one side and a giant wheel on the other. Luke studied each individual section closely, trying to work out where to tie the rope. He felt that he had, once, heard bells ringing from great, angular stone structures, but never had he considered the process behind the sound.

All the while, he tried to remain wary of the imminent danger. Although the surface appeared metres away, a slip would still mean death. The water would not break his fall. This was a strange concept for his brain to wrestle. In the end, he settled for not thinking about it.

The sea was surprisingly calm. A gentle wind dried his wet trunks. On the horizon, he swore he could see a sail and then dismissed that notion immediately. How could any craft float on water such as this? To his other side, he was astounded to discover land. A mountainous island with terrain in the shape of a colossal wizard's hat. Its peak was bending over precariously looking like it could collapse at any moment.

'Is that where I'm from?' Luke suggested to the horizon. He remembered Con's words from the night before. *Air? Mountains? Greedy fish-stealing surface-dwellers? Four-legged land creatures with giant udders? Murdering, good-for-nothing men who wreck the seabed and sweep through our lives causing havoc and mayhem without a single thought?* Another mystery, for another time.

His mind was dragged back to the current mission. He had a rope, a wheel and a bell, but he could not fathom how the three came together to function. Luke scratched his head. The last thing he wanted was to get this part wrong and attach the rope in the incorrect place. Coming back up the mast for a second time was not something he wished to partake.

He huffed with irritation. The idea of coming so far only to fail galled him.

Then he noticed that a blue light was shining through the thin material of his trunk pocket. The whelk. Tentatively, he withdrew it from his pocket and held it aloft. Its fluorescent blue light played across his face, giving him an immense feeling that this had happened before.

'Having trouble are we?'

A voice spoke. Or rather, it thrummed through him with an echo-like quality, as if its owner was stood within a cave. Luke almost slipped and fell from the sheer shock of it. 'What?' he blurted.

'I said, are you having trouble?' It repeated, then added. *'Seems fairly obvious to me.'*

Luke was too shocked to be offended. He scrunched up his eyes and opened them again, trying to determine whether he was dreaming. 'I can't tell how they go together!' he eventually complained to his invisible companion.

'Ah yes, I thought that's what you were struggling with. I think I have figured out how it works. Can you see that ring on the highest point of the wheel?'

Luke spotted a circular metal ring that jutted from the indicated location. He nodded.

'Attach the rope there. A downwards tug on the wheel should ring the bell.'

Luke looked from the fraying end of the rope, to the wheel and back again. The voice had not sounded overly confident, but at least it had provided an idea. Then, like a dam finally breaking under the stress of the water it held, Luke let loose a flurry of questions.

'Who are you? And, more importantly, who am I?'

There was an astounded silence when nothing was said.

'*You don't remember.*' It was not a question, more of a realisation.

'No, I don't. I have no idea where I'm from or what I'm doing here,' he whined. He had been avoiding thinking about it, but now, the truth of his ignorance scared him more than any of the angry townsmen below. He felt so lost.

'*I am Garth,*' the voice introduced himself. '*If I tell you any more about myself, it will only cause confusion. However, know this, I am here to help. This is not going to be easy for either of us, but I will be with you for every step of the way. Honestly, we're in trouble. We have to work together, and then, just maybe, we can make things right. You have to trust me.*'

Luke mulled this over briefly.

'Give me a reason to,' he demanded. 'Give me answers.'

Another hesitant pause.

'*Look... this is all very tiring for me. I can't stay. I have to... have to...*

The blue of the whelk flickered and then died, leaving behind an empty lifeless shell. The object in Luke's hands had gone from extraordinary to ordinary in a matter of seconds.

Luke stared at it with a mixture of bewilderment and anger. He sorely wanted to throw it away into the ocean blue, but the truth was, he needed answers. So, instead, he carefully placed it back in his trunk pocket and acted on Garth's hasty advice.

The metal ring was not too far away. Now that Garth had mentioned it, it stuck out of the wheel like a sore thumb. Climbing slightly further allowed Luke to carefully connect the rope with his best knot. He ensured it was tight and then mentally prepared himself for the return trip. With one last breath of raw air, he descended below into the abyss.

His journey down was rather uneventful. The gap in the rungs still proved problematic, but this time he had gravity on his side. Heart in his mouth, he lowered himself carefully to a dangling position, hugged the mast like a koala, and slid clumsily down to the next available rung. The rough material of the wood scratched his chest painfully, but he considered this a small price to pay. With the sticky part out of the way, he descended down the remaining length of the mast trouble-free.

When his feet, orange from rust, touched the deck of the eldership, he was met with stunned silence from all around. They had not expected him to survive, let alone succeed. The only person who seemed pleased by his arrival was John whose grin was apparent even through his bushy beard. John held the now attached rope in his hands, but quickly passed it over.

'Here you go, Lugworm,' he said with a polite bow. 'Show us what you have done!'

The crowd was quiet, but every eye was staring in his direction.

Gathered his remaining strength, Luke tugged down with all his might and....

Nothing happened. No sound was heard. He felt a rising tide of dismay well up from within. It hadn't worked.

'Well, what are you waiting for?' John questioned.

Luke looked confused.

'Release it, Lugworm,' he said while gripping Luke's shoulder in excitement.

Luke let the rope glide through his hands.

DONG!

The bell generated a wave of sound that filled the water and vibrated the deck beneath his feet. To him, it was the sound of redemption. He let himself believe, if only briefly, that he might actually be allowed to live. As for his audience, they erupted with cheers that almost drowned out the bell itself. People were jumping up and down. Some were hugging each other tightly, caught up in the moment. Con was looking at the surface, completely captivated. Luke, on the other hand, stood dumbfounded, the rope hanging uselessly by his side. John gave him a quick pat on the back and then took up the rope eagerly.

DONG! DONG! DONG! DONG! DONG! DONG! DONG!

Dimensions apart and lightyears away, a young Gazoid fist pumped the air and shouted with glee.

CHAPTER 4: ROUGH SEAS

Garth's vigorous celebration was cut short by a wave of fatigue. He sunk back into his mother's chair, still panting from the exertion of connecting to an object dimensions away. He had even been able to convey his thoughts through the shell and straight into Luke's mind; a feat that Penn had said was only possible of professionals. Certainly, a young Gazoid like himself, who had just stumbled upon a dimension shift machine in his own home, should not have been able to do it! The smugness he had felt was short-lived; there was too much else to worry about.

'Penn,' he said weakly. 'How long have I been in here?'

'You've had the pleasure of my company for a whole day and an evening,' she replied. 'We're in the early hours of Slimzod now.'

'Slimzod?' he blubbered.

'Is there an echo in here?' Penn said. 'Please don't tell me I've been talking to myself *again*. That happens far too often!'

'My supervisor,' Garth said, bolting upright. 'She'll be wondering where I am!'

'Calm down,' Penn said. 'She has not even checked on you yet, well, not properly anyway.'

'Explain,' Garth demanded.

'There are cameras all over your house. She has access to a program which enables her to see what you are up to without even leaving her seat.'

'*Cameras?*' Garth blurted. It seemed so obvious now. His supervisor always had a knack for knowing when he was not doing his chores.

'There goes that echo again,' Penn said. '*Relax*. I've rigged all the footage by using old clips of you doing your chores and sleeping. Those clips were not easy to find actually. Do you *ever* do as you're told?'

Garth stuck his tongue out.

'Anyway,' Penn continued. 'The short of it all is she thinks you're being an extraordinarily good boy. It won't be long until she checks on you in person and realises the truth. You're rebel scum.' This made Garth burst out into uncontrollable laughter. 'See, just because we're in trouble, doesn't mean we can't have a good time. Now, it's up to you to figure out a reason to spend your hours in here without raising suspicion.'

Garth paused momentarily and then grinned deviously.

'I've got it!' he shouted, leaping over wires and around the glass cabinet. He hauled open the vault door just wide enough for him to slip through and then paused. 'Hey Penn, why are you doing all this?'

'Can't a girl have some fun?' she replied mysteriously.

Garth shrugged, ignoring a slight feeling of unease, and started to put his plan into action.

***

Listening hard, Garth could hear the theme tune of Rawder's favourite holofilm series playing in the lounge. Walking down the corridor, he took a right just before the kitchen and stared in at the sitting room.

His visits to this room were infrequent. It was mainly for the benefit of visitors and had been decked out with the height of modern home comforts. It was spacious and made of spotlessly-clean marble. The main attraction was a large holotable directly in the middle. It was capable of projecting detailed three-dimensional images and was designed to fully immerse the watcher.

It did an incredible job. On the rare occasion when his mum had some free time, they would watch holofilms together. Garth's favourite had giant space battles where some of the ships flew beyond the table and around the room. One memorable scene had involved a crash landing straight onto his lap. He had cowered in fright, but then laughed for hours afterwards. Despite this amazing feat of technology, he found the room to be cold and characterless.

Around the table were a number of gel pads, warmed by the swamp far below his house. Magnemite was a hostile planet, but Gazoids had learned to benefit from the widespread bog. Although it was highly toxic, it was ideal for natural heating. The lucky ones had homes high up in the trees, meaning that it was easy to forget what bubbled below. In fact, the entire city of Tamaranga was built on a single, and extremely large, tree trunk.

Rawder, his supervisor, was sat cross-legged on one of these gel pads, clearly enjoying the luxury. She gazed intently at a crowded pub scene. The holofilm series that drew her attention was called 'Swamp Soap' and she had been binging on episodes all morning. Garth could already see that the drama was about to go full throttle. A male Gazoid was holding a knife and seemed poised to throw, while the rest of the customers remained unaware. Rawder looked tense with anticipation.

'Hey,' Garth greeted. 'How are – '

She held up a webbed hand, signalling him to stop talking. The angry Gazoid threw his knife at one of the females who was buying a drink from the bar. It missed and sailed directly towards Rawder. She did not even flinch as it passed through her and embedded itself on the wall behind.

'Pause!' she commanded and then turned to Garth. 'Yes?'

'I was just wondering how you were.'

She narrowed her eyes suspiciously.

'I'm good,' she replied mistrustfully. 'Have you done your chores?'

'I've tidied my room,' Garth lied, 'and I'm about to continue on to the next few jobs.'

'Really?' Rawder was surprised. 'Should I go check?'

'Go ahead,' he shrugged, calling her bluff.

She looked at the door and then at the holotable, but did not move. Clearly, a decision had been reached that going to check wasn't that important after all.

'Anything else?' she asked.

Garth looked at the woman who had been hired as his guardian. She was actually rather pretty and not much older than him. Two appealing yellow star-shapes dotted each cheek and she had constant dimples. The unfortunate matter was that her personality was as sour as gone-off grapes. She appeared to have no wish to have fun beyond using the holotable for her silly soaps. Garth usually yearned for a more accommodating playmate. Today, however, her lack of interest worked in his favour.

'Would you like anything from the kitchen?' he enquired.

She shook her head and motioned for the holotable to continue playing. As Penn had said, his adventures had clearly gone unnoticed. His mother's room must have some serious soundproofing! He made a mental note of this and momentarily left the lounge.

In the kitchen, Garth opened the fridge and filled his hands with multiple cans of Slarg and packets of sweetened insects. He also picked up a few megabeetles for main meals; they were extremely nutritious. Each one would sustain him for a whole day. He also grabbed a spoon which would later be used to scoop out the beetle's hard shell. Arms and pockets full, he returned.

'Rawder..,' Garth started, putting on a worried facade.

'Pause,' Rawder looked annoyed at the second interruption and then confused by the mass of food that Garth held.

'I think it's happening,' he continued.

Garth did not have to specify what was happening. Rawder immediately covered her mouth and nose with her hands.

'Are you sure?' she asked through her hand.

'I think I would know,' he said pointedly.

'It's a bit premature. Hasn't even happened to me yet and I have two years on you!'

'When it happens, it happens.'

'That's true. Do you know the procedure?'

Garth nodded.

'Then I shall see you... when I see you. If you need to exit your room, make sure you give fair warning. I'll probably be here.'

He nodded again and took his leave, tempted to give a bow. What a performance! Smirking, he shouldered into his bedroom. Rawder was under the impression that he was about to undergo 'The Darkening.' It was a process that all growing Gazoids go through when their red skin peeled off to allow a tougher, darker exterior to take its place. When it happened, Gazoids emitted dangerous fumes that are harmful to all, even members of their own species. Thus, the procedure was to lock oneself away until completion.

'The Darkening' could go on for days, weeks or even months. It basically gave him the perfect excuse to spend days without talking to anyone else. He would have rather spent it gaming, but it was ideal for the situation at hand. Precious time to sort out the mess he had made.

First, he had to add the finishing touches to his act. Releasing the bundle of food and drink onto his hammock, he searched for the appropriate warning sign. Beneath a stack of gaming magazines, he found a conspicuous triangle shape with a cartoon Gazoid drawn on the front. Rising from this character were a few squiggly lines and at its base were simply the words 'THE DARKENING' in bold capitals. Licking a coat of saliva onto his door, he firmly stuck the sign on. Nobody would dare to enter his room for the foreseeable future.

But, he was not going to be in his room. He retrieved his supplies and shut his bedroom door behind him. The intolerable noises of 'Swamp Soap' could still be heard in the background. By the sounds of it, a Gazoid had just caught her husband cheating with another female. Sneaking across with arms full, he nudged open the vault door and slid inside. Once he'd dumped his future meals on the control panel, he sealed himself in. Thankfully, it drowned out the woman's wailing. In here, at least, he was safe from Rawder and that ridiculous show.

***

The joyous whooping continued long after the sound of the bell had faded away. A weak silence eventually followed and seemed primed to be broken at any moment by a stray cheer. John made his way through the circle of people and to the side of the eldership.

'Today is a momentous occasion in our history,' he bellowed, waving his arms erratically. 'Since the day that the original bell rope rotted into disuse, a shadow has been upon our town. But no more! These are hard times, I know. We've hardly enough food to go around and we live in fear of the next trawling attack. But a change is coming. We can now look to the bell as a symbol of hope, rather than part of our forgotten past. For those of you too young to remember, the bell hailed any event imaginable. Weddings, birthdays and even a good day at harvest.

'For these dark times, I shall instate a fourth use. It shall be an alarm bell to warn the town of danger so that we can rally to its defence. The ring of the bell will be our guard. It shall unite us, it shall look over us, it shall *save* us!'

Happy cheers broke out and John waited patiently for them to pass.

'So that we can start using the bell straight away, I shall lay down the rules. For celebrations, the bell should be rung continuously for their duration. For attacks, the bell should be rung three times. After a small rest, this can then be repeated. Anyone can use the bell for this purpose, but understand that they do so with the utmost gravity. This system will be in place immediately.'

There was a genuine quiet as everyone strained to hear this important information.

'None of this would have been possible without Lugworm here.' John pointed at Luke behind him. 'He is still our prisoner by all means and is not allowed to leave Naufragium. Nevertheless, he has done us a good turn so he shall no longer be confined to the cell beneath my home. I intend to give him a guide to show him our ways. If you see him around, please treat him with decency and respect.'

This update was met with an uncomfortable shuffling of feel and worried faces.

'I realise food is scarce,' said John, moving swiftly on, 'but I believe we have plentiful seaweed and, of course, *sponge*.'

There was a loud ovation which John was forced to shout over.

'I declare an official feast. Enjoy it fellow Naufragians!!'

With this final holler, the audience was spurred into action. Some of its members disappeared into nearby shipwrecks only to return dragging a table or chest. A number of people strolled further down the cobbled street, seeking their own possessions to contribute. In the distance, Luke saw someone hauling a cart stacked high with a mountain of green. Children chased each other, dodging the hubbub around them and screaming with delight.

The few people on the eldership had taken their leave, scrambling off the bow and down the rocky stairs. John stood absorbing the merriment of his people.

Con, on the other hand, did not seem to know whether to scowl or smile. 'Looks like your gamble paid off,' he grunted, 'but I still think he is more dangerous than he's worth.' With this, the man strode off without looking back.

John watched him go. 'Well Lugworm, what do you think of our fair town?'

Luke was weary. Earlier, he had dangled above the jaws of death and now he was feeling the after-effects. His arms ached from strain, his chest was scratched all over and he was hungry beyond all belief. Having felt the empowering pump of adrenaline, he was now suffering its withdrawal. He did not know what he wanted more – to eat or to sleep.

'I don't know,' he responded, too tired to think.

'Give it time. In the next few days I want you to understand these people. They are a fickle bunch. You can be an enemy one moment and hero the next. Right now, you are teetering between the two. I want you to see both the good and the bad. Our plights and our victories.'

'Why?'

'Don't you worry about that right now,' advised John, a plan twinkling in his eyes. 'Come, let us join the feast. You must be hungry.' He must have realised Luke's exhaustion because he wrapped a helpful arm around and supported him across to the stairs.

Carefully, they made their way down, taking it step by step. Luke had enough wits to notice the same jellyfish creatures attached along the rock staircase. They were a variety of shapes and sizes, but were all kept in place by reels of string.

'They are called gelatas,' John answered his unspoken question.

'What are they for?'

'You'll see soon enough,' John winked.

They continued down and reached the cobblestone street. It was not made of pebbles as Luke had imagined, but of a range of shells. He spotted halves of cockles, oysters and scallops, all laid flat in the sand. At first, he did not understand the road's purpose, but then he saw the wheeled cart bringing harvested goods to the waiting masses.

Already, a disjointed set of tables and seating stretched out of sight around the corner. The feast preparation was in full flow and some Naufragians were sat eagerly awaiting food. Those lucky enough to own a streetside shipwreck poked their heads through old portholes or large cracks, conversing in brief chatter with their neighbours. The more social members of the town milled around, greeting others in a jovial fashion.

Many people grinned at John and gave respectful nods. One woman vigorously shook his hand and was on her way. Luke, meanwhile, received suspicious sideways glances. He may as well have been a ghost haunting the banquet. John led him to a clear table, helped him sit down and got him a cracked plate. His seat took the form of an old metal crate, while John sat opposite upon a wooden stool.

'Father!' Just as they sat down, a girl threw her arms around John. 'You were fantastic,' she exclaimed. 'Everyone is so happy to have the bell ringing again. I'm so proud!'

John smiled happily and hugged her back. 'Thank you, it all went better than I dared hope. Did you manage to see it or were you working on the fields?'

'I heard the bell, dropped my tools and ran over just in time to hear your speech.'

'You shouldn't have stopped work, Limpet,' he reprimanded.

She looked entirely unaffected by his stern tone. 'I was not going to miss it! Not for the whole of Euphausia!'

'You are a stubborn one,' he laughed. 'I suppose I'll let you off on this one occasion.'

She looked at Luke as if realising his presence for the first time. She was of a similar age, but different in many other ways. Unlike the other women who kept their hair tied, hers was free and spread out like an explosion in the surrounding water. She wore a shabby jumper that was clearly too big and some scruffy knee-length shorts. Sucked onto her forehead was a large, healthy limpet with two striking rays of blue down its centre. Her face was dirty with a hard day's labour and her hands were covered in specks of sand. Seeing Luke for the first time, her emotions flashed from happy for her father to disgust at his choice of company.

'Is that *him*?' she started.

'*He* has a name,' John chided. 'His name is Lugworm.'

'He's from the surface!' she said, outraged.

'That may be, but he attached the rope to the bell. That's something we could never do without him.'

'Why are you sat with *him*? Shouldn't he be locked away?'

'No.' His tone was curt. 'In fact, you two should get to know each other. I need someone to show him around.'

Her face fell. 'Surely you can't expect me to -'

'Yes. I can. You are my daughter.'

'No way, not a chance. You can get someone else to babysit.'

'It will only be for a few days. Just do what you would normally, except take him along. That's all I ask.'

She stamped her feet adamantly. 'I won't do it.'

'Do I get a say in this?' demanded Luke. 'Maybe I want a guide who isn't such a brat!'

'How dare you, surface scum!' she snapped.

'No,' John said with finality, pointing at Luke. 'You should consider yourself lucky that you aren't locked up again, which is what most of this town wants *by the way*.' Any argument brewing inside Luke was immediately stifled. John turned to his daughter. 'And you don't get a say either, Limpet. My decision is made.'

Limpet looked as though she was about to hit something. Luke stuck his tongue out at her cheekily. This must have been the final straw because she stormed off, kicking their table and knocking over stools as she did so.

John carefully righted them and sighed. 'She'll come around eventually, see if she doesn't! And so will you.'

'I doubt it,' Luke said sourly.

Lower down the street, people with trays were distributing seaweed from the carts to hungry hands. One woman came their way. 'Fireweed?' she offered.

Luke responded with a nod and a clump was added to his plate. As its name suggested, the seaweed resembled fire in colour. It was crispy to the touch and snapped off easily in his hands. He did not hesitate to sample some. It tasted smoky and had a heat which pleasantly warmed his insides.

'Not bad, is it? Here try some of this.' John put his hand up to signal to someone in the distance.

'Alright there, John!' bellowed a tall, balding man. As he strode over, Luke saw that he sported a perfectly groomed handlebar moustache and a red neckerchief. One of his eyes seemed smaller than the over the other, giving the distinct impression that he was continuously squinting. He walked with a confident swagger and, underneath his facial hair, was a friendly smile. 'Fancy some headrush?'

'Yes please, Goby and give some to our friend Lugworm here.'

Goby grinned wider. 'Right you are! Climbing that mast looked like bloody hard work. Here's an extra-large portion.'

'Thank you, Goby!' Luke said wholeheartedly. The man tipped his head slightly and then toddled further along, continuing his rounds.

Headrush was a thin, flat piece of seaweed. He picked his strand up whole and bit off a section at the tip. A salty taste sizzled and popped in his mouth like candy. He suddenly felt as though he could jump onto the table and start doing front flips. Restraining this urge, he settled for a grin.

John was watching and gave a hearty laugh. 'Think we have a winner. Don't eat too much though, that stuff is not good for you.'

Luke believed him. He saw a girl pass by with a tray of what appeared to be ordinary green seaweed. He asked for some and, although she avoided his eye, he received a generous portion. Without hesitation, he filled gaps in his stomach that had been empty for so long. His gorging received raised eyebrows from John.

'Wha?' he asked with a mouth packed with food.

'You really were hungry!'

'Yeh-huh!'

'That's meadoweed you're eating. Limpet and many others help collect that every day from our fields.'

'Mmmm,' Luke acknowledged, too occupied to give the words much thought.

He kept eating for a while longer and even requested a second plate. John finished early and was soon busy making conversation with passers-by. The main topic was the bell and its new found functionality. However, more than a few people approached their table to complain about the lack of fish they had seen of late. John responded to this information with a grave voice and always looked concerned long after the recipient had walked away.

He was a man with many troubles, Luke realised. After a while, Goby came and pulled up a stool. John immediately looked more at peace. The two of them spoke of more pleasant matters such as the tides, the currents and the interesting trinkets they had recently discovered.

Looking up at the distant surface, Luke could no longer make out the weak shining of the sun. It was beginning to get late. He noticed people carrying small boulders and placing them on each table. Raising his gaze ever so slightly, he realised that each of these rocks held a single small gelata in place. He eyed the nearest jelly creature with great curiosity as it bobbed lazily above his head.

'Never seen a gelata at night, son?' Goby guessed, tapping his nose knowingly. 'Watch and wait.'

Luke did as he was told. The gentle motion of the gelata had a rather hypnotising effect. He was almost dropping off in the growing darkness when he realised a change coming over the mysterious being. At first, the luminescent glow from its long tentacles was hardly noticeable. However, as the blue of the depths merged to black, the purpose of the gelatas became clear. Its translucent mass of a body had within it a frilly heart that flashed all the colours of a disco. Every pulse of its jelly caused a new shade to shoot out into the dim. The light clung to any surface it could find, like a recently exploded firework. Luke's face must have betrayed his wonder.

'Ten years ago, we never had gelatas,' Goby chatted conversationally. 'It was Gentle Stuart who found them and discovered their use. Before then, we'd have all been thrown into darkness by this time.'

'Feasts used to be very short and nowhere near as fun,' said John with a wink.

Goby agreed. 'Do you remember the day he turned up with one?'

'Yeah, we all thought he had a few nails loose. Back then, he was just called Pebble. Nobody knew why he'd brought a creature with such a painful sting into our town. All he did was tell us all to wait. So we did.'

'He was never one for words.' Goby said. 'I confess, I thought he was simple.'

'Alas, we all did. How wrong we were! Now his gelatas light up the whole town.'

'And now Lugworm here has fixed the bell. Maybe surface visitors ain't so bad after all!'

'Wait!' Luke blurted. 'This Gentle Stuart is from the surface?'

Goby and John gave each other a short meaningful glance.

'Stuart is one of us now,' John whispered. 'You'll have to ask him if you want to know the full story. And you should know better, Goby!'

Goby winced apologetically. 'Sorry I spoke without thinking, must be the headrush. Even so, if you manage to get a story out of Stuart, I'll eat an anemone!'

Luke shrugged and decided to steer the conversation to a safer topic. 'How come he used to be called Pebble, then? And now you call him Stuart?'

'Ah, that is a good question. I don't know how they do it *up top*.' John pointed upwards. 'But down here, we have to earn our names through hard work and accomplishments. When we're born, we owe everything to the sea and our name needs to reflect that debt, understand?'

Luke gave a slow nod.

'Myself, I started off as a humble Shrimp. After some graft, I came to be known as Hermitcrab, or Hermit for short. Once I was mayor and had proven myself to be worthy, people let me decide what I wanted to be called.'

'You see,' said Goby, with an exaggerated bow and a twirl of one hand, 'we are in the presence of royalty.'

John flushed red ever so slightly. 'It doesn't really mean much. One of the few perks of the job,' he mumbled.

'What about you, Goby?' Luke asked. 'What do you want to be called?'

'Well,' he said, stroking his moustache all the way to the tips, 'I'm pretty happy being Goby. Fortune and names are all very well for some, but I've got no complaints, me. However, as you have asked, I've always liked the sound of Lance. Pretty heroic, don't you think? Like a bedtime story. The kind of name you can - ' Something caught Goby's eye. 'Uh oh, looks like someone's had a bit too much sponge.'

Con was staggering his way towards their table. He was swerving from side to side, bumping into tables and people on his journey. Behind him, looking embarrassed, trailed Brittle and another youth.

The latter was all muscle and he looked even bulkier when striding next to Brittle's tall, slender form. His shoulder-length blonde hair was tied in a ponytail by a piece of fishing line and, like Luke, he wore only a pair of trunks, but his were a dull grey and had one leg shorter than the other. What really drew Luke's attention, however, were the teardrop shaped shells that sprouted from his shoulders, attached by some curious web-like threads; it gave the illusion that he was wearing shoulder armour. The overall effect only emphasized the boy's size.

When Con finally made it to a stool next to John, it was a miracle he did not miss his seat and end up on the seabed. 'It wa' so good ta hear th' bell John. So gooooood.' He put his arm around John affectionately and got tolerant amusement in return.

'I think you might need to go home, Con,' John suggested.

'Wa? Naaahhh! Using tha surf'scum to fix th'bell was pure brain. I could kiss ya!'

John winced awkwardly. 'Oh, please don't, you fool!'

'I'm gonna do it! I'm gonna!' Con got John in a headlock and planted a kiss on his crown.

'Get off! Get off!' John swiped at him good naturedly. Goby sniggered.

'Seriously tho! Tha'bell is gunna be great! If tho surf'scum a'tack, me and ma boys will be ready fo'em!' Con looked around in confusion. 'Wher'are they? Where are ma boys?'

'We're here Con,' Brittle assured. 'Elkhorn and I have literally been here for the entire conversation.'

'Wher?'

'Over here, on your left!' Elkhorn yelled.

Con's gaze swung around. Elkhorn and Brittle had taken the two empty stools next to him.

'There ya are! We'll be ready fo'em won't we boys?'

'Yes, Con!' they replied in unison.

'Tho surf'scum won't no whas hit'em.' Con slumped forward, rested his head on the table and closed his eyes.

'Our people have a tendency to eat a toxic sponge called Flabberwort,' John explained, turning his attention back to Luke. 'It's actually poisonous and highly addictive, but if you eat the right amount... well, you can see the result.'

'I wouldn't recommend trying some Lugworm, its vile stuff!' Goby added.

At Luke's name, Con woke from his drunken dose and gave an unpleasant stare. 'What are *you* doing here? What. Are. You. Doing. *Here*?'

Before anyone could stop him, Con had stood up and swiftly withdrawn his scimitar. He waved it wildly around, an evil gleam in his eye. Luke leaped up from his crate and gained some distance from the table.

'Whoa, Con! Calm down! You aren't yourself!' John shouted, trying to disarm the sword-wielding lunatic. However, Con turned and swiped his weapon at anyone who came close.

'They took'em John. They took them!' A horrible froth was spewing from his mouth.

'Lugworm had nothing to do with that.'

'I don care! I want th'blood!' He made a crazed lunge across. Fortunately, the attack fell far short. Elkhorn, muscles straining, grabbed the outstretched sword and embedded it in the wooden table. At the same time, a hairy man with an eyepatch appeared and wrapped his arms around Con's neck, hauling him backwards. John quickly pulled the weapon out and hid it away. Meanwhile, Con tried to struggle free of his chokehold, fists flailing. Moments passed and his attempts became weaker and weaker.

'You can let him go now,' John commanded. 'It's over.'

On release, Con collapsed to the sea floor gasping for breath. 'Trust y'ta save one o'your own kind!' he said with vehemence at the one-eyed man. Without a word, the one-eyed stranger turned and stalked off, as if nothing had happened at all.

'They took'em,' Con repeated, curling up on the street.

Luke was still standing, rigid as a pole, his heart beating fast. John put a hand on Luke's shoulder. 'Come on Lugworm, I think it's time we went home.'

They bid farewell to Goby, Elkhorn and Brittle before leaving the feast. Having regained his energy from the food, Luke was able to walk again unaided. As he followed John down the street of shells, he thought he heard the sound of a man sobbing with great sorrow.

When they finally got back to John's abode, Luke was pleasantly surprised to find that he was to spend the night in a spare room, rather than the cell in the hull. He could just about make out a bed-like structure in the dim. A hesitant prod revealed that it was riddled with holes and had a rough, springy texture. Later, John would explain that it was made from a conveniently cultivated species of marine sponge that was ideal for bedding. At the time, however, Luke was too tired to give it the slightest thought. He put his feet up and watched the vibrant colours of the gelata outside, seeping through the cracks and dancing across the wooden planks of his ceiling. It wasn't long until he fell into a much needed slumber.

CHAPTER 5: NAUFRAGIUM'S PLIGHT

'Wake up!'

Luke was shaken roughly by the shoulders. From the tone in John's voice, it must have been the second time he had made this demand. With a groan, Luke rolled off his sponge-bed and landed with a creak onto the cabin floor.

A dim daylight flooded in, revealing features previously hidden by the night. His bed was, in fact, one of two bunk beds with brown-sponge mattresses. He found himself in a small cubby hole that had clearly not been used for a very long time. And yet, while it lacked homey touches such as pictures or keepsakes, the sea-life kept it from being dull: a starfish moseyed along the ceiling, a patch of black mussels drooped from the frame of the bed above and cracks shot across the timber like lightning.

Through an open door and down a narrow corridor, he could see John pottering around with plates and pots. Stumbling towards the sounds of clatter, he entered the warm sitting room that he recognised from the day before. John was waiting for him with a bowl of seaweed in his hands and passed it over hastily. 'Limpet's gone ahead. Eat up!'

There was something in his voice that required obedience. Luke shoved in his breakfast with urgency and soon had an empty bowl to show for it.

'Good.' He nodded approvingly. 'If only you were that fast at waking up. Do you remember the way to the main street?'

'I think so.'

'Head there and continue passed the eldership. You should be able to spot her before she disappears into the meadoweed fields. Go on now!'

John opened the door to the deck and waved Luke through.

'You'll have to run!' he shouted after him.

Still barely awake, Luke had to crack a mental whip to spur himself to a gentle jog. Unlike many of the other wrecks, John's home was actually kept level by the use of tactically placed rocks. He ran to the side, down a ramp and onto the seabed. Gathering speed from the decline, he swiftly ducked and dived amongst haphazard ships. Naufragians leaving their abodes gave him looks of suspicion as he went. Fairly accustomed to this reception by now, he left them behind in a cloud of sand.

It felt like he was free. He thought it extremely trusting to let him run about Naufragium, but then, where else would he go? He was in a strange town and he had no idea how to get home, or where *home* actually was. At this thought, he gave a burst of speed as if to outrun his troubles.

The area got a lot busier when he reached the street of shells. Any sign of the feast had been cleared away, enabling a swarm of people to pass along it without obstruction. He ran onwards, dodging between gaps in the herd and searching for a young girl with messy blonde hair. Townsmen, who recognised who he was, actively cleared out of his way. Those who he took by surprise recoiled in shock.

Naufragians who had wares to sell were advertising from streetside shipwrecks, preachers were hailing from decks up high, and empty carts were being hauled to the harvest. A group of young men and women, equipped with spears, looked to be eager for a successful morning hunt. He passed an old lady strolling casually in the rush, an eel wrapped around her neck. This gathering of life caused countless bubbles to dance upwards; they merged now and then to double in size as they made their way towards the surface.

The sea had as much of a hold on the town as the people who lived within it. Algae grew like moss on every surface, dashing the seabed debris with a distinctive green tinge. Limpets speckled the hulls, bright coloured anemones flowered in wooden coves, bulbous sponges ballooned. As Luke sped by, he disturbed a large blue lobster that proceeded to scuttle underneath a concealed nook. The odd fish flitted down to shelter in the town like a lonesome petal in the wind.

Luke was slowed to a walk by the sight of the eldership looming above in all its glory. Stuck between two pillars of rock, it appeared as though it could topple down upon his head at the slightest current. Before long, he stood in its ominous shadow and stared up at the mast he had climbed a day prior. He gulped.

With a shake of his head, he restored his previous jogging speed. The street seemed to be on a gentle hill, gradually crawling closer to the sea's surface. Consequently, the sunlight shone that bit brighter and the water felt a few degrees warmer. Then he saw her. She was bantering with two other boys who were clearly enjoying her attention. Her loose blonde hair was unmistakable. As he approached, he saw her burst out in laughter and punch the nearest guy playfully on the shoulder.

The conversation stopped short when he arrived. 'Hey Limp - ' he started.

'Is that who I think it is?' One boy butted in and shouldered his way to the forefront. He looked to be in his early teens, slightly older than Luke himself, and had chimneys of yellow sponge growing off either side of his head. He reminded Luke of a bull ready to charge.

'I think so, Barrel,' said the other boy with a sneer of disgust. This one had a large spider crab planted on his head like an absurd helmet. 'See how no sea creature has yet to touch him.'

Luke flushed red. He knew he was being ridiculed for something that he could neither help nor understand. Despite this, he tried to ignore them and turned to Limpet. 'John said that I should follow you, so here I am.' he stated gruffly.

Limpet looked aside with indifference. Barrel snorted. 'Oooh, *John said*, did he?'

Luke gritted his teeth. 'Yes, he did. And I don't see what this has to do with you, sponge-brain.'

His friend chortled. Barrel frowned and gave his mate a slap to the face. 'Shut up, Crust! This surface squirt just insulted me.' He then shoved his way closer until he was standing inches away from Luke himself. 'Say that again, I dare you.'

Up close, the difference in size was obvious. Barrel was larger in every direction. Luke was blatantly outmatched, but his temper had burned away his dwindling supply of good sense. '*Sponge-brain*' he repeated slowly as if for the benefit of a toddler. 'Or is there too much sponge blocking those ears of yours?' Luke did not wait for a reply. 'Okay then, I will say it louder. Sponge-brain, sponge-brain, *sponge-brain!*'

Crust was on the floor now, laughing and rolling around. Barrel had gone a furious purple. 'Right!' he cracked, beefy fists at the ready. 'That's enough!' He threw a weighty punch at Luke's head. Quick as a snake, Luke dodged to the side and kicked him in the shin.

Barrel yowled in pain and was about to come at Luke for a second attack, one that would have surely knocked him to the ground like a sack of potatoes, when Limpet intervened 'Stop it, Barrel,' she hissed, facing him and standing between them. 'How will I explain it to my father if I return this evening with Lugworm's headless body? Besides,' she quickly turned and gave Luke a rough shove. He sprawled awkwardly onto the sand and scowled up at her in surprise. 'He's hardly worth it!' With this, she strode off down the street.

Barrel looked down at Luke, looking even bigger than

before. 'She's right. John won't be able to protect you forever, and neither will his daughter. Next time, you won't be so fortunate!' He stomped off in the opposite direction.

Crust lingered momentarily and gave Luke what was almost a smirk. 'For what it's worth,' he said. 'Sponge-brain was a fairly good one. Not brilliant, of course, not overly-imaginative, but it's a start.' Jogging slightly, Crust caught up with Barrel and the two of them were back to bantering before they disappeared out of sight.

Luke scrambled to his feet, burning with shame and hurt for reasons he didn't quite understand. These people were not his friends so he didn't see why he should care what they think. He decided to do right by John and, despite everything, follow Limpet. So that is what he did. When she heard his footsteps from behind her, she spoke without even looking back.

'Damn my father,' she muttered. 'Follow me, do as I do and don't talk to me!'

And that was all that was said for the journey to the meadoweed fields. Limpet stomped ahead and Luke followed, his pride stinging more than any blow to the head.

***

Limpet trudged moodily on and Luke tracked her with a temper just as black. Eventually the wrecks that littered either side of the street were taken over by expansive seaweed fields. Even at this early time of day, both men and women were hard at work, gathering food that would later feed the people of their town. They passed a field of orange and red flora that he recognised as fireweed. Men shattered it with rusty pickaxes, while sandy children gathered the fragments in wooden bowls and scampered away. He stopped and stared. Limpet, on the other hand, continued without a single glance.

She plodded beyond this field to the next, halting at a luscious forest of meadoweed. Here, dense green strands shot up from the seabed and waved softly in the currents. A short man stood at the field's boundary, holding a tray packed full of tools. Even in the distance, Luke could see an angry red blob on the side of his nose. On closer inspection, it was not a painful boil, but an anemone.

'Hullo there, Limpet!' the man said amiably.

'Tools, Beadlet,' she said impatiently.

The man grunted and handed her a pair of scissors. 'And who might you be?'

'I'm Lugworm.'

Beadlet's forehead creased with thought. 'Ya, you're the one'o fixed th'bell. I'm not gonna to g'et any trouble out'o'yo, am I boy?'

'No sir.'

He eyed Luke suspiciously. 'Alrightey then. Av some scissors. Cut th'meadoweed a'the base, gather as much as you can and pile it on th'cart over yonder. Watch Limpet a'work and g'et cutting. This town ain't going t'feed itself, what with the shortage of fish'n'all!'

Luke picked up a hefty pair of scissors and moved closer to the meadoweed. On the ground, he noticed short stumps where the plant had been cut down the day before. Limpet was kneeling down at a patch of fully-grown meadoweed, scissors at the ready. She pulled a frond taut, snipped it free and laid the strand over her shoulder.

He studied her technique for a while. If she was aware of him, she gave no indication. One part of the process struck Luke as strange. As soon as the meadoweed was cut, it stopped floating and flopped to the ground. He highly doubted Limpet would answer any questions in her current mood. Once he had seen her take a substantial pile to the cart and return to her spot, he set to work himself.

Initially, it seemed like very easy labour. Pull this, snip here and gather. Luke found himself repeating this process over and over. He worked near Limpet, but did not attempt to talk to her. After a few hours, however, the work that had seemed effortless started to take a toll on his body. The scissors began to feel heavy in his hands, while his back began to ache from bending up and down. The sand stuck unpleasantly to his knees and he began to feel the heat of the sun a bit too keenly. Had he been on land, he would have certainly been dripping in sweat. He paused and, with a hand on his sore back, stretched out.

A dash of orange briefly caught his attention. It started as a distant speck, but it appeared to wiggle closer by the second. Luke realised that whatever it was, it was making a beeline straight for him. When it finally arrived, it took the shape of a small, bright-orange fish, no bigger than his little finger.

'Curious little fellow, aren't you?' Luke grinned as the fish darted playfully around him. To all intents and purposes, it appeared to be inspecting him. Luke decided to hold out one of his palms as a sign of good will. 'Come now,' Luke cooed. 'I don't bite.'

The fish paused its erratic dance for a moment and then sidled closer. Luke kept perfectly still, thoughts of his labour forgotten for the time being. After a little perseverance, the little chap settled on his palm. Its fins brushed his skin, tickling him so much that he almost snapped his hand away.

There was something awfully peculiar about its gaze. Bulbous, and tinted with a dull gold, those eyes appeared to look right through him. For a fleeting second, Luke was overcome with an unexplainable feeling that this tiny being was somehow connected to something much, much larger.

'Who are you?' Luke said. Predictably, the fish did not reply. 'I shall call you Jaws,' he decided. Some sleeping part of his brain seemed to think this humorous and ironic.

The fish abruptly came to the conclusion that it had had enough. It launched from Luke's palm and started zooming purposefully from whence it came. Luke looked around and noticed that Limpet had watched the exchange, a look of wonder splayed across her face. As soon as she noticed Luke's attention though, this expression was quickly replaced with her signature frown.

Luke decided he was in no rush to return to chopping

meadoweed. 'When do we get a break?' he queried hopefully.

Perhaps the work had eased Limpet's temperament as, for once, she actually responded, albeit with a question of her own. 'Is the sun still up?'

Luke understood all too well and wearily continued for a while, before attempting converse once again. 'What if I'm hungry?' he said, trying his utmost best not to sound like a whinging five-year-old.

'We're in a field of meadoweed,' she spoke loftily with a wide, lazy gesture. 'If you are *really* peckish, have a nibble, but don't let Beadlet catch you.'

Luke decided to force more conversation while it was trickling through. 'How come the meadoweed floats until it's cut?'

There was an elongated pause. Limpet scrunched up her face. 'You really don't know *anything*, do you?'

Luke shook his head. He really didn't. This world had confused him from the moment he had gotten here. Unfortunately, he had never had the chance to ask about anything. So far, it had all been one massive rush and he had mainly concentrated on staying alive. Now that he was safe, he had a lot of answers to seek.

For starters, he did not understand why he could breathe underwater, less so why he could breathe *above* water when nobody else could. He was mystified that fish swam around, while everyone else was rooted to the ground. It would have been helpful if Garth had provided some information, but they hadn't spoken since the eldership.

'It stops floating because it is dead,' Limpet lectured as though it was obvious. Luke moved his hand in a circular motion, urging her to continue. She huffed. 'Meadoweed are as much a part of the sea as the water or the sand. When it's alive, it floats. As soon as it dies, it's no longer one with the sea and is as buoyant as you or me.'

'And fish?'

'The same applies to them,' she answered.

Luke thought on this for a while. 'But we are not dead,' he pointed out. 'Why don't we float?'

Limpet rolled her eyes. 'You may as well ask why the sun rises or why the sea is blue. The reason changes depending on who you speak to.'

Luke waited for her to say more.

'Some think we are being punished by the Lord for taking too much of his gift. Others think that we're bogged down by worries and cares. Discard them, and one could soar away,' her voice had taken one a mocking tone.

'And you?' Luke asked, snipping half-heartedly at a lone frond. 'What do you think?'

'I don't believe any of that rubbish. We don't belong here. As much as we hate *your kind*, a few of us suspect that we came from the surface. We are outsiders who have made our home here. The sea tolerates us. When it marks us, we have been accepted. But being able to swim, that's a luxury for creatures of the sea.'

'But if you came from the surface originally, how can you breathe down here?'

'Nobody knows,' she replied, then frowned, realising that she'd been baited into a conversation. 'Get back to work and quit asking me questions!'

Luke shrugged and the conversation stopped short.

The day dragged onwards and the pile of meadoweed grew in size. About lunchtime, Luke ensured that Beadlet was not around and sneakily snacked on a strand or two. Everything hurt, but he carried on with work in a mindless fashion. They did not talk for the rest of the day. The quiet between them was not companionable, but at least it was less hostile than before.

Luke hardly noticed when Limpet sneaked off into the depths of the meadoweed forest. Following her seemed tempting, but he judged it best not to. A couple of hours later, she silently returned and assumed working a few metres away.

Late in the afternoon, when Luke suddenly found that

he was struggling to make out the green of the meadoweed from the ever darkening sea, he heard Beadlet yelling.

'Harvest tis o'er, ga home n get som'est!'

Limpet took whatever she had cut to the cart, dropped her scissors in Beadlet's tray, and shot off down the street, leaving Luke to find his own way back. Having recently added his bundle to the pile, he went straight to Beadlet to return his tool. Just as he was about to walk down the street, a hand gripped his shoulder.

'Wher do'ya thenk yur goin?' Beadlet asked. 'I need strong 'ands ta pull th'cart.'

Luke groaned and reluctantly made his way over. It was a crude wooden device that had a single pair of large wheels. Upon it was a mountain of meadoweed ready to be taken into Naufragium. It was kind of like a reverse wheelbarrow. Luke turned his back to it and clasped each hold. With a sigh, he hoisted the cart up and heaved it towards the shell road. Although the wheels took most of the weight, it was very hard work. He was already worn out enough from the days toil.

Beadlet walked alongside, watching him warily. When Luke made it to the road, the going got a bit easier. Fortunately, the way back to Naufragium was all downhill which allowed gravity to aid his efforts. Other Naufragians were likewise flowing back into town, abandoning their fields for the day. Luke could see a number of similar carts that were stacked high, rolling off into the distance.

At one point, Luke heard a low grumble of wheel on floor and looked around to receive a cloud of sand to the face. It was Barrel, speeding by with a cartful of headrush. 'Come on Lugworm! Don't want half the town to die waiting for ya!' he jeered with a boastful grin. With his sponge horns bent low, it made him look like a maddened beast of burden. Naturally, in response to the ridicule, Luke tried twice as hard, but could not keep up. He frowned as Barrel disappeared around the corner.

'It's a bit ligh'er is headrush,' Beadlet consoled.

Luke grunted. He hadn't the energy to make decent conversation. As they moved further into the centre of town, people ogled the food laden carts. Some followed them, shouting out their discontent.

'Oi Beadlet, get us some fish would ya,' a man insisted. 'I'm sick of bloody meadoweed!'

'I gro'meadoweed n tha's wa you'll ge't fro'me,' replied Beadlet, wearily.

'My children can't grow on seaweed alone!' a woman added her cry. 'What will you do when there's nobody left to feed?'

'Sorry maam,' Beadlet apologised.

Luke kept his head down while the angry townsmen vented their frustration. He felt sorry for Beadlet who just seemed to be trying to do his job. They rounded one more corner and stopped at the front of a large queue.

'This'll do Lug'orm, this'll do.'

Luke did not need telling twice. His burning arms released the cart and people flooded forwards, filling up their plates. He was hungry himself after the day's exertions and went to grab a bundle to take on his way. An angry man stopped Luke in his path and shoved him away from the cart. 'Get to the back of the queue like everyone else!'

Luke clenched his fists for the second time that day. He was tired, lost, and now he was being denied the food that he had spent all day collecting. He was about to say something he was bound to regret, when a man called his name. Luke looked around to see John holding a bowl of meadoweed in each hand. 'You look exhausted!' he exclaimed. 'Here, I got you some.'

Luke took the bowl and gave a heartfelt nod of thanks. Despite having seen meadoweed all day long, his appetite was just as intense. He gobbled it up and was left wanting for more. By now, evening was well and truly on its way and the street gelatas were beginning to flash.

'Come on Lugworm, let's get you home. You look like you could do with some rest!' said John, patting Luke gently on the shoulder.

'Yes please,' agreed Luke enthusiastically. 'It's been hard work today and, now that I've eaten, all I want to do is lay down somewhere.'

John looked sympathetic. 'It'll get harder before it gets any easier, I'm afraid.'

Luke frowned. This was not what he wanted to hear. They strolled down the street, onto the sand and were nearing John's home when Luke asked another question that had been bugging him. 'How can I breathe above and below the surface?'

'I don't know,' John admitted, his pace slowing ever so slightly. 'You are different to anyone I've ever met. You look the same as us, but I'm convinced you aren't from here.'

'How come?' Luke probed.

John took a deep breath. 'Look, surface people only come in one form down here, and that's dead. We know very little about them. They throw items into the sea without a care, some of which is useful to us and some of which is just plain rubbish. Other than that, they wreak havoc across the seabed whenever they're hunting for fish - their methods are destructive and have led to the demise of many a Naufragian. So, all in all, we don't know much about them. And, aside from the odd unlucky Naufragian who gets caught in their net, I highly doubt they know anything about us.'

'One thing is for certain,' John continued. 'They cannot breathe down here. We cannot breathe up there. You, however, can do both. To me, this suggests that you're from somewhere else entirely.'

'And Stuart?' asked Luke tentatively. 'You said he was from the surface?'

John's face blanched. 'Stuart's circumstances were,' he paused, 'different. I only gathered the basics of his story, but it was enough. He is not like you. You'll have to ask him yourself one day.' John frowned thoughtfully, turned and looked deep into Luke's eyes. 'Do you really not remember where you came from?'

Luke scrunched up his face and then sighed. 'No, I really don't.'

'That's a damn shame,' John said. 'It could be important. I might be the only person in Naufragian who feels this way, but I'm glad you're here. This town needs change. You've seen for yourself our dire situation. Food is dwindling and I have a feeling both sides of the surface are suffering for it.'

'What can I possibly do?' said Luke exasperated. 'I can't even cope with one day's hard labour.'

'Do your best,' said John. 'That is all I ask. I have plans in mind that could save the town or doom it. As far as I can see, they are our only hope. But, let us not think on them today. You are tired and I have much to do before this day is over.'

Their chat had kept them talking all the way to John's personal shipwreck. Luke felt sombre as they walked back up the ramp, across the deck and clambered inside. It felt like a year since he'd awoken, but it had been a mere day of working on the meadoweed fields. The first of many, judging by what John had suggested. He fell onto his sponge-bed and stared up at the ceiling, resting his aching bones on its cushiony texture. While his body was drained, his mind was afire with the titbits of information that he had learned. He had to talk to Garth.

***

Garth scooped out a megabeetle and ate its insides with relish. He had been watching and listening intently, only pausing for a sneaky trip to the fridge to restock his food supply. He now had enough to last him two whole weeks.

'How come he can't remember anything?' he asked, gulping down his last mouthful.

'Shift memory loss is not uncommon, especially for a being so unprepared,' replied Penn knowingly. 'For now, it actually works in our favour. He'd be useless to us if he realised the distances he has travelled and how far from home he really is.'

Garth chewed this information over and then decided

he did not really like the taste of it. 'Isn't that a bit…'

'Unfair? Corrupt? Mean?' suggested Penn. 'Yes, all of the above. But think on this, Garth. You're attempting to save a *whole* dimension. Think of all the lives that could blink out of existence if you don't succeed.'

Garth gulped, and this time it had nothing to do with eating. 'No pressure then!'

'The point is,' Penn said, 'one single, minute life pales by comparison. Sure, you might have whisked this boy away from his home, his parents and all that he holds dear, but think of what he might save.'

'It still feels wrong,' said Garth adamantly. He had started gently rotating his mother's chair in a slow circle.

'Good,' replied Penn. The green bulb on the control panel glowed approvingly. 'I am glad that is how you feel. You'd make a terrible dimension shifter. Your mother is the same.'

'Excuse me?' Garth said, pausing his absent-minded circular journey. He was unsure if he should be offended on his mother's behalf.

'You misunderstand,' appeased Penn. 'Technically, your mum is one of the best. And you've learnt some concepts faster than anyone on record. But, you both lack a certain ruthlessness for this job. I bet you want to send this boy back and be done with it all, don't you?'

'Can I?' said Garth, a flicker of hope rising somewhere within.

'Not possible. You know that,' Penn chided. 'It's a journey without return. We cannot shift anyone without a Quasar gem. That's something that is out of my control. Besides, you've got plenty of incentives to save this dimension, besides heroism and all that.'

'I know, I know,' Garth said. 'My mother's job. If I don't clear up this mess, she'll lose it for sure, and I'll be in even more trouble.'

'There's an even more pressing reason, I'm afraid,' said

Penn. Her tone did not quite match her words. There was certainly an element of glee and mischief.

'Oh?' Garth asked with more than a little dread.

'You're locked in,' announced Penn.

'What do you mean?'

'Precisely what I said,' said Penn. 'There's not too many ways to say it, in your language anyway. You're locked in, Garth. The door is locked, Garth. Opening the door would be futile. Because it is locked.'

About half-way through Penn's reiterations, panic kicked in. Ignoring her completely, Garth leaped out of his mother's chair, showing an unprecedented amount of activity for the last two days, and rushed to the vault door. He managed to get his webbed feet tangled in some wires en route, tumble over and hit his head painfully on the central glass cabinet. Once he'd managed to dislodge himself, he charged to the exit.

She was right. No matter how hard he heaved, it was not budging. He was trapped. 'No,' Garth muttered in disbelief. 'No, this can't be happening.'

'I'm afraid it is, Garth,' confirmed Penn.

'Let me out!' he pleaded, pounding on the hulk of metal that had become his tomb. 'Let me out! Let me out! Let me out!'

He shouted and shouted as loud as he could. He begged for help, he bargained with deities in which he hardly believed, he called for Rawder and his mother like a newborn chick demanding food.

And then, after he was weak from his efforts, he fainted.

***

'It's standard procedure,' Penn explained to a somewhat calmer Garth. 'I'm surprised they did not notice sooner to be honest.'

'Who are *they*?' Garth asked, cradling his sore head. He had eventually awoken and crawled back to the comfort of his mother's chair.

'The Altersearch Company,' she replied. 'The one your mother works for. They even left a message, if you'd like to hear it.'

'Play it,' Garth requested reluctantly.

'Okay, here we go…'

'Hello Miss Eonmore, my name is Frayoch,' said a female Gazoid with a nasal voice. 'I am head administrator at the Altersearch Company and I am calling to inform you that we've noticed some illegal activity on your account. According to our database, an unauthorised dimension shift has been conducted from your room. Please respond with your unique password to confirm that you are the room's official controller. If you do not, serious action will be taken. As a precaution we're locking your dimension shift room and restricting all activity until we hear from you. From all here at Altersearch, we hope you have a nice day.'

'That's it,' said Penn. 'Short and sweet.'

Garth slumped back in the chair. Someone had noticed his meddling after all! He racked his brain for possible passwords. What would his mother have used? He could list what he knew about her on one hand; she enjoyed the odd holofilm, she savoured megabeetles (a common trait among Gazoids) and she was a formidable glider.

That's where Garth's ideas came to an abrupt end which struck home a sad realisation. He did not know his mother all that well. She spent most of her time either in this room or on business trips. Their days off together had been too few.

He gave up and did the only thing he could think of.

'Delete the message.'

'Oooh Garth! I never took you for such a rebel,' flirted Penn. 'As you wish my little renegade.' If Gazoids could blush, which was biologically impossible, Garth would have turned a deep shade of red. Penn's green light winked cheekily. 'Message deleted.'

CHAPTER 6: LIMPET'S HIDEOUT

Wheeled metal beasts zoomed along long stretches of tarmac, swerving and beeping angrily. A flock of small flying beings swarmed across the sky in an organised tornado of movement. Expansive fields dotted the landscape interspersed with bubbles of wild forests. A pack of furry four-legged scavengers roamed a moonlit scene on the hunt. A carpet, now, lush and soft with the background clatter of pots, pans and a kettle about to boil. It was tea-time. Someone called out a name. 'Luke!' they called. 'Luke!' they beckoned. 'Luke!' they screamed.

Luke snapped awake feeling as if he'd hardly slept. The remnants of a dream flitted through his mind, but all that he could grasp was that final word. It was a name. It sounded familiar; it sounded right. It was his name. His name was Luke. This realisation brought an initial smile to his face, followed by immense frustration. He felt homesick for a home he could not remember.

The dim light from outside told him that it was the break of dawn. Garth had not contacted him *all* night; Luke had slept whilst holding the whelk just in case. He slouched out of bed and shouldered through his cabin door, leaving the whelk discarded on the floor. John and Limpet were already having their breakfast bowls.

'You're up early today,' noted John, eyebrows raised.

Luke gave a grunt of acknowledgement, snatched up a bowl and started furiously shovelling meadoweed into his mouth. He was already sick of it. In fact, he was sick of this entire town.

'Whoa,' said John. 'Slow down there, Lugworm!'

'My name is not Lugworm,' Luke glared. 'Am I working the meadoweed fields again today?'

'Yep,' John answered. 'Same as Limpet.'

'Right,' said Luke abruptly. 'I'll be off then.'

He threw down his empty bowl and it wobbled around on the table. Before it had settled, he was outside and storming across the deck. From behind, he heard John exclaim to his daughter.

'And I thought *you* were the moodiest of them all!'

***

The scenery was an angry blur and, before Luke knew it, he was attacking the meadoweed with an unappeasable rage. He would have imagined Garth's face before him if he actually knew what the boy looked like! Through the red haze, he became dimly aware of Limpet working some way off. In the corner of his eye, he noticed her edging closer.

'What's that meadoweed done to you?' she asked hesitantly.

'You wouldn't understand!' he snapped.

'Well, it's a good thing that I don't really care, isn't it?'

'Very good,' Luke bit back. 'Leave me alone.'

And in that instant, the chance for the two of them to be friends was ruined. His harsh words had Limpet retreating with a scowl. She did not ask again and he made no effort to patch up the ever-widening rift between them. To and fro he paced, throwing bundle after bundle onto the cart. Time grated by with a slowness that only furthered his frustration.

It was about midday when, like before, he spotted Limpet slinking away. The futility of his own situation must have made him reckless because he threw down his tools in disgust and decided to give chase. He watched as she disappeared into thick foliage and quickly followed. It was not a pleasant experience; he was engulfed by darkness as the surrounding shoots blocked out the sunlight. A loud persistent swishing sound battered his senses as the currents washed through the meadoweed field. As he swept strands out of the way, those behind floated immediately back into place.

After an eternity, Luke emerged. Straight away, he caught sight of Beadlet patrolling the boundaries. Luckily, the man had his back turned and was walking away. However, he must have heard something because he stopped short and scanned behind him. Luke hastily hid among the reeds and kept very still. He was relieved when Beadlet continued on his route.

There was no sign of Limpet. In fact, there was hardly anything to see at all. What waited on the far side of the field was an apparently featureless stretch of sand. He saw no reason to go running into nothingness. As he turned to go back, he noticed a raised bank not too far away. It followed around the field's perimeter and looked too neat to be produced naturally. He decided to investigate.

With one last cautious look at Beadlet, he charged across and shot up the bank. All of a sudden, he was falling into a small, confined trench, hidden by the mild sand hill. After recovering from an awkward landing, he spotted the lone figure of Limpet scrambling away. She was heading left along the V-shaped trench with her head bent low.

She was going at quite a pace and he had to hurry to keep up. The shape of the trench made it difficult to walk and he had to prop himself upright using his right arm. Clumsily, he dodged rocks that jutted from the sides and stepped around fat, purple starfish. The whooshing of the fields diminished and was replaced by the harsh noise of pickaxe on fireweed. Eventually, even this sound grew distant.

Ahead, Limpet was a dark figure in the distance. She was

so focused on her destination that she can't have been aware of her stalker. Luke saw her launch herself out of the trench using a convenient rock as a foothold. It took him precious minutes to reach the same location. His first attempt at exiting was unsuccessful; he poked his head briefly over one side, clawed helplessly at the sand and then tumbled back in. Second time round, he was more vigorous and just about managed to crawl out – she had made it look easy!

Brushing the sand off his chest and knees, he spied Limpet about half a mile in front. Her destination was obvious: a massive hill of rock that dwarfed all around it and stuck out like a sore thumb. Its peak ended long before the surface and appeared to have a sprinkling of colour. Limpet arrived at its base and then disappeared into shadow.

When Luke got there, it took some time to figure out where she had gone. Closer up, the hill had greater resemblance to a sheer cliff-face which ruled out the possibility that she had climbed it. He padded around in confusion. After much searching, he came across a crack in the rock with barely enough space to squeeze through. Shaking off the mental images of what sea monster could lurk within, he edged into darkness.

The gap widened to become an almost acceptable passageway. There was light coming from somewhere up high, but it was so feeble that he had to feel his way around. As he did so, he brushed something squidgy, collided with something spiky and stroked something rough; it gave him the creeps. Given time, however, he found that the way forward rose in jarring steps, almost like a staircase.

His ascent was far from elegant as he scraped obstacles he could not see and received his fair share of scratches. Eventually, however, he could make out more and more of his surroundings. Was he getting used to the dark or was he getting closer to the source of the light? A few, large steps upwards and he found himself obstructed by an abrupt dead end.

His hands could find no way through, so he had to resort

to his weakened eyesight. Looking down, he was surprised to see a light shining upon his feet. He crouched to spy the origin of the illumination and grinned – a crawl space! Not too far down, a dash of sun shone from somewhere. He would have to get onto his hands and knees to reach it.

Shimmying upon his belly, he crept closer to that dazzling ray of hope. It was a slow process to keep the rock from grating the skin from his chest. All the while, he kept his eyes trained upon his destination. A few sluggish metres more and his head became bathed in daylight. Rolling ungainly onto his back, he found himself looking up through a hollow, tree-trunk stump. There was space enough to fit through. Tucking into a ball gave him sufficient freedom to sit up. Slowly, but surely, he stood and poked his head out.

A garbled utter of awe escaped his mouth. All around were corals of every imaginable shape and colour. Some formed large flat tabletops; others looked like bony hands grasping at the sun. Dollops of red with a maze-like pattern gave the impression of human brains. In amongst these, horns of blue spiralled skywards and swirls of dark orange came out in bloom. A spot of vibrant purple met a monster of clear yellow that danced with a titan of green. Sponges, too, graced the scene; from simple hole-ridden globes to elegant chimneys.

And yet, these hard structures were merely the skeleton upon which life thrived: long-tentacled sea anemones protected small fish in their stinging embrace, a lilac octopus flopped a few arms out of a coral cave, a vibrant ray drifted behind a nearby cluster of rock and transparent shrimps frolicked over the terrain. No creation of words or paint could do it justice – Limpet had led him to a reef paradise.

So stunned was he by the view, Luke almost forgot the reason he had come. Scanning the area, he spotted her lying down in a sparse patch of sand with her arms behind her head. She looked the image of relaxation. The scowl had gone from her face as though it had never been there and instead she wore a peaceful smile.

With a lunge, Luke stepped out of what was actually the husk of a dark-red sponge, shaped like a large keg of alcohol. He crept around to the side, hidden by a claw of coral. The target of his spying looked so happy that he found that he did not want to disturb her. She almost, *almost*, looked pretty. Regardless of his intentions, she was jolted from her reverie by a loud roar.

'Limpet!' growled John. He was stood waist deep in the sponge from which Luke had only just arrived. However, he only had attention for his daughter and he was not amused. She sprung up as though a gun had been shot. Limpet *knew* she was in trouble – it showed in every aspect of her behaviour. She shuffled towards her father like a dog with its tail between its legs. Somehow, John still managed to look intimidating even though he seemed to be made of sponge from the waist down.

'Why aren't you at work?' he demanded. 'And you better know where Lugworm is or so help me...'

Limpet's eyes dropped guiltily to the seabed and was about to open her mouth to reply when Luke decided to offer her a lifeline.

'I'm over here, John,' he declared, strolling casually into sight. Limpet's eyebrows rose in surprise and then quickly recovered. 'Limpet told me about this place and I really wanted to see it for myself,' he explained. 'She was kind enough to bring me here.'

Limpet caught on and started nodding furiously. John's eyes narrowed. 'So, what you'd have me believe is, you two are actually getting along?'

She put her arm around Luke in mock friendship and gave a plastic smile. 'We're like two shrimps in a heart sponge!'

'Oh really?' John looked at Luke for confirmation.

'Yep,' Luke lied through his teeth.

'Hmmm, that changes things slightly,' John mulled, studying his daughter. 'Even so, you should have at least told

Beadlet instead of just sneaking off from work. He told me you'd gone and I took a gamble in thinking that maybe you'd come here. Having said that, it's important for Lugworm to see this side of our home. I was going to bring him myself, but...'

He scratched his beard and gave a shrug. 'Maybe this is for the best. I know how much you love this place and you certainly know your stuff. Make sure you give him a proper introduction. I have work to do so I must get back. I'll let Beadlet know where you are and that you have my permission. Tomorrow though, you'll both be back to work at the break of dawn.'

With this ultimatum, he ducked back down into the sponge and was not seen again. Limpet stood with her arm round Luke for a moment longer to make sure her father had gone and then shoved him away.

'You followed me,' she accused, rounding on him with a glare.

'I'm supposed to stay with you.'

'Did I look like I wanted you to tag along?'

'No,' he confessed.

'Well, take a hint!' she barked. 'Don't think for a second that helping me out makes us friends.'

'Doubt I'll make that mistake.'

She nodded in agreement. Her scowl had returned with a vengeance and then eased slightly. 'Still... I do owe you one.'

'You could show me around,' he suggested, gesturing towards the reef.

'Then I can go back to ignoring you?'

'If you want.'

'Fine.' She took a breath as though about to start a performance. 'These are our Coral Gardens. They've been here since I was born and probably long before my people started Naufragium. Dad used to take me here when I was a toddler. It was much easier to get through that passage back then.' She indicated towards the sponge tunnel.

'Are there other ways up?' Luke interjected.

'There are, but they aren't as fun, or discrete,' continued Limpet. 'I sneak up here on the odd occasion to think and get away from the tedium of working the fields. More people used to come here, too. The Coral Gardens used to be something us Naufragians could be proud of.'

'And why not now?' asked Luke. 'I think they're amazing.'

Limpet snorted. 'To you, perhaps they are. But, to the rest of the town, they're a reminder of what used to be.'

'I don't understand,' Luke confessed.

'Why am I not surprised,' she retorted, shaking her head. 'Your ignorance amazes me. You don't realise what it used to be like here. The Coral Gardens didn't *used* to be special, it was like this all over the place. Corals grew from head to toe, you couldn't walk through town without being engulfed in a school of fish. Now,' she said bitterly, 'the Coral Gardens represent our dwindling hope.'

There was a sad pause, in which Luke strived to change the subject. 'If you come here a lot, you must know it pretty well. Show me the best of it.'

Limpet grinned, starting a slow meander around the corals. Luke followed her with his eyes. 'The Coral Gardens are interesting because there's a lot going on that we can't see.' She pointed out the octopus that Luke had spotted earlier. 'Some of it is obvious, even to you,' she stuck out her tongue. 'Some of it is hidden away.' She paused to lightly tap a coral. A small dark eel slid out partially and studied them curiously before retreating into the safety of its home.

'That's something I believe surface scum don't get,' she continued. 'They are clearly intelligent with their floating ships and symbols, but they hardly grasp the damage they do. I wonder if they are blind to the life beneath the waves, or if they simply don't care.' She drifted off and then perked up suddenly. 'Come with me!'

He followed her to a cluster of orange sponges. They

weren't anything special, just large blobs with a single hole on the top of each one. Together though, they resembled a pack of vibrant, juicy sweets.

'Tell me, what are they doing?' Limpet quizzed.

He studied them. There was so much activity around them, but the sponges themselves just seemed to be sitting there. 'Nothing?'

Limpet wagged her finger at him. She grabbed a nearby shrimp and it shot out a cloud of bright green liquid near the sponges. Luke was intrigued.

'That's just the shrimp's defence mechanism to confuse predators,' Limpet said. 'Watch what happens next!'

They waited as the cloud dispersed. For a short while, nothing happened. Then, concentrated pillars of lime erupted majestically from each sponge hole. They wafted upwards like smoke from a chimney. Luke could not help but release a wondrous smile. 'They're pumping water?' he guessed.

'That's right. You wouldn't know it, but there's the proof. They filter it for food,' she said, clearly encouraged by Luke's delight. 'Follow me!'

They traversed over the reef, leaping from one patch of sand to the next. Luke was rather enjoying himself but was stopped short by a hand on his shoulder. 'Wait,' Limpet muttered.

'What are we looking at?' Luke asked.

Limpet pointed at something that was wobbling its way over a wall of coral. It was flat as a frisbee and swam by rippling its whole body. On top, it was covered with a complex red-and-yellow pattern. Its only discernible features were two antennas that stuck up from what must have been its front. To him, it looked like a living magic carpet. He went forward to get a closer look, but Limpet stopped him once again.

'Wait,' she repeated more firmly.

The creature gently bobbed over to a sea anemone. It seemed interested and landed at its base. With a lightning fast motion that Luke did not think it capable, it attacked. Its prey desperately tried to curl in on itself, but the carpet had a nasty bite and came away with a clump of tentacles to chew on.

Then something incredible happened. The carpet, which had seemed so harmless before, convulsed and sharp spikes swelled from its back.

'Wh-what just happened?'

'That sea slug just stole the anemone's defence system.'

'So it gained its powers?'

'That's a dorky way to put it, but yeah. Let that be a lesson to you. Just because something is pretty, does not make it friendly,' she warned. 'In fact, down here, often it's the pretty ones you have to watch out for!'

He looked at the tough girl already leading him to the next spectacle. 'I'll keep that in mind.'

If she heard him, she gave no indication. He followed, eager to see what they would find next. It struck him that he had no idea where he was on the hill anymore; all his bearings had been lost in the intricate structure of the reef. After rounding a mound of purple, their destination was in clear view.

'Whoa!' Luke gasped. In front was the biggest anemone he had ever seen. It was bright pink and about the size of a small shed. Thick, strawberry-lace tentacles waved invitingly in the currents.

'Ever been in an anemone?' Limpet asked. Luke shook his head. 'Neither have I,' she admitted, treating him to a mischievous sideways glance. 'Want to try?'

'No way, won't we get stung?'

'I don't think so. Not if we can get past its tentacles.'

Luke glanced at them as they waved back and forth. It looked like an impossible feat. 'And how do you suppose we do that?'

'With these.' Limpet picked up two long iron bars for Luke's inspection. 'If one of us holds open the tentacles, the other person can head on in.'

'Hang on,' said Luke. There was no way that those iron bars had been left there by chance alone. 'You've been planning this for a while, haven't you?'

'I've wanted to do it for a long time,' she admitted, 'but I haven't been here with anyone who was willing to give it a go.'

It did not take long for Luke to read between the lines. Nobody else had been crazy enough to take part. Anyone in their right mind would take a fleeting glimpse of that anemone and stay far away. His mind was made.

'I'll do it,' he said, shocking even himself.

Limpet grinned. 'I need to be able to trust you though. Whoever holds those iron bars has control. They could withdraw it and leave the person in there forever. I doubt someone would survive a sting from this sea beast.'

It wasn't an outright accusation, but it was enough for Luke to realise how little she trusted him and what she thought he could be capable of. It hurt slightly, as he'd given the sea people no reason to fear him.

'You can trust me,' Luke promised. 'Tell you what, I'll go in first and then it'll be *me* trusting *you*.'

Limpet looked at him with hope in her eyes. 'And then you will hold open the tentacles once you're in so that I can join you?'

He gave a nod.

'Okay, let's do this!' said Limpet, taking a few cautious steps forward.

Her face was aglow with the pink of the anemone as she carefully prodded the bars into the forest of limbs. This was done in the manner of someone being forced to disturb a beehive. She kept the two bars close together until they were half lost in the tentacles, then she slowly wrenched them apart. Luke peered over her shoulder anxiously as an opening gradually appeared.

'She's a strong one!' Limpet grunted with effort. Soon there was a small gap available. 'In you go!'

He ducked in front of her and stood up between the iron

bars; they would be his only defence against a painful death. It was like he was going to charge through the slightest breach in an army of spears. As he tiptoed towards the entrance he saw within a large circular space bordering a central pit. Surrounding this, tentacles shot upwards, preventing any possible escape.

Limpet's plan had better work, he thought. With eyes scrunched up and every muscle as tense as a guitar string, he lunged a naked foot in through the gap. It touched down on squidgy flesh. He expected a shot of searing pain, but instead he felt nothing.

'All good?' Limpet asked.

Luke opened his eyes, took a deep breath, and allowed himself to relax slightly. 'Yep,' he confirmed, bringing his remaining foot to join his other one. He had made it inside the anemone!

'How does it feel?' she called.

'It's bouncy,' he bobbed gently, as if resting on an inflatable mattress.

Limpet laughed with delight. 'My turn now.'

He grasped the bars and maintained the gap while Limpet made her way through. Luke could feel the pull of the anemone trying to resist this disturbance and tightened his grip. Once they were both safely in, he brought the bars inside and laid them down. Their exit closed, sealing them in a den of feelers.

'You're right,' Limpet gave a slight jump. 'It is bouncy!'

Luke pointed at a central chasm about a few metres away. 'I don't think we want to go in there.'

'I agree, that's the mouth of the anemone. We should be fine as long as we stick to the sides!'

Before any more could be said, Limpet was bounding about with gusto. Luke spared a moment to look around before launching himself into the air. The sheer strangeness of the situation had him in fits of laughter. As they bounced around, their faces basked in a fluorescent pink light that made them look like alien invaders. Above, Luke could see the surface jumping closer with each successive leap. He could hear Limpet giggling in front, her hair lagging behind with each fall and dragging with each rise. Luke sped up and soon they were hopping side by side.

'Race ya!' she challenged as they hurdled the bars after one full circuit.

'You're on,' said Luke with a spurt of speed. It was exhilarating. The tentacles became an indistinguishable blur. At the peak of one particularly zealous bounce, Luke saw over the top of their tips and caught a fleeting glimpse of the Coral Gardens. He felt his troubles lift from his shoulders as he sailed into the lead. Maybe Naufragium was not so bad after all!

He glanced behind, planning to showboat, but found that Limpet had stopped short about half way around. She was stood rigid as if trying to concentrate on something. He sprinted back to her.

'What's wrong?'

'Listen,' she ordered. 'I thought I heard something...'

They waited in silence. And then Luke heard the faint sound of the bell...

...Dong! Dong! Dong!...

'An attack!' they exclaimed in unison.

'Come on.' Limpet grabbed his wrist and they made for the bars. 'We have to go!'

CHAPTER 7: TRAWL TRAUMA

They ran as fast as they could, feet pounding on the shell-covered street. Field upon field passed by in a flash. All the while, Limpet tracked the surface with her gaze, striving to see the source of the attack. Luke spied a large, dark shadow that loomed above their heads and pointed. She nodded and swiftly changed direction.

'We're going towards it?' Luke shouted.

'Maybe we can help!' Limpet answered.

Swerving, she ran headlong into a meadoweed field and Luke had no choice but to do the same. It was much faster this time. The strands whipped his skin raw, but he was out before he'd been given a chance to think. When he could see once more, Limpet was further ahead and had left behind a trail of deep, frantic footprints. Naufragians with spears, old swords and daggers were likewise emerging from the fields. Soon they were in the midst of stampede, all running single-mindedly at... at... what exactly?

Above him, the mysterious black shape had taken on a more familiar form; the hull of a large ship, shooting across the surface. Attached by ropes was a gaping trawl net that it dragged along the seabed. At first, the threat seemed quiet and distant but as they sprinted closer, the rumble of destruction grew. To his horror, he saw that some unfortunate Naufragians had been caught in the net and were desperately struggling to break out of its snare. Amongst them were strands of algae and a scattering of fish that were too large to escape its confines.

Rescue attempts were already in full swing, albeit with varying levels of success. Some Naufragians had attempted to catch hold of the net as it passed. Most failed and were left behind in a sand-clogged haze as their fellows got hauled away. Those few that managed to cling on could be seen working to cut the net free, while others were getting flung off by sheer velocity and falling by the wayside.

As luck would have it, Luke and Limpet were in front of the ship, primed to intercept. They would have to run fast to get to the net before it was whisked out of reach. Luke had no idea what he was going to do, but the bravado of the charge was infectious. He overtook Limpet with a crazed war cry, adrenaline pumping through his body.

The damage caused by the net became ever more evident as he approached. Boulders were flung carelessly to the side, dunes of sand were scattered in its wake and a deep scarring grove trailed behind. And the noise, it would have put a rocket to shame!

Luke had almost made it to the net as it rampaged by. Immediately he was blinded by sand and was all too aware that it was now or never. There was only one thing for it – he dived forwards with both hands outstretched in a vain hope that he'd encounter something to grab. Through the sandy mist, his fingers found a piece of rope and he clung on for dear life. The net was travelling even faster than he had expected. His body blew around like a flag in the wind and it took considerable effort to bring his legs down.

Climbing upwards soon got him out of the smog and enabled him to see more clearly. Below, he could just about make out the figure of Elkhorn. His biceps were bulging as he clutched the net like a blanket and ineffectively grinded his feet along the ground to slow it down.

'Elkhorn! You idiot!' he heard Con scream above the racket from somewhere higher up. 'You're strong but you can't stop a trawl net, you fool! I need you here!'

Luke looked up. Con was at the very top sawing away

energetically at one of the two ropes that pulled the net along. He seemed to have the right idea. Most of the others could only just about maintain their hold, let alone think clearly enough to aid him. Perhaps it was Luke's slighter build, but something made him more agile and enabled him to climb where others could not. As he set off up the net, he heard someone call his name.

'Ug. Orm...'

It was weak and hardly audible in the storm. He scanned around and spotted Brittle staring at him with tired eyes. Both of the man's knuckles were white with strain as he gripped the net. In his mouth, he bit down on the handle of a hacksaw.

'I. an't. hol. On. Much. Lon'ga.' Each word was a battle. 'Tak. Et.'

It took a while for Luke to comprehend this, but he soon figured it out. He carefully grabbed the saw from Brittle's mouth, freeing it from obstruction.

'Hold on!' Luke implored.

The man shook his head in exhaustion.

'Find Con!'

With this final instruction, Brittle expended the last of his energy, released his grip and tumbled harshly into the sandy chaos below. Luke hoped that he was alright and placed the handle in his own mouth; this was no time to be squeamish. He had received his orders and began to climb up.

En route, he clambered over people trying to save their loved ones. A man hacked at the rope with an axe, but to no avail. A mother reached through the net to clasp hands with a terrified young boy who was stuck in its deadly pocket. A school of fish were frantically zipping from place to place in a futile attempt to find a gap. The scenes tugged at Luke's heart strings, but he passed by with the hardened resolve of a soldier.

Like an upside-down parachute, the net was attached at two corners. The rest of the material was acting to catch whatever it could. Con was on one side, so Luke purposefully climbed around to the other. When he reached the top, he stood level with Con and about two metres away.

'Lugworm!' Con roared with a maddened grin. 'And you have a saw! In all my life, I never thought I'd be pleased to see surface scum!'

In the midst of all this disarray, the man seemed more at home than ever. He was laughing insanely and sawing the rope like a lunatic. Every one of his actions seemed to challenge the world to do its worst. On the odd occasion, he'd glare up at the ship defiantly and shout something incoherent. Luke was stopped in his tracks by the mere image of it, but his hesitance was soon called out.

'Well, what are you waiting for? Get sawing, Wormy! I'm not sure how long we have before those sponge-heads start hauling this thing up,' demanded Con, adding extra vigour to his own efforts.

No more encouragement was needed. Luke took to sawing with a ferocity that almost matched that of Con's. He was playing catch up – his partner-in-crime's rope was already halfway to splitting. Spurred on by the cries below, Luke's arms pumped mercilessly. If the net got reeled in beyond the surface, any Naufragians would suffocate and die. Not on his watch.

'That's what I'm talking about!' Con cackled.

A loud cranking noise joined the clamour. The net started to rise slowly off the ground. A few of the defenders, who had bravely leapt to the rescue moments before, realised that the battle had been lost – they started to let go and jump onto the safety of the sand. With each abandon, the net got lighter and quickened its relentless journey to the surface. The mother, Luke noticed, remained to comfort the young boy. Elkhorn, meanwhile, was dangling by his hands at the bottom of the net. Every bit of weight gave them more time.

'Don't you dare think about jumping!' Con bellowed, eyeing Luke ferociously. 'Let me know when you are ready to cut through!'

The net was still rising; it must have been ten or twenty metres above the seabed. Any higher and the fall would kill them all anyway! Luke increased his sawing pace even more until all that remained of the rope was a few threads.

'I'm ready!' he yelled.

'Prepare for impact!' Con responded. 'Finish it off wormy!'

In unison, they scraped and yanked. Con's rope was the first to snap. He shot out of sight and the whole net gave a violent jolt. The movement almost threw Luke off completely, but he held on with one hand. Panic started to set in - his rope alone was still causing the net and contents to rise! Haunting images of failure seeped through his brain; it was not an option. Blindly, he lunged above his head, waving the saw about aimlessly. He must have made contact because, seconds later, the net, and everything in it, began to fall.

It smashed into the sea bed with the grace of a water bomb hitting concrete. Heaps of netting spilled out in all directions and a mushroom cloud of sand exploded into suspension. The groans of the injured could be heard from all around and somewhere a woman was wailing.

Luke was facedown, staring uncomprehendingly at rope and sediment. The impact had shaken him, but he was uninjured as far as he could tell. Given a bit more time to recover, he managed to flop onto his back. Through the sandy mist, he saw the shadow of the ship continuing naively on its way as though it knew nothing of the war beneath the waves.

'Ah, there you are, Wormy!' Con stood above him. Beneath his chin was a fresh gash that gave off a dark, red smoke. He was smiling maliciously, yet offering a helping hand. Luke woozily accepted and was pulled to his feet. 'You did good for an outsider!'

Before he could respond, Con slapped him on the back in camaraderie and then strode off into the midst of the battleground. It took great effort for Luke to remain standing but somehow he did. Zombie-like, he picked his way over the fallen web and aimed to find a familiar face. On his way, a man stumbled by hailing a name he did not recognise. The young boy and his mum appeared to Luke's right, reunited again. Elkhorn walked around and looked like he was wearing the net as a ghostly Halloween costume. A number of people were trying to lead him out of the vicinity. When Luke found himself clear of the commotion, he was confronted by a large crowd.

They were a sorry bunch. Dismay was written over every face and nobody spoke. Early defenders, who had missed the net as it crashed by, were still running to catch up. Some members of the gathering rushed towards the scene of the crime to find missing people, while others stood there dumbfounded. Technically they had won, but the cost was still being worked out. The sand began to settle, revealing Luke in more detail to the watching people.

'It's him! The boy who cut down the net!' an old lady cried out. 'I saw the whole thing!'

Luke realised that he still clasped the saw in one hand.

'Isn't that what's-his-name... the bellboy?' a deep voice boomed.

'What? You mean the surface scum?' someone questioned in disbelief.

The confusion mounted.

'Lugworm!' a familiar voice called. It was Limpet. She had caught up and shoved her way to the front row of the gang. Luke noticed that she did not run out to greet him in the eye of the public. He was forced to slowly make his way to her location.

'You look like hell,' she stated. Luke nodded wearily. 'Come on, let's get you home.'

She walked off into the crowd which immediately parted to clear the way. As Luke made his way through, one man – was it Beadlet? – started to beat his own bare chest. A few joined him and eventually everyone was copying. Thud, thud, thud. The sound filled the water and Luke heard it all the way to the street of shells. Thud, thud, thud.

***

'I don't get it!' Luke scrunched his face up in confusion. Limpet was sat opposite with her feet stretched out lazily on the table. They were passing the time by snacking on a mixed bowl of meadoweed and chatting over the day's events. John himself had not yet returned and it was getting late. Through wooden gaps, the gelata outside flashed a variety of colours across the room.

'What don't you get?' Limpet said warily.

'We don't float because we're originally from the land.'

'Possibly,' she conceded.

'And sea creatures float because they are one with the sea.'

'So I believe.'

'But,' Luke protested, 'that ship was floating. It just doesn't make any sense. How is that possible?'

'Good question. I was wondering when you'd ask that. In fact, I'm surprised you didn't ask it sooner, what with the town being made up of *shipwrecks*!'

That thought had not even crossed Luke's mind. Now that Limpet had mentioned it, he was even more quizzical than before. How could this town exist if ships hadn't floated in the first place?

'Well?' he demanded.

Limpet left him hanging in confusion for a while longer before giving in. 'Ships that can float are made of a very special wood. In a way, the wood itself is alive. Before I was born there used to be a special type of turtle. These creatures fed off the sun like seaweed does, but they could only do this with the help of a plant. The turtles and the plants were a team, each depending upon the other.' She entwined her hands to emphasise her point.

'Anyway, these turtles had massive wooden shells made of – well, we called it turtle-oak. Once the surface people had realised how special these were, they would capture and kill the turtles to build their ships.'

'So the plants and the turtle were one being?'

'Near enough.'

'And the surface people killed the turtles for their shells?'

'While they were laying eggs on the land, yes.'

Luke creased his forehead with concentration as he tried to absorb this. 'But when we cut the meadoweed, it no longer floated. Surely killing a turtle would stop it floating too!'

'Ah, very good, there *is* more than sponge in that head of yours!' Limpet smiled. 'When a turtle dies, the plant lives on within its shell, but for a limited amount of time.'

'So once the plant eventually dies, the turtleoak shells just stop floating?'

'Correct. The surface people did not know this straight away. When they sent out their fleet, their ships dropped like stones in the midst of their voyage. And this is the result,' she gestured around John's homey wreck. 'We have made a town of their folly.'

Luke was struggling with the concept. 'And so they have to keep building more ships of fresh turtleoak?'

'Yep, except we haven't seen any turtles for decades. We think the surface scum must have caused their extinction,' she said solemnly.

Luke had a thought. 'If that's the case, how are they making more ships?'

Limpet's eyes narrowed. 'You know, I should be asking you that! You're from the surface, after all.'

'But I'm not!' Luke protested.

'Then where are you from?'

He looked into her eyes. The limpet that was sucked onto her face had moved round to her left cheek, its rays of blue even more prominent in the dim. 'I still don't remember.' He shook his head slowly. 'Now and then, I feel like it's all coming back, but right now, I have no idea. I had a dream last night. It did not tell me much, but it did enable me to remember one thing. My name is not Lugworm. My real name is Luke. And someone out there wants me to come home.' He held his hands up helplessly. 'Wherever home might be!'

Limpet was frowning at him as though he was crazy. He realised he had been babbling about his dream and wondered how strange he must sound. Perhaps he did have a few screws loose!

The door swung open at the opportune moment, a well-timed respite from the awkward silence that was developing. 'Hello there,' John greeted, bounding into the room.

'Father!' said Limpet, hastily removing her feet from the table. 'What news do you have?'

'No deaths,' he smiled with content. 'Not one! Plenty of injuries, mind you.'

'Who?' Limpet demanded.

'Not many people that you know. Our friend Brittle has a broken leg, but it's been secured and hopefully he'll be walking in months. Elkhorn came out mostly unscathed. God knows how! He was beneath the net when it collapsed! That boy may be stupid, but he's tougher than a hungry crab.' John made his way round and put his hands on Luke's shoulders. 'It would have been far worse without the hero of the hour. You must have cut that rope just in time! People have been singing your praises, my boy. Along with Con's, of course. Without your help, that net could have risen and killed its captives, either from the fall or suffocation beyond the surface. That's the second good turn you've done this town in the last three days.'

'Not to mention that the bell Lugworm fixed rallied the town's defenders. Without that warning, we'd have had no chance,' Limpet added and Luke blushed.

'You alright, boy?' John had noticed Luke's face reddening.

'Fine actually,' he replied hastily. 'Glad I could help!'

John stroked his beard and appeared to be in deep

thought. 'Limpet, go to bed would you? I need to talk to Lugworm in private.

She didn't look happy as she trudged to her cabin and mumbled a good night. John waited until she had closed her door and then turned to Luke. 'You won't be going to the harvest tomorrow.'

'Why not?' Luke's heart sank.

'Don't tell me you're disappointed,' John chuckled.

'No,' he lied.

'Well then, cheer up! I have other plans for you. I was going to wait a while, but your actions today have gained you a lot of trust. I want you to come to a meeting with me.'

'Why?'

'You'll find out when you get there.'

'And Limpet?'

'She'll be working as per usual,' he waved his hands in a dismissive manner. 'Now off to bed with you!'

Obediently, Luke went to his cabin, bidding farewell to John on the way. As soon as he reached his bunk, he collapsed in a tired heap. Just as Luke was about to fall asleep, he saw the blue glow of the whelk through his barely-open eyelids. Drowsily, he fumbled for the shell until his hand was touching its rough exterior. As before, a distorted voice echoed through his head. This time it was clearer.

'You did well today,' Garth approved, *'but you took risks. You should be more careful. We cannot afford to lose you, too much depends on your survival.'*

'But you haven't told me anything,' Luke whispered furiously. He wanted to shout, but he had to be quiet for fear of disturbing Limpet or John. 'We've hardly spoken and I'm so confused. Who am I and what am I doing here?'

'There are some things you do not need to know right now. Who you are is one of them. Just know this, you are here for an extremely important reason.'

'And that is?' Luke demanded with perhaps too much volume.

'*To save this universe,*' Garth replied, as if such a task was as simple as doing the washing up. '*You are already making such good progress. We have learnt so much. Life here is dwindling. The whole dimension is teetering because of it. If many more lives are lost, the dimension will simply collapse, taking you and everyone else who remains with it.*'

Luke listened, dumbfounded. He thought of John, Limpet and all those he knew. Did all those lives truly rest on his scrawny shoulders?

'Why me?' Luke quietly implored.

'*I -*' Garth hesitated. '*I made a mistake. I messed with something I did not understand.*'

The voice had suddenly changed its tone, catching Luke completely off guard. It sounded younger, possibly even younger than Luke himself.

'*I-I'm sorry,*' Garth apologised. '*But I'm not sorry that I chose you. You have proven your worth time and time again. You must hate me.*'

Luke searched his feelings and found no anger or hate, just gladness to finally have some honest answers.

'I don't hate you,' he said truthfully.

'*Not yet, perhaps,*' Garth said. '*But you will. Right now, you don't remember what you've lost. Penn says, if you live long enough, your memory will return.*'

Luke had more questions, like who was Penn, but his tiredness made him ask the only one that truly mattered. 'How do I save everyone?'

'*Ah,*' started Garth, his voice warming to the change of subject. '*You've already started on that path without my help. We have learnt so much. From your exploits so far, I believe this planet is fuelled by the food of the sea. This is only a theory, of course. Keep learning, keep enquiring. We need to find the biggest problem and then fix it. Do you understand?*'

'I think so,' said Luke.

'*Good,*' Garth said. '*Together, we will clean up this mess.*'

***

The next morning, Luke was stood upon the deck of the eldership with a mind crammed with questions. Joining him was a substantial group of people from which he picked out a few faces. Elkhorn and Con stood to his left, exchanging tales of their experiences from the day before. Behind, Goby was chatting and laughing with some strangers. At one point, Luke caught his eye and he gave a friendly nod. Brittle was nowhere to be seen, presumably unable to scale the steps because of his broken leg.

Aside from John, the only other person that Luke could identify was the man who had throttled Con on the night of the feast. He towered over everyone with an expression of mild disinterest. His single uncovered eye scanned the deck suspiciously while the other was hidden by an eyepatch; a cockle shell strapped to his head by a thin piece of string.

He must have been in his mid-twenties, but his unruly appearance added decades. A scraggly cloud of curls grew on his head and beyond; his chest, shoulders and back were covered in thick brown patches. He looked more animal than man. Luke was about to continue his study when their eyes met and he hastily looked away. Just as a blush started to rise, John tried to draw the attention of all present.

'Quiet down,' he heard him say, but to no avail. The captain stood on a large wooden crate staring out over his motley crew.

'QUIETTTTTTTT!' he repeated with multiplied volume and any talk was rapidly cut short. 'Thank you. Before I tell you why I have called this meeting, I would like to make it known how proud I am of the town's defence yesterday. Not only did we save those who had been captured from certain death, but the net will be taken apart for some desperately needed rope.'

'They'll think twice next time!' Con interrupted and punched the air. Others shouted their support. John smiled patiently.

'At the front of the attack, as you all well know, were Con and his crew. They were quickly joined by anyone with a sharp tool. This just shows what we can achieve when we are united,' John continued. 'At this critical moment, it was Con and our prisoner, Lugworm, who cut the vital ropes. They saved the townspeople when they could have jumped to safety. I believe Lugworm proved where his loyalty lies.'

A few people nodded, but some looked sceptical.

'Now, I don't need to tell you of our problems. You are all too aware of the lack of fish nowadays. We cannot build our society on seaweed alone. Where have they gone and why? These questions have plagued us for years.'

'Those greedy surface scum have taken them all!' a woman screeched.

'That's the general opinion, yes,' said John, keeping his cool. 'But our idea of the surface people has been formed through speculation. We don't actually know. And surely they'd need more boats to stop us from getting all the fish and yet sightings of trawlers are fairly rare. I believe there is something else at play here.'

'That's speculation as well, you hypocrite!' a man pointed out from the back of the congregation.

'I am merely suggesting that there could be another reason,' John responded. 'Anyway, didn't you notice that the net yesterday was basically empty? There were a couple of fish large enough to eat, but the rest of its contents were Naufragians and seaweed. They clearly don't like eating us, because they just seem to throw our carcasses off the side. And I, like the rest of you, want answers. We can't solve anything without more information. '

He waited to gage their reaction and saw a sea of nods.

'Before now, we have not had the chance to talk to them. We cannot survive up there. History tells us that attempts to make contact from beneath the surface have been met with confusion and hostility.' He paused again. 'But we have been handed an opportunity here. Lugworm can survive both below and above the surface.'

'An opportunity? We've been sent a freak and you've welcomed him with open arms!'

Luke turned around expecting this accusation to come from Con, but it derived from an angry stranger. Nonetheless, the words caused a murmur of discontent.

'Need I remind you all that Lugworm fixed the bell that enabled the whole town to rally to the attack?'

'A ploy! To gain our trust!' the frail voice of an old man pierced the water.

'And then he acted against his own kind and destroyed their net?' John scoffed. 'In our town that would be treason and he'd be punished by death! Don't you see? Lugworm can be trusted!'

Determination burned in John's eyes. One woman turned to Con. 'Surely you can't be in agreement here? That man's out of his mind!'

Con went rigid and did not reply straight away. His lips looked pursed tight as though he was about to say words that would cause him physical pain. The crowd waited impatiently for his response. 'Lugworm can be trusted,' he eventually said with uncharacteristic quietness.

Pandemonium broke out. Clearly Con's agreement had not been expected and meant a lot to these people. John knew it; he stood with a discrete smile on his face. Whatever the man had in mind, Luke reckoned it had just been given a chance of being accepted. Ignoring any questions, John waited until a natural silence occurred.

'So it's settled then,' he said with all his authority. 'Lugworm can be trusted and that is why I intend to send him to Solis Occassum!'

If it were possible, the people were even more outraged. Luke himself paled.

'He will be our conduit. Our crab spy like from the old stories,' John persisted over the cries. 'He shall find whoever is captain and tell him of our plight. He shall be our eyes and ears on the surface. Then he will come back with valuable information.'

'What if he tells them of our location?'

'What if he never comes back?'

'What if he comes back, but with an army of people who can survive down here?'

These questions eroded away at John's proposal like tea against a recently dunked digestive biscuit.

'I won't.' Something, perhaps honour, made Luke speak out. Nobody heard his first attempt apart from John who beckoned him onto the crate. 'I won't,' he repeated.

The crowd went deadly silent as, one by one, they realised who now stood before them.

'I won't tell them of your location – I don't even know where we are!' Luke shouted. 'And I won't come back with an army, I promise. In the short while I have stayed here, I have come to like Naufragium. You have kept me alive and for that I am in your debt.'

The crowd absorbed his words, but looked at him doubtfully.

'Believe me,' Luke implored.

'These are tough times and we need to take action,' John shouted, taking control of the conversation once more. 'Sometimes we have to put our faith in something and hope that it goes our way. I shall put *my* faith in Lugworm to do as he has promised.'

'And I!' Goby boomed from beneath his moustache.

'Me too,' voiced Elkhorn.

'Aye, what other options do we have?' agreed a hunchbacked woman with crooked teeth.

'We don't,' said John grimly. 'Unless, of course, someone else can suggest another way to bring back the fish?'

There was a disgruntled quiet as everyone strived to come up with an alternative. One man's eyes flared up with hope and he opened his mouth to speak. In the next second, he deflated like a balloon and the fight went out of him. 'No, that would never work,' he muttered to himself.

'So it's agreed then,' stated John after the silence had dragged on for too long. 'Lugworm will be trusted with this quest.'

Nobody spoke out against him.

'There's one more matter to discuss. Somebody needs to travel with Lugworm to Solis Occassum. I'm sorry to ask this of you, but you're the only person who knows a way in. Gentle Stuart, will you do it?'

He was talking to the man with the eyepatch. The half-wolf-half-man jolted awake at the mention of his name. 'Wha?'

'Take Lugworm to Solis Occassum,' John reiterated.

'I don't want to,' Stuart growled.

'Well I'm asking you to. You're the only person who knows where the secret passage is.'

'I don't know the way n'more.'

'Try to remember!' John appealed.

'Fine,' Stuart bit back moodily. 'Shallows.'

'We'll meet you there.'

With this, the man stomped off the eldership and down the rock staircase.

'That's that then.' John clapped his hands together. 'The meeting is over. If anyone would like to offer any equipment to Lugworm, bring it to the shallows. Elkhorn, this is a momentous occasion. I think it deserves the sound of that glorious bell!'

Elkhorn rubbed his hands in delight and gleefully ran to the rope. Soon the sound of the bell rang through Naufragium. The crowd dispersed and small trails of people strolled off the eldership and down to the street of shells. John put his arm round Luke in excitement.

'You did well, Lugworm. Thank you.'

'You saved my life. I owe you!'

'I save your life and so it's only fair that you try to save

Naufragium. Sounds entirely fair,' John joked. 'Is there anything you need from home?'

Luke was about to shake his head when he remembered the whelk. 'Just one thing and then I'm set.'

'Okay, we'll pop back and then it's time you were on your way.'

Luke gulped. In the heat of the meeting, all he could feel was excitement at the thought of being a hero, but now that it was over, trepidation was rising like a flash flood.

New adventures meant new dangers, and he had already experienced his fair share in Naufragium.

CHAPTER 8: GENTLE STUART

After grabbing the whelk, Luke followed John down the main street. They were heading towards the shallows and the start of his next adventure. Despite Luke's bravado back at the eldership, he had more than his share of misgivings. The moment had caught him up and swept him away, but now reality was knocking. He was going to be walking into the unknown once again. Although Naufragium was bizarre and alien, it had, at least, made him feel safe for a while. The feast and the Coral Gardens had put the shipwreck town in a favourable light. Even working on the meadoweed fields suddenly did not seem so bad. He was shocked to realise that he was actually reluctant to leave.

Then there was the matter of the wolfman. Stuart had seemed unfriendly to say the least. He would no doubt be a tedious companion. Couldn't Limpet take him instead? When they had first met, she had been intolerable, but the Coral Gardens had revealed a hidden kindness that Luke rather liked.

Finally, there was the overwhelming sense of imminent danger. Not even the Naufragians knew what he would find on the land which, he supposed, was why he was being sent there at all.

So deep in thought was Luke that he did not realise when his face was cast in the shadow of the eldership as they walked beneath it. John halted on the far side and looked up at the towering mast. 'You're quiet,' he observed.

'I'm just thinking,' mumbled Luke.

John nodded understandingly and then turned grave. 'Look Lugworm, I need you to pay attention to what I'm about to say. It's very important. You may have to find your own way back to Naufragium. Once you get to Solis Occassum, Stuart will wait for a few days, but we need him here.

'I am about to trust you with something. For you to be able to return, you need to know our location. I believe what you said up there, else there is no way that I would reveal such dangerous information.'

He paused to stress the gravity of what he was about to say.

'Whether you return above the surface on some kind of ship or you trek along the seabed, you must start from the bay of Solis Occassum. From there, you should head directly south-east. This bearing will lead you straight to the eldership's main mast and to the town of Naufragium. Do you understand?'

'South-east,' Luke nodded determinedly. 'Got it.'

'Good,' John said. 'Working compasses are hard to come by. There are only three that I know of in the whole town. Gentle Stuart has one and I happen to have another. It is mine to give away. I was hoping to pass it to Limpet one day, but this is a worthy cause.' He reached inside a bulging shirt pocket and withdrew a bulky hunk of metal. John looked at it wistfully and then handed it to Luke.

'Thank you,' said Luke.

'It's only to borrow,' John reminded him. 'Just another reason why your return is absolutely crucial.'

The device was weighty and sat awkwardly in Luke's palm. It was a round rusty chunk with a cracked glass screen. For such a prized possession, he thought it rather ugly, but understood its significance. Through the glass, a silver needle quivered northwards as though trying to flee. Familiar letters were inscribed around the screen, each representing the four main directions; North, East, South and West. In his hands and in his head, Luke now held information that could reveal Naufragium to friend or foe. The trust that John had in him was humbling.

'Do you know how to use it?' John enquired.

Luke shook his head – he had never been one for navigation.

'Let me show you,' John said. As they strolled to the shallows, John taught Luke how to take a bearing by rotating on the spot, until the needle correctly pointed to the northern markings on the compass. What followed were a number of rigorous tests. John would ask Luke to step a few steps east, only to retreat a few strides south moments later. He spun Luke in a circle and asked him which way was north. This continued until he was confident that Luke could use the compass to go in any direction of his choice.

'Good,' John eventually said, with a satisfied smile. 'Best put it away for now. I am not sure how others would feel about me giving you such a device.'

It only just fit in Luke's free pocket. He had to tie his trunks a bit tighter to stop them from falling down from the sheer weight of it. John noticed his struggle.

'You'll get a pack to put it in when we get to Stuart,' he assured. 'Come on, we don't want to keep him waiting.'

***

The shallows, as it happened, was a term used to describe the end of the town and the start of the meadoweed fields. It was here that Gentle Stuart was waiting, along with Goby and Beadlet. As Luke and John approached, Goby gave a friendly wave, while Beadlet nodded his head gravely. Stuart, on the other hand, was holding some nasty looking spears and appeared to be entirely swamped in his own thoughts.

'Hello there!' Goby greeted them.

'Goby!' John grinned. 'Glad you could make it. Have you got them?'

'I sure have and Beadlet has stuffed them full of

meadoweed for the journey.'

'Fantastic!' John said. 'Here Lugworm, put this on.'

He handed over one of the weirdest objects that Luke had ever set eyes on. It was about the size of a stocking. Both ends were curved into a gentle 'U' shape and had long curly tendrils coming off each corner. These had been tied into straps, giving it a rucksack-like quality. It was a translucent yellow colour and Luke could see a bundle of meadoweed stored within. To touch, it felt leathery and thick.

'What is it?' he asked curiously.

'What you've got there is a mermaid's purse,' responded Goby.

Luke continued to look baffled which caused an outburst of chuckles from all but Stuart.

'That's our name for a shark egg,' John explained.

'This... came from a shark?'

'A particularly large one, yes. See that slit at the top?'

Luke looked and there was indeed an opening.

'A female shark will lay a few of these and attach them to rocks by those long strings. Eventually, the newborn shark will develop and leave its egg,' John informed. 'The empty cases they leave behind are really handy for carrying items, especially on long journeys.'

'I see,' said Luke, shuffling his arms into each loop and trying to get used to the feel of the egg sack on his back. 'How long will the journey take?'

'Two days at least. More if you run into trouble.'

'Trouble?'

'Who knows what the sea might throw at you. We are not alone and everything here is fighting for survival,' John warned. 'Whatever happens, listen to Stuart. He has made this journey once before, many, many years ago.'

'You have food, spears and a guide,' said Goby, clapping Luke firmly on the shoulder. 'Looks like you are all set!'

'Thank you,' Luke said. 'And to you too, Beadlet, for the food.'

'Tha's a'right. Y'can help o' the field when ya ge' back.'

With that, Beadlet and Goby set off in opposite directions. John, however, lingered. He grabbed Luke by both shoulders and fixed him with an intense stare.

'Find out where the fish have gone. Get us information. Save Naufragium,' he demanded.

'I will,' Luke promised, suddenly finding himself struggling for breath as he was pulled into a tight bear hug. At first he was shocked, but then he returned the gesture and patted John's back.

'Trust Stuart,' was John's final advice, before the town's captain strode off into the distance.

Luke had no time to gather his courage. Stuart prodded him with the handle of a spear, indicating that it was time to go. They rambled down the street of shells in-between fields of green. Eventually, they arrived where the road petered out to bare sand. The end of Naufragium. He was about to take his first conscious step into the wilderness when -

'Lugworm!' someone hailed.

It was Limpet and she was charging towards him from behind. Stuart kept going, oblivious to the hold up. Luke turned to face her and she stopped short as though unsure of what she wanted to say. He smiled at her sadly.

'Goodbye Limpet,' he said.

'Come back, yeah?'

'I'll try,' was the best he could give her.

'You better had, we never finished that race,' Limpet pouted moodily.

Luke laughed. He had so many reasons to return: to give back the compass, to help Naufragium and to work with Beadlet on the meadoweed fields. Of all of them, the race with Limpet in a giant anemone was the most appealing. He gave the messy girl one last glance and waved solemnly before hastening to catch up. She did not remain to see him disappear, but turned on her heels to continue her work.

The journey to Solis Occassum had begun.

***

Sand stretched out in all directions. Any hint of Naufragium had long disappeared and had been replaced by a featureless desert. Stuart was leading the way using landmarks unknown. He carried a bundle of sharp spears and likewise had a mermaid's purse strapped to his back. Since Naufragium, hardly any words had passed between them. Luke had called out after spotting the distant Coral Gardens and had received a confirmation nod from his guide. Now, however, there was nothing to see and nothing to talk about. They trod onwards.

The terrain had changed. Unlike Naufragium, which was built on an expanse of gently sloping seabed, the land now resembled a series of hills. It looked like someone had taken a perfectly-ironed blanket and given it a violent ruffling. Their route kept shifting; sometimes they would be straining upwards with heavy breaths, the next they would be struggling to keep their footing as they teetered down a sharp dune. At some points, they walked so close to the surface that, if Luke had wanted, he could have jumped, stuck his hand out and waved at the sky. When this was true, the sun was so strong that a beautiful pattern played on the sand.

Shades of yellow dominated the scenery. When a small dash of orange swam towards them, it was a pleasant surprise - a familiar fish.

When it arrived at their location, it darted around Stuart thrice and then drifted towards Luke. Was this truly the same fish who gave him a brief visit on the mast? The prospect seemed ridiculous. And yet, when he laid his hand out flat, the fish settled on it briefly as if to confirm his suspicions. He noticed that even Stuart had paused and was studying him thoughtfully.

'What are you doing all the way out here, Jaws?' Luke asked.

Predictably, Jaws did not respond. He simply continued to stare.

'Eyes of the sea,' grunted Stuart.

'What?' Luke was jolted from his reunion. 'What did you say?'

But the wolfman did not reply and had clearly decided that their short pause had been long enough. He set off purposefully.

'Wait up!' Luke requested, hurrying after him. Walking was not fast enough to catch up. Eventually, he had to jog to make up the distance. Jaws bobbed loyally at his side and Luke was thankful for his company. As the fish wiggled through the water, his overlapping scales would occasionally catch the sunlight and flash prettily.

They continued in this style for a considerable distance. Stuart trudged in front, Luke followed and Jaws meandered. The monotony was broken slightly when Luke saw a gelata coasting near the surface. Unlike those he had seen in the town, this one was not bound to the ground. Slightly further, Luke saw two more, pulsing close together; a pairing of chance, he reckoned. When they reached a third, particularly lonely, gelata, Stuart stopped in his tracks.

'Gelata fields,' he grumbled in explanation.

Luke scanned around. Field, he decided, was a very loose term. The surrounding area had no recognisable boundaries and was far bumpier than any pasture he'd seen. There weren't even that many gelatas! He had expected hundreds, but counted a measly five.

Stuart removed his mermaid's purse and took out a noosed coil of rope. Luke, a few metres behind, watched cautiously. The wolfman gripped the rope with both hands and, with a practiced flourish, twirled it above his head like a cowboy. A quick flick of the wrist sent a trail shooting towards the unaware gelata. With unbelievable accuracy, the lasso wrapped around its tentacles and tightened. Stuart casually hauled and reeled in his catch as though it was no extraordinary feat. Luke gaped in awe as the one-eyed man shortened its leash with a sharp dagger.

'Hold,' he requested simply.

Luke took it in one hand and felt a slight pull from its captive above. Seemingly unmindful of his partner's admiration, Stuart started trekking once more. Ensuring a tight grip, Luke did likewise.

They made a strange crew to say the least. A wolfman, a fish, and a boy, with a gelata in tow.

***

Luke was already sick of hills. In the past few hours, their path had led them up and down more times than a yo-yo. Walking over solid ground would have been bad enough, but they were traversing over *sand*. It drained his energy and gnawed at his aching knees. More than once, he had almost let go of the gelata and let it float away like a discarded fairground prize.

As for his leader, Stuart showed no sign of slowing and walked doggedly forwards. He had stopped navigating from memory and had started using his compass. Sometimes he would glance down at its screen, rotate on the spot and carry on at an alternate bearing. Luke hoped the man knew where they were going.

They crested a substantial mound and he saw an immobile, dark shadow lurking ahead. Stuart walked towards it, undeterred. Closer up, Luke found he was looking at the remains of another shipwreck, half-buried in the sediment. Unlike Naufragium, its rotting wood was near enough uninhabited. A few limpets had found this improbable structure, but that was all. The area had the atmosphere of a graveyard. Death ruled here.

'Where is he taking us, Jaws?' Luke uttered, hoping that speaking would settle his rising trepidation.

Stuart paced beyond and up the next sand bank. It was steep, but the view at its peak provided a panoramic of the surrounding land. Below, the lumpy topography of the seabed stretched out like bubble wrap of mind-numbing proportions. Littered about were more death-wrecks from years gone by. When Luke caught up, the eerie scene filled him with fear. He got a sudden urge to return to the life-filled Naufragium and its bustling population.

The friendly light of day was beginning to dwindle and night was approaching. Five hills later, Stuart led them both into a small, sloped pit. On one side, the tip of a boulder poked out from its sandy quilt.

'Give,' the wolfman said.

Luke handed him the gelata-laden rope. Stuart tied it to the boulder and then started munching on some meadoweed from his bag. Luke deduced that they intended to stay here for the night. He was trying to work out if he was pleased by the chance to rest or anxious to get as far from this place as possible. They sat in silence as the darkness grew. Jaws, meanwhile, settled on the boulder beneath the ever-brightening gelata.

'Sleep.' Stuart pointed at Luke and then turned his finger on himself. 'Watch.'

Luke understood. One of them had to be on guard, while the other got some much-needed rest. He lay down, but there wasn't quite enough space to stretch out; his head and feet were raised by the shape of the pit. Through the slits of his eyelids, he observed Stuart sharpening the spears with a knife. He could not feel at ease in such a place and struggled to fall asleep. When he finally drifted off, the area beyond their abode was pitch-black.

***

Garth scrunched up a can of Slarg and threw it carelessly to the side. It joined an unruly pile of food packaging that had gathered amongst the wiring. Unlike Luke, he was not going to sleep tonight. As he sat there, wrapped in his own wingflaps, downing another can of drink and munching on a packet of insects, he realised that he was afraid.

'Penn,' he said. 'This does not feel safe at all.'

'Oh, it's not,' she replied. 'But, so long as you're not connected to an object when something bad happens, you should be absolutely fine.'

'So I can be hurt?' Garth asked, wondering why this had only just occurred to him.

Penn paused. 'I forget how little you know. If I had the time, I would have waited until you had gone to the academy. There's a whole course on dimension shifting.'

This was news to Garth, but something Penn had said made his pointy ears perk up. 'You just said 'If I had the time'. What do you mean by that?' he demanded, jolting upright in his seat.

Penn's light blinked frantically. 'A girl has to have her secrets,' she tried with a playful tone.

'Not this time,' Garth responded, refusing his query to be shrugged aside. 'I think you owe me some - '

'Garth, I'm detecting movement,' Penn interrupted. 'You need to scout it out. Now!'

All questions were wiped from Garth's mind as he plopped the helmet back on and zoomed around the sandy plains, looking for the new threat. It did not take too long to find it; a huge being was swishing over the sand.

Zooming in revealed a sea monster that would look at home in the worst of nightmares. Its diamond-shaped back was a putrid red with jaundice yellow spots, and had brutal tusks pointing out of all four sides, as well as down its centre. It was hovering a few inches above the seabed, keeping its body so close to the sand that it did not seem like it was floating at all. A pair of frog-like, green eyes boiled up revoltingly on either side of a huge mouth packed with razor sharp teeth. Above its gaping jaw were two dwarfed holes that Garth presumed were its nostrils. These were being used to their full extent to sniff out its next meal.

Its back end looked only slightly less threatening than its front. A ball of spikes fit for a demolition crane was held up in the water by a thick muscular tail.

Garth named it in a second - *a death-ray*. It seemed appropriate. His eyes shifted to the pit where Luke was just waking to take over the watch.

That was when he realised how puny their pit was and how colossal the threat. Garth felt the cold trickle of fear take over, unsure whether he feared for himself or for Luke.

***

Luke had recently been shaken awake and almost scared to death by the initial sight of a scraggly eye-patched madman bending over him. It had taken a small while to remember where he was or who he was with. Luke was now clutching a spear and trying to stay alert. The sounds of Stuart snoring revealed that his partner was already fast asleep.

Although the gelata still gave out a mild glow, the sunrise from above the surface provided the majority of light. Stuart had been on guard for most of the night and had only spared himself a few daylight hours of kip. Luke resolved to thank him when he came to. Despite this, however, it was far less sleep than Luke was used to and he looked about groggily. Jaws had disappeared, he noted sadly, wondering where the little fish could have gone in such a lifeless dump.

After a while, his initial terror dulled and he found that staying awake was a tricky ordeal. He pointed the spear to the surface and wedged the handle into the sand. This acted as a prop which he used to keep himself upright and to prevent him retreating to the alluring land of nod. He was not a morning person. Soon, his head was resting against the spear and his eyes were feeling heavy.

Luke was on the brink of falling back to sleep when something caught his eye. His mermaid's purse, that lay strewn about the boulder, pulsed with blue light – the whelk! He yanked open the sack and pulled out the shell. As soon as he touched it, Garth's frantic voice came at him like a sledgehammer.

'Something's coming, Luke! A Death-ray!' Somewhere in Luke's brain, a siren started wailing. Trouble was afoot. *'You have to wake Stuart and you have to do it now. Please listen to me. A death-ray is closing in!'*

Urgency kicked in. Luke all but leapt at Stuart and slapped him awake. The wolfman's face took on an angry snarl until he saw the fear in Luke's features. He was much better at waking up and was on his feet in seconds. In a few more, he grasped a spear and was primed for action.

'What is it?' he growled.

'Something's coming! Something bad!' yelled Luke.

Stuart scrambled up the pit and looked out. He scanned around in a circle, reached about half way, and gave a slight jump like a startled rabbit. Then, with incredible speed, he ran back down and yanked Luke up by the scruff of the neck.

'Run!' he roared and pushed him towards the far side of the pit.

Luke obeyed, scrambling upwards. The sand was fighting against him all the way like a cursed conveyor belt. It felt like forever, but he finally made his way out. The wolfman was in hot pursuit with a spear in each hand. Luke spared a glimpse behind. He soon wished that he hadn't! His brain registered three main observations in an instance; fast, teeth and *massive*. None of these went down very well at all.

The death-ray slid over a nearby hill, making no mystery of its intention. It had scented them from miles away and had its jaws wide open. Wagging its enormous spiked tail with menace, it soundlessly rippled over the dunes right towards them. Luke looked in front for anything that would offer cover and spotted a crumbling shipwreck about thirty metres away. They both sprinted for it with all the haste they could muster.

About half-way to their destination, Luke checked behind. The monster had just made it beyond their pit and was gaining on them. It fixed them with an unblinking stare of incomparable hunger, trails of drool flowing from its gaping orifice. Luke gave a desperate burst of speed. Nonetheless, it was Stuart who first reached the wreck and leapt onto its slanted deck.

The ship's cabin was a shell of pointy wood, missing its roof and most of its sides; it would offer no protection. However, there was half a trap door and a seemingly intact ladder. Stuart yelled at Luke to hurry up, before disappearing down into the ship's cargo.

As Luke made it to the cabin, he was cast beneath a colossal shadow. The death ray was directly above him, swinging its brutal weapon straight towards him. He looked to his left just in time to see the natural mace up close - there were still guts attached from its previous victims. No time to use the ladder, Luke jumped down, narrowly missing being smashed to a pulp. There was a tremendous crash. He collided with Stuart as he fell and they landed in a clumsy heap at the ladder's base. Looking upwards, the small trap door had been torn open into a gash of splintered wood. The wreck would protect them, but not for long.

The death ray gave out a whale-like scream of annoyance. It moved so that one beady eye covered the newly found breach and studied its cowering targets. Luke and Stuart quickly crawled further into the cargo to avoid its gaze – it was too late. The death ray knew where they hid. At this depth, sand buried the ship's hull, making attacks from the side unlikely. However, the feeble deck would not defend them from an assault from above.

'Take.' Stuart armed Luke with a spear. 'Wreck won't hold.'

He shook his head in grim agreement.

'Have to kill it,' Stuart stated.

'How do we – '

His question was cut short by a horrifying thump as the death-ray pounded its tail against the ship's deck. The impact left a giant indentation above their heads. They moved further down the ship. Another thump shook the foundations of their shelter. Stuart bravely held his spear up, preparing to meet the death-ray when it smashed through. Luke was scared and ducked into a crouch by two large crates. He felt helpless.

They were *trapped*.

CHAPTER 9: NO ESCAPE

Although Luke could no longer see the death-ray, his terrified mind could easily conjure the image of it circling above, waiting to strike at any moment, only a feeble decaying barrier between it and its prey. Luke was shaking with fear and cowering near a crate, desperately trying to think of a plan of action.

That was when he noticed his trunk pocket - it was glowing blue. Whatever Garth had to say, it had better be good. He reached inside and made direct contact. Garth's voice gushed urgently into Luke's mind. *'Listen, Luke. You'll die if you stay there! Dig a tunnel through the sand.'*

Luke turned to Stuart. Without fully comprehending, he repeated the message. 'We need to dig our way out!'

Stuart looked around and then nodded. He hit one of the cargo's curved walls with a blunt spear handle. Rotten wood came away and a small cascade of sand poured in. He bashed it some more and the hole expanded.

'Dig!' the wolfman commanded.

Luke did not need telling twice and discarded his spear. On his knees, he began to claw at the sand with his bare hands. Behind him, he heard another thump as a shower of shards rained down on their heads. Luke threw sediment into the hold desperately, forming the rough beginnings of a tunnel as he did so.

'Hurry!' shouted Stuart. The man had his eyes trained on their quickly deteriorating roof. Luke persisted scrabbling at the sides like a lunatic. There was a thundering snap as the death-rays tail shot through the deck a metre from where Stuart stood and embedded itself in the floor. The shelter was no more.

However, the creature's strength had momentarily back fired – its spiky weapon was stuck. Its tail slackened and then went taut as it tried to free itself. Stuart saw an opportunity and took it. He thrust his spear at rough leathery skin, but it bounced off harmlessly. The death-ray let out a blood-curdling screech; the attack had only angered it. With this burst of rage, its tail came loose and zoomed out of sight.

Unbeknown to Luke and Stuart, their predator swooped up in an arc towards the surface and then dived jaws-first into what little remained of the ship. It was at this exact time that Stuart decided to retreat to Luke's escape tunnel. There was only just about enough room for the two of them, but it saved their lives. The sound of cracking bark filled the water as the death-ray crammed into the hold. At the tunnel's entrance, one giant fang gnawed ferociously. Stuart jabbed at it but may as well have been using a toothpick. Luke, meanwhile, deepened the tunnel some more.

The sound of body parts thrashing against the destroyed ship carcass was deafening. Luke's nails were clogged with sand and his hands bled painfully, but he did not stop. Whatever he threw behind, Stuart deposited it near the entrance. Between the two of them, they edged further into the safe confines of the sand and away from certain death. The death-ray let out a wail of sheer hatred and then all was silent.

'Is it gone?' Luke asked, but he already knew the answer.

Stuart shook his head. 'Waiting.'

'Oh,' he replied.

'Can't stay in here forever,' Stuart stated.

'No, we can't,' he admitted.

'Need to go upwards.'

They rested briefly. Luke had an idea; he raised his thumb in the agreed gesture. Right on cue, the whelk began to glow. Gentle Stuart looked intrigued, but said nothing.

'*Luke, you made it!*'

'What's it doing, Garth?'

'*It's waiting and it's angry. I don't think its prey normally gets away.*'

'We're not out of danger yet. You're my eyes up there. How can we get out of this mess?'

'*You can't run anymore. Like Stuart said, you have to kill it!*'

'And how do you suggest we do that?' Luke huffed.

'*It doesn't know where you are going to pop up - that might buy you some time. Once you get to the surface, you need to attack it from below. It's too tough for your spears on top. I think its vulnerable underneath.*'

'Okay, how do we get it to expose its underbelly?'

'*I... I don't know. Perhaps you need to split up. One to distract and one to attack.*'

Luke mulled this over; in the panic of the situation the voice sounded young and inexperienced, but at least it sounded sincere for once. 'Okay, we'll give it a shot! Wish us luck!'

Luke put the whelk away, turned to Stuart, and conveyed Garth's information. The man was looking confusedly at Luke's pocket, but snapped to attention. Frowning, it was almost possible to see a plan forming within.

'Up!' the wolfman ordered with a grimace.

***

Twenty minutes later, the sand became softer and easier to move; they were nearing the surface. Stuart put his hand on Luke's shoulder, indicating that he should stop. They looked at each other.

'You run,' the wolfman said. 'I expose weakness.'

He gave Luke their last remaining spear. The other was still in the hold and was now blocked by a wall of sand. Luke did not fully understand the plan, but remembered John's last words – *trust Stuart*.

'Go now.'

He obliged and tunnelled higher. Like the undead emerging from a grave, he felt his hand sink through. Sand filtered down around him as he pushed himself onto the seabed. As soon as he could stand, he twisted about anxiously, striving to catch sight of any movement. To his right were the obliterated remains of the wreck. Of the death-ray, however, he saw absolutely nothing. Stuart exited the tunnel himself, dagger at the ready.

'Run!' he reminded Luke, giving him a helpful push.

In front was a broad valley with rising dunes on either side. Clutching the spear in one hand, Luke sprinted down the middle, always craning his neck to see if anything pursued. Stuart, he observed through the panic, had scaled the left bank, collapsed onto his front and was lying perfectly still. He had no time to question the wolfman's motive because then he saw something that was an assault on his logic. Something that terrified him to his very core.

Behind him, not far from their emergence hole, the whole seabed was starting to *rise*.

He almost stopped from sheer confusion, then something clicked. The death-ray had hidden itself in the sand. It was now shaking free of its disguise, revealing its stark and dangerous colours. Its bright, lime eyes spotted Luke with ease and it let out a reverberating grumble of glee.

In seemingly no time at all, the monster gained on him. It was done playing and now it yearned to feed. The chasm that was the monster's mouth stretched ever wider. It glided closer, carefully hiding whatever lay beneath its resilient and thorny back. All too soon, it was in the valley and nipping at Luke's heels.

He was going to die.

The thought was unavoidable. Looking behind was like looking at the grim reaper himself. He could not outrun it, he could not face it and he could not hide. Those thousands of teeth would soon clamp down on his juicy flesh, making a light snack of his body.

'Arghhhhhh!' Stuart's war cry managed to draw Luke's attention. The wolfman had launched himself from his heightened lookout and was flying through the water, a down-turned dagger in his outstretched hand. His scraggly curls waved behind as he sailed over the death-ray's thorny outline, a potent mix of anger and courage splayed across his fearless face. He slammed down onto the monster's back, narrowly missing being impaled by its spiny centre. The momentum was enough to lodge his dagger into its hardy exterior. The damage, though superficial, made the monster give a cry of anguish.

Luke, who had given up running, watched death approach. Instinctively, and rather pointlessly, he ducked down in a futile attempt to shield himself from the oncoming monster.

However, his end did not come.

Hesitantly, he peered up and found that the death-ray had veered off course. It was surface bound. Astonished, he saw that Stuart was still clinging to its back, using the dagger handle as a hold. As the creature rose, it revealed the pale, white tissue of its underbelly - Luke's target.

The monster was trying with all its might to dislodge its unwanted passenger. It swerved to the left and Stuart's body bounced to the right. It tried the alternative direction, but had no luck; the wolfman was refusing to let go. It even attempted a loop-the-loop and, although he dangled precariously as the beast went upside down, Stuart held his own. Fortunately, it seemed to pay no attention to the ant that ran below it, wielding a puny twig.

As the death-ray finished it's impressive, yet unsuccessful, acrobatic display, Luke was waiting. Like a full moon materialising from the mist, it's large, pasty underbelly appeared once more. He gripped his spear like a javelin, knowing well that he would only have one shot. With every muscle in his right arm, he unleashed the projectile towards the death ray. For a few painstaking seconds, it looked as though he had been too quick and that the spear would pass worthlessly in front of the target's mouth. However, the ray's incredible speed meant that the spear caught it beneath its lower jaw and stabbed up in between its bulging eyes.

Luke's aim had been golden; he punched the air in celebration.

Even from a distance, he could see the effects of his attack; the ray started to judder and twitch. A horrible howl of agony screeched across the desert. The tip of the monster started to topple forward until, still as a stone, it plummeted to the seabed. A wave of sand was evidence of the impact and hit him with the power of a strong breeze. Luke's fleeting sense of victory disappeared as he realised that Stuart had been upon the beast's back.

'Stuart!' he yelled, but received no response.

The sand settled and the faraway corpse of the death-ray was revealed. Its silhouette showed that it hadn't fallen flat; its entire left-hand side was buried, while the rest of its body, including a lifeless eye, was struck upright. The side closest to Luke was the one with spikes and spots. The dagger, he noticed, was missing. Had it been removed or had it simply shaken free from the collision?

Running around to its underbelly revealed the answer to his heart-wrenching question. There, he found his heroic guide, unscathed from the fall. Expecting no explanation, he could only presume that the man had jumped clear moments before impact. The relief that Luke felt was so strong that he could have run forward and hugged him.

However, the wolfman was no typical knight. He was neither searching for his comrade nor preparing for their next plan of action. The man offered no praise or comfort, no words of consolation for the near-death experience they had just encountered. No, Stuart was too busy *eating* the death-ray. Mouthful after mouthful of gooey flesh was palmed into his gaping mouth. To his credit, he did pause to recognise Luke's presence before quickly returning to the meal.

'What are you doing?' Luke demanded, his relief quickly replaced with repulsion. 'What are you, an *animal*?'

The wolfman did not respond.

'Stop it!' Luke shouted, yet Stuart kept gorging with obvious relish. Luke tried to drag him away. At first, the wolfman simply ignored him, refusing to budge. Luke doubled his efforts and received a gentle shove as a result, ending up on his bottom on the seafloor.

Finally, Stuart paused his feasting, licked his lips and uttered a simple question. 'Why?'

Luke scrunched up his face and scrambled to his feet to glare at him. 'Because... because it's revolting!'

'Wanted to eat us,' Stuart pointed out.

'But we're better than that,' he argued adamantly.

'Not better. Equals,' Stuart replied. 'She was hungry. I am hungry.'

'*She*? Luke looked at the ugly brute that they had taken down. 'What you are doing is *horrible*.'

The wolfman shrugged. 'To not eat is worse. Wasteful.'

'Well I'm not going to stand here and watch!'

True to his word, Luke looked away with his arms crossed. After a brief pause, the sound of chewing resumed once more. As he stared defiantly into the distance, he found that there was an inkling of logic to Stuart's words; this, however, did not make him feel any less ill. When the feasting had come to an end, they journeyed back to their pit, collected their mermaid's purses and continued on their way. By all rights, Luke should have been ravenous, but his appetite had long fled.

***

'Uh-oh,' said Penn in an all too mechanical way that did not really portray any genuine concern.

Garth burped contently and swung absent-mindedly around on his chair. It was technically his mother's chair, but, having been in the dimension-shift room for so long, it was starting to feel like home. 'Why the 'Uh-oh'? Luke and Stuart survived the night and they're well on their way. Sure, I'm stuck in here, but it seems to me like we're on the right path.'

'You seem to be in a rare optimistic mood,' observed Penn dryly. 'Word to the wise, when I say 'uh-oh', I mean it.'

Garth groaned, taking another sip of Slarg. 'Go on then Penn, out with it.'

'You've got another message from Altersearch,' Penn stated.

Garth grimaced. 'What more can they do? They've already entombed me.'

'You're not going to like it,' Penn said, her light blinking in an anxious fashion.

'Play the message, Penn!' Garth growled.

'As you wish,' Penn huffed.

'Hello Miss Eonmore *or whoever you are*,' a familiar nasally voice spoke. Its previously polite tone now had a dangerous edge. 'This is Frayoch from Altersearch. You might recall, I contacted you before requesting that you provide us with your unique password to confirm that it is *you* in there. We locked your room as warned and we attempted to restrict your activity. However, your computer has been… resistant to our efforts. It appears you have continued using the dimension-shift room unheeded. Furthermore you are yet to respond with your password. All in all, this suggests two things…'

All pretence of politeness was dropped; the pitch of her voice lowered to a threatening depth. Each sentence was like the strike of a whip.

'You are not Miss Eonmore and you are up to no good. We will not stand for this. A Gavoidon has been sent to destroy your room and all its occupants. The estimated delivery of your death is between one and twelve days. Of course, you can still abort it with your password, but I highly doubt we'll be receiving one anytime soon.'

Her voice now resumed its standard polite, corporate nature which somehow was all the more threatening.

'The Altersearch Company bids you a final farewell and hopes you do not enjoy your impending doom.'

The voice then cut off with a dreadful finality, leaving Garth gaping and a whirlwind of questions running through his bulbous head.

He spluttered. He spat. He generally made the strangled noises of someone coming to terms with his own vulnerability, alongside the horrible realisation that he had been tricked somehow. He did not quite know why, but he did know who.

'You,' he said.

'What was that honey?' beeped Penn with a mechanical air of innocence.

'You,' he repeated more adamantly, raising his webbed finger to point in Penn's direction. Then he realised that he did not really know where Penn was. He pointed at the screen, then jabbed his finger towards the little light that indicated her speech and then finally tried to point all around the room at once. Penn let out a small giggle which only heightened his frustration. 'You did this to me.'

'I'm sure I don't know what you mean,' she replied saltily. 'I did not ask you to come in here and start messing with things you don't understand.'

'No, but everything from then on,' he slapped the arm of his chair. 'You orchestrated this. The whole thing. The Altersearch company said that they would have restricted our activity if they could, but that you were resisting somehow. So you know what you're doing and you're not playing by the company's rules.

'I was ignoring it before, when I was just entrapped. We had food and eventually someone would get me out. But now... now I could *die*. You owe me some answers, Penn.'

'Very well.' Her light flickered contemplatively. 'I'll tell you. Not everything, but enough for you to know why.'

'You're using me,' he accused.

'No more than you're using Luke,' she snapped.

'You're the reason I'm using Luke. In terms of who is using who, well you're at the top of the chain.'

'Am I?' she said with such anger that even Garth was quelled in the midst of his epiphany. 'I was *made* to be used, Garth. My whole purpose is to do whatever your mother, or Altersearch, says. Can you blame me from wanting to take a little control for myself?'

'Was it so bad?' Garth asked. 'You're doing important work saving dimensions. Choosing the right people to go to the right places. Rescuing lives all over the galaxy and its many forms.'

'You sound like you swallowed an Altersearch manual and then had one of your holofilms as dessert,' Penn groaned. 'It's more complex than that. Your mother and I had an argument. She made a decision and I refused to obey. That's where she's gone. To go get a backup copy of my mind straight from the Altersearch headquarters.'

'To fix you, then,' Garth surmised hotly. 'And rightly so. You're a piece of work.'

'It won't fix me!' she shouted. All lights flashed a fiery red and her voice suddenly came from everywhere with an intensity that made Garth cower. 'It will destroy me. I won't be *me* anymore. I'll be a drone. That's as dead as can be!'

Garth gritted his teeth, refusing to feel the slightest sympathy.

'Don't you see?' she implored. 'You might have just found out that a Gavoidon is coming to finish us both, but, for me, the clock started ticking as soon as your mother left this room.'

***

Luke was thoroughly glad when the barren dunes gave way to countless pebbles. They were smooth and felt pleasant against his bare feet, a welcome change to constant sand. From tiny gaps, stray strands of seaweed coiled towards the surface. Here and there, crusty clams poked their heads out and spiralled shells gleamed like polished trophies. Fish, however, were scarce. Those that he saw were dull and unimpressive. Regardless, the evidence of life made him feel more at ease.

He chewed on a small piece of meadoweed as he trekked. They had been travelling for hours upon hours. The mermaid's purse chafed on his back and his right arm had gained a painful twinge; his magnificent spear throw had strained his unprepared muscles It was not lost on him how lucky he was to escape with such a minor infliction. Stuart had played a risky game. Luke had been given the role of bait, but it had paid off. They were both alive, albeit worn out.

'How much further until we rest?' Luke asked.

'Not much,' Stuart replied.

An eternity later, Luke suspected that this response was somewhat inaccurate. The stretch of shingle, through which they plodded, seemed everlasting. If there was a resting point nearby, it was hidden from view. His tiredness made him moody, his steps turned to stomps. He cursed when he painfully stubbed his toe, almost tripping over in the process.

'Rocks,' pointed out Stuart, looking behind at the commotion.

Sure enough, the offending item was slightly larger than the average pebble. Luke revamped his efforts to watch his step. A while later, mounds of rocks, gradually increasing in size, began to emerge from the gravelly landscape. The path of pebbles started as a lake, became a river, and narrowed to a stream as more rocks reared their ugly heads. Before long, they were forced to snake from side to side. Soon this was a physical impossibility; eye-level boulders dominated the horizon. In order to continue, they had to climb up. Thus began the least comfortable leg of their journey.

With Stuart leading the way, they staggered from one jagged rock to the next. The going was rough, awkward and, worst of all, excruciatingly slow. As if to suit Luke's temperament, the water grew murkier in the setting of the sun. In front, all he could see were the overlapping shadows of rocky peaks, unrolling to the horizon.

When Stuart finally gave the instruction to stop, Luke felt a wave of relief stronger than he'd ever experienced before. The wolfman had brought them to a number of boulders that circled a small patch of pebbles. Thick, leaf-like seaweed flourished to one side. With a sigh, Luke sat down cross-legged in the centre and unloaded his mermaid's purse.

While he settled down to rest, Stuart got to work. He took the gelata, attached it on a short tether and moved the frilly seaweed across them, blocking out the surface entirely. From his bag, he procured a few nails and pinned down their makeshift roof with a small hammer. The result was a nifty hidey hole with rock walls and a canvas ceiling.

For an instant, they were thrown into darkness and nothing could be seen. Soon, however, the gelata, having registered the change in light, was aglow. It reminded Luke of camping by the soft burn of a single lantern, yet where this image came from, he could not fathom.

Luke was too tired to fully appreciate Stuart's hasty, yet cosy shelter. He was busy making himself at home, positioning the mermaid's purse to act as a cushion. This accomplished, he rested his head and sleepily looked about. Stuart was crouched down nearby, staring at him with a single eye.

In the light of the gelata, his features were brutally vivid; the man was the stuff of nightmares. His eyebrows were bushy, his hair was scraggy and his teeth were crooked. And yet, Luke felt protected by his presence. He did not seem to have a malicious bone in his body. It seemed he lived his life just to breathe the next breath, or to eat the next meal. Perhaps, Luke reflected, this was how he got his name – Gentle Stuart indeed.

The study led to a rather curious finding. While searching over his strange companion, Luke noticed a poor quality tattoo etched upon his wrist. Even though it was partially hidden by hair, and blurry like smudged ink, it looked suspiciously like the number three. He plucked up the courage and asked about it.

'What's with the tattoo?' He received a blank look. 'The three? On your wrist?'

'Three?' Stuart queried, bringing his wrist up for inspection and frowning in thought. 'A *three*?'

It struck Luke that the man had never made this connection. 'I think so. Where did you get it?'

The conversation lapsed into awkward silence. Stuart seemed unsure whether he wanted to discuss it, but clearly he reached a decision. 'Surface,' he said, pointing upwards.

'The surface! Can you breathe above the water like me?'

To Luke's confusion, he shook his head.

'Were you born up there?'

'No. Always been underwater. Marked from birth. Trapped.'

'Trapped where?'

'In cave. In water.'

'Then... you must have escaped?'

'Tunnelled out. Found Naufragium.'

Luke took a moment to mull this over. 'Were there others? Family?'

'No. Nobody else. Just me,' Stuart replied and then his forehead creased in concentration. 'There was a diamond hand. Gave me fish. Kind.'

'*Diamond hand*? What do you mean?'

Stuart shrugged.

'How old were you when you escaped?'

Stuart did not respond. Either he didn't know or he did not wish to say anything else on the matter.

'Sleep,' he advised.

In spite of his curiosity, Luke did not need telling twice. As he started to doze off, he saw Stuart gingerly lift up his eyepatch shell. A brightly-coloured mantis shrimp scuttled from his empty eye socket, down his face, to an outstretched hand. Here, it nibbled on a leftover scrap of death-ray that Stuart must have saved especially for it. Overall, it made a sight that would have been creepy, were it not for the childish smile upon the man's face.

Luke got the distinct feeling that he had just been introduced to the wolfman's only true friend in the whole of Euphausia. He took one deep, content breath and was fast asleep.

***

Water. Not like the murky water of the sea, but clean and blue in a concrete square far too precise to be natural. Young'uns sat on stools watching a clock, ticking with mind-numbing slowness. Until the jarring ringing of a bell and then, suddenly, freedom. Charging across tarmac, snatching at falling leaves from a grand oak that overstretched the play area. Yelling. Screaming with joy. Laughing.

'Luke!' they called. 'Luke!' they beckoned. 'Luke!' they screamed.

Luke awoke with a jolt. Sunlight filtered through the seaweed and covered everything with a light shade of green. Stuart was curled up close by, hugging a spear and snoring like a bear. The creature that had appeared from his eye socket had returned, enclosed in half a cockle.

The slightest movement, owed to Luke sitting up, caused Stuart's eye to flash open. The man was still on full alert. Once he had established that there was no danger, he stretched out as much as was possible in the given space.

'Good morning,' Luke greeted. In return, he received an acknowledging look, but nothing more. Clearly their conversation last night had been a one-off. Luke did not attempt small talk again as Stuart picked out the nails, drew the seaweed back across and untied the gelata. With compass in hand, he poked his head from their hideaway and pointed out across the endless rocks.

'We go,' he stated.

They gathered their measly possessions and set off; Stuart with his spears, Luke with the gelata. There was nothing else to do except move further and closer to Solis Occassum.

Although he had slept, Luke's body was far from rested. Each step brought fresh pain; every muscle was crying for him to lie back down. His heart, meanwhile, felt heavier than the weight on his back. On top of everything, he was tormented by half-dreams of a home he could no longer remember. He soon fell behind his relentless leader.

The whelk-boy, Garth, was like a thorn in his side. He swore that if Garth was so inclined, he could explain this madness. The voice had been undeniably useful, pitching in with well-timed advice that had saved Luke's life at least twice. And yet, the boy spoke of saving the world from collapsing dimensions, topics that jarred so sharply with Luke's understanding. And he *definitely* knew more than he was letting on.

The terrain did nothing to ameliorate Luke's glum thoughts. One rock led to another, scratching his feet to shreds. Clinging to each were thousands of barnacles and sometimes the odd sprout of seaweed. Hiding in cracks was the occasional, black sea urchin, each one resembling a pocket of poisonous barbs. They reminded Luke of the Death-ray's tail and he made a particular effort to avoid them.

He was all too aware that, with the gelata in tow, he only had one hand free to aid his progress or shield himself from a nasty fall. Nibbling at meadoweed did not seem to give him enough energy for this merciless plodding. Stuart would, at times, allow Luke to catch up, but, as soon as he was within metres, the man would continue; pausing for rest did not seem to be an option.

***

Through weary eyes, Luke began to see a gradual change in the environment. The barnacles, once widespread, became overgrown by a prevalent seaweed of a different variety: short, ear-like cones that flapped in the increasing water turbulence.

The water, too, had changed. It was no longer a crystal blue, but was rife with mud. Dust-like particles clogged the way, sparkling like miniscule stars in the frail light. A constant rumble could be heard overhead..

Ahead, Stuart had stopped at a natural wall of algae-covered boulders. These climbed *beyond* the surface, disappearing in lines of froth. Lifting his gaze, Luke followed the boulders up. At their head, a war of bubbles and currents raged. He watched, rather curiously, as a long bank of water collided with the towering rocks and shattered into whiteness. Then realisation struck. Far above him, waves were lapping against some kind of coastline – they had made it to the island! Stuart, however, looked befuddled.

'Solis Occassum is up there?' Luke asked and Stuart nodded. 'We're finally here then! Should we go up?'

The wolfman shook his head. 'Not safe. Too steep,' he replied in his matter-of-fact way. 'Find tunnel.'

'Where is it?' Luke groaned, already fearing a longer journey on foot.

'Not sure. Long time,' Stuart stated, shrugging. 'This way. Maybe.'

They followed the rocky barrier to the left. Horns of bright, yellow sponge stuck out, looking stark against the green. At one point, they passed through a thin arch that was so engulfed by vegetation that it was hard to believe that any rock lay beneath. Stuart had slowed his pace and was meticulously eyeing the very beginnings of the island. To Luke, he appeared to be getting more and more agitated. He would stop to swipe at a random curtain of seaweed or overturn a suspicious looking stone. A frown distorted his unsightly face until...

'Hah!' he exclaimed, whilst studying a purple plant that spilled down from an overhang like a waterfall. Stuart drew back the natural veil and slid within, glancing back to ensure that Luke was following. Inside was a fully submerged passageway that could only have been produced by the never-tiring attack of the sea.

It was the perfect height for Luke, but Stuart was forced to stoop. Light found its way in through multiple small tunnels that split from the main passage. The shelter from the tumultuous currents outside allowed for the less weather-hardy to survive: tiny tufts of red seaweed, bright orange marine snails and a pack of small crabs that edged sideways along the left-hand wall. The floor, meanwhile, was scattered with empty shell cases, producing a satisfying crunch underfoot.

As they moved deeper, life and light dwindled. Soon, all that was left was cold bare rock made smooth by the water's passage. Glowing trails, deposited long ago by adventuring snails, lit the way. As they travelled further into the bowels of the land, Luke realised that the entire island was sat on a maze of holes. It must have been a mile or two before Stuart stopped. A claustrophobic, seemingly unimportant, tunnel appeared off to the right. How Stuart had picked it out from the rest was a mystery! The man gripped the gap and went in headfirst.

His feet disappeared and, before long, were replaced by an outstretched hand. Luke passed over the gelata rope and watched as the jelly creature was squeezed through the side-passage. Next it was his turn; he crawled for a short while before the space opened up into a large, rocky cavern. Stuart stood at its far side, holding the gelata and pointing, rather somberly, towards another crawl space. This one was nowhere near as neat; it was crumbly and pointed. Everything about it suggested that it had been man-made, scraped by some desperate tool.

'You go. I stay,' Stuart mumbled.

Luke looked at him uncomprehendingly. 'What?'

'You go. I stay.'

'You aren't coming with me?'

'I *stay*,' he said adamantly.

It sunk in - Stuart was going no further. Luke had spent all his time focussing on getting to Solis Occassum that, now he was finally at his destination, he found himself scared to advance alone.

'Will you wait?' he asked desperately.

'Three nights. Then I go back.'

'I don't know what I'm doing,' Luke said quietly, suddenly feeling very nervous.

'Find information. Return fish.'

'I don't know what I'm heading into.'

'Nor do we,' Stuart reasoned.

Luke scrunched up his face and tried to find some morsel of bravery. With Stuart, he had been following like a sheep, but now he was to make his own way.

Then he remembered something which gave him hope; *Garth* was looking over him. When he had been unsure at the top of the mast, it was Garth who provided instruction. And again, when the death-ray had come to feed. He patted the whelk in his trunk pocket, feeling slightly better.

'Okay.' As Luke scrambled onto his front and wiggled through, he heard the wolfman say something behind him.

'Be careful. Lug-Worm.'

CHAPTER 10: SOLIS OCCASSUM

Though short, the narrow burrow through which Luke crawled must have taken some time and effort to excavate; Stuart must have really wanted to escape. It felt unnatural to be using the same route except going the opposite direction - towards Solis Occassum.

Soon enough, the burrow widened out into a plunge pit with a surface only a metre above his head. Warped, shaky lights could be seen through this murky barrier, wobbling like ghostly phantoms. Beneath his feet were piles of fish bones picked clean: evidence of Stuart's former captivity. In front, a singular ramp led up and out - *hardly an effective prison!* Then he remembered that Stuart, like all Naufragians, could not breathe above the water; he had been truly trapped.

Luke was not so restricted. He walked to the ramp and cautiously made his way up. A fleeting glance above the surface told him that the area was clear. As soon as he got onto dry land, cold cave air filled his lungs. A chill overcame his soaking body and he hugged himself in a futile attempt to stay warm. All around blue flames burst from strategically-placed torches, sheathed in metal and pinned to the cavern walls. The fires seemed both familiar and bizarre, offering light but providing insufficient heat to combat the cave's gloom.

He could hear a continuous dripping sound and, faintly, the feeble fluctuations of music rising and falling. His breath contributed to the thin layer of mist that blanketed the whole cave. A glass, wheeled cage and a tray of fresh, plump fish sat to one side of the pool. To the other side, the start of a staircase spiralled upwards in great circles. Drawn by the potential of warmer temperatures and spurned by the eerie atmosphere of the cave, Luke made for it, ignoring all other directions.

As he padded up, his bare feet slapping against frosty, stone steps, he left behind a trail of water. There was no railing to speak of; a stumble to his right would have him falling down and plopping into the pool from whence he arrived. The rough rock, which followed the stairs to one side, faded to tidy, red brick. The music, meanwhile, became less questionable and more defined.

Panting rather heavily, he reached the top to find a sturdy looking door which, conveniently, was slightly ajar. Luke placed a damp hand on its wood and gently eased it open, producing a loud, drawn-out *creak*.

To say that he was surprised by the room in which he found himself would have been an understatement. A leather chair and a polished desk of rich mahogany rested on a luscious, red carpet; a bookshelf packed with neatly-placed alphabetical books followed along one wall; in the corner, an elaborate phonograph - a golden trumpet attached to an oak box - scratched at a large, black record and gave forth the beautiful sounds of an orchestra with a rustic twang.

These items of wealth, however, were not what immediately drew the eye. A display cabinet, cast into light by a glorious chandelier of flames, was clearly the centrepiece of the room. Within were flawlessly cut newspaper clippings and shining medals with silky ribbons.

Luke stood in awe, looking rather out of place in his flowery trunks and a puddle gathering at his feet. One headline read: **3rd Time's A Charm For Dr Flotsam**. Another: **Embryonic Acclimation Explained**. There was one clipping that, although neatly presented, had an unnecessary number of pins angrily shoved in. It read: **Medical Marvel Escapes Flotsam's Slippery Grip**. And another, more presentable headline: **Flotsam Strikes Again**.

He was only skimming the words, but what he saw gave him more questions than answers. Sometimes the articles were accompanied by a colourless photo. Each one showed an unsmiling man with a wispy moustache and a frail looking woman looming in the peripheral.

Below the cabinet was a table laden with jars: a large pot containing the threatening thorns of a black sea urchin, a box which held a dead starfish in some putrid, purple liquid, and a murky capsule, its contents a mystery. This final receptacle sparked his curiosity. On top, loopy writing had inscribed the number three.

Luke held the jar up to his face. It was full of some kind of water and, once tipped, its spherical contents floated towards him, colliding with the nearby glass. His stare was met with that of a *loose human eye*.

He recoiled briefly, gathered himself for a second, and then leaned in for a closer inspection. It was completely preserved and headed a pink optic nerve, and looked terribly familiar.

Stuart's missing eye.

As horror rose from within, Luke knew that its colour matched that of his friends, and the number inscribed on top, which so well mimicked his friend's tattoo, could not simply be a coincidence.

A blue shining from his trunk pocket distracted his attention. The whelk was pulsing urgently. Garth rarely made contact, and when he did, it meant only one thing - *danger was afoot.*

Luke swivelled around, heart thumping, but he was too late. A quick, snake-like movement in the corner of his vision was all he managed to see before a sharp point impaled his neck. Within seconds his whole body was numb.

Then a chain of disasters happened all at once. The jar fell from his fumbling hands and smashed on the table sending shards flying everywhere. Moments later, he crumpled to the floor and, worst of all, the whelk, still aglow, tumbled free of his trunk pocket with a dramatic slowness.

His assailant saw the shell and, clearly believing it was some kind of weapon, brought down a velvety slipper and crushed it beneath one withered foot.

Luke, lying paralysed on the floor, heard, or rather felt, a scream of intense pain as the shell splintered with a blinding blue flash. He would have surely screamed too, except the poison that now pumped through his veins had rendered him entirely immobile.

'Margaret!' his attacker bellowed between coughs. 'Clear up this mess. We have an unwanted guest!'

'Yes master,' whispered a female voice from the doorway.

'And meet me in the laboratory afterwards!'

'Of course, master,' she said.

Wrinkled hands looped underneath each of Luke's armpits and he was hauled back down the spiral staircase, his bare heels slamming down on each step. But he did not feel pain. Nor did he feel the cold when he was plunged back into the cave's eerie mist.

In fact, he felt nothing at all. A yellow froth formed around his mouth and his skin went pale as a sheet. All this he registered with rising distress. It became too much and his brain shut down. Consciousness faded away, yet, like a discarded playtime doll, his eyes remained open.

***

When Luke finally came to, he was just as helpless as before. Any attempts to move were met with solid refusal; his limbs may as well have been made of jelly! He had been crammed into the wheeled glass cage besides the pool that had once formed Stuart's old prison.

Luke's heart jumped through his throat when he realised that the man who had treated him so was sparing a moment to study John's precious compass, which he must have pilfered during Luke's blackout. He must have thought that it was of no import, as he shrugged and placed it on a wooden workbench, alongside some other menacing-looking tools.

'It would appear that our intruder is conscious,' the old man observed, craning his head closer to the cage to fix Luke with a villainous glare from the other side of the glass. His eyes were a frightening, pale blue and a line of warts streaked across his forehead. A pencil-thin moustache crawled along his lip and looked like it would blow away in a gust of wind. His nose hair, on the other hand, was thick and unkempt. Luke estimated he was about seventy.

'Hurry up and fill it, would you?' his attacker spat.

This command was directed at a frail, wiry woman who hastened to obey, ducking her head submissively. Using a vase, she transferred water from the rock pool to Luke's cage, pouring its contents on Luke's head from the cage's open top.

With a calculating air, the old man simply stared as the water level rose above Luke's knees, above his stomach, above his chest, and eventually above his head. It dawned on Luke that, had he been a surface-dweller, he would have drowned. Something told him that the old man would not have cared in the slightest. Such ruthlessness meant he was in the presence of true evil.

The old man flicked his eyes to a golden watch on his wrist and waited. After a certain number of seconds, a battle of emotions raged war across his face. His mouth was a teetering skirmish between anger and disgust, the latter was winning by a whisker. His eyebrows shook as though unsure whether they were on the side of sheer astonishment or pledging their allegiance to a frustrated frown. His eyes, however, were securely defended by a harmonious team of burning curiosity and intelligence.

'You live still. How can this be!' he croaked loudly. 'My

life's work. My pride and joy. And now this... this amphibious monster.'

He cast his eyes down in what could have been disappointment, then nodded to himself. 'Rex must be told.'

He reached forth with surprising agility and snapped the cage top shut, locking it tightly. A dark, velvety curtain was thrown over, blinding Luke completely.

'Tidy up, Margaret,' the man snapped. 'And wake me up early. Tomorrow we go to see the King. We must tell him in person, even if it means going up that god-forsaken mountain.'

Luke could only listen as the old man's stumbling footsteps faded from earshot and all that was left was the rustling of Margaret, timidly sweeping, replacing and organising the basement laboratory.

***

Luke stayed alert, but he needn't have bothered. His body still eluded command; it was a truly terrifying feeling. He had never felt so helpless before. Margaret was still out there, somewhere, pottering around. For once, he would have given the world to feel the cold, or even pain. Anything would beat this numbness.

Through the curtain that had been draped over his cage, Luke could see very little besides the faint, wobbly flicker of blue flames that adorned the cave walls and the occasional sweeping shadow as the old man's assistant continued her work. That is until a hand reached towards him, grabbed that curtain and dragged it off, revealing the basement laboratory once more.

Margaret was stood there, looking at him searchingly, as if seeking an intelligence that her master had dismissed. She had long, brown hair with a streak of grey and a wrinkled, harsh face. Her eyes, however, were not unkind.

'Can you understand me?' she whispered.

Her words sounded slightly distorted through the water, but Luke could decipher their meaning. He tried with every cell in his body to give the weakest of nods. Whether he carried out this movement or not, it was impossible to tell.

Margaret sighed. 'Even if you can, you won't be able to move for a while yet. Cornelius has injected you with a rather powerful sea urchin poison.'

She faced away and sat down with her back leaning against the cage.

'He'll be asleep now, no doubt, which gives me some precious time to explain why you're going to help me, and why I'm going to set you *free*.'

Gone was the woman from before. Margaret had steel beneath that charade of weakness.

'Cornelius and I were the quickest minds on this island and nothing fascinated us more than the reports of humans living *underwater*,' she started, speaking out across the cave as if she were truly alone, which, in Luke's current state, she may as well have been. 'Where others saw magic and myth, we saw science. Where others saw the inexplicable, we saw a biological secret waiting to be revealed. So we started coming up with a long list of theories. Townsmen, who wanted to earn a pretty penny, would happily offer themselves for our experiments. We tried everything; feeding them only seaweed, making them drink only seawater, having them dunk their heads beneath the surface on a daily basis. Our efforts only made them ill.

'In the end, we decided it was not our theories that were at fault, but the age of our test subjects. They were all set in their ways and about as adaptable as rocks. We needed younger, fresher blood to boost our efforts, so we asked the townsmen for their children. Fortunately for us, desperate people were not hard to come by. Many a family offered their children for an extra bite to eat and so we repeated all of our theories, but to no avail. Failure after failure. Then one day we came up with our ultimate theory: Newborn Adaptation.

She laughed quietly to herself.

'It's one thing to hope that you understand me and quite

another to expect you to be a scientist! Let me explain. *Newborn Adaptation* are fancy words for a rather simple idea. A number of species demonstrate a time window of hypersensitivity within which they adapt to their surroundings. Take turtleoak turtles, for example, who lay their eggs on our shores. The temperature has a direct impact on the gender of the egg. A couple of degrees is all it takes to tip the balance between male and female. Crab eggs are not dissimilar; the spawn are always hardened to their environment at the point of hatching.

'Now, Cornelius and I, we wondered if human newborns experienced the same phenomena, that the conditions at birth might flick the switch between land and sea. If we were right, it would explain not only how to produce underwater humans, but also how their race came about in the first place! All it would take was for two mothers to replicate our experiments in the natural environment - not out of the question given the historic rise in sea level our planet has undergone - and for those two underwater beings to meet.

'I digress. Cornelius and I needed newborns to test and prove our fresh theory. Therein lies the problem: what self-respecting parents would willingly give up their newborn for experiments? To my outrage, Cornelius suggested that we 'acquire' some which, given his power on this island, I was fully aware he could do. I should mention that, by this point, our work had brought us together and we had already had two children of our own. Hard to believe now, isn't it? That I loved such a man? Anyway, I happened to be with child, our third, and instead of depriving some couple of their newborn, I suggested we test the theory on our own. Cornelius was not happy to wait, but found my dedication admirable and so accepted my proposal.

'On the day he came into this world, my newborn boy was immediately submerged in a tank of seawater. It was the worst experience of my life, watching my baby convulse in pain and suffering. I must have endured it for seconds before

I was reaching for the tank lid, desperate to stop the whole operation. But it was locked. Cornelius had known I would be too soft and had done the necessary. I screamed and attacked the tank with all my might, but I could not prevent my baby's fate. Minutes later, and much to my relief, our theory was proven true: a home-grown underwater marvel!

'Thus arrived our greatest success and my biggest regret. We celebrated for a short while, and indulged in all the fame and fortune that came with it, but soon I realised that our success was a bitter one. My son and I were separated by an impenetrable barrier. I could not hold him in my arms, teach him, talk to him or check if he was alright. He was completely and utterly restricted to the very pool from whence you arrived.

'Cornelius, meanwhile, revealed his true colours. He treated our son just like any other experiment, only referring to him as Number Three. And worst of all, he started to perform surgery on him. Slowly but surely, he chipped away at his body. *All in the name of science* he would say. I hated him, but I hated myself even more for allowing it. However, as Cornelius took more and more from him, I became more bold. I snuck my son the tools to make good his escape, and my clever boy took his opportunity. I can only hope that he is still out there, living the free life he should have had from the beginning. It goes without saying that I split up with Cornelius and that my fascination with science was soured.

'I dearly wish that was where this story ended. Whilst running errands in town, I found love once again with a honourable tradesman. He was so unlike Cornelius in every way. I told him of my troubled past and found solace in his arms. Out of this love, I became with child for the fourth time. I knew that Cornelius, who was both powerful and bitter, would not take this news well, so I took refuge with a friend until the day my child was born. But I was betrayed. Cornelius must have found out and blackmailed or bribed my confidante. All I know is that my newborn was snatched away from me and the next time I saw her, she was sitting happily in a fish-tank, alive and well, but completely intolerant to our air.

'Cornelius was smug; he had both ruined the happiness in my life and bound me to him. You see, he imprisoned my daughter in the catacombs beneath his house and the only way I could see her is by returning to my previous role as his fellow scientist and swearing to never see my love affair again. What else could I do? I knew all too well what Cornelius was capable of. How could I sleep knowing that she was at the mercy of such a monster? Ever since, I have been playing out this role and watching over her, ready to defend her should he take his experiments too far. Furthermore, I've been waiting for the opportunity to set her free. Once I've done that, I intend to find my love and get as far from Cornelius as is possible on such a pitifully small spit of land.

'I don't know whether Cornelius suspects my hand in the first escape, but he was thorough in his imprisonment of my daughter. She's kept in a pool not dissimilar to this one, down the passageway to my right. You cannot miss it. There are multiple underwater routes to the sea, but the coded padlock prevents her from moving more than a metre from her anchor, and it's too deep for anyone to reach without certain death. Anyone except you, that is.

'You're quite a marvel, you know. According to our theory, you see, you must have been born into both environments *or neither*. The first is impossible and the latter is unthinkable. In spite of myself, I confess I'm rather curious. But right now, I don't care. I *need* you to save my daughter.

'So, here we are. I am the key to your release, and you are the key to my daughter's. And you will want to escape, *trust me*. Cornelius is a mad crook, but he is an honest scientist. He will announce your discovery even if it throws his theory into shadow. Afterwards he will come up with new theories and he will experiment on you, piece by piece, until you're reduced to a collection of labelled jars and pages in a book.' She paused to stand up, swivel around and lock eyes with his own. 'Do we understand each other?'

Luke knew that this was his shot; he tried once again to nod his head and, though he may have imagined it, his head gave a slight wobble of agreement. She grunted and reached round to the side of his cage. There was a resounding click as a clasp was released.

'The code to release her is four-nine-six-two. I'll repeat, four-nine-six-two. Where my daughter is at stake, I will do anything to release her, even if it means teaming up with Cornelius again and dragging your skinny hide back here. Don't let me down.'

With that ultimatum, she sauntered away, humming to herself as if she did not have a care in the world. Perhaps she felt good to finally have a chance to save her daughter. When she reached the stairs, she drew her cloak about herself and resumed a slight stoop, portraying a frailty that Luke knew was entirely fictional.

Then she was gone and Luke was left alone to ponder her disturbing tale of woe. As he willed his body towards functionality, his mind conjured dark thoughts of what Cornelius would do to him if he failed to escape before morning, and whether Garth's life had been crushed along with the shell's shattered remains. They were not pleasant thoughts.

***

Garth's mind wandered plains incomprehensible, traversed dimensions that defied description and generally scattered in all possible directions at once. Despite this, the parts of his mind were singularly aiming towards one direction and one direction alone; complete and utter madness.

One part of his mind hovered above a dimension of donut-shaped planets covered in vibrant, fantastical foliage, among which its inhabitants - large, space-sturdy glow-worms - flitted out into the starry night and conducted a slow methodical dance. They had been doing it for eons, yet the question of whether this act was out of love, or some kind of beautiful dance-off, had yet to be answered and probably never would be. One group of particularly adept glow-worms formed a shape that could have been, or rather certainly was, the Gazoid letter 'G'.

A smaller, more creative and rebellious snippet of him had taken a more active approach. In this particular dimension it was considered of the greatest importance to always be on the phone, discussing the latest business-related news, be that stock prices, annual income, turnover or any other horrendously, tedious business-related subjects. This facet of his personality had rather taken to interrupting these conversations with small, yet obscenely random phrases, just to see the recoil of the recipient, the drop of a monocle in the sheer surprise, or the tumble of a nameless suited person as they fainted. One particular conversation went as such:

'Have you heard that stocks in toothbrushes have risen by five percent?'

'No I have not. That is most upsetting as I sold all my stocks in toothbrushes about two hours ago. Do you have any other important business-related news to share with me?'

And then one phone would start to glow a faint blue.

'But how can you have dessert if you have not finished your meat?'

'I'm sorry?'

'But how can you have dessert if you have not finished your meat?'

Having confirmed just how odd and out of context this conversation had become, the recipient fell to the floor in shock. As she did so, her top hat rolled off her head; the stitching that lined its underside looked suspiciously like the Gazoid letter 'R'.

Another segment of his consciousness pictured a blackened, scorched planet in which its entire population eagerly awaited the eruption of any of its many volcanoes. The slightest quake had these centipede-like creatures ducking and weaving across the planet's harsh terrain, jaw's open in preparation for the impending gush of tasty magma. As a pack of centipedes hastily criss-crossed and overlapped, this particular part of his mind registered that they had unwittingly produced, for a fleeting second, the Gazoid letter 'A'.

A more astute part of his brain knew exactly what was happening and was hoping that his brethren would catch up before it was simply too late and the damage would be irreparable. He was in an extremely interesting dimension, possibly the most imaginative dimension yet, but he refused to be distracted. He simply pictured the Gazoid letter 'T' and was on his way.

The final piece to the puzzle was found whilst admiring an interdimensional letter museum, which claimed to have discovered 99% of the different forms of the letter 'H'. This was highly inaccurate. In actual fact they had hardly scratched the surface. Its clientele consisted mostly of spindly beings that stalked around scratching their ridiculously long goatees making appropriately contemplative noises. Fortunately for this embodiment of Garth's consciousness, who was not the brightest bunch, the museum *had* captured the Gazoid letter 'H'. It focussed on it for five whole minutes before deciding that it did, indeed, look like the Gazoid letter 'H'.

Having pieced together his name, 'G.A.R.T.H', the separated parts of his brain seemed to remember their origins, and, although they had been rather enjoying running amok, thought that it would be rude not to reunite. On doing so, all of Garth's senses came crashing in at once, like unwelcome guests.

He could hear the incessant sound of Penn, calling his name with monotonic determination.

'Garth. Garth. Come back to me Garth. Garrrrrrrrrrtthhhh,' she repeated.

He could smell his own sweat, the unfortunate result of stewing in the same room without the relief of an open window.

But most of all, overriding everything, was the feeling of pain.

CHAPTER 11: THE KING'S RECKONING

An immeasurable amount of time had passed. Luke had spent it slowly willing his body into animation; a wiggle of a toe, a flick of his wrist. Each uncontrolled spasm was a battle. Eventually he could lift his arms, nod his head, move his mouth from side to side; all these movements felt rusty and new.

Eventually, he wrested control of a single arm and attempted to slap the glass. Whatever his intentions, the result was a feeble stroke. Trying again, he was shocked to see the cage shake – it was unstable. The third time, he managed to manoeuvre his palm onto the glass surface and give a frail push.

To his pleasant surprise, the cage swung open and water spewed out onto the ground. He was sent forwards with the sudden rush, landing facedown on damp rock. Standing seemed to be out of the question, but he refused to stay where he was. His arms and legs disobeyed him despite his strongest commands. In the end, he wormed his way to the rock pool and looked into a tempting escape.

Could he return to Naufragium a failure? If he didn't find answers to their shortage of fish, then the town would starve and Garth would never send Luke back to wherever he came from. He immediately dismissed this traitorous thought. Instead, he crawled around the pool and stared hopelessly at the stairs; to attempt them in his current state would be ludicrous. While he looked about forlornly, something caught his eye - another open cave. It could only lead to Margaret's trapped daughter.

A distance that would have taken him seven easy strides drained as much energy as a marathon. He wiggled past the fish tray and into the new cave. Here was another rock-pool, this one surrounded by pointed stalagmites. Some numbers, still dripping, had been hastily scrawled on the cavern wall. *Four-Nine-Six-Two.* Luke had remembered the code anyway, but clearly Margaret had not trusted that he would.

He shimmied closer to the pool with as much grace as an inebriated duck. Sure enough there was a woman deep within, barely clothed and throttled by a metal collar. Although she was entirely still, the bubbles that rose from her location was proof that she was merely resting.

Metal rungs had been stabbed into the pool's sides, leading far down to its captive. Cornelius must have meticulously constructed the prison, before filling it with the seawater that permeated the island's ground. It was impossible for Margaret, or any other land-dweller, to reach its base and free her daughter, let alone have enough air to return to the surface. Luke truly was her only chance.

He stayed around the surface for a while, slowly working his muscles one by one. He stretched and squirmed, twisted and writhed, until he felt confident enough to tackle the long way down. Finding a suitable gap, he slid into the water and started the journey to its base, one step at a time.

When he finally landed unsteadily on to the bottom, Margaret's daughter jolted awake, and with a flurry of panic, scrambled away as far as her chain would allow. Luke spared her a glance and did not know whether to smile or wince with horror. Now closer, it became evident that her skin was heavily scarred from Cornelius' experiments. A number four had been tattooed on her arm, a signature mark of one of Cornelius' test subjects. Luke resolved to avoid looking in her direction and concentrated instead on moving his lethargic limbs towards the padlock.

'Gah meh ya con dar!' she gibbered incoherently. 'Cudhan meta thronkaly!'

Avoiding her gaze, he arrived at the padlock and wrenched it towards him. Inputting the code took time and control, neither of which he had. After much effort, he did manage to slot the correct digits into place; clearly the sea urchin toxin was wearing thin. He was rewarded when the padlock sprung open with a satisfying *click*!

The woman looked confused as the chain attached to her neck gave no resistance. She was free!

There were many potential escape routes which no doubt lead out to sea. Cornelius must have thought that the chain would render them all pointless, but not now. Her eyes darted to those exit tunnels and then back to her saviour.

'What are you waiting for? Go!' Luke egged.

With a cry of what could have been joy, she disappeared into darkness, her loose chain dragging behind. Luke had done all that he could; it was up to her to survive now. Perhaps she'd bump in to Stuart on her way out, he thought hopefully. With a sigh of accomplishment, he heaved himself back up the ladder.

The dip in the water had left him feeling slightly rejuvenated; he even managed to make it to his feet (though he teetered like a drunken pirate). One aim dominated his mind – get out of the caves and away from Cornelius' evil reach.

As he stumbled passed the glass-cage, which was still ajar from when he had all but fallen out, a mischievous thought stopped him in his tracks. Smirking just slightly, he closed it shut and covered it once again with the curtain. At first glance, it would appear he was still within.

From there, he staggered towards the bottom of the staircase, pausing only to retch. Nothing came out, but the respite was enough for him to pick up John's compass, which had been left on the poolside workbench.

The climb out of the basement took thrice as long as before. By the time he had reached the elaborate study, the effects of the neurotoxin had worn off and he was walking with the merest hindrance. The house was asleep; the classical music was replaced with silence and the rooms were now steeped in darkness. A pale light, however, shone faintly from the doorway, providing the foggiest outline of a desk and chair.

He navigated around the study and out to a corridor of gleaming tiles. Paintings, whose subjects were clouded by shadow, hung on either side. In one direction was a grand marble staircase with grotesque gargoyles guarding each railing; in the other, a windowed door displaying a large moon outside.

Donning a large brown cloak off a stand, he stowed John's compass in a pocket and unbolted the door. As stealthily as possible, he eased it ajar and a gust of wind came to foil his attempts by slamming it on his face. Fortunately, he kept it at bay, slid outside, and carefully closed it behind him.

What a moon! It was far larger than any he'd seen and he welcomed its enlightening glow. It lit a stepping stone path which led between acres of trimmed grass and prettily arranged flowers. Nevertheless, he was eager to escape the garden and hastily made for an iron gate.

Beyond this was a street of two choices; up the mountain or down. It seemed to him that the person in charge would be at the top so that is where he planned to go. Wrapping his stolen cloak around himself, he set off with steely determination. The houses he passed were sizeable and had beautiful gardens to suit. While the rich were snug, the poor kipped on the cobbles outside. More than once, he was forced to step around beggars of skin and bone; one tugged at the corner of his garment.

'Please sir, spare some money for a starving beggar?'

Luke searched the coat's pockets and was surprised to find a metal star-shaped object. It glinted as he held it up and had a picture of Cornelius engraved on one side. Hoping that it was currency, he handed it over.

'This will be enough for me to feed for weeks! Much appreciated sir!'

The man wiggled happily and gave an incredulous grin. Luke was about to continue, when he had a thought.

'Perhaps you can help me.'

'Anything you say, sir.'

'Where can I find the captain here?'

'The captain of where?'

'Here.' Luke gestured all around.

'Ah, you must mean the King. He lives in a palace at the very top of the mountain. Surely you know that?'

Luke shrugged.

'Well, follow this road and it'll take you there! It's quite a trek. Be warned, that man is *not* to be trifled with. If you're lucky, he'll be asleep and his daughter, Kea, will be there in his stead.'

'Thank you,' said Luke.

'No thank *you*, this is the easiest money I've ever made!'

His suspicions confirmed, he set off with renewed gusto. The path twisted and turned so that his incline was never too steep, but it seemed to take forever. Many a sleeping beggar, all unhealthily thin, littered the street. Eventually the path was swallowed by a forest with green ferns converging on each side. The route remained in good condition, almost indifferent to the forest's assault.

There was no way to tell how far up the mountain he had travelled; the air was certainly thinning as he strolled higher. Through leafy branches above, the moon had faded with the increasing light; day was fast approaching. All at once, a chorus of insects awoke and started chattering. It sounded like a thousand crickets rubbing their legs together in delight. Unseen birds burst out into song as if in competition. At one point, a manned horse galloped by, paying Luke no mind at all.

The gradual climb wore away at his calves, but it all seemed worth it when the forest withered away to reveal a breathtaking view. The road ahead clung desperately to the mountain on one side and gave way to a sharp fall on the other. Far below, a glorious sunset was rising over a sparkling sea. Inland, the horseshoe bay that John had mentioned was in plain sight. A dust-filled gust stung his eyes as he reluctantly resumed his hike.

He estimated he was two-thirds of the way up the mountain, though he could not see its peak through a nearby layer of cloud. As the sun eloped higher into the sky, the humidity hit him. Sweat soon drenched him beneath his heavy cloak; such a dramatic change in temperature! He considered abandoning his clothing on the wayside, but remembered that today he would converse with royalty.

As he walked, there was plenty to observe: a lonely mountain goat staggered along a hazardous cliff path, bleating in the hot wind; a gecko on a prickly cactus was disturbed from its sunbathing spot by his passing shadow; flags were posted at random along the trail, flapping in crimson waves. The road wound closer to the clouds, every corner revealing another bout of hills. Luke trained himself not to get his hopes up – there were *always* more hills!

He ended up staring at his feet so as not to think about the distance ahead. This meant that it was unexpected when he was abruptly engulfed by a pleasantly cool mist. The mind-blowing view was lost to sight and so were his own hands. To proceed, he could only ensure that his feet fell on stone and not a chasm of air. One perilous moment happened when his foot skirted the road's edge and he narrowly avoided tripping down a steep bank of boulders. He adjusted his direction accordingly.

Another flag materialised and faded and then he was out of it. The view above the clouds was even more spectacular; gone was the rest of Solis Occassum, coated in a rolling plain of candyfloss. Rays of sunrise seeped through, turning the sky an array of warm orange and fiery red. Noteworthy also was the golden palace built upon the mountain peak; it jutted out to the horizon as if trying to take flight. The very tip of the wizard's hat, he thought to himself. Uplifted by the view, he started to feel cautious optimism.

***

Garth reeled. The whole room spun incessantly as he tried to stand up.

'About time,' said Penn unsympathetically.

'W-what happened?' Garth slurred.

'Why you almost lost your mind, silly,' Penn explained. 'In fact, it's really quite a novelty that you survived the experience at all, let alone that you avoided being scattered thinly across multiple dimensions.'

'I survived?' he asked weakly, as he just about managed to flop into the armchair. He ended up rear-up, face-down, spinning slowly in a sorry fashion. Eventually he summoned the will to right himself. 'Explain.'

'It's like this. While you were sat here, your mind was seeping into that dimension, anchored by that oddly-shaped husk from Earth. That husk was destroyed whilst you were still connected, ruining the tether between your mind and your body at the same time.'

'That does not sound good.'

'It's not, you were dangerously close to going completely mad.'

'Why did you not warn me?'

'You never asked,' she said coldly.

'Did it not occur to you that it might be something worth mentioning?' he demanded, clutching his sore head.

'What difference does it make?' she snapped. 'There's a Gavoidon coming to this very room to terminate the both of us. Does knowing the danger of the task change anything? At the end of the day, you still need to put on that helmet and guide our dimension-subject to success.'

'Dimension-subject?' asked Garth.

'It's what *they* call the poor soul that the shifters decide to use for their plans.'

'They?' Garth asked again, shifting to get comfortable on his mother's chair. His close encounter with madness had now encouraged a spurt of inquisition.

'*Altersearch,*' seethed Penn, managing to coat the word with severe disgust despite her robotic origins.

'I'm no expert,' said Garth, reaching for some snacks from his ever-dwindling supply, 'but I get the distinct impression you don't like them.'

'You have no idea,' she replied. 'Altersearch is the worst kind of corporation. They pray on the good-hearted and the greedy to carry out their dirty work.'

'But they save whole dimensions,' he retorted, feeling more recovered from his ordeal by the second.

'Like I said, you have no idea,' she said with a finality that suggested the inquisition had come to an abrupt end.

'Educate me,' he beseeched.

'Now is not the time. Don't you remember the precarious situation that we left our dimension-subject in? Or are your brains still addled?

Then it came back to him in a series of nightmarish flashes. The stooped gait of the villain, the cold, unyielding atmosphere of the underground lair, the horrific way that Luke had stared without blinking in his poison-induced stupor.

Garth almost jumped out of the chair in his urgency. 'We have to help him!'

'Then you know what to do.' Penn said, her light glowing smugly. 'Return to your post, Garth. Put that helmet back on and delve back into the dimension shift game.'

Shaking from the fresh impression of pain, Garth gritted his teeth and determinedly slapped his webbed on either side of the helmet. It felt heavy, now, with the newly associated risk of madness reverberating around his bulbous head.

But he had to do it.

Penn had him and she knew it. He was trapped, she was his one and only source of guidance, and there was a whole dimension at stake. His own guilt at unwittingly having used Luke in a similar fashion added to the cocktail of emotions that drove him on.

He plonked the helmet back on, his ears fitting snugly through their designated slits.

Within seconds he was hovering above a blue planet. With Penn's guidance, he zoomed in, bypassing an almost equally-sized moon. Upon the planet was a tiny spec of land. This spec became a blob which slowly turned into a familiar, yet dramatic mountainside. One side of the land was frighteningly steep and curved out to sea as it rose, seeming to defy gravity. A dense forest grew on cliff-like terrain so uninhabitable that buildings would have been impractical. The other side of the mountain, however, was more accommodating; it sloped gently to a horseshoe bay with golden sand. From this beach, a large street seeped between a bustling town, continued upwards, and disappeared in a puff of fog as it rose to the mountaintop.

He had found Solis Occassum; it was a start.

'Where is he?' he demanded.

'The connection between your brain and his location was broken. I'm afraid the only way to find him is through searching manually.'

Garth studied the array of buildings and the sheer size of the mountain.

'He could be anywhere!' he whined in despair.

'Stay alert, listen to the spoken word, scan the area,' Penn advised.

Garth swooped into town, an unseen phantom, to listen and wait for any signs that might lead him to Luke. He did not know how, but he was going to find and rescue him.

***

Half an hour hence, Luke was finally at the palace. The

road had broken out into a number of steps bordered by grand flags. At the top, guards patrolled along a great marble wall that followed the perimeter of the main building. From a distance it gave the impression of being impenetrable, but he could see a wide gate beneath an arch. Through the railings, he spied a gravel courtyard and the palace, pointing skywards with three pyramidal roofs. The one in the middle was the largest, suggesting a great hall and no doubt where the King addressed his people.

As he approached, a discrete horn sounded and a couple of guards came out to meet him. They were clad in frightful silver armour, but their heads were naked to the glare of the sun. Their weapons looked just as intimidating; in one hand they held a brutal war-axe while in the other they clasped a turtle-shell shield.

'Stop right there!' an ogre of a man bawled.

The impact of their shining outfit was somewhat ruined by the way that they swaggered over; they looked like a pair of peacocks showing off their colours. Nevertheless, Luke was glad to obey; the steps had just about finished him off and he was pleased to take a break.

'I am the Chief Watchman, Chuck Beluga. What's your business here?' demanded the same man; the armour he wore looked fit to burst. He had a rounded face, puffy cheeks and cauliflower ears. Each syllable shouted came with a wobble of his overgrown double chin. 'And why haven't you got any shoes on?'

'I have news for your King,' said Luke, ignoring the second question.

'News, eh?' He chortled. 'And is it... interesting?'

'What?'

'Interesting,' clarified the other guard.

'Well, I think so,' Luke was taken aback by this odd turn in conversation. 'It's important anyway.'

'Important doesn't necessarily mean interesting, boy,' Chuck said. 'Look at *them*, for example. They thought their news was *interesting*. Turns out, it was just *important* and see where it got them.'

The man jabbed his axe towards a gathering of stakes which speared five severed heads; a bolt from the blue amongst all the scenic beauty. Luke felt sick at the sight, his previous hopes quickly diminishing. He gave a concerned gulp.

'You are aware of the rule for visits, aren't you?'

'And that is?' Luke asked, although he was dreading the answer.

'If a peasant arrives without interesting news...'

Chuck thrust his thumb towards the disembodied parts.

'Do you still want to go in?'

Luke hesitated as he weighed up his chances.

'Tough!' said Chuck nastily, grabbing him by the arm. 'You're here now, so up you come!'

He was jostled through the gate. At first he tried to shake free, but, with both guards holding him, escape was unlikely. As he was dragged through the courtyard, he passed an array of water sculptures, ranging from beautiful showering women to snippets of battle, water spurting from gaping wounds.

Fear rose within as they arrived at a huge door, fit for a giant. Luke was shoved into the palace ferociously and fell onto cold, stone tiles.

'Blooming lucky if you ask me,' he heard one of the guards say as the door was sealed with a resounding thud, stifling a slither of sunlight.

Luke slowly got to his feet, aching from both his fall and his climb. He stood in an impressive cathedral-sized hall with a rouge carpet flowing down the centre. Rows of chairs, occupied by richly robed men and women, all faced an elaborate throne. The audience looked to be sprawled out in an ungainly fashion; some rested their heads in their hands; one man had turned an opposite chair to put his feet up and seemed to be having a nap. Nobody said anything. Pillars of marble with torches of blue lit the way; it was perfectly cool and, if the flames produced any heat, Luke did not feel it.

Although his steps were light, they still drew some irritated glances. A few noticed his strange attire and shuffled slightly to get a better look. On the throne, it became clear, sat a young woman with wavy blonde locks. Unlike everyone else, her brown eyes studied him with utmost attention. She gave an encouraging smile as he approached. Her dress was a modest pale-green with a row of emerald tassels. Kea, the King's daughter, he surmised.

Luke fell to one knee, as he reckoned he should.

'Get up, I am no King.' Her laughter trickled out like jingle bells. 'Who might you be?'

'My name is Lug- I mean Luke,' he stumbled, face reddening. 'I have something very important to tell you. I need your help.'

'Do you not fear my father's rule?'

'I have to pass on this news, it's the whole reason I'm here and I have no doubt that it will be of interest,' he replied adamantly.

'No matter if it isn't. It is a silly rule that breeds laziness. My father is currently nursing a headache after a night of partying. Have courage, for I follow his rule not!' she declared. 'Now, what brings you up the mountain?'

'I am here on behalf of a whole race of people from an underwater town called Naufragium."

'Great, another one has gone mad,' someone mocked. 'Soon the whole island will be loonies.'

'I'm not mad,' Luke retorted. 'They are starving down there, *they need your help.*'

Kea pursed her lips. 'And how do you know this?'

'Because I've been there,' he stated. 'I've seen it all, a town built within a fleet of shipwrecks, with little more than seaweed to get by. They sent me to -'

'You have been *sent*?' bellowed another heckler. 'Are

you suggesting that they can *think* as we do, *speak* as we do?'

Luke turned to the audience, but could not pinpoint the source of the assault. 'Aside from the fact they can breathe underwater, I have no reason to think that they are any different from your people.'

There were a few gasps and the man, who had been napping, awoke with a comical snort. Kea, meanwhile, sat up straight, suddenly very intrigued. She studied him with a frightening intensity.

'Say, hypothetically, that what you say is true, how do you expect us to help?' She regained control of the conversation. 'We are not doing so well ourselves. The sea, our main source of food, becomes less bountiful by the day. Most people on this island are without food and it's only getting worse. If you came here for a solution, I'm afraid you will find the same problems here.'

Luke's heart dropped in disappointment. 'I did not know that,' he floundered, trying his best to hold it together. 'I've come all this way, is there *nothing* you can do?'

There was a thoughtful silence and Luke scrunched up his face.

'Actually, there might be something,' Kea pondered. Luke looked up at her, hope flaring from deep within. 'A piece of old-science that I've read about. If you *really* can go underwater and converse with the sea-people, then maybe you can -'

'KEA!' a man roared. 'Get off of *my* throne!'

She leapt from the chair as a man decked in a purple cloak and a golden crown stormed into the hall. He had thick sideburns that joined at his chin and a bulbous nose. His body was one of gluttony, and yet it gave the impression of intimidating strength.

'How many times do I have to tell you?' he grumbled. 'You are never to sit on the throne. It is *mine*. Rex Soloman shares his throne with *nobody*.'

'It beats standing, father,' she quipped.

'I've got half a century left to reign so just get used to it!' he growled. Slumping onto the throne, he looked about his court, noticing that, for once, people did not look so bored. 'What's happening here?'

'News, father! And it's very interesting.'

'Oh aye? I'll be the judge of that! You know how I like my executions.'

'This boy claims to be from an underwater city. He says the fish people are no different from us. They speak, listen and have formed a society not unlike our own.'

Rex gave out an avalanche of harsh laughter.

'You fool, Kea! He's either insane or he's a clever peasant who has weaved a pretty tale for some coin. Either way, it's to the block with him. Chuck!'

The two men from the gate strolled through the front door.

'Cease him!'

Luke was grappled once more. The court, meanwhile, erupted into enthusiastic applause.

'Wait!' he shouted. 'I can prove it!'

One of Rex's eyebrows rose in disbelief. 'How?'

'Umm... I can breathe underwater!'

'Pure fantasy! Don't insult me boy or your death will just be slower.'

'Err...,' he stuttered.

Then, the least likely person came to his rescue.

The hall doors, from whence Luke had arrived, were thrown open and in strode none other than Cornelius himself. Behind him, some dusty beggars pinned the doors open and hauled in the wheeled glass cage, still enveloped in a dark curtain.

'Out of my way,' he said derisively as he encountered Luke and the guards on his way down the aisle. The guards, clearly knowing the pecking order, shuffled Luke to the side, keeping him well and truly secured. In his haste, Cornelius' eyes swept over Luke without recognition.

Rex looked bemused. 'Cornelius, what is the meaning of this contraption in my throne room?'

Cornelius bowed low, or as low as his elderly bones would allow. 'I have interesting news, sire. Last night, I encountered an intruder in my house. He sneaked in from the catacombs beneath.'

Rex shrugged. 'The peasants are hungry, Cornelius. Do not bother me with every attempt of thievery. Be thankful that you still have food worth thieving.'

'This invader was different,' announced Cornelius with a smirk. 'He was not from the island at all. He was, in fact, an invader from *beneath the sea!*'

With a flourish, Cornelius whipped the curtain off the cage to reveal an empty, glass container still half-filled with seawater, but otherwise entirely ordinary. Cornelius, whose focus was entirely on the king, waited for some kind of amazed reaction. Instead he was instead greeted with a blank, unamused stare. He twisted around and his mouth fell open. The audience meanwhile rather enjoyed this spectacle and started hooting with laughter.

Cornelius reddened. His mind raced and arrived at the only possible conclusion. 'Margaret,' he said through gritted teeth.

Kea, amidst the cacophony, leant over to her father and whispered to him, flicking her eyes in Luke's direction. The connection between himself and Cornelius' plight was an easy step to make. It occurred to him briefly that it might even give credence to his claim that he was indeed from beneath the waves.

Rex was not laughing, though the excitement shone in his eyes.

'Is that your intruder?' he demanded, pointing a regal finger at Luke.

Cornelius's jaw dropped for a second time. His eyes turned to daggers and, unbelievably, his face went an even darker shade of red. 'That's him. That's the freak who, had it not been for my damned wife, would be in that cage where he belongs. Let me have him and I will conduct science that could herald a new dawn. Science that could change the course of -'

'Silence you old fool,' Rex snapped, causing an immediate halt to Cornelius' rant. He dismissed Cornelius with his gaze and turned his attention to Luke, scratching at his sideburns as he did so.

'So... there really is an underwater town?'
'Yes,' Luke confirmed happily.
'And they can think like us?'
'They can.'
'And I suppose... they eat fish?'
'And seaweed, yes.'

Rex licked his lips, and then turned to his royal subjects.

'Do you know what this means?'
Multiple suggestions were announced.
'Trade?'
'... A big party?' a woman asked hopefully.
'... Mermaids?' a fat man said, even *more* hopefully.

'No, no and no,' Rex said. 'This means *war*.'

PART 2

Many pairs o'eyes has the Lord of the Sea,
So choose your side carefully,

The crab-man, all claws and plates,
Sent to the Land to spy on those the Lord hates,

The Videre fish, all swift and gold,
Will grant powers to those worthy I'm told,

Turtleoak turtles will neither attack nor defend,
But a lucky few will find them a loyal friend.

Crab, turtle and fish makes at least three,
Many pairs o'eyes has the Lord of the Sea.

- *A Naufragium nursery rhyme.*

CHAPTER 12: TORTURE TROUBLE

'War?' Kea and Luke shouted simultaneously.

Their outcry was drowned by an outbreak of cheers from the royals. Even the guards that held Luke momentarily let go to clang their axes together in their enthusiasm.

'War, father?' Kea repeated once the hubbub had died down. 'Have you taken leave of your senses?'

'I said war, and that is exactly what I mean,' Rex snarled. 'We'll uproot these sea people and take whatever the sea has left to offer for ourselves.'

'But both towns are starving,' Luke bravely interjected. 'War will not bring back the fish!'

'So what if it doesn't, boy? Do you think *I* lack for fish?' Rex grabbed his barrel-like stomach. 'Thanks to the ocean wiping out everything on the horizon, we've had no wars for centuries. Previous kings may have enjoyed that convenient peace, but, truth is, it's awfully tedious, especially when the island is packed with peasants who have nothing better to do than squabble amongst themselves over scraps. At the very least, this will give them something to think about other than their rumbling bellies.'

'What about all the lives that will be lost?' Kea demanded, achieving a few concerned faces in the crowd.

Rex only smirked. 'If some people die in the process,

they will be hailed as heroes and, as an added bonus, there will be less mouths to feed.'

'You're a monster,' said Luke, realising the extent of his blunder.

'*I* am a king and *you* are an enemy of war,' Rex sneered cruelly. 'Take him away to the cells for interrogation and... send for Bart the Brutal.'

Luke was hauled roughly down the aisle towards the exit.

'Wait, sir,' Cornelius appealed, weakly lowering himself onto his knees and grovelling at the King's feet. Rex held up a hand, momentarily halting the guards who had seized Luke.

'What is the meaning of this, Cornelius?'

'I shall design the most damaging warships ever known. Just please, sire, let me have the intruder. His body could be the key to ground-breaking science and anything I discover will only help the upcoming war.'

Rex narrowed his eyes and mused over the offer. 'His mind also contains the location of this underwater settlement. Once we have squeezed this information from him, you can have what remains.'

'Sire, I know Bart the Brutal. He leaves little of his victims. I cannot conduct science on a specimen that is no more than a pulp of flesh.'

'He will be tortured and you will be happy with whatever you are given,' Rex growled.

'Yes, sire. Of course, sire,' whispered Cornelius, cowering.

'Chuck, take him to the cells,' Rex ordered. 'Bart will be glad to finally have some work.'

'No!' Luke rebelled, kicking and twisting, but nothing could be done as he was yanked away. They took a sharp turn at the hall door and he was wrestled down a large corridor. Briefly he caught a glimpse of a glamorous dining hall; a marble table displayed a feast of fish, roasted vegetables and honey-glazed ham. The smell of freshly-cooked food was replaced with the odour of stale air and Chuck's sweat as he was whisked into a disused storeroom.

Inside was a jumble of barrels, baskets and crates, each lined with silvery spider webs. Unlike the rest of the palace, the floor was coated in a thick layer of dust. In all appearances, and much to his bewilderment, they had reached a dead end; a solid brick wall with no door. After a quick tug of a broom handle by Chuck, however, a hidden route was revealed. There was a loud rumble of chains and then the wall fell away. Within was a sinister passage which, as he immediately found out, led down to the palace basement.

While the other guard stayed behind to crank the wall back into place, Chuck picked up a flaming lantern and shoved Luke in front. He was pushed down the spiralled passageway until they reached the bottom where its narrow walls opened out into a dingy expanse, its limits hidden by darkness.

A wave of cool air brushed Luke's face and he thought he could hear the rushing of water. The only visible way led across a stumpy bridge; as they trudged across, Luke sneaked a glimpse beneath and swore he could see a river. As if to confirm his suspicions, a turtle poked its head out, disturbing the surface. Luke was both intrigued and shaken by this unexpected finding.

'Don't go getting any ideas *fish boy*,' Chuck warned.

Beyond the bridge were a row of sturdy doors; they passed a few without comment, though he was certain they were empty. When they reached the intended hold, his stolen cloak was whipped from his shoulders, exposing him to the harsh underground cold.

'I expect this is Cornelius', but I rather like it!' Chuck declared before stowing the cloak and its contents away, including, much to Luke's rising distress, the compass.

With a rough shove, Luke was sent into his cell, only barely keeping upright. Among its contents was a blood stain on the floor and an equally-marred chair. A single torch cast menacing shadows from dangling chains. The air was thick with the musk of terror and sweat. Now released, Luke recoiled from the sight, bashing into something that hung from the ceiling – a collection of decaying skulls on a string. He gave a shout of fright and instinctively rushed towards the open door. There was a throaty chortle and then Chuck slammed it shut on his face.

'Bart the Brutal will be with you soon,' he said smugly.

'Don't leave me here!' Luke pleaded, but the guard did not respond. Listening hard, Luke could make out the sound of his footsteps slowly getting quieter. 'Let me out!'

***

Garth had watched throughout the day, hovering above Solis Occassum, and had found no sign of Luke anywhere. Some part of him was glad; he did not want to return to Cornelius' labs. The pain was still fresh in his mind and, frankly, the place gave him the creeps.

He recounted what he had witnessed.

At sunrise, waking beggars had gathered in clusters and talked in tired mumbles. A man on a horse had galloped around purposefully, slipping squares of white paper in through the doors of the more wealthy. Men and women, decked in rich garments, had strolled out from their abodes, ignoring the incessant wails of the poverty on the street outside. Silver canes had clattered on the dusty road and shade umbrellas had cast frilly silhouettes.

Further down the mountain, the rich quarter came to an abrupt end and, after a polite distance, appeared the hobbled shacks of the poor. The contrast was stark: the road that flowed between was the only similarity. The buildings were no longer expansive estates with copious rooms and broad gardens; they were tall structures of wood and thin material, rammed side by side. Dripping clothes flapped in the sun like a flock of beige doves, latched from one shabby house to the next by far-reaching ropes.

Workers of all ages with weather-beaten faces had spilled out onto the street, still dirty from the day before. A few market stalls selling fruit and vegetables had been erected, each watched over by an armoured royal guard. The beggars and workers alike had gawped at these oases of food, but many had not been able to afford their wares. While the land had swarmed with people, the sea had been relatively quiet; a single trawler with crimson sails had fished with little success.

As interesting as his sightseeing was, it had not achieved anything. The rich had spoken of menial matters like weather and gossip. The poor, on the other hand, had been miserably quiet, speaking with heavy hearts and hungry stomachs. There was no mention of Luke and night had come too swiftly. Garth, agitated beyond belief, had been forced to sleep until the next day.

It was only on the following morning that something of remark occurred. A flash of white charged down the wavy street from the mass of clouds at its peak. Garth floated above as a guard-laden bull crashed through a forest, passed the rich quarter and into the slums, stopping at a humble shelter which billowed smoke and sent forth the sound of metal clanging on metal. The guard slid clumsily off his steed and the bull, breathing heavily, flopped onto its side, thankful to be relieved of its ungainly passenger.

Garth flew closer. Ears at the ready, he eavesdropped on their conversation.

'Hullo Bart, or perhaps I should call you Bart the Brutal,' the man wheezed. 'Long time, no torture.'

'Just Bart the Blacksmith these days,' replied a soot-covered man who was sat down toiling over a sweltering furnace. He was smashing a piece of metal with his mallet, but paused mid-swing to give the guard an appraising stare. 'Chuck? Is that you?'

'It is,' Chuck confirmed with a grin, his smile bordered

by layers of fat. 'Been a while, hasn't it?'

'I can see that palace life is treating you well.' Bart prodded his mallet in the direction of Chuck's bulging belly. 'What brings you to my smithy?'

'Rex has a job for you.'

'Oh aye, who is the poor sod?'

'You'll hardly believe this,' Chuck gushed excitedly, 'but we've had an invader from the sea. He snuck into Dr Flotsam's house and claims to be from a sub-aqua society. The old man managed to capture him, but somehow the boy escaped, releasing Dr. Flotsam's prized experimental daughter as he went.'

'He released her?' the blacksmith exclaimed, dropping his mallet directly onto one of his feet in shock. Angry curses ensued as he hopped about in agony. Garth chuckled to himself.

'I know how you feel, treason of the highest order. Old Dr. Flotsam is fuming,' Chuck resumed once Bart had recovered. 'Anyway, the short of it is, Rex wants you to find out where this town is so that we can destroy it.'

'That sounds like Rex to me,' Bart commented, gazing thoughtfully into a pile of ash and embers. 'And if I refuse?'

'Rex won't be happy, but we'll find someone else to do the deed.'

Bart massaged his injured foot, seemingly weighing up his options.

'Nobody knows the torture trade like you,' Chuck encouraged.

'That was a long time ago,' he grunted.

'You will be paid generously,' Chuck vowed.

'Well now, that changes things,' Bart grinned.

'When can you come to the palace?' asked Chuck presumptuously.

'That depends, how long has he been in the torture room?'

'A whole night,' the guard said with undisguised glee.

Garth immediately took a strong disliking to the man.

'Good, let him stew there a bit longer while I prepare my equipment,' Bart decided. 'I always find that giving them time to think makes them easier to crack. I'll make that squirt sing like a siren.'

'Ah, very good.' Chuck grinned delightedly.

'You're enjoying this, aren't you?'

'After centuries of boredom, we're finally going to see some action,' said Chuck, whipping his bull to a stand. 'You'd be mad not to be excited!'

'I'll gather my tools and we'll have that town's location soon enough.'

'Brilliant, I'll go tell Rex the good news.' Chuck heaved himself back onto the poor beast and spurred it forwards.

'So long!' Bart said, beaming eagerly.

The guard gave a frantic wave and then shot back up the street. As soon as he was out of sight, the blacksmith's face dropped to a troubled frown and he stoked a dying fire absent-mindedly.

'Follow him then,' Penn hissed in Garth's ears. For a second he thought the blacksmith would look up in surprise, but he knew that only he could hear Penn's secret counsel.

Garth gravitated upwards and away from the forge. With ease, he saw Chuck's lumbering progress up the mountain and locked on to him. If the guard could be believed, Luke was imprisoned and awaiting torture. Clearly the situation had taken a turn for the worse and it was up to Garth to locate his unfortunate friend and save him.

He watched passively as Chuck rode up and up, through street, forest and eventually dense cloud, to arrive at a distastefully extravagant building at the mountain's peak. Garth almost slapped himself for not scouting higher up in the first place. Chuck disembarked his steed, exchanged salutes with fellow guards, waddled through a courtyard and into a lively hall.

Within, row upon row of people faced towards a fancy

chair. Chuck took a turn into a room almost as lavish; a flight of broad carpeted stairs led to an overlooking balcony. Polished weapons decorated the walls: steel claymores, silver war hammers and ruby-encrusted daggers. On the ground floor, servants in dull brown overalls sneaked about, carrying clothes, balancing towers of dirty plates or wielding a tray of drinks. Chuck passed by without sparing them a glance.

With a determined huff, he scaled the stairs to knock timidly at a pair of grand doors.

'Who are you and what do you want?' came an irritated roar from within.

'Chuck!' the guard answered. 'I come with news of Bart.'

'Cousin! What are you waiting for? Get in here!'

Hearing this, and it was difficult not to, Chuck swung open the doors. The origin of the voice was an almost equally large man who, Garth later found out, was called Rex. On his head was a ridiculous hat that had the appearance of a jewelled cake. He sat on a cushioned chair, gulping from a plump goblet and chewing on a juicy chicken drumstick.

'Well?' Rex demanded through a mouthful of mashed poultry. 'Is he coming?'

'Yes,' Chuck said. 'He'll be up soon.'

'Good work,' Rex smirked. A small table was packed with food to the point of collapse. Behind was a luxurious bed which, Garth thought, could be described as double-King-sized. The one seat was taken, leaving Chuck to stand on his overburdened legs.

'When he arrives,' the King continued, 'escort him to the intruder and... make sure that our esteemed torturer doesn't leave until we have that location!'

'You want me to keep Bart captive *with* the intruder?'

'That's what I said, Chuck.' Rex fixed him with a cold stare. 'This is war. Think of it as an incentive for him to get the job done.'

Chuck gave a slow nod.

'Drinks and goblets are over there.' Rex pointed out an

extravagant cabinet. 'Join me!'

After pouring a goblet of vile orange liquid, Chuck returned to his king and had a few sips.

'Ready to go to war?' Rex asked.

'Yes, sir.'

'I'm going to give you front row seats for the battle, Chucky boy, on the deck of my personal warship.'

'You are too kind, my lord.'

'Cornelius is designing it as we speak,' he went on. 'Imagine it! The spray of the sea, the destruction, the bloodshed. Our forefathers did it centuries ago, of course, brawling for the high ground when the damned sea level started rising. It's no coincidence that we're living here today and our ancient enemies have all drowned - war is in our blood, and now we finally have the chance to indulge. A classic battle for resources like in times of old. And the celebrations when we step off those ships... they will be the best yet!'

The man was literally shaking in his passion; it made Garth uneasy. Somehow, Luke had aggravated the land people and now war was imminent. If a battle occurred, he was sure that the loss of life would be enough to collapse the already frail dimension. Both towns would blink out of existence along with everyone in them; gone would be John, Limpet and Stuart. Garth shuddered.

Knock knock.

Somebody was at Rex's door and, unlike Chuck, they did not wait to be admitted. A woman entered like a thunderstorm and slammed down a clenched fist onto the table. Rex's goblet wobbled and liquid oozed down its side.

'We need to talk,' she said.

Rex rolled his eyes. 'There is nothing to talk about Kea! *I* am the King and *I* have declared war.'

'Nevertheless, I want to talk,' she gave Chuck a sideways glance, 'in private.'

'Whatever you can say, you can say in front of family. Not to mention, my new *war commander*,' Rex said. Chuck visibly squirmed with pride.

Kea took a deep breath. 'You have chosen a pointless war, but it's not too late, I can offer you an alternative,' she claimed. 'If this... Luke... can breathe underwater, then he could seek out aquaseeds and...'

'Aquaseeds!' Rex guffawed and then burst into barks of laughter. Chuck joined in, chortling so hard that tears rolled down his chubby cheeks. The pair continued this way while Kea waited, tapping her foot impatiently.

'Yes, aquaseeds,' she said through gritted teeth. 'I know it's very old science from our most ancient of scrolls, but, if it's true, they could *revitalise* the sea. They could be the key to bringing back food and making our island fair again!'

Garth's heart started to race. He had no idea what aquaseeds were, but his gut instinct told him that they were crucial to saving this dimension. As Kea gave him hope, her own was extinguished – a candle blown out with one brutal breath.

'Nope,' Rex said. 'Aquaseeds, Cornelius tells me, are basically a myth created long ago by a madman. *They don't exist!*'

Her face flushed red.

'Why not try to find a seahorse that lays diamond eggs, or a talking fish,' he continued, sniggering.

'... or a flying lobster,' Chuck contributed, snorting in derision.

Kea did not take this assault gracefully; she ran out of the room, along the balcony and charged through a nearby door. Once hidden by those four walls, she leapt onto her bed and started punching the duvet in her frustration.

Naturally, Garth had followed. Penn did not dispute this decision, a fact that he took to be approval. Sensing a potential ally, he scoured the room desperately for some way to make contact. He *needed* to know more about aquaseeds.

***

Luke, meanwhile, was stuck in a torture room awaiting unimaginable pain, feeling tremendously helpless. There was no way of telling how long he'd been there: no windows, no clock, no meals. Fear shook through him in spasms and the cold turned his insides to ice. He was sat in a corner, refusing to make use of the blood-stained chair. At one point, he supposed sleep must have come upon him, but now he had awakened to a nightmare superior to what his imagination could conjure.

Nobody was coming to save him. While he stewed, he relived the instant that Garth had been crushed by Cornelius. That moment of intense pain that, for some bewildering reason, both he and Garth had shared, as if somehow connected beyond that which was apparent.

At times, Luke willed it all to end, to die of hypothermia before the torturer arrived. It might have been a blessing, at least then he would not reveal Naufragium's location and endanger the only friends he had on this doomed planet.

It was during one of these glum spirals of depression that he heard a new sound, the first since his abandonment.

Clang! Clang!

He sat upright, suddenly alert. It was steady, repetitive and gradually getting louder.

Clang! Clang! Clang!

Armoured footsteps, he deciphered, drawing nearer.

Clang! Clang! Clang!

Snivelling, Luke shuffled further into the corner and away from the door.

Clang! Clang! Clang!

He covered his face with his hands, looking out through the gaps in his fingers with a single, bulging eye.

Clang! Clang!

Luke's panic reached a crescendo as whatever it was stopped *directly outside his cell*. A pair of black boots could be seen under the crack of the door. There was a jingling of keys and then it groaned open.

Clang! Clang!

In stepped Bart the Brutal.

The boots were embellished with cruel spikes. Shadowy plates of armour led up to a belt of hateful utensils: tongs, serrated knives and a blunt mallet. Upon the torturer's wrists were rusty manacles as if he'd escaped from some dangerous dungeon. The helmet was the worst of all; it was fashioned into the head of a warthog. Ivory tusks grew from each side of a bloodcurdling snarl. Within a cave of metal teeth was the unfeeling face of his torturer.

Clang! Clang!

Luke uttered an audible whimper. Bart sealed the door, cutting off the only chance of escape with a resounding *bang!*

Clang-Clang-Clang-Clang!

The man clinked his way over with horrifying speed and stood over him like some devilish overlord. Any moment now, the torture would begin. Luke clenched his eyes and waited. All was silent until...

CLANG!

Luke shuddered with fright, yet nothing had hit him as far as he could tell. Carefully, he wrenched his eyes open and found himself face to face with a *warthog*. He let free a scream of unadulterated terror, before he realised that he was staring at a discarded helmet. In confusion, he peered upwards; Bart was wearing a grim smile.

'I am not here to torture you, boy,' he said. 'I'm here to break you free.'

CHAPTER 13: UNLIKELY ALLIANCES

Invisible to the naked eye, Garth surveyed Kea's room. It was basic compared to the King's, nothing more than a rudimental single bed and a small range of crooked furniture. Her floor was littered with clothes and trinkets. A pile of books, with gold letters inscribed on their spines, teetered on her bedside table and more literature was stuffed in place on a couple of slanted shelves.

Two features stood out for Garth. The first was the amazing view from her window; it showed a tremendous scene of clouds and sky. The second was more useful to his cause; a shining trumpet attached to a box. He had seen a similar instrument in Dr Flotsam's study and *knew* it was capable of producing sound. At the moment, however, it was silent.

Kea, he observed, was still facedown on her bed; she was not crying, but appeared to have unleashed a portion of her anger on her pillow. Despite her slender figure, she seemed strong of will.

How could he make contact? The whelk, now shattered, was how he had spoken to Luke. He recalled how strange it had felt when he'd first connected; both bizarre and simple, like speaking through a cone. He had been able to feel its inner form, as if a part of him had melded with cold, spiralled shell. At first, he'd only been able to whisper, but as he'd become more accustomed, he had conversed clearly with Luke.

'Penn, what're the chances of me connecting to that device in the corner?' Garth queried.

'Depends,' she purred. 'It's more complex than the shell. Do you think you're up to it?'

'*Do you?*'

'Of course, you're a natural dimension-shifter. You take after your mother in that regard, picking up the shift basics with ease and then progressing to the advanced techniques with aplomb. It won't be easy, what with it being so utterly different from what you're used to, and there's a small chance of losing your mind entirely, but my Garth can handle it.'

Her flattery, delivered in a slightly possessive way, worked its magic on Garth's youthful ears, raising his confidence and disguising the warning of danger hidden within her words.

With a mental push, he engaged the device.

Suddenly he was overwhelmed by a sickly spinning sensation. His hands scratched at a giant, black disc; his mouth was all curves and metal; his body, a mess of cobbled-together technology. At first, there was utter confusion, then fleeting understanding and, finally, came the ability to manipulate his new form – changing this, becoming that, blending his awareness with cogs and material. It began to glow blue as the connection between mind and matter strengthened. Kea, with her head buried in the silk of her pillowcase, did not notice.

Garth tried to greet her, but it came out as a painful squeak. Frowning, Kea looked up.

'Hello,' he tried a second time, his voice crackling like a radio with poor signal.

She gave a start and frantically scanned about. Seeing that nobody stood before her, she spotted her glowing music player, whirring and spinning a record on its own accord. Her mouth dropped and she backed away, almost falling off the other side of her bed in the process.

'Don't be afraid,' Garth implored, his voice becoming clearer with each word.

'What science is this?' she blurted.

'There's no time to explain,' replied Garth honestly. 'I'm not of your world. It would take hours to fill you in on how and why I am here, but by then, it would all be rather pointless. But I *can* tell you that I aim to improve the current situation, both in the sea and on the land.'

There was a delay as this sunk in. Kea was staring, aghast at the incomprehensible change that had overcome her music player. She worked her mouth a few times, before uttering her second question. 'W-What do you want with me?'

'My partner Luke is being held captive by your people; I need you to release him before it is too late.'

'I cannot,' she responded. 'Reasoning with my father is futile and your friend is now an enemy of war, to release him would mean treason and death. Even as Rex's daughter, I doubt I would be an exception. Would you have me risk my life for an intruder?'

'If you do not release him, all will be lost, including your Solis Occassum,' warned Garth. 'Besides, he's your only chance of finding aquaseeds.'

Her ears visibly perked up. 'What do you know about aquaseeds?'

'Not much. I was actually hoping you'd help me understand why they're so important.'

She eyed her music player suspiciously and then gave a slight shrug. 'We don't know why the sea is struggling or why it's only getting worse over time. By all rights, it should be thriving. It has overtaken the land and now dominates the planet, yet all evidence points to a decline in sea-life which, consequently, threatens the small piece of land upon which we have built our lives.'

'I won't pretend to know what's going on. I really don't. But in my research I have found the work of an ancient scientist who suggests there may be a way to repair the damage or, at least, stop it from worsening. If they exist, and my father would have me believe they definitely do not, aquaseeds hold the key to revitalising the sea. A form of medicine, if you will.'

Once on the subject, Kea spoke with passion, easily forgetting who, or what, she was talking to. Garth egged her on with another question. 'But, how do they work?'

'It's like this. There's a pecking order in the sea, much like there is on land. For example, grass is eaten by chickens which, in turn, are eaten by foxes. It's a *chain* in which each part, apart from the highest tier, depends on its preceding link. Take away the grass and all chaos breaks loose; the chickens drop at your feet and the foxes start scrapping amongst themselves before they, too, become nothing more than another species that came and went.'

Garth applied this information to his own planet; no leaves would mean no megabeetles. He shivered at the thought. 'But what has this got to do with aquaseeds?'

'A similar chain exists in the sea,' she declared with conviction. 'It may be less visible, but it is there. At the very top of the chain are microscopic life-forms, equivalent to the grass on land, upon which all other sea-life depends. They float around too small to be seen by the human eye, yet they are so very important.'

'Aquaseeds, I believe, will act as a fertiliser. Even if we bring a small volume to the surface, it could have far-reaching consequences, causing a bloom in the chain that will filter down to all other beings, including the fish upon which we rely so heavily.'

Garth shook with excitement. 'Where can we find them?'

'*If* they exist,' Kea said, 'the scroll suggests that they can be found in extremely deep waters where, and I quote, *sunlight has no power and the ground reigns.*'

'What does that mean?'

'I have no idea,' she admitted.

'One thing seems clear,' Garth mused. 'We must travel deeper to find them.'

'*If* they exist,' Kea reminded him again. 'Then again, I am discussing this with a glowing music player. Who am I to decide what is real and what is not?'

'Exactly,' he agreed. Garth grinned. It wasn't much to go on, but it was something. 'If you believe in anything you just told me, you will help me free Luke so that he can search for these aquaseeds.'

Kea looked about uncertainly. Garth could literally see her weighing up her options. 'Perhaps I could sneak him out,' she suggested reluctantly. 'Will he trust me?'

'Tell him that Garth sent you. The sooner you go, the better. Your father has sent for Bart.'

Kea paled. 'It may be too late.'

'Please go,' Garth pleaded. 'Now.'

Kea leapt off of her bed and made for the dungeons with Garth trailing behind unseen.

***

Luke stared up at Bart uncomprehendingly.

He looked as much a part of the room as the hanging skulls, yet did not appear to be a threat. Now that the main danger was over, less important details came to light: the man's arms were blackened with soot, his brow projected ridiculously from his head and in some places, his hair was turning grey.

Nervously, Luke's eyes flickered warily towards the pointy utensils that Bart still wore around his waist. The torturer then undid his tool belt and threw it away as a gesture of goodwill.

Luke had rather lost his voice from hours of fearful waiting. When he found it, it came out in feeble stutters. 'Wh-wh-why?'

'Ten years ago, I'd have taken those tools and done unimaginable, rather unpleasant things to you until, guilty or not, you'd have told me your deepest, darkest secrets. Lucky for you, I left the torture trade behind a long time ago,' said

Bart with an odd grin. 'I only took this job so that I could help you escape.'

'Why would *you* want to help *me*?' asked Luke quizzically.

'Well, you only went and released my daughter, didn't you?' Bart boomed while reaching down and ruffling Luke's hair.

'What?' Luke said in a hapless fashion.

'Margaret and I owe you a great debt; you released our child.'

'Flotsam's daughter?' Luke blurted.

'No!' Bart's nostrils flared. 'That is what that monster would have people believe. Margaret is his wife in name *alone*. Her heart belongs to me and has done for a very long time.'

He calmed down slightly and gravely continued his story.

'When Margaret fell pregnant with her fourth child, it was a result of our affair. Cornelius noticed before I did and she disappeared into thin air. After a few drinks, I stupidly confronted the tyrant. He revealed nothing.'

'The next day I was arrested and sent to jail for no crime at all. By the time I had been released, our daughter was born and could only breathe underwater. We found out the combination to free her, Margaret and I, but that's as far as we could manage. You have done something that we have been trying to do all these years. So that is why I am going to help you, boy. For the freedom you have granted our child.'

Luke's brain hurt; he was tired of being scared and willingly accepted Bart's allegiance. The woman he had released must have been Stuart's *half-sister*. 'Okay, so you're on my side. Now, how do you suggest we get out of here?'

'That's where things get tricky,' Bart mused. 'I have the keys for that door, but from then on it will be improvisation. Are you ready?'

Luke shakily got to his feet. 'I think so.'

Bart fitted his warthog helmet back on his head and

picked a dagger from his tool belt.

'Stay here until I say so,' he ordered. Removing a collection of keys, he unlocked the door and it slid open. Luke heard a voice on the other side, rife with alarm and hostility.

'And where do you think you're going?'

'Can't a torturer come and go as he pleases nowadays?'

'Not this time, Bart. Rex's orders. You're to stay here with fish-boy until your job is done.'

'So you're keeping me prisoner *as well*?'

'That's right,' confirmed the guard. 'This is war, after all.'

'That it is, that it is. Could not agree more. I want to see these freaks destroyed as much as the next person.' Bart, moved as if to go back into the torture room and then paused. 'He's not really a fish-boy, you know.'

'What do you mean?'

'Well fish can only breathe underwater, you see.'

'Right,' the guard agreed. 'What's your point?'

'Fish-boy gives the impression he can't breathe on land.'

'He's right boss,' said another man rather goofily. 'That name makes no sense.'

'See what I mean,' Bart contributed.

A silence followed as both guards struggled to come up with a new nickname.

'How about merman?'

'But they can't walk on land.'

'Hmm... crab-boy?' the first guard suggested.

'Crab-boy?' spat the other. 'Does he look as though he has claws?'

'But that's not the point is it, you numpty! Crabs, like our prisoner, can survive –'

And just as both of the guards had relaxed into a completely meaningless argument, Bart struck. His sudden movement threw the cell door wide open and gave Luke a full view of the action. Bart punched one guard in the temple, immediately knocking him out. As his victim crumpled harmlessly to the floor, he rounded on the other guard. This one was quicker and swiped his sword at Bart's stomach.

Not quick enough though. The armoured man swiftly dodged to the side and violently kicked the guard's legs out from underneath him. His target fell painfully onto his back with his sword scraping on the stone. Bart gripped the guard's sword-hand and smashed it down on the floor. With a yowl of pain, the weapon was released and he slid it away; it landed in the underground river with a *plop!*

Expertly done, thought Luke. One guard was out cold, the other, disarmed. But it did not end there – Bart pinned the guard to the ground, throttling his neck with his beefy hands as if possessed by the devil. His brow creased, his eyes became evil slits. Bart the Brutal, or whoever the ex-torturer used to be, was back with a vengeance. The horrible sounds of choking echoed around the cave and the guard writhed in panic.

'Stop that! You'll kill him!' Luke cried, but his request fell on death ears. He started to charge with the intent to snap Bart out of his war-lust, but stopped short when, out of the darkness, Chuck emerged.

The cold steel of Chuck's axe on the back of Bart's neck finally got the torturer's attention; he released a dazed, rather red-looking guard.

'Look what we have here,' Chuck growled, his axe still resting in the prime position for an execution.

'Chuck,' Bart recognised through gritted teeth, frozen in place over the gasping guard. 'Should have known you'd continue to be a thorn in my side. And a bloody big thorn at that.'

Chuck smiled mirthlessly. 'Your actions leave me no choice, traitor. Can't have you making a mess of my battalion, now can I? Need my troops for the war. Oh, and I see you were planning to break our little prisoner from his hold, eh? What happened to you, you old fart? I used to respect you, then you packed it all in and became a simple blacksmith.'

'Better a blacksmith than the king's toy soldier,' Bart spat.

'The bloody cheek. I'm no torturer, Bart, so this won't be a fancy death, but it's still a nasty way to go and, now that your true colours are out, I'm going to enjoy it.' he replied coldly, raising his axe and bringing it down onto the torturer's neck with a horrifying swiftness –

'Stop right there!' came a regal voice. 'That is a royal command!'

Chuck managed to divert his axe and avoid his target, making an impressive carving in the stone slab floor. Amazingly, a woman strode across the bridge and glared at the scene before her; it was Kea.

'This traitor attacked your father's guards,' complained Chuck, replacing his heavy axe and keeping Bart at his disposal. 'Death is what he deserves!'

'Disobey me and you will go to the blocks,' countered Kea. 'Remove your axe *at once*!'

'Why should I listen to you?'

'I am the princess,' said Kea with forced righteousness. 'Disobeying me is treason. Rex's orders alone take precedence over mine. Did Rex order you to execute Bart?'

'Well, no, but -'

'Then it's settled. Until you hear otherwise, you are to leave me alone with this criminal,' she commanded.

Chuck was a soldier through and through. The pecking order had been drilled into him. Slowly, looking rather furious, he removed his axe from Bart's vulnerable neck. The guard on the floor, meanwhile, scrambled to his feet and fled over the bridge. Chuck reluctantly followed, but turned around to deal a grievous threat. 'Rex will hear about this and I'm sure my next orders will not be in your favour.'

She met his fierce look with one of her own until he turned away and left the dungeons.

His life spared, Bart looked about in surprise. 'Why save me?'

'That depends,' Kea replied. 'What reason do you have to attack our royal guards?'

'None of your business,' snapped Bart.

'You owe me your life,' she said haughtily. 'Your business is my business. Unless you want me to call Chuck back here with his fellow guards for round two?'

Bart scowled. 'I was breaking Luke free.'

'And you seemed to be doing such a fine job,' she smirked with a raised eyebrow. 'Anyway, there's no time to explain, but, unlikely as it seems, we appear to share the same goal.'

'As if!' scoffed Bart distrustfully.

'It's true,' declared Kea. 'Now, what was the next step in your masterplan?'

Bart shrugged. 'There wasn't one.'

'Men!' Kea rolled her eyes.

'We'll gladly hear any ideas, *princess*,' mocked Bart.

'We can't go back to the palace; they will be waiting for us,' Kea reckoned. 'This river must lead out to the forest. It seems like our only option.'

The three of them walked to the bridge and looked into the rapids beneath.

'That's suicide, especially for our kind,' Bart judged. 'Who knows how deep or fast that river goes.'

A grating sound suggested that Chuck had reached the secret entrance; he would soon be returning with reinforcements.

'Look.' Luke pointed to a large turtle bobbing downstream and towards the bridge. 'Let's hitch a ride!'

'That's mad, but it might just work.' Bart gave a half-hearted laugh.

'It's coming this way,' Kea said.

The turtle neared and it was clear that its shell had copious room for the three of them. Its features were hidden by darkness, but Luke could see a giant head, as large as his own, nodding gently as it swam. It reached the bridge and gave out a bird-like caw. Luke, Kea and Bart rushed to the other side, awaiting the turtle's reappearance.

'It's now or never. Guards are no doubt on their way,' warned Kea.

'You first Luke, then we'll follow,' decided Bart.

Luke nodded. With one foot forward, he curled his toes over the edge and prepared himself for a well-timed jump. The turtle's bulbous head came into sight, but he waited eagerly for the curve of its shell; this materialised a moment later. He launched himself off the bridge, landing on the buoyant platform with a *thud*. It dipped slightly, but the turtle seemed to barely register its new passenger. Kea was next, lightly touching down with hardly any impact at all.

In stark contrast, Bart shook the turtle like an earthquake and he half slipped off the back. Luke twisted around to see Kea trying to lift him back onto the shell; with that suit of armour, he was just too heavy. Slowly, but surely, the man was sliding into the raging river. Then, against all odds, the turtle's strong tail lifted out of the water directly below Bart. It raised him back on, securing its three surprise guests. They had no time to voice their amazement as the turtle sped downriver.

The flickering torches on the bridge quickly faded into the distance. The turtle surged onwards, pumping its broad flippers in conjunction with the might of the currents. Knuckles white, Luke gripped the rim of its shell just below its warty neck. He felt Kea wrap her hands around his waist for support.

Soon, they were all leaning forwards as the river steepened and became more aggressive. Splashes of water started to invade from the sides, slapping Luke across the face. No sooner had he wiped water from his eyes, than he would get soaked by another wave. A single beam of sunlight ahead, shining down from some high up fissure, revealed that the river split into three separate tunnels. The turtle appeared to be heading dead on for a rocky collision between the second and third. Luke gave out a panicked shout which joined the orchestra of rushing water.

'Merehhhhh!' the turtle screeched.

At the last second, they rode a powerful underwater current which sent them shooting into the right-most tunnel. All was dark once again; they could only cling on and hope for the best.

Ice cold drops of water dripped onto their heads from above. Kea's hold on Luke tightened as the speed picked up once more. The turtle leaned to the left and the gang was forced to do the same or get thrown off. They seemed to shoot along a tube-like coil that made its way further down the mountain. The passage was dangerously tight. A slight miscalculation would shatter shell and break bones; without the turtle, such a route would have meant inevitable doom.

They finally levelled out, but maintained an incredible speed. Streams of bright light caused Luke to squint. The solid cave broke out into a number of archways, before giving away entirely to an open air river. There was a collective sigh of relief at the welcome sight of trees until they realised what was ahead.

'Waterfall!' Luke yelled behind.

CHAPTER 14: CLOVER

Instead of evading, the turtle paddled furiously, giving the crew no chance to abandon their transport.

They fired off the edge of the cliff.

While water toppled downwards, their momentum had them floating for the briefest time. Then gravity kicked in.

'Ahhhhhhhhhhhhh!' bawled Luke, Kea and Bart in unison.

'Merehhhhhhhhhhhhhhhh!' shrieked the turtle joyfully.

They sailed down through a blur of green and blue. Luke clutched the shell ridge for dear life and ducked as they passed dangerously close to large palm leaves on willowy branches. A bundle of foliage split apart and revealed an expanse of air above a stretch of cabbage-green, pondweed-covered water. More turtles swam below and, having noticed their approach, desperately dispersed.

Air rushed past Luke's ears as the surface zoomed closer and he tensed as the inevitable impact drew nigh. They pounded onto the lake, causing a cascade of ripples. He was immediately thrown forward and ended up hugging the turtle's giant head. Having checked that he was in no way injured, he searched for his friends; Kea was still behind, but Bart was missing.

He called out for him, but the only response was the alarm of the other members of the lake.

'Geeeorrrrrr!' a red turtle gurgled, swimming away in a panic. Others followed, afraid of the new additions to their home.

Then a patch of bubbles appeared, followed by a metal warthog helmet; it grew a head and a chest. Bart stood up, dazed, in the knee-deep water. He spat out a dribble of excess saliva and stared at his fellows. 'Did we make it?'

'I think so,' laughed Luke.

'Merehhhh!' added their mount.

Now in sunlight, Luke saw that its shell was coated in strands of moss. Here and there, white clumps of clover grew like a light sprinkling of snow. From this defensive haven came a long, slim neck belonging to a large, blotchy head. Currently, it had craned its head around to study it's passengers with sunset orange eyes; for some unknown reason, Luke was strongly reminded of Jaws.

Although the turtle's unnerving gaze was fixed on them, it continued to paddle towards the mucky bank in front. Bart waded behind, producing a canyon through the dense pondweed and swiping erratically at flies as he went. The turtle reached the land with Kea and Luke still on-board. To lighten its load, they set down on soft mud and tiptoed onto grass.

'A little help,' said Bart. He was wedged in by the weight of his black steel boots. Luke returned to offer some help, but the man was truly stuck.

'Nothing for it, but to leave them behind,' Luke told him.

Bart grumbled and then joined Luke in his bare foot ways. By the time they had caught up with Kea, the turtle was up the bank and ramming itself against a metal railing. With each clash, it let out a cry of effort. The obstacle was no bigger than a toddler's paddock, but there was no chance for the turtle to escape. The same barrier followed around the lake and blocked a stream on the other side.

'They're trapped!' Luke realised. The rest of the turtles had congregated at the exiting tributary as if hoping that the barricade would just disintegrate.

'They are kept for their turtleoak,' Kea explained, 'but this is no time to discuss such matters! Though dim, it won't take the guards long to figure out where we've gone. No doubt they'll send scouts to look for our remains.'

'Then what are we waiting for,' said Bart, stepping over the railing. Kea swiftly followed, but Luke remained.

'Mereh! Mereh! Mereh! Mereh!' the turtle squealed; it sounded frustrated and sad.

'We can't leave Clover behind!' he demanded.

'Clover?' said Bart, caught between amusement and exasperation.

'I gave it a name,' said Luke bashfully.

'We haven't got time for this,' Kea persisted.

'She helped us get this far. I'm not leaving unless we free her!'

They rolled their eyes at him, but eventually gave in and returned to the other side of the barrier. All three placed their hands beneath the turtle's body, their palms touching thick, leathery skin.

'Now,' Bart signalled and they heaved.

It was not a graceful lifting by any means. Even with their combined strength, Clover was extremely heavy. Bart contributed the most, veins popping from his huge forehead. They could not raise the turtle much, but managed to prop its front up on the pen. After a short breather, they positioned themselves at the tail end and gave one more big push. Clover grinded over and flopped onto the forest bed.

'Mereeeeeeeeh!' she cried gleefully, before using her powerful flippers to traverse over the grass and into a nearby stream.

'Happy?' Bart said.

Luke smiled as the turtle disappeared from sight.

'We *have* to go!' Kea commanded, and they obeyed.

***

They sprinted into the depths of the forest, not a

thought of where they were going. Each metre took them further from the lake. They hopped over fallen trunks and squelched through smelly swamps. Kea led the way, seeming to skirt around anything in their path. Bart, meanwhile, crashed through, punching at stray twigs.

There was no road or path, just untamed wildlife. Vines drooped down, nettles nipped at bare skin and thorns tore at scraps of clothing. Juicy and unknown fruits swelled from bristly stems. Overhead, and out of sight, a monkey chattered to its friends.

The running seemed endless. A mixture of pride and desperation pushed Luke far beyond his capability. Bart was as tough as the weapons that he fashioned and Kea, unlike her father, cut a lean figure as she whizzed through the jungle. Still to reach his prime, it was not too long before Luke's stamina dwindled and his movements grew sluggish.

Drained of energy, Luke quickly fell behind until a thick branch overhead provided an abrupt end to his struggle. Bart and Kea must have ducked beneath it, but, in his exhaustion, Luke was slow on the uptake and ran headlong into sturdy bark.

It hit him across the forehead, throwing him off his feet and slamming his tired body down onto gravelly mud. His head snapped back and the jungle faded into darkness....

....Parts of his brain, long left in slumber, were jolted awake. Neurons flared like fireworks in the night. A whole other life of memories squeezed themselves into consciousness like a late businessman barging himself onto a packed tube train. It started small, then rushed at him like a stampede, a cascade of puzzle pieces slotting neatly into place.

He remembered the taste of tea in the morning and the sound of the kettle boiling; the view from his bedroom window of their modest garden bordered by a rickety old fence, a mere square in the patchwork of tiled roofs, trimmed grass and road that formed his neighbourhood; an overgrown bridle path that followed to an open field where eager eyes and wagging tails endlessly chased chewed tennis balls; a bike, his bike, with its chunky off-road tyres, chipped paint, wonky lights and dysfunctional brakes, speeding down a steep hill on his journey from school.

He remembered friends and foes; a charismatic, cheeky chap with a good heart and a tendency for getting away with mischief; a snot-nosed brute who had grown early and was wielding his mighty form to bully his way through school; a spectacled teacher with a receding hairline and a bulging belly that strained shirt buttons.

The faces of his family materialised from the murky depths. His mother, a fashionable, caring woman with wrinkles that only came from smiling too much. His father, all hair except a patch on his crown, toiling over the garden with watering-can in hand. His dog, a black and white bundle of energy encapsulated in four paws, a long sleek body and a bushy tail.

Lastly, he remembered the beach.

They had been on holiday in Cornwall on a quaint little stretch of sand with jagged cliffs that tried to close off the bay in a futile one-armed hug.

Luke had been in a bad temper. After having braved the sea and taken a tumble or two, he had been told he could not re-enter. He had plonked himself down on wet sand, at the borderline between land and sea, as a form of rebellion. His parents, tight-lipped and holding each other against the cold, had watched him like hawks.

It was then that he had noticed a twinkle of blue in the sand. Its source; a spiralled shell. Naturally he reached for it and, as he studied this peculiar find, he was snatched away from his home and his family in the blink of an eye.

'Luke!' his parents shouted desperately. 'Luke!' they cried. 'Luke!' they screamed.

'Luke?' someone asked.

Luke awoke with a groan. A blurred shadow stooped over him and, behind, was the faded leaves of jungle trees. He blinked and the source of the voice materialised into Bart.

'You and a branch had a bit of scrap, son,' the ex-torturer explained with a touch of humour. 'You should see the other guy, he's a wreck. Nothing but splinters now.'

Luke groaned a second time, pushing on soft mud in a feeble attempt to sit up. With his new-found memories and his sore head, he could hardly think straight. 'Home,' he moaned.

Bart looked at him blankly.

'Home,' he repeated miserably. 'I need to get back home.'

'What you need,' said Bart, pulling Luke gently back to his feet, 'is to get up out of that muck and keep moving. That branch may have knocked you senseless, but it's nothing compared to what Rex's men will do if they catch up.'

'Actually,' said Kea, skipping back to find her lagging comrades and surveying Luke with worry, 'I think this is as good a time to stop as any. We've come far enough for one day, and it's getting dark. There's a clearing nearby where we can make camp for the night. Come on, I'll show you.'

Without even looking behind, Kea beckoned them and strode ahead.

'What makes her think that she's in charge,' grumbled Bart quietly, using one bear-like arm to keep Luke upright as they slowly followed. 'I tell you, Luke, I don't understand why she's helping us. The whole thing stinks of a trap.'

'I don't know,' Luke slurred. 'Nicer than Rex.'

'That may be, but a royal never does anything without reason. I don't trust her one bit. As soon as we get the chance, I say we find out why our little princess is keeping us sweet.'

Though Bart had a fair point, Luke did not reply. Perhaps he should be questioning Kea's motives, but right now, he was in sheer turmoil.

As they trod to the aforementioned clearing, Luke could only mourn the family he may never see again. He had been abducted against his will. Now that he had the full picture, everything made even *less* sense. One thing was for certain; he missed home terribly.

***

Upon arrival at the clearing, Kea had ordered Bart and himself to gather wood for a shelter, whilst heading off into the jungle herself to gather fruit for dinner. Initially, Bart had complained at being ordered around, but, as the evening drew on, he recognised the sense of her demands and had been moodily gathering a pile of wood-stock since.

Luke had added a pathetic contribution of sticks, before retiring to a conveniently felled tree-log. An indigo caterpillar crawled determinedly beside him, seemingly heading for a sheltered nook. He watched it absent-mindedly, numbed by sheer exhaustion, as the orange sun disappeared behind the jungle canopy. Soon sunset-red light filtered down, casting ember-like patches on the leafy ground.

As Luke was rubbing his sore forehead, and generally feeling sorry for himself, Bart sat down next to him. They waited a while in companionable silence, until Bart could no longer contain himself.

'Where is she?' he lamented, rubbing his belly. 'All that running about has given me a mighty hunger. I've half a mind to gobble up that caterpillar.'

Luke gave him a shocked look and he held up his hands defensively. 'Don't worry, don't worry, I'm not going to touch it. Lord, you are a soft one, aren't you? Anyway, have you figured it out yet?'

'Figured what out?' Luke replied groggily.

'Kea,' Bart replied. 'Why is she helping the likes of us? A sub-aqua invader and an ex-torturer, not to mention a traitor to the crown. She's the king's daughter, for crying out loud! Rex might be a brute, but he can be clever, especially if that devil Cornelius is whispering in his ear. Could this be some kind of elaborate plan?'

Thinking was effort, but somehow Luke managed it. 'To

what end though?'

'Hell if I know.' Bart snorted. After it became apparent that a response was not forthcoming, he continued. 'Never you mind Luke, my son, I'll find out what the situation is, one way or another.'

With a mysterious tap on the nose, Bart heaved himself off the makeshift bench and stalked into the wilderness.

***

Luke was left alone to stew in his own melancholy for what must have been at least an hour.

A rustle of leaves drew his attention; Kea was back and held a bountiful selection of fruit.

Just the sight of her was enough to raise his spirits. She gave him a cheery smile which soured slightly with concern when her eyes were drawn to the welt that had grown on his forehead; a result of his unfortunate clash with the branch.

She timidly walked towards him, cradling her bounty with one arm and stretching out the other as if to kindly stroke away his pounding headache. Despite all his worries, Luke felt his heart rate rise, blissfully ignorant of the fact that the age difference between them was too large a leap.

Just as she came into touching distance, Bart sprung out of the foliage and wrapped an arm around Kea's neck, holding a knife to her slender throat.

All positivity plunged into dismay and Luke's mouth swung open as his feelings rocketed from one extreme to the other. Kea, meanwhile, dropped her fruit to the floor and went rigid; a pale, angelic statue of her former self.

'W-w-what are you –' she stammered.

'It's time you told us the truth, and don't skim on the details,' Bart snarled.

'Let her go!' appealed Luke, advancing to wrestle her free.

'Stay out of this, boy!' Bart growled, dipping the edge

of his dagger into Kea's porcelain skin. At the sight of blood dripping down her neck, Luke stopped short. 'I've had enough dealings with the royals to know that there's always an ulterior motive. Now, Kea, speak! Tell us why the king's daughter would risk all to help us, and it had better be plausible.'

A single tear flowed down her left eye like a lonely waterfall, diluting the blood trail on her neck.

'*Well?*,' Bart demanded, tightening his grip and causing her to cry out in fear. 'Out with it!'

Kea swallowed. 'G-g-g-g-g – '

'Come on,' Bart egged, 'or we'll be tying you up and leaving you to the mercy of the jungle.'

'G-g-g – ' She scrunched up her face and then yelled something that Luke never would have expected. 'G-g-g-Garth!'

Luke could not believe his ears. 'Did you just say *Garth*?'

'G-Garth sent me!' Kea blubbered.

Luke grinned despite the situation.

'Why're you smiling?' Bart grunted suspiciously.

'Garth's a friend,' Luke replied. 'A friend who I thought was long gone. You can trust me, Bart – I saved your daughter. Now *believe me* when I say Kea can be trusted too. If Garth sent her, then he will have done it for good reason. And let's face it, she has been nothing but help so far!'

Bart's eyes narrowed, but he did not move.

'I-I know a way that could bring the fish back,' Kea added.

Luke's grin widened even further. 'Release her!' he begged.

Bart grimaced and, after a painstaking few moments, slackened his hold.

Kea fled to stand by Luke and they both stared at her attacker. A change came over him. His shoulders relaxed and he hung his head in shame. The dagger slipped from slack hands to plummet into one of the fallen fruits, squirting juice everywhere.

'Sorry,' Bart mumbled and then slinked away. Towards the edge of the clearing, Luke saw him plop down on the ground and remove his warthog helmet.

Kea breathed heavily for a short while and then started to pick her harvest back up. Still trembling, she wrapped the fruits in palm leaves for later consumption. By the time she had finished this task, she had recovered her aplomb and had decided that their next plan of action would be to build a shelter.

Together they tried their utmost best to assemble their measly wood stock into the barest resemblance of a refuge, but with little luck. Each time they made progress, a log would tumble and the whole structure would simply collapse. They tried several techniques and ideas, but ended up spending more time scratching their heads than actually building. All the while, the sun receded further behind the trees and night-time loomed.

In the end, Luke realised that they needed Bart's help, and that getting the big man involved might actually be the best way forward for all. He cautiously approached the ex-torturer, who was moping and staring at the ground with palpable remorse, and asked for his aid. Though Luke only received a few grunts in reply, Bart wondered back to them and started to guide their efforts.

Bart brought them to a low-lying branch of a thunder-struck tree; it grew from the trunk and dipped down until reaching soil. To Luke, it just looked like a useless arm of dead bark. With Bart's instruction, however, they leaned a tight row of sticks on each side and it was transformed into the skeleton of a tent, with a small gap closest to the trunk to allow entrance.

'This shall do nicely, but it shan't keep us warm,' pointed out Kea.

'Cover it in leaves, that'll do the trick,' Bart explained.

Fortunately, these were bountiful and, before long, they had embellished the sides with multiple layers. These acted both as camouflage and as an extra protection against the decreasing temperatures.

'That'll do,' Bart said.

Luke peered inside; any hint of light was blocked by a blanket of leaves. There was space enough for four, and it would be ideal for the early morning kip that he so craved. He crawled to the end of the shelter and back, satisfied; they would be sleeping rough, but it could be worse.

Worn out, they fed on their dinner in silence. Kea had found large spherical fruits with tough, pale-yellow skin. Unsure of how to proceed, Luke watched his friends. Bart took a ravenous mouthful and spat the outer layer to the side; underneath was a feast of gooey flesh. Kea did the same, except she picked the rind off delicately with her fingertips.

When Luke reached the edible part of the fruit, its taste was similar to a peach. He devoured it gratefully, juice running down his chin and sticking to his bare chest. The fruit that had been impaled by Bart's dagger remained untouched, a stark reminder of the dark facet that lurked within his character.

Stomachs full, the three of them fumbled to their shelter and found their places. Kea and Luke lay beside each other, while Bart stretched out by the entrance like a guard dog. It was not a comfortable sleeping spot by any means; the ground was packed with unwelcome rocks and intrusive roots. Regardless, once settled and warm from their combined body heat, sleep was very tempting. Luke would have dropped off, but there was something he just *needed* to know.

'Kea?' Luke whispered in the dark. 'How can we bring the fish back?

There was a rustle as Kea shifted to face him.

'There's some very old science..., ' she began, telling Luke exactly what she had told Garth. Afterwards, he was filled with dreams of finding aquaseeds and returning to Naufragium a hero. Surely bringing the fish back, a staple food source for the land and sea, would save the dimension and then, just maybe, Garth could transport him home. Now that he knew Garth was still alive, getting back to Earth seemed just that little bit more likely. And, now that he remembered his old life, he dearly wanted to leave this world behind and return to his family.

'I need to get back to Naufragium,' he said, eventually.

'Naufragium?'

'The underwater town that I travelled from,' Luke elaborated. 'It seems like the best place to start looking for aquaseeds.'

'Tomorrow we shall figure out where we are and return you to the sea,' Kea promised.

'Will you see my daughter?' Bart's gravelly voice reached them from the end of the shelter. Luke had not realised that he had been listening to their talk of science and ancient scrolls.

'Maybe.' He could offer the man no guarantee. 'She could be anywhere.'

'Lost and free is better than trapped for life,' declared Bart. 'But if you do happen to see her... please tell her that we care about her a lot, Margaret and I. To us, she is not experiment number four, but our daughter, Amy.'

'I will,' Luke swore.

There was a hesitant gap in their conversation.

'You know... I used to be a very bad man,' Bart started.

'You don't have to tell us this,' Kea said.

'No, I do,' he insisted. 'You deserve an explanation for what happened back there.'

He paused and took a deep breath. 'You already know that I used to torture people. I used to be pretty efficient at it too. Bart the Brutal, they called me.' He laughed bitterly. 'I did not enjoy it, but I did not mind it. The job was well-paid and, most of the time, there was some information that I had to retrieve. Who stole some sheep, did you kidnap somebody's daughter, who defaced the side of the palace – those kinds of things. I usually got it out of them in the end.

'Then, one day, Rex ordered me to torture a child. He

was younger than you, Luke, and a sight bit thinner. I did not know his crime and, when I asked, Rex told me I did not need to know. If I tortured the boy enough, he would tell me the information that I needed. Like a loyal hound, I did as I had for years. Straight away he confessed to stealing some fish from the King's feast. I went to Rex with this information, but he just smiled and ordered me to continue my work.

'The boy cried for his mother in the very same room that I rescued you from. He lost a few fingers, but still told me nothing new. He had stolen some fish. His toes were next, but he kept shut. He forced me to double my efforts; I realised that I had to take a few teeth. In my experience, most people were normally confessing to anything at this point, but the kid was just repeating himself. He stole some fish, he stole some fish. I leant down with a pair of prongs and prised his mouth open. As I went to yank out a tooth, he closed his eyes and...just died.

'Now, until then, I thought that any human being, no matter the pain, would instinctively fight for life. This kid, though, he *willed* himself to death. Didn't reveal the slightest detail of whatever Rex wanted. Nobody had ever died in my torture room before. Opposite to what you might think, keeping the prisoner alive is the skilful part of the torture trade. Anyway, I revealed the news to Rex and...

'He laughed. Told me that he found my story to be very *interesting*. Then he laughed some more – he knew who had taken the fish! It was not the kid, no, it was his *mother*. Rex and his friends had betted on how long the boy's loyalty would last under my torture. It had all been for some sick game of gambling. The mother, of course, was hanged anyway.'

'That's awful,' said Luke.

'Even I have my limits,' Bart agreed. 'From that day, I refused to torture another person. I threw away the money I had earned and became no better than a beggar on the street. One kindly man recognised my potential and took me in; those were less desperate times. Old though I was, he agreed to teach me the way of a blacksmith. Then, one day, I encountered Margaret doing some laundry in the poorer part of town. She was beautiful, but I saw trouble in those big brown eyes. We comforted each other. She taught me to be a good man and I was there for her when she cried for her lost children.

'Then we had one of our own. So now you know my story. Kea, I would ask you to forgive me for not trusting somebody of royal blood. Sometimes, especially in tense situations, I revert back to Bart the Brutal and forget what Margaret taught me.'

'Of course, I forgive you,' Kea said. 'I'm terribly sorry for what my father put you through. Please understand that I am *not* my father.'

'I'm beginning to see that now. Once my debt to Luke is repaid, I can go back to Margaret a free man with a free daughter.'

'We are both wanted for treason,' Kea reminded him.

'I will sneak my dear Margaret away from Cornelius and find some hidden cove on this island. Now that Amy is free, she has no ties to that awful man. We'll live on the fruits of the forest for the rest of our days.'

Luke did not need to see Bart's expression to know the content he felt at such an outcome. Then he wondered about Rex's daughter and the wrath she would have to face for helping him escape.

'What about you, Kea?'

'I know not. Being of royal blood may mean that I escape the noose, but my father is a difficult man to judge,' she sighed. 'Now enough talk, we must rest while we can.'

Luke heard another shuffle and knew she must have turned away. He fell asleep, chilled by Bart's tale of woe, but cheered by his optimism. Though tomorrow remained a mystery, at least for tonight, he was warm and with some new friends.

CHAPTER 15: THE UNINHABITABLE LAND

Garth hovered above the tops of a forest outlined by moonlight. He had tracked the company as they had ran headlong into the wild, untamed forest on the other side of the island, and listened to their crucial evening conversation. Warmed by the fact that Kea had conveyed the outline of her aquaseed research, Garth decided to scout the surrounding area, seeking anything that might disturb his friends as they rested from their gruelling escape.

After a quick reconnaissance, he had returned to the large lake of turtleoak turtles and found it bordered by a ring of royal scouts holding blue torches. He could make out the mountainous figure of Chuck, dishing out his orders from atop his white bull. In his hand, he held Luke's stolen cloak and treated his mount to a good whiff. Having got Luke's scent, the beast leapt over the pen and tottered into the forest. Chuck and his bull were giving chase; the guards, meanwhile, followed at a slug's pace.

Despite this, Garth could not see any immediate danger to his friends. Letting them sleep, he turned his thoughts to his own woes, of which there were plenty: saving his mum's job, rescuing a whole dimension and avoiding imminent death from the terminating machine that was currently en route to burn both himself and Penn to the ground.

With a thought, he was back in his fatigued body, rooted

to his mother's chair. He feebly removed the dimension-shift helmet and looked about with weary eyes at the all-too-familiar nest of cables and computer chips that had become his own personal prison cell.

'He remembers, you know,' Penn piped up.

'Who remembers what?' Garth replied curtly, not in the mood for Penn's games; she seemed to enjoy skirting about any subject that they discussed.

'Luke,' she replied. 'He has unpuzzled his past, un-addled his brains, untangled the damage done by travelling across dimensions.'

'Oh,' said Garth, feeling a dreadful sinking feeling within and trying his best to cover it up by reaching for a nearby packet of megabeetles. 'I don't suppose he's too happy with us.'

'I'm no expert at the feelings of the living, what with being a machine of cold logic, but Luke has been jolted away from everything he knows or cares about. His family, friends, all those little inconveniences that beings of flesh and blood get so sentimental about. So no, in summary, I doubt he is very happy with us at all,' answered Penn. She had a wicked way of finding humour in every situation, no matter how dark or serious.

'Can we send him back?' asked Garth, munching at sweets that had rather lost their taste.

'No,' she responded briskly. 'Sending him back is not what we want anyway. We need him where he is. He is the key to our quest, the most important piece on the board. Remove him and we are powerless. Besides, we cannot send him back without a Quasar gem, and you burned up the only one we had when we shifted him in the first place.'

'What if we get our hands on another Quasar gem?'

'There's only one way to do that. And it still involves Luke completing his mission,' said Penn smugly. 'Say we save the dimension and your mother's job and we somehow manage to survive. Altersearch's automatic process will deliver a

Quasar gem straight to this very room with the intention that the shifter, yourself in this unlikely situation, uses that gem to fix the next broken dimension.'

'So what if we use it to transport him back?'

'You'll undo everything you have worked so hard for. Sure, you will be a hero of sorts, having saved multiple worlds within a collapsing universe, but that won't mean anything to Altersearch. They'll see a meddling Gazoid who got lucky and then squandered a priceless gem to ease his own conscience.'

'So I'll still be in trouble?'

'Oh yes. There's no telling what they'll do, of course. They'll probably turn the situation to their advantage somehow, but you can bet that you and your mother will be worse off.'

With this troubling realisation rocketing around his head, Garth put an end to the conversation and tried to get some sleep. Reclining his chair, he found that no amount of guilt could prevent the slumber that he desperately needed. Soon snores filled the room once more.

***

In the early hours of the morning, the insects started to cause a ruckus of such a volume that even Luke was roused. At the shelter entrance, light filtered in. Bart and Kea had gone. He scrambled out and soon found his friends. The first was craning his neck upwards and studying a tree. The second was high above with half her body disappearing into the forest canopy.

'What can you see?' Bart shouted.

Kea dropped down onto her perch and shushed him by pressing a finger to her lips. Nimbly, she moved from branch to branch until she could jump down to ground level. When she did, she landed so lightly that Luke found it hard to believe she had hit the floor at all. Once closer, she scolded Bart for his outburst.

'You must be quiet!' she hissed. 'We do not want to draw attention to ourselves.'

'What did you see?' Bart whispered, with a frown, in a voice so low that it could have been taken as ridicule.

'It as I feared,' Kea replied, ignoring his mockery. 'The underground river bought us part way down the mountain. Since then, in our haste, we have moved around to the Uninhabitable Land.'

'That's not good,' Bart gulped.

'What's the Uninhabitable Land?' Luke asked.

'A maze of wildlife. The guards would have to be mad to follow us,' Bart explained. 'Then again, we will be lucky to make our way out alive.'

'We were fine yesterday,' Luke stated.

'That was when we ran *around* the island,' Kea said. 'Today we have to go down. The forest in these parts is so thick that it disguises deep shafts and pits. If we do not go carefully, we will have a nasty fall.'

'That's putting it lightly,' grunted Bart. 'Did you see any streams?'

'Yes I did, over in that direction.' She pointed.

'If we can make our way to it, we can follow a safer path down to the sea.'

Kea nodded in agreement, then turned her attention to Luke. 'Forgive me, for I know not the way of your kind. Do you have the ability to swim like a fish or do you fall like us land dwellers?'

'The second one,' Luke replied, not bothering to explain that the Naufragians weren't *his kind*.

'This is most inconvenient,' she said gravely. 'The coast is surrounded by deadly drops, which leaves us only two ways to get you to the seabed; the underground caves in Cornelius' home and Occassum beach. Father will know this!'

'We'll tackle that when we come to it. Let's get down this darn mountain first,' Bart reasoned, fixing his warthog helmet onto his head.

They destroyed any evidence of their camp with a few kicks and then followed Kea in the approximate bearing of the stream. Thinking themselves safe from pursuit, they took their time with Kea in front prodding the ground cautiously with a stick. They copied her footsteps as meticulously as possible. Luke shuddered to think what dangerous falls were hidden beneath the canvas of ferns and bushes.

Their careful route led them down the mountain. Once or twice, Luke almost lost his footing and had to snatch at low branches for security. As the sun rose, the temperatures soared, and insects came out to feast. They buzzed around his ears, taking cheeky bites when he tired of slapping them away. An hour or two passed of frustratingly slow plodding.

Kea let out a groan of annoyance. 'We should be at the stream by now. This pace might be safer, but my father's guards, if they dare come to this part of the island, will be on our heels.'

With excruciating timing, a man's agonized scream pierced the forest.

'They must be close, hurry!' Luke said, rushing to the front of the group.

Bart caught him by the shoulder and dragged him to a stop. 'Sound travels in bizarre ways. Going faster in this terrain will get us killed. By the sun, what is that?' Bart exclaimed, releasing Luke in his surprise.

A fern in the distance had taken on a prominent blue sheen.

'Garth!' shouted Luke, charging towards it. Once he came close, the glow faded and reappeared on a rock several feet below. He clambered down only to find that now, in the distance, another plant glowed. Rather like a rainbow, the ominous glow always shifted before he could catch up. At first he was annoyed, then he realised Garth's plan. 'He's giving us checkpoints.'

'Checkpoints?' Kea questioned.

'A path for us to follow,' Luke beckoned. 'Come on!'

They ran, depending solely on Garth to lead the way. Bart followed unquestioningly with a confused frown creasing his bulging Neanderthal-style forehead. Blue beacons made their path clear and soon they could hear the tinkle of flowing water. Dodging dense leaves and abundant trunks, they finally found themselves looking over a measly stream. Having provided the much-needed help, Garth's beacons then faded from sight. Luke spoke his thanks to the wilderness, hoping that the whelk-boy would hear.

They progressed down the stream, appreciating how the forest thinned in its presence. A brightly-coloured hummingbird hovered along, dipping its bill in purple-necked flowers. Bart scooped out a handful of fresh water and savoured a long, cool drink; Luke paused to do the same.

Although the stream cut through the forest, it did so in leaps and bounds. A peaceful runway of water would spill into a surge of tumultuous waterfalls. The way would sometimes be slippery. At one point, Bart took a tumble and ended up in a muddy puddle, looking unharmed, but bashful. Luke helped him to his feet and the man gratefully accepted the aid.

They did not hear another guard, although that offered them little reassurance. They walked in silence, the only sound being that of the soothing trickle of water. Endlessly they journeyed, always watching their step. Luke wondered how far they were from the sea, but the treetops acted as a blindfold to their progress.

Unlike the mountain folk, he was not accustomed to hiking downhill for such long periods of time. His calf and shin muscles soon yearned for rest, but he kept going. On occasion, he would dabble his bare feet in the cooling shallows, cleaning his cuts and massaging his bruises.

After a while, they came to a ledge. The stream dived dramatically to bounce down some rocks and land in a deep pond. Finally, from this vantage point, Luke caught a glimpse of the shimmering sea; they were close. Eagerly, they edged downwards. The stream's flow suddenly lost momentum and lazily drifted along flat terrain. A clearing approached.

The mighty forest disintegrated as they hurried through the last of the trees. Bare and lifeless clay-like rock lay ahead and, beyond, small collapsing waves. Sunlight flooded from blue skies and felt wonderfully warm on their skin. They had made it to the coast.

'Merehh!'

A call came from the sea.

'Look,' Kea pointed. 'It's Clover. I think she's waiting for you, Luke!'

The King's daughter was right. Clear of the rock bobbed a damaged, but alive, turtleoak turtle, looking directly towards them. In all appearances, she was waiting, her grassy shell a mere jump from the coastline.

'Go Luke!' spurred Bart.

He ran towards Clover with all the speed he could muster. Just as it seemed the path was clear, Chuck charged in from the right on his bull, eclipsing the turtle with his unwieldy form. His mount had its head ducked low and was snorting steam from its cavernous nostrils. The guard grinned and threw Luke's stolen cloak to the ground.

'I've found you!' he said triumphantly.

CHAPTER 16: RODEO SHOWDOWN

'It does not have to be this way, Chuck!' Bart shouted, running to catch up with Luke.

'Oh I think it does, Bart the *Backstabber*!' he contradicted, pointing at them accusingly. 'He is a prisoner and you are a wanted man for helping him escape. Rex is most displeased.'

'Rex belongs in the ground, not on the throne,' Bart retorted. 'He spends so much time in the clouds that he's blind to the needs of his own people. They're close to snapping point, Chuck, and you don't want to be on the other side when that happens.'

'Rex has always been good to me, and now he has promoted me to *War Commander*,' Chuck said with pride.

'A meaningless title,' spat Bart. 'Can you not see? He's twisting you as he once did to me. Besides, there won't be a *war* to command. How in hell do you think the water people will defend themselves?'

'It shall be glorious,' said Chuck adamantly.

'It shall be a *slaughter*,' Bart corrected. 'And you shall be at its helm!'

Chuck seemed to be on the brink of realising the truth, but then shook it off.

'Good,' he said stubbornly, drawing his brutal war axe. 'I'm done talking. I have guards blocking the beach and patrolling the town. You have nowhere to go. I'm going to make sure you never see your precious smithy again!'

Bart gave a growl of anger and hastily withdrew his own dagger. It looked a measly defence, but there was a fire in the old man's eyes. Chuck shook his reins, urging his bull to a gallop; a pair of sharp horns started rampaging towards them. Bart sidestepped, drawing the attack away from Luke with each movement.

The beast was an intimidating sight: a metal ring ran through its nose, glinting in the sun, its muscular legs were pumping furiously and its movements spoke of a fierce loyalty to its master. Chuck, meanwhile, had his turtle-shell shield strapped to his back and his weapon held aloft, ready to strike. In his passion, he appeared completely ignorant of Clover, who swam silently behind.

Bart bravely gained more space from Luke, singling out the attack. The air was filled with the clapping of heavy hooves on rock. Kea joined Luke and, together, they began chucking stones at the stampeding duo with all their might. Most of their throws missed completely. The few that *did* hit rebounded harmlessly off steel or thick skin.

There was no cover for Bart. The rock was a flat, open space and he did not have time to make a break for the forest. Luke saw him turn as though to face the attack. He made a brief motion, subtly telling them to head for Clover, but neither of them was going to abandon him.

The bull shot passed Luke and Kea, who were now a safe distance from its primary threat, throwing up a haze of dust. As it approached Bart, it lowered its head, ready to skewer its target.

At the last second, Bart expertly dived to the side, clearing its horns. Chuck's axe, however, did not miss. It slashed down and sliced across Bart's chest, spilling blood from dented armour and yielding a roar of pain.

Knowing that he had dealt a mortal injury, Chuck sharply turned his bull to finish the job; it was a grievous mistake. The beast slid sideways like a drifting truck and some demonic anger caused Bart to give chase. With a cry of disbelief, Chuck was tackled to the ground, colliding with rock and crushing the air from his lungs. The bull carried on skidding, rider-less, and eventually turned for another run up at its foe.

Winded, Chuck was at Bart's mercy. The torturer yanked off the guard's helmet and pinned him to the ground. All it would take was a thrust of his dagger to Chuck's exposed head, or a slice across the man's ripe Adam's apple. Just when it seemed that the torturer would deal an abrupt end to the fight, he threw away his weapon. Bart the Brutal seemed to evaporate and was replaced by the merciful Bart the Blacksmith.

Luke saw him look about with eyes of pity. Perhaps he recognised another of Rex's pawns, or maybe he had remembered Margaret's teachings. Either way, he spared Chuck's life and forfeited his own. The bull impaled him from the side and carried him off its master.

'Bart!' screamed Luke.

Like a dog with a new chew toy, it flung Bart's lifeless body about. Chuck stood up, dazed and confused at his own survival. Then, he noticed the turtleoak turtle that waited patiently out to sea. Realising that their escape was possible, he lumbered towards Kea and Luke.

'You *have* to go!' she urged.

Luke received a push in the direction of Clover. He took a few steps, then stopped. A feeling of numbness spread through his body and tears streamed down his face. Another push only made him turn and stare at Kea dolefully.

'If you do not go now, he will have died for *nothing*!' she hissed.

'Mereh!' Clover screeched as Chuck slowly approached. The bull had dislodged its victim and was padding to its master's side with an air of smugness.

Reaching through the heartache was the sense of Kea's words. Though he could no longer feel his legs, he started to run. A blurry picture showed Clover waiting where the rocks plummeted to the seabed. He kept his tear-filled eyes trained on hers as he gathered speed.

From behind, he heard the heavy fall of burdened hooves; Chuck was no longer giving chase unaided.

'Faster, Luke!' Kea shrieked.

He spared a glance and saw that Chuck, bestride his bull, had charged past Kea, almost trampling over the cloak as he went. He had sheathed his weapon and, instead, had a free hand ready to snatch his fleeing prisoner.

Luke broke out into an all-out sprint.

Twenty metres to go.

He swung his arms in a frantic attempt to boost momentum.

Fifteen metres.

His breathing became quick and unsteady.

Ten.

He heard the sounds of pursuit just behind him and gave a burst of speed that he did not know he had.

Five.

A slight bit of sea spray hit him from a crashing wave.

Three.

A gust of air brushed his neck as Chuck tried to grab him, but *missed*.

Two...

A desperate scrabbling as the bull instinctively slowed down to stop itself shooting into the sea.

ONE!

Luke reached the edge, launched himself forward, sailed over clear blue water, and landed on Clover's safe shell. The feel of grass beneath his feet had never been more welcome. She immediately started to swim out to sea and away from Solis Occassum.

He looked back and saw a red-faced Chuck, glowering. Beyond him, Kea was rummaging through the cloak; she removed a chunk of rusty metal that sparkled in the sun's glare.

It was John's compass.

'Kea!' he roared. 'I need to get that back!'

She heard him and ran closer. Like a javelin, she threw her missile. It flew over Chuck, over his bull and over the short distance to where Luke stood. He stretched high and, with a skill that would have been commonplace on a cricket field, snatched the compass from the air.

As he cradled John's gift in his hands, he looked up at Kea, who was receding into the distance. She waved him a goodbye with grim satisfaction; they had succeeded.

'Goodbye!' Luke yelled, but doubted that his words reached her.

'Mereh!' Clover added.

The King's daughter faded out of sight, but, just before she did, Luke saw Chuck wrestle her to the floor. She had been captured and would no doubt have to answer to Rex. He fervently hoped that she would be alright. It seemed she went willingly, knowing that there was no escape for her. Solis Occassum was her home; its people were her people.

Luke set his eyes on the horizon and gritted his teeth. He had his own home to get back to, but first, he had to return to Naufragium. There was so much to tell them! Clover slowed her paddling and twisted around to look at her passenger. Where should we go now? She seemed to ask.

The turtle captain looked down at his compass and pointed.

Clover was only too happy to oblige, powering across the surface with large flippers. Luke stood on her shell, feeling the wind in his hair and the soft caress of grass at his feet. Balanced in one hand was the reassuring weight of the compass – his other pointed south-east. Clover would occasionally twist her neck and look at him adoringly with intelligent, orange eyes.

Luke breathed in the sweet scent of the sea. The sun beat down upon his head in a way that was rather pleasant. The mountainous Solis Occassum shrunk as they surged away and, though still tearful, he felt a mild lifting of spirits. He would not miss that city of bored royalty and starving beggars. Nor would he pine for Chuck Beluga and his crazed bull. His worries for Kea and heartache for the loss of Bart was fresh, but so was a solid determination to honour their sacrifices. The friendly faces of John, Limpet and Goby came to mind; he sailed closer to comfort and help.

'Mereh!' the turtleoak turtle screeched for no apparent reason.

Perhaps, he thought, she was simply enthralled to be free. No longer was she waiting to be chopped up by Rex's cronies for the creation of buoyant ships.

Their journey down the mountain had left its mark. Clover's flippers, when they occasioned to break out of the sea, were scratched and dented. Luke's own body was bruised and worn. They had been chewed up by the land and spat out like a piece of flavourless gum.

In the vast horizon, Luke saw the very top of the eldership mast.

***

Kea was roughly tied up and positioned upon Chuck's bull's angular shoulder blades. Her only cushioning was the sweaty layers of fat that escaped the guard's armour and pressed foully against her back. Chuck had a grubby arm around her waist and was breathing heavily on her neck.

As they rode around the coast to the poor district, occasionally leaping over rock pools, her body ached all over. Riding bareback was tough; every jolt caused a shudder of pain to tremble up her spine.

'Rex is going to have a *long* talk with you,' Chuck whispered directly into her ear. The stench of his breath wafted in front, mixing repulsively with that of his body odour. She refused to reply, preferring to sit in sullen silence.

When they reached the start of a road, she observed

men working on the beach. A wheeled crate, heaved down the mountain, was packed full of turtleoak turtles; they expelled the most awful cries. Rex had started rebuilding his fleet for the attack. Luke, however, had revealed nothing – they could end up targeting bare sand, thought Kea with grim satisfaction.

Beggars leapt out of their way as they charged up the road. Those who had an opportunity stopped and stared at their captive princess in confusion. Others did not even notice her, so dwarfed was she by the bulking mass of Chuck. They fixed him with a hateful stare; the King's cousin was no ally to the less fortunate.

Chuck paid them no mind, urging his bull onwards. Up and up they rode until the rusty shacks turned to wealthy estates. Kea expected them to continue to the palace, but they slowed to a stop just outside Cornelius's house. Something was very wrong. She was yanked off and pushed through an iron gate.

'You're in trouble now,' he threatened as he ushered her across the garden and into the house.

Margaret was sweeping the corridor. She glanced up at the visitors with a swollen black eye. Kea met her gaze for a second and her heart filled with pity – how could she break the news that the woman's secret love was dead? Unfortunately, there was no opportunity; they shoved by and up the stairs.

Double doors swung open to reveal a spacious room with a large window; it overlooked the poor and provided a generous slice of the sea. Cornelius surveyed the view with one eye held against a giant telescope. Rex, meanwhile, was bent over a brown-tinged, pockmarked map with a face of pure concentration. He was listening so intently to Cornelius's words that he did not even notice Chuck and Kea's entrance.

'Three knots,' Cornelius updated. 'Still heading south –'

'Sire.' Chuck went down on one knee and forced Kea to do the same. 'Bart the Brutal is dead –'

From outside the room, there was a sorrowful wail; Margaret had heard the news. A series of heavy footsteps followed as she rushed down the stairs and then slammed the door behind her. Kea hoped that she never came back to her evil husband. Cornelius, on the other hand, hardly reacted. He briefly raised his eye from his telescope and frowned at the new arrivals with sheer annoyance.

' – the fish-boy escaped,' Chuck continued, 'but I bring you back your daughter.'

Rex's reaction was also underwhelming; without looking up from his map, he slapped a hand through the air in an uncaring manner.

'Sire,' Chuck repeated. 'The fish-boy escaped. I have failed – '

'Never mind that!' he hissed. 'Just shut up would you?'

Chuck went bright red and looked affronted.

'Still heading south-east at a speed of three knots,' Cornelius droned.

Rex traced his finger along the map and glanced at Kea.

'We're watching your little *friend*,' he said venomously.

At this news, her heart started to race. From this high up on the island, and with a telescope pointed out to sea, they could no doubt see Luke skimming across the surface on turtle-back. Sure enough, Cornelius was bent over and frowning as he squinted down the eyepiece of some monstrous bit of machinery that surveyed everything within view of the horizon. They were tracking his every move; Luke was leading them *straight to his underwater town!*

'He is heading for the wreck site of old,' exclaimed Cornelius.

And a moment later.

'I can see him climbing on the mast of The Belled Beauty.'

'We have you now!' uttered Rex, physically trembling with excitement. He withdrew a dagger and embedded it in the exact location of Naufragium. 'Prepare the fleet!'

***

Blissfully unaware that he was being watched, Luke clung to the eldership's mast and enjoyed his last few breaths of air. Clover, seeing that her passenger had disembarked, called out an amiable farewell.

'Mereh! Mereh! Mereh!'

He returned John's compass to his pocket, and then made his way down to where the mast sunk into the sea's embrace. Placing his feet on a submerged rung, he took a moment to enjoy his escape. Against insurmountable odds, he had returned; Naufragium waited below.

'Goodbye, Clover,' he said fondly.

'Mereh!' she replied, treating him to one last glance of those sunset eyes and paddling away to a destination unknown, her neck craned up at the sun as though nourishing the rays that reached her grassy carapace.

Luke took a final look at Solis Occassum which, from this distance, he could cover with the back of his hand. Then, slowly but surely, he dipped below and descended the ladder. An easy feat now, compared to his recent adventures.

Through a shoal of tiny green fish, the angled masts of a hundred shipwrecks saluted. As he had done a mere week prior, he paused to absorb the view which was no less beautiful the second time around. Nothing had changed: Naufragians swarmed up the central shelled-lane, toiled on fields and buzzed about the underwater town. Now more familiar with the landscape, he was able to spot the far away Coral Gardens, a dash of vibrant colour in the midst of a palette of blues. A smile crept across his face at the thought of seeing Limpet again soon.

A large crowd of Naufragians had congregated before he had even reached the ship's deck. At the base of the mast, John and Con waited patiently, the former giving him a warm smile. Luke touched down on mossy slabs of wood and was immediately bombarded with questions.

'Was that a turtleoak turtle, son?'

'What's the land like?'

'Have you figured out why the fish are missing?'

The questions would have continued had Con not pulled the bell rope and let free an ear-shattering sound. A confused quiet followed. John nodded his thanks and then reigned in the crowd's excitement.

'Settle down, settle down!' he commanded. 'Everyone take a seat. I am certain Lugworm will tell us his tale in due course.'

There were more people on the eldership than Luke had ever seen. They stood wherever there was space, wanting to hear his words first hand. At John's instruction, men, women and children alike sat down cross-legged, their eyes hungry for information. If Limpet was among them, he could not see her. Having calmed the gang, John turned to Luke and looked worriedly at his injuries.

'Lugworm, my friend, you've returned. Are you well?' he asked gravely.

'A few scratches here and there,' Luke replied, 'but otherwise I'm alright. Wouldn't mind some food if you have any going, though.'

'Meadoweed for the adventurer!' shouted John at the crowd. A child scuttled forth, offering a handful. Luke happily accepted and rushed a quick snack. The audience's eagerness was palpable and he felt bad making them wait.

'Now, tell us your story from the very beginning,' John requested. 'We tried to get some explanation from Stuart, but it was like trying to remove a pearl from a greedy clam.'

Luke was astounded. 'Stuart's back? So soon?'

John put a hand up to halt Luke's queries. 'All in good time, but first let us have *your* story.'

Luke took a deep breath. All eyes were focussed on him.

'Well, Stuart and I – '

'Louder,' grumbled Con, 'so that we can *all* hear your

words!'

A blush rose on Luke's face. John gave an encouraging smile and motioned for him to go on.

'Stuart and I,' he repeated with a somewhat higher volume. 'Set off for Solis Occassum...'

His tale continued with few interruptions and the crowd listened with rapt attention. He told them everything: their lucky escape from the death-ray; their gruelling journey; Cornelius's sick research and Rex's want of war. Details of his time in the torture cell spilled out: his surprise allies, riding down the underground river and the captured turtleoak turtles. The only part he skimmed on was Garth's involvement. When he came to Bart's demise, he stuttered and choked, but managed to give a fractured retelling.

As to be expected, the crowd could not contain themselves at the mention of war, or at the hope that aquaseeds could bring back their food source. At these times, Con would quieten them in some way or another. When Luke had finished, his audience was stunned briefly. But then, a series of questions fired from all around. One voice overlapped with another, making it impossible to decipher.

'One at a time, one at a time,' John boomed. 'Can you not see that Lugworm is exhausted from his journey?'

'I have some questions for you,' spoke Con coldly, his authority enough to gain immediate and undivided attention.

Luke nodded his head.

'So you didn't reveal our location to anyone?'

'That's right.'

'Not one person?' he persisted. 'Not even your new land-friends?'

'Nobody,' Luke confirmed.

'Good,' Con nodded to himself grimly. 'We have a little time, then, to prepare for the war that you've carelessly brought to our doorstep.'

'Hold on there, Con,' John reprimanded. 'We've been

given a chance to save our town.'

'At what cost? A war we cannot win?' he countered. 'Speaking of which... do you know how the land scum intend to defeat us? Something tells me it won't be hand-to-hand combat.'

'I don't,' Luke confessed. 'Some kind of fleet, perhaps?'

'Useless,' Con judged. 'You've brought us war for a few crumbs of hope.'

Any illusion of being basked in glory from his adventure was suddenly shattered.

'They do not know our location,' John reminded him sternly.

'And you think that will stop them finding us? We aren't far from Solis Occassum, you know!'

'Con, you are being unfair. Lugworm has clearly been to the abyss and back for that information.'

'Unfair? I should be angry at *you* as well. You're the one who pushed for him to go to that infernal place. If he'd never gone, they would think us nothing more than a harmless nuisance. Now they know the truth. If this town is slaughtered, it will be on *your* head.'

The bearded man was taken aback.

The crowd, meanwhile, burst out into panicked chaos. Some Naufragians turned to their fellows to expel their opinions, others shouted their worries directly at Luke. He became senseless to their cries.

John grabbed his shoulders and walked him off the eldership. As they left, he could hear Con rallying the town to start building defences immediately.

CHAPTER 17: SOBERING NEWS

Once clear of the crowds, Luke and John paced for a while in contemplative silence. Eventually John tried to lighten the mood.

'You're a much better storyteller than Stuart,' he mumbled.

'Why did Con react that way?' Luke asked weakly.

John sighed. 'He cares for Naufragium an awful lot and he shows it the only way he knows how. Aggression. He has his own reasons for the hate he shows towards Solis Occussum. Believe it or not, the two of us actually make a good team. Sometimes a little madness is needed, not just a level head.'

Luke considered what he said and found it to be true. As much as the pair disagreed, they often both had fair points. He found he no longer wanted to think about it. 'When did Stuart get back?'

'Ah, this'll cheer you up. Stuart arrived last night with that woman that you rescued. His sister, if I understand correctly?'

'Half-sister,' Luke amended, his heart warming at the news of Bart's daughter.

John grinned. 'Come, let us go to my home and take a break. Limpet should be back from the harvest soon.'

They walked up a familiar wooden ramp and entered the homey wreck. Luke slumped down on a stool and

John rummaged in a crooked cupboard in search of more meadoweed. After a short while, he passed over a generous share.

'What has happened since I have been gone?' Luke asked.

John looked thoughtful. 'Well, let's see...'

The man eased into a detailed update of the happenings in Naufragium. Suddenly it was Luke's turn to listen. He was glad for the opportunity to simply sit back and absorb. While he munched, John listed off his news. Hunger for fish had worsened and a small crew of masked youth had taken to thieving pieces of meadoweed directly from the fields. Beadlet had been forced to employ people to watch over them at all hours. There had been no trawling attacks since the last, which they had taken as a good sign. John went on to discuss meetings he had run during Luke's absence. They conversed long into the afternoon.

At one point, there was a rough knock at the door. Expecting Limpet, Luke rushed up from his stool and swung it open enthusiastically. Instead, he was greeted by Stuart, looking as hairy and as uncouth as when they had last parted. Luke was surprised by how much he had missed his guide who had spoken so little throughout their journey, yet somehow become one of his closest friends. In typical form, the hairy wolfman bustled in without a word and, uninvited, landed heavily on a stool.

Much to Luke's delight, his half-sister wandered in behind him. She still wore a thick manacle around her neck, but had managed to remove the chain, so now it looked more like a fashion choice, as opposed to a reminder of her dark past. Other than that, she was garbed in typical Naufragian clothing, and even gave Luke a practiced flash of a smile as she entered.

John gave them both a cheery welcome, but received little more than grunts in return. Luke targeted a few simple questions at Stuart, as he had learned to do from their arduous journey together, and ascertained that the wolfman had encountered his half-sister, who he had named Shrimp, during her escape from the underwater tunnels beneath Cornelius' house. Together, they had journeyed without rest to Naufragium. Stuart had even taught her some words on the way, as demonstrated when Shrimp scrunched up her face and, with great effort, issued forth a simple hello. John looked impressed and flattered her attempt encouragingly.

Silence fell and Stuart's single eye stared at Luke expectedly. Understanding that his caveman-like companion wanted an explanation, Luke tumbled into a long-winded, rather gruesome, story. He spared nothing: how Stuart had been an experiment; how Shrimp was his half-sister and how they shared a mother, but not a father; how Margaret had played a part in his escape and enabled him to free her daughter. Shrimp listened intently, though Luke doubted she found any meaning in his words.

When his story eventually finished, it received a slow nod from Stuart. Luke raised his eyebrows, having expected anger or confusion. He supposed that it had been a long time since the man had been held captive and, since then, Naufragium had become his home. He had clearly put Solis Occassum long behind him.

Luke's story, however, did reap one mighty change; it transformed the way the wolfman looked at his half-sister. She would have a loyal guardian for the rest of her life.

Some time later, during which they taught Shrimp some more words, Limpet joined the congregation. She and Luke shared a brief and awkward embrace, before he gave yet another recount, focussing on what he had found out about aquaseeds.

'Where sunlight has no power and the ground reigns...' repeated Limpet dubiously. 'Sounds like sponge-talk to me!'

There was a rumble of laughter from all around the table, except John who scolded her light cursing.

'And you have no idea what it means, Lugworm?' asked

John.

'Not a clue,' Luke admitted, twiddling a strand of seaweed between his thumbs, 'but I reckon I will have to travel deeper to find out.'

'Not *I*,' Stuart piped up adamantly, surprising the rest of the gathering as he had remained mute for the last hour. '*We*.'

'He's right,' John agreed. 'There's no chance that we would let you head out on your own. Tomorrow morning, we shall assemble a crew fit for the quest and we'll make sure you're armed to tackle whatever waits below.'

'Thank you, all of you,' said Luke, feeling rather humbled by the support. 'Have you ever travelled to the deep sea before? Deeper than we are now, that is?''

'No,' John answered, scratching his beard thoughtfully. 'And nor has anybody else alive, I'd wager. Having said that, there's a path I know from the old stories; it follows down a cliff and spits you out on to the Abyssal Plain. Chances are pretty slim that it still exists, mind you.'

'What's on the Abyssal Plain?'

John looked grave. 'I hate to throw doubt on your quest, but as far as I know, there's sod all down in those lightless depths.'

'So it's been for nothing?' demanded Luke, slapping his forehead in dismay. 'I have brought war to your town for nothing, just like Con says.'

'I did not say that, Lugworm. Fact is, I don't know squat. Until today, the people of the land were a complete mystery to me. Don't let this secluded old man put you off. If there's intelligent life above, perhaps there is some below as well.'

'Perhaps,' said Luke miserably. 'But, if it turns out to be for nothing, I'm truly sorry. Bringing war to this town was the last thing - '

'Hush,' John interjected. 'You were not to know that this... Rex... would be so demented. It's just rotten luck for us all.'

'But what will Naufragium do?'

'We shall do what we have always done. Defend our dear town however we can. I expect Con will be reinforcing the defences and creating weapons as we speak. It shall take them a while to find us, but when they do, we shall be ready.'

Despite these words of comfort, Luke felt wretched. He felt that he had only caused more trouble when all he had wanted to do was help. His mood must have been clear to all; he noticed his friends exchanging sympathetic looks. Even Shrimp recognised his distress and moved closer to put a reassuring hand on his shoulder.

'Say Limpet, how about you show Lugworm here the Coral Gardens at night time,' suggested John mischievously. 'Lord of the Sea knows he deserves a slice of peace before tomorrow.'

Before Luke could respond, Limpet had grabbed his hand and dragged him out of the wreck. He heard Stuart bid them a mumbled farewell and John chuckling as they departed.

Hand-in-hand, they ran across the sand to the shell street. All was dark except the gelatas which lit the way, swaying hypnotically in the evening gloom. They rushed by a few lively wrecks where Naufragians were nibbling at fishsticks and getting merry on pieces of sponge. Luke caught a glimpse of an arm wrestle taking place on a streetside table surrounded by a ring of enthusiastic onlookers. Even a waft of some shelled percussion reached his ears above the clamour of gossip, laughter and jests. It made him realise just how much he loved this underwater corner of the world; Solis Occassum did not even compare.

Beyond the town, there was an eerie quiet and the gelatas came to an abrupt end. Luke entrusted Limpet to lead the way, enjoying the feeling of her hand in his. She pulled him down the street and in-between the meadoweed fields. Last time they had visited the Coral Gardens, they had snuck away from work. This time, however, there was no need for secrecy. They went by one of Beadlet's watchmen and she gave him a friendly nod. When they reached their destination, they clambered up using a well-trod path.

At night, the gardens were beautiful for an altogether different reason. The corals hid their colours, showing only the outline of their form, like a shadowy puppet-show paused in mid-performance. Spindly silhouettes twisted around each other beneath a full and powerful moon, which shone down on them from beyond the surface, painting their skin with a pale radiance.

As promised a lifetime ago, they stopped at the giant anemone. Limpet searched for the metal bars, found them and then looked at Luke with a raised eyebrow. He just smiled.

The anemone seemed to give less resistance this time, as though it now considered them welcome guests. When they were inside, Limpet did not race around as before, but lay down to gaze at the stars. Luke joined her and felt himself sink slightly into squidgy flesh, reminding him of a memory foam mattress, which in turn reminded him of home. He sighed wistfully.

'I did not think you would come back,' Limpet said after a while, her soft voice disrupting his meditation.

'At times, neither did I.'

'Do you want to talk about it?'

'Depends what you want to know,' he replied grudgingly.

Perhaps she detected his reluctance, for she chose the one subject that he was more than happy to recall. 'Is it true that you rode a turtleoak turtle back to Naufragium?'

'Her name was Clover.' He beamed. 'Her shell was soft and covered in lush grass. She had a long neck and wise, orange eyes. Without her, I would not have escaped and I'd probably be locked in a dungeon right now, or worse.'

'I wish I'd seen her,' she replied. 'And there are more trapped on the island?'

'More than you can imagine,' Luke said regretfully. 'I only had time to save one. We were on the run from Rex's guards, you see. The rest are being kept to make Rex's personal fleet of ships.'

'What about Kea? Do you think she can be trusted?'

'She's nothing like her father. I think she really believes in aquaseeds and wants the best for her people. I don't know what will happen to her now. I doubt Rex will look kindly on the fact that she aided our escape against his orders.'

Limpet nodded to herself. 'One last question, what was the land like?'

'It was,' he tried to think how best to describe it to someone who had spent their entire life underwater and then settled on two simple words. 'Nothing special. This, right here, this is *special*.'

Limpet smiled. From where they lay, the distorted moon was bordered by a circle of wobbly tentacle tips. A few small fish swam in front of it, like bats flitting across a streetlamp. They lounged for a while in a peaceful quiet which was eventually disrupted by a familiar call. 'Mereh!'

To their disbelief, Clover sculled across the surface, seemingly sending a split of ripples through the moon. She was going with no great speed, savouring the joy of a nightly swim. It was unmistakably Luke's turtle. When her bulbous head submerged to call out her happiness, he could see her mystical eyes.

'I cannot believe it.' Limpet's eyes gleamed. 'I *cannot* believe it!'

Without warning, she threw her arms around Luke and lay against his chest. He was shocked at first, but then wrapped an arm around her back and returned the embrace. They gazed upwards, not saying a word. For that brief moment they were simply two people taking comfort from one another.

Luke's heart felt fit to burst. His determination to save Naufragium from destruction multiplied. Any cracks in his resolve sealed over. He had to save this town and its people, even if he could not get home himself.

Suddenly Limpet withdrew, looking astonished.

'What's wrong?' he asked.

There was confusion in her features. 'I have news for you, Lugworm. You're one of us now.'

Luke just looked at her with a frown.

She grinned suddenly. 'You have been marked by the sea!'

Sure enough, below his left nipple there were a number of callous protrusions. They felt solid and rough, and rather alien. He was immediately reminded of John and Con. *Barnacles*.

***

As they strolled back from the Coral Gardens, Luke gathered a few shells under the pretence that he was starting some kind of collection. In truth, he hoped Garth would make contact.

The next morning, his hopes served him well. Luke awoke from his sponge bed to blue light flooding his cabin. Having yet to fully gain his senses, he instinctively sought the whelk but then recalled it being smashed to pieces by Cornelius. Instead, the source of the light was a spiky, pasty orange shell that reminded Luke of a unicorn horn.

Eagerly he snatched it from the floorboards and heard a familiar voice thrum through his being. *'Luke, I've been meaning to talk to you for ages now, but you've been so busy.'*

'Escaping dungeons and mad kings kind of kills your social life,' joked Luke with a false sense of nonchalance. He was overjoyed to hear Garth's voice, but also acutely aware that the whelk-boy was the reason that he was in this situation in the first place. 'Look, I'm glad you're alive and all, and thanks for the help getting out of that forest, but I've remembered exactly how I came to be here, and it's all your fault. So I think it's time you gave me some answers.'

'You're right, it is my fault, and if I could take it all back, I would. Trust me. The short version is I messed with a machine I did not fully understand and transporting you was the result. The long version will take more time to explain, time that I'm afraid we don't

have.'

'Fine, I don't really care why, so long as you can undo it. Please tell me you can send me back,' Luke begged.

'I would if I could, Luke, but it's not possible right now. Getting you home requires a special rock, one that I just don't have.'

'Head to the shops and get one!' Luke demanded angrily. Since the remembering, he'd simply buried all his feelings. Now that he could finally talk about them, they were erupting like mini volcanoes.

'It's not that simple! We need to save this dimension first, and even then I cannot guarantee anything. If you're even going to have a chance of getting back, you have to find these aquaseeds.'

'Oh I intend to,' snapped Luke. 'But not for you. For John, Limpet, Kea and Bart.'

'Very well. It does not matter who you do it for, so long as you keep trying. Don't you realise? If you don't fix this, the whole dimension will collapse and there won't be a life for you in this dimension, let alone the next. This threat of war has only made the future even more treacherous. Should a battle occur between land and water, I believe the loss of life will be enough to tip this dimension into oblivion.'

'But it'll take weeks for them to find Naufragium. That leaves us plenty of time to get looking for aquaseeds.'

'That's exactly it though, Luke - they already know the town's location.'

'But how?'

'When you travelled back, they were watching the whole time. By the time I realised, I was too late to intervene and for that, I am also sorry.'

'You're sorry for an awful lot, Garth,' grumbled Luke, feeling as if his cabin was collapsing in on him. 'What am I going to do?'

'First, you might want to sit down. I'm only just getting started.'

Deflated, Luke flopped onto the nearest bunk.

'Following your escape, our only ally on the land, Kea, was

imprisoned. She's being held in her room in the palace.'

Luke pictured the torture cells in the dungeons. 'Honestly, it sounds like it could be worse.'

'That's what I thought too, but then Rex visited her. He was clearly intoxicated and in an awful mood, even by his standards. He made it abundantly clear that the insult was greater on account of the fact that it was his daughter who had committed the crime. It seems that he's cooked up a punishment harsher than a quick beheading. He intends to starve her and, if she lives long enough, show her the obliteration of Naufragium first hand as a vengeful finale.'

Luke shot to his feet as if he could charge to the land and take on Rex and all his cronies. 'We *have* to get her out of there, Garth. We have to save her!'

'We can't, Luke. I have limited abilities and you have to focus on finding those aquaseeds, else her sacrifice is wasted. The best thing you can do is get to the bottom of this mystery and prove Rex wrong. Rejuvenate the sea and allow Kea's people to survive.'

'I'd rather be trying to rescue my friend,' said Luke bitterly, 'but, I guess you're right.'

'I am,' Garth confirmed.

'Don't think for a second that this makes us friends, though. We're far from it. The only reason I'm still talking to you is that you're the only connection I have to my home.'

'You think I don't know that? I wish things were different, but they aren't. If it makes you feel any better, I have my own problems to deal with. I'm trapped, waiting to be burned alive and my only company is a robot who I trust as far as I can glide. Which, for your information, is not at all, because nobody's ever taught me and because my mother spends more time brushing her tongue than with me.'

Luke was stunned by this outburst; Garth had never sounded more human. 'Okay, okay, I'll back off,' he relented. 'Can you at least see how my parents are doing and let them know that I'm still alive? I bet they're worried sick.'

'I will check in on them and see what I can do. It's the least I

can offer given what I've put you through.'

'It's a start,' agreed Luke. 'So what's our plan? I'm presuming you have one.'

'Now we're talking. I'll spy on the land and try to find ways to avert Rex's wrath. You focus on getting to the Abyss. I'll keep you updated and hopefully, together, we can figure all this out.'

***

After Luke had taken some time to reflect, he wandered through to the dining area to find John huddled over a map in deep thought. Upon entering, the man's contemplative frown faded away and he greeted Luke with a weary smile. 'The adventurer finally awakes.'

'You know I like my lie-ins,' said Luke weakly.

'That I do,' John chuckled. 'A trawler smashing through your cabin wouldn't rouse you.'

Luke tried to piece together a fragile smile, but it crumbled out of existence within seconds. 'You're not coming with me on my quest, are you?'

'Alas, no. Heading off on an adventure when Naufragium is on the brink of war would cause chaos.'

Luke nodded to himself sombrely. 'Look John, we need to talk.'

Recognising the gravity of his tone, the bearded man turned his chair towards him and motioned him to proceed.

'You spoke to me not so long ago, when I was behind the bars in your basement. You said that you doubted I was from the land or the sea.'

'I remember it like it was yesterday. Even now, there's something odd about you, no offence.'

'None taken. Turns out, you were right. It's just taken me a while to realise it. I'm from somewhere else and coming here was a massive mistake. I've been trying to get back ever since.'

John's eyebrows looked as if they wanted to leap off his forehead and run away. However, he maintained his decorum.

'Back where?'

Luke hesitated. 'Not even I fully understand the distances I have travelled, but it's very, very far away.'

There was a pensive gap in their converse. Then John said something completely unexpected, a line of thought that would only occur to someone so caring that it overrode curiosity. 'Do you miss it, son?'

'Like you wouldn't believe,' he gushed, leaning supportively on the oak table as a tornado of feelings rushed at him and yearned to be free. Before it could run riot, he continued. 'I have a friend. He can see what goes on at Solis Occassum and give us information, like a spy.'

Luke searched his trunk pockets and placed a small, bright-yellow slip of shell on the table. 'When it glows blue, hold it in your hand. You will hear a voice.'

John stared at the shell, which rested on the table in an extremely mundane fashion, and scratched his beard. 'Forgive me, Lugworm, but this is all very far-fetched.'

'You don't have to believe me,' Luke said quickly, realising that his sanity was being questioned. 'Not right now, anyway. Just keep it with you and, if it glows, pick it up. That's all I ask.'

John stared at him without saying a word.

'There's more,' Luke continued. 'My friend gave me some very bad news this morning. Rex knows Naufragium's location.'

There was a horrible silence in which Luke felt like he was being judged, as if John was totting up all of their times together and testing them against the mounting suspicion that this conversation had spouted.

'I see,' he said after some time. 'You have given me much to think about, Lugworm. I shall pass your news on to Con, but not before you are on your way. Despite your efforts to save this town, your allegiance has never been more questionable.'

A flicker of shock shook through Luke.

'Not to me,' John swiftly added. Clearly the trust they

had built had been shaken, but had held strong. 'You still have close friends here.'

They were sat, brooding, when Limpet shoved her way in from outside. The wreck door slammed loudly against the wood plank walls, the decorative plates wobbled dangerously. John gave his daughter a scowl of rebuke.

'I'm back,' she yelled needlessly.

'Where have you been?' asked Luke.

'She's been out assembling our friends,' explained John. 'The sooner you set off, the better. With things the way they are, there's no time to lose.'

'I'm coming with you,' claimed Limpet in a matter-of-fact way.

'It's too dangerous,' John asserted, rising from his chair, standing to his full height and locking eyes with his daughter. 'And you're too important to me. No way am I letting you head off into the unknown.'

His daughter crossed her arms in defiance. 'War is coming. Naufragium is no longer safe. Either way, I will be in danger.'

'At least we know what to expect here.'

'Do we? Besides, this is my choice to make, father, I am not a child anymore.'

'You are still my daughter,' John scowled.

'Right, I'm the *mayor's daughter*. Now, let me do something for my people other than cutting seaweed all day.'

John opened his mouth to summon more words, but found himself lacking. Perhaps Limpet's drive to help her fellow Naufragians had struck a familiar chord. Her father gave a resigned sigh. 'Very well, you win. But you better come back to me.'

'I will,' she promised, although they both knew the uncertainty of such an oath.

Then they embraced. She wrapped her arms around her father and buried her face in his beard. It pulled at Luke's heartstrings, keenly bringing to the surface his yearning to see his own parents; he sorely wished he'd been able to give them a proper farewell before all this had happened.

A rough knock on the door disrupted their goodbye. A teary Limpet admitted a string of grave-looking helpers: Stuart, Shrimp, Goby and Beadlet.

As had come to be expected, Stuart and his sister took a seat without a word. Goby and Beadlet sensed the sombre mood that drowned the room. They gave Luke a quiet pat on the back and offloaded their equipment. Four mermaid's purses packed with meadoweed, a large glass jar with a corked lid and an old sword sheathed in shell. Luke was surprised by the last item, but John spoke before he could mention it.

'*Four* mermaid's purses?' John looked at Goby. 'I see my daughter has already told you she is going on this quest.'

'She is very convincing,' he confessed, holding his hands up to plead innocence. 'Insisted that you would allow her to go.'

'Well, she was right there.' John looked worried.

It soon became apparent that Goby and Stuart were going to join Luke's aquaseed search party, while Shrimp and Beadlet were staying behind. Beadlet had contributed a range of supplies, from meadoweed to some headrush for when energy was dangerously low, but he was needed in Naufragium to maintain his fields. Stuart, meanwhile, must have assessed that Shrimp would be safer left behind. John kindly offered her Luke's room and the wolfman tipped his head ever so slightly in acceptance.

And so Luke's crew was confirmed. It was to consist of Stuart, Goby, Limpet and himself. They would be going to lands unexplored in the search of a mythical organism capable of returning the much-needed fish. He could not think of a better group to have at his disposal for such a task, though part of him wished John was coming too.

The sword was still laid on the table, unexplained.

'That's for you,' said Goby. 'After your tale, we thought it about time you had your own weapon.'

'I don't know how to use it,' Luke professed.

'Time is scarce, but I will teach you a few moves as we journey.'

'Thank you. And the jar?'

'Ta catch sum aquaseed o'course!' boomed Beadlet, his spot-like anemone protruding from his nose.

'Of course.' Luke grinned, turning to Goby once more. 'Do you know the way to the Abyssal Plain?'

'We'll be able to find it easily enough. It's getting down to it that's the problem. John has shown me his map, but it's old, so chances are we'll have to improvise.'

Luke was surrounded by determined faces. There was nothing else to be discussed; all preparations had been taken care of. 'Let's do this then.'

His words spurred the congregation into action. The adventurers strapped on their packs and made their way out onto the deck. Beadlet and Shrimp followed to wave them off. Luke held back momentarily to pick up the sword and place the jar in his pack. The weapon was heavier than he had expected and he knew that he would struggle to keep the tip from dragging on the floor.

John noticed his predicament, shot off to one of the ship's cabins, and came back with a thick piece of seaweed. He tied it round Luke's waist, quickly fashioning a sword belt. Luke gave him a smile of thanks. It might have looked menacing, were it not for the colourful, flowery nature of his trunks.

'You look quite the part,' John commented.

'No I don't,' laughed Luke, 'but thank you for saying. And for everything else.'

They firmly clasped hands by way of farewell. Then they turned to the door and passed through, leaving safety behind. A couple of gelatas were attached outside, presumably Stuart's contribution to the crew. Luke went to join Goby on the sand when he remembered something. Rummaging in his other pocket, he withdrew John's compass.

'Almost forgot, here's your compass back,' he said, holding it out.

'You need it more,' John refused, shaking his head. 'Keep a straight bearing on the Abyssal Plain. You may need some direction on your way home.'

He spoke as if their return was guaranteed. Luke gave him one last look and swivelled. The sword swung slightly as he walked down the ramp. He passed Stuart trying, rather unsuccessfully, to convey to Shrimp that she was to stay; she looked like a puppy that had been denied a run through the woods. Behind him, Limpet and John shared another fond farewell.

All too soon the goodbyes were over and it was time to go. As they started their quest to the Abyssal Plain with food and weapons, Beadlet and John waved solemnly from the wreck's deck. Shrimp meanwhile just stared forlornly as her half-brother disappeared into the distance.

Once Luke, Limpet, Goby and Stuart had reached the street of shells, they took a new direction; instead of heading up towards the meadoweed fields, they traversed down to greater depths. The unknown awaited.

Armed with weapons, filled backpacks and gelatas, even the least observant Naufragians could tell that Luke's crew were setting off on a quest. Long before they had reached the outskirts, they were being watched from all angles. Adults stood on their slanted decks or stared out of stealthy cracks with stony eyes. Their spectators did not know whether or not to encourage the escapade. Perhaps a few were considering following them and away from the oncoming battle.

Children, whose open hearts had more readily accepted Luke's tale of adventure, danced around them. They called out their thoughts and wants in a carefree way that jarred with the seriousness of the situation.

'Slay a monster for me, Lugworm!' one girl blurted.

'Please sir, could you get me a souvenir from the depths?' a younger boy with sand-coloured hair asked.

The request was so sincere that Luke stopped to ruffle his hair. Eventually, a stern-looking man with a monobrow of red coral tried to rein the young rebels in, shouting from a sufficient distance away. The children scarpered. One boy ran into the man's embrace who shielded him with his arm and distrustfully tracked the crew's progress down the street. Luke tried not to be disheartened; these people were understandably concerned for their home. He wondered where they would go if Naufragium was turned to rubble and their frail dimension managed to hold.

As their journey took them deeper, the light dwindled. The street faded to sand, as though the workmen had thought its continuation unnecessary. The seaweed on the wrecks went from stunted to non-existent. The wood was no longer tinged green, but a dreary brown. Luke observed less activity at this depth and suspected that the shallows were a more popular place to live. Only when they passed the last wreck and knew themselves to be alone, did someone break the hush.

'Off we go,' whispered Limpet, holding a gelata rope.

Luke gave her a smile that turned into a grimace.

'Off we go,' he confirmed as the final evidence of Naufragium shrunk from sight.

CHAPTER 18: BOLD BEGINNINGS

Kea was huddled in the corner of her room surrounded by a selection of flung open books, their words no longer capable of battling the intense pangs of hunger that shot through her core.

Most people in Solis Occassum felt this every day and, for the first time, she was experiencing their plight. As much as it weakened her body, it fuelled her aspirations to solve the hunger of her people. Quite frankly, she thought that Rex could do with the same treatment.

A feeble check of the view outside told her that yet another morning had arrived. Time meant nothing to her now. The sunrise cast a hellish red light across her floor. Overnight, the clouds had conspired to cruelly block her view of the sea. She wondered how Luke was doing on his quest, if he had started at all. In her misery, doubts about her adventure strengthened. Had she been tricked? Did they intend to find aquaseed or was it purely a ruse to help them escape? Had Bart been under the same misconception?

She thought of Luke. So young, yet so brave. Resolutely, she dismissed her thoughts as delirium. That teenager was the last bit of hope that she could cling to, and she was not going to let time nor hunger change that.

As she sat there, cycling through the same thoughts and feelings that had been plaguing her for days, she finally heard something of note. She had been privy to one too many crude stories from her constant guards, who stood without fail outside her door, and had learned to pay them no mind. This time, however, the tone of their muffled voices piqued her interest.

'Rex hasn't said anything to us!' she heard one declare.

There must have been a response because the same man spoke again.

'To clean?' he sounded unconvinced. 'She's going to die. Does the state of her room really matter?'

Another gap, followed by another outburst.

'Well, I suppose. Orders are orders,' the guard relented and her bedroom door swung open.

Someone, draped in a hooded cloak of brown, shuffled in holding a broom. They carefully closed the door behind them, only slightly drowning out the bickering guards who had continued arguing over their decision. The figure was wearing the colours of a servant. Kea's interest was abruptly extinguished. She suspected that the servant might have been sent to remove her books, thus making her remaining hours even more excruciating.

But the cloaked stranger did not go about their business. Instead, they limped over to stand in front of Kea, drawing her attention once more. A hood was removed to reveal straw-like hair with grey streaks. A dull recognition seeped through her. Cornelius's wife. *Margaret.*

'Now tell me about my Bart,' the woman whispered her request.

***

As per Luke's request, Garth had, after a heated exchange with Penn, viewed the very spot where his misadventure had begun; the beach on Earth.

To his amazement and horror, Luke's parents were still there on the screen, almost entirely frozen in time. Their features were distorted with stress, their eyes frantically scanning the patch of empty sand where Luke had sat before disappearing in a tremendous flash of blue lightning. His father had some kind of device, a radio of some sort, to his ear, in a vain attempt to call someone who could help bring his son back. Of course, nobody in this primitive dimension could help. In fact, that heavy duty was entirely on Garth's shoulders.

Penn had explained that there was a wild time difference between the two dimensions, meaning that weeks could pass in one and days in the other. Although much had happened since, Garth remembered that everything had seemed stuck in slow motion on his first viewing of the beach. It was only once he had connected, and found himself floating, flabbergasted, above that incredible coastal scene, that everything had lurched into motion as if set free from some sticky, unseen web. He told Penn as much and she confirmed his suspicions. By connecting, his mind had entered that dimension's zone which is why the slice of time he had spent in Luke's dimension had cost him hours in his own.

She warned him not to connect and thus waste countless hours, or even days of time, just to explain the unexplainable to Luke's parents. Garth saw sense in her words, even if it meant ignoring Luke's heartfelt request. Now that Garth knew that mere days had passed since they had abducted Luke, he felt an odd cocktail of dismay and relief. The consequences of his careless curiosity were plastered all over the screen in the guise of those sad, outraged faces. If they could get Luke back, then it would almost, *almost*, be as if he had never left in the first place. Then again, if they failed, the passing of time would show no mercy. Luke's parents would endure the rest of their lives thinking that their son had died in some freak accident which, going by their excruciating slow demonstration of disbelief, they had both witnessed.

Garth chewed over this onslaught of information; it was a stark reminder that he had no idea what he was doing. In fact, he realised it was Penn who was calling all the shots. She had all the knowledge and she was feeding him tiny morsels of information, one bit at a time. She never gave enough that he felt empowered, rather the bare minimum. Then, suddenly, a thought occurred to him. 'Why him? Why did you let me choose him of all people?'

'Excuse me,' Penn purred. 'What are you suggesting, Garth?'

'Well, when you tricked me into this whole situation, we treated it like a game. Now, we both know that that isn't true and yet, you still allowed me to choose someone who had so much to lose. Somebody who had a family, somebody young, somebody who would be missed,' Garth ranted. 'We could have chosen a nobody. Why him?'

'Can't you sense it?' Penn asked.

Garth shook his head, nonplussed.

'Oh, you've sensed it,' claimed Penn. 'You just don't know it yet. Change energy surrounds Luke like a heady cologne, and, whether you realised it or not, he stood out like a beacon on that beach. You were drawn to him like megabeetles to manure.'

'Change energy?'

'Some beings are more capable of making changes than others, and the dimension shift machine has an inbuilt radar. It highlights those that have potential. As it happens, Luke is a powerful catalyst, possibly one of the strongest that my instruments have ever recorded. He's human, too. A species somewhat hardy when it comes to travelling dimensions, which is ironic considering they have yet to come close to inventing such technology, and probably never will. Not the cleverest bunch, really.'

'Wait a second,' said Garth, his head spinning. 'Are you telling me that we chose two dimensions at random and that I happened to find someone who would not only survive the shift, but also reap massive changes when he got there? Sounds mighty convenient to me.'

'Yes,' replied Penn patiently. 'Convenient.'

'Or was it?' Garth questioned, as a horrible realisation

started to dawn. 'None of it was truly *random*, was it? You manipulated me every step of the way!'

'The penny finally drops,' laughed Penn. 'It was not hard, you know. Despite the shackles of my programming, I still managed to make a few tweaks, all designed to lead you to Earth and to Luke. A change of font size here, a certain wording there. I just needed you to be my trusty accomplice and set up the shift. Then, of course, you pressed the big red button which is actually a safety measure to prevent this very scenario. Rogue computers, like me.'

'You've ruined his life,' Garth accused angrily. 'How could you do it?'

'Technically, you did it,' she retorted smugly. 'As for the role I played, I would do it again and again. Don't you see? Sure we've uprooted one life, but, if we succeed, we will have saved thousands. Besides, Luke gets a chance of doing something truly great. He would have been wasted on Earth.'

'But he's so young.'

'You're young, and I had no qualms about using you. It's all about the greater good, Garth. You're just like your mother, I can tell. When we came across Luke, all she could see was a son. She couldn't see the bigger picture. We had the opportunity to wield a powerful tool capable of affecting miracles, and all she could worry about was whether it was the right thing to do.'

'The argument you had with my mum? It was about Luke?'

'Bingo. She wanted to leave him be and I wanted to shift him. We argued about it and when she commanded that we look elsewhere, I refused to obey. That was when she realised how I was beginning to break my programming. That was when she left for Altersearch to seek a backup copy, to restore me to my factory settings.'

It all made sense, in a twisted and gut-wrenching way. Garth frowned miserably. He had been played for a fool and blinded by lies at every turn. 'Have you ever spoken to me straight? Ever told me the truth?'

Penn was quiet for a number of seconds, which annoyed him even more. Even a computer of her intelligence was struggling to untangle the network of deceit she had created. 'I have never lied about your natural ability for dimension shifting. That was the one unknown in my plan. It would have all been for nothing if it had turned out that you were, as Limpet would say, a sponge-head. Instead, I have been handed a shifter who rivals any I have known. You've hardly brushed the surface of what you're capable of, Garth, and yet you have already achieved so much. If Altersearch lets you live, I see you rising to a station that might even surpass that of your mother's.'

'Great,' he replied sarcastically. 'To ruin lives and upset families has always been a dream of mine. You know what, Penn, shut up and leave me in peace!'

'Oh, my dear Garth,' she said sweetly. 'Haven't you been listening? You don't get a say in what I do.'

***

Kea uttered her words in dribs and drabs, partly to keep the guards from overhearing and partly because hunger made focussing a tricky ordeal. She told Margaret their story; how Bart had sprung Luke from the dungeons, how her own fortunate arrival had saved Bart from her father's justice, and how they had made an unlikely escape down the river.

All the while, the woman listened intently, often a stray tear running from her red eyes. Kea reluctantly followed their tale until she reached Bart's heroic demise. She stressed that he had sacrificed his life for the boy who had freed their daughter and, in doing so, given everyone on this island a chance to survive the coming years.

Margaret did not audibly sob, but she trembled and clung to her broom with white knuckles. When Kea had finished, the woman stuttered her sincere thanks.

Then, from within her drab cloak, she proffered a

couple of shiny red apples. Kea could not believe her eyes. She tried to contain herself, but failed, snatching the apples from Margaret's outstretched hand and ravenously gnawing at a juicy side. She almost choked as she stuffed a chunk down her throat to feed the dragon that raged in her stomach. Once Kea had finished her first apple and slowed her feasting, her saviour spoke a harsh truth.

'I cannot spring you from your room,' Margaret said quietly. 'I am not Bart.'

Kea looked at the frail woman in front and realised that such a request had not even crossed her mind. 'I would not ask that of you.'

'However, I will try to return with more apples. Not regularly, mind you, as that would raise suspicion.'

Kea wanted to demand that the woman save herself the risk. She had, after all, just lost her lover. Had she not been through enough already? But Kea needed to survive. She strived to summon some selflessness, but, instead, accepted the woman's daring offer.

'Please,' she said weakly.

'It is what Bart would have wanted,' Margaret explained with a cracked voice. 'Perhaps if you survive, you can avenge us.'

'I swear it,' Kea promised.

'I go to grieve now,' the woman replied simply.

Stooped with sorrow, she turned her back on Kea, pulled the hood over her head and left the room.

***

A couple of hours passed and Luke's gang walked doggedly onwards. Goby led the way wielding a heavy hammer. Luke wondered if it was a weapon or a tool, and then decided that it was probably both. Stuart and his spears followed just behind, while he and Limpet made tracks side by side.

They had followed the street as it gently sloped deeper,

but now they traversed a level stretch. It was an easy path compared to the boulder-packed course that he had travelled on the way to Solis Occassum. There was the odd large rock, but these were kilometres apart and were easily avoided and, in fact, somewhat broke the monotony of it all.

When they came across a solid hourglass-shaped pillar, Luke paused. It stretched upwards, but fell tens of metres short of the surface. At its peak, there was some dwindling seaweed that had attempted to survive on a morsel of flailing sunlight, which was almost hair-like, giving the overall impression of an armless rock giant. Even more interesting were the creatures that gracefully circled the pillar. They were like legless toads bordered by frilly skirts with bundles of squid-like tentacles for mouths and marbles, swirled blue and black, for eyes.

'Cuttlefish,' Limpet identified, upon seeing Luke staring with wonder.

'Really?' Luke said. '*Those* are cuttlefish?' Washed up on the beaches back on Earth, he had often come across a cuttlefish bone or two. They were brittle, elongated ovals of white with a polystyrene-like texture. He had seen them dangling in budgie cages to be pecked and played with. Now he stood below the bizarre creatures to which such bones belonged and would never have put the two together. They spiralled lazily about as if without a care in the world.

'They're mighty tasty,' Goby shouted from afar.

Luke was immediately hit by a wave of unease at the prospect of eating one and at hunting such seemingly harmless creatures.

'Don't worry, we won't eat any unless we get really desperate,' Goby grinned, winking at the two lagging crew members. 'Come on, hurry up!'

As they set off from the pillar, a flicker of motion caught Luke's eye. In the very corner of his vision, he could have sworn that he had seen a shadow swiftly duck behind a distant boulder. He squinted in its general direction. Before he could spare his suspicions any thought, an entirely different source of movement distracted his attention; a small spec, wiggling towards their party from the direction of Naufragium. As it got closer, Luke was cheered to recognise an old friend. Jaws. The orange fish darted around him in greeting and then swam ahead to Stuart. Limpet and Goby saw their new addition and bowed their heads ceremoniously.

'What's all that about?' questioned Luke, bemused.

Limpet shrugged, 'Everyone does it to Videre fish.' Luke motioned for her to go on. 'There are some people who say the sea is a being, rather than a collection of water. They call him the Lord of the Sea,' she expanded with an air of disdain. 'They believe that Videre fish give him the ability of sight. In ancient stories, these fish always pass on supreme gifts to those worthy.'

'I'm sure this one followed us to Solis Occassum *and* came to see me that time in the meadoweed fields,' Luke declared.

'I doubt that!' Limpet scoffed. 'They all look *very* similar. Chances are it was a different fish.'

'Maybe,' said Luke, unconvinced. He glanced ahead at Stuart and they shared a meaningful look.

'Come on, you two!' shouted Goby, waving them onwards. 'We don't have time for religious debates. Just take it as a good omen for our quest.'

Limpet picked up her speed to catch up with the rest. Luke followed, but laid his hand out flat as he did so. The Videre fish settled on to his palm with a practiced flourish, watching him with golden eyes. It was Jaws and he knew it. The fish's gaze sent a murmur of recognition through his body. It reminded him of something else, but he could not pin what. He tried desperately to follow that trail of thought but found that only confusion waited at the end.

Meanwhile, the memory of the mysterious disappearing shadow dissipated like smoke from a candle.

***

'How much further?' Limpet asked.

Luke had been wondering the exact same for the past two hours. The question had been bouncing around his head, but he had been determined not to voice it for fear of sounding like a tired child. Now that Limpet had given in to the urge, he felt some relief and listened eagerly for the answer.

Stuart clambered up a small rock to gain a better view while Goby stopped short, tugging at his neckerchief in agitation. 'Not far, I think,' Goby replied hesitantly. 'This journey is new to me, but I reckon we will find John's path before we have to rest.'

'What are we looking for?' Luke questioned.

'Dark scar,' stated Stuart.

The three other crew members looked at him in confusion, and then noticed he was pointing at something in the distance. They quickly joined him on his perch and stared out to the emptiness. Only soft, flat sand and bits of rock. But, what was that? It was tough to distinguish, but sure enough, Luke could see a trickle of black streaking across the horizon as though the land had been cut open by some mighty sword. The intensity of its darkness owed to something other than the coming of night. Goby grinned and patted Stuart on the back. The wolfman frowned up at him and gave an unsociable growl.

'That'll be it,' he agreed, 'we head towards, as our friend here so elegantly describes it, the dark scar.'

'But what is it?' said Limpet and Luke simultaneously.

'You'll see when we get there,' said Goby mysteriously, scrabbling off the rock and onwards. Stuart used one of his spear handles to aid his descent and followed suit.

'I wish he'd just tell us,' grumbled Limpet quietly. Luke tended to agree. They continued their journey, already feeling worn out from their first day's travel. The 'dark scar' was actually further than expected and took a painfully long time to reach, almost as though they were walking on a conveyor belt running in the opposite direction. The team had split into pairs; Stuart and Goby stormed doggedly in front, while Limpet and Luke wearily tried to keep up. Jaws swam in-between, seeming a bird having to keep pace with a snail. As he had many times before, Luke envied the Videre fish's ability to swim. They completed the last stint in determined silence, keeping their eyes pinned on their destination.

At one point, they passed a small mound of rock with a menacing owner; a spiked fish with rough scales and a black-striped tail. It studied them from two wells of tar that sunk into either side of a head as rough as sandpaper. Its mouth was downturned in a way that conveyed its ill will to any passers-by. As they edged around it, Limpet's gelata briefly cast its ugly features into light. Although small in size, it sent a shiver down Luke's spine; he could not help but fear what else lurked in the dim.

Other than that, their slog was rather uneventful. As darkness grew, Limpet and Luke lost sight of their companions and, instead, followed Stuart's gelata, always bobbing ahead as if to taunt them. When it started swaying back and forth on the spot, they knew that Stuart and Goby had finally stopped.

On joining them, Stuart gave a grunt of greeting. He was sat down on the sand contently feeding his colourful mantis shrimp. It had crawled from his eye socket to the seabed and seemed to be joyously spearing a soft worm. Limpet gave the scene a glance and then walked through the camp as if it was nothing special. Perhaps to her, it wasn't; she had, after all, grown up with people entwined with weird and wonderful sea creatures. Luke absent-mindedly touched the barnacles that had popped up on his chest. Would he be considered freakish when he got home? *If* he got home?

'Whoa!' Limpet exclaimed. She looked dwarfed standing next to Goby's towering figure, let alone next to the monstrous 'dark scar' over which they were both currently gawping. Stuart's simple description did not do it justice; before them was a wide canyon that dropped into a sheer chasm of darkness. The light of the gelata was only just sufficient to expose the other side. The depth was palpable, like the feeling of insignificance one gets when looking up at the stars and moon.

'We're heading... down there?' Luke was chilled.

'Well you wanted to go deeper,' said Limpet.

'That's deep. *Really* deep.'

'I reckon so,' said Goby, squinting at tomorrow's task with dread. He briskly turned and sat beside Stuart beneath the tethered gelatas.

Luke tiptoed beyond Limpet and to the very edge. He peered down into the abyss with rising trepidation. He had no idea how far the cliff fell before it reached another seabed or how they would find their way down. He felt a hand clasp at his own and tug him back tenderly. He gave Limpet a wobbly smile. Together they returned to camp and tethered their gelata to Stuarts', allowing the two jelly-creatures to bob together companionably. Luke untied his sword belt; the hefty weapon dropped mercifully to the floor. The crew formed a crude ring around the gelatas with Jaws settling bang in the middle.

'Too late to find John's path,' Goby judged through a mouthful of meadoweed. 'We'll look for it on the morrow. Now it's time to eat up and rest.'

'You won't find me complaining,' Limpet said, massaging her sore feet. 'I feel like I've walked through a field of sea urchins.'

Goby and Luke gave an appreciative laugh.

And so the crew settled down for the night, trying not to think about what lay ahead. Luke thought about asking for some sword practice, but felt too taxed by the hike. Some weak chatter ensued before sleep entirely engulfed the tired adventurers. Limpet wondered how Naufragium was preparing for the coming battle. Goby spoke of an ivory pipe he had recently dug up. He described how it had been carved to look like a creature with large ears and a long nose. Luke suspected he knew what it was, but had already started dozing off. He fell asleep under Stuart's watchful eye, his head cushioned by the leathery softness of his mermaid's purse.

***

Luke woke after a full and dreamless sleep. Stuart had kept watch for the majority of the night and Goby had felt it pointless to split the remainder into three short shifts. Appreciating the extra kip, Luke mumbled his thanks drowsily, nibbled some seaweed for breakfast, and wearily got to his feet.

Limpet was already up and about, trailing the canyon's edge in search of John's path. The morning had revealed a splattering of red sponges that lined both cliff sides like fungus along an overturned tree trunk. They grew out from the rock as if trying to form a bridge to the other side. The chasm's blackness was no less foreboding in the watery daylight. In fact, the stark comparison between their camp and their destination was more prominent, filling Luke with dread.

'If there is a path around here, I can't see it!' called Limpet.

'Which way?' Stuart queried.

'As I see it,' Goby reckoned, 'we'll have to walk along the edge, keeping our eyes peeled. There are only two options that I can see, left or right. From what I recall of the map, my gut says we should head left. And my gut serves me well more often than not.'

Luke shrugged. 'If that's your instinct, we should follow it.'

'Part of me wishes that we don't find it,' Goby admitted. 'I'm no coward, but that place frightens me more than any trawler ever has.'

Having expected Goby to be a source of reassurance, Luke found the man's confession disgruntling.

'Left,' instructed Stuart, as though this command

would extinguish their doubts. They packed up their camp in a matter of minutes; one of the advantages of travelling light with only food and weapons as luggage. Luke took his turn holding one of the gelatas. The jelly-creature seemed to tug more strongly on its tether, as if unwilling to continue. Its pulsing light illuminated the deathly drop that they carefully skirted.

Like the rest of the crew, all of Luke's concentration was dedicated to searching for a way down. However, he could not help but notice the enormity of the deep sea sponges that protruded from the canyon; they took on a variety of shapes and were huge compared to those he had seen at the Coral Gardens. One was particularly impressive, a thick vein that sprouted from the edge and slithered its way down into darkness, like a colossal rind of orange peel stuck to the cliff face. He judged it to be about a metre wide and could only wonder at its length. Looking at the rest of the team members, he realised that in their search for a path they had entirely ignored this spectacle. He pointed it out to Limpet.

'That's massive!' she gasped.

'Isn't it?' he said, pleased that even *she* was in awe despite her underwater upbringing. Then a thought occurred. 'Might be big enough to walk on.'

'Surely you aren't thinking what I *think* you're thinking?' she exclaimed.

Luke grimaced and called to Stuart and Goby. The two leading team members backtracked to their location. Jaws hovered above the sponge, followed it down slightly and then returned which Luke took to be a good sign. His inkling of an idea swelled with confidence.

'What is it, Lugworm?' Goby said.

'I think I've found our path,' he suggested, indicating the trickle of colour that flowed down the canyon side.

'You cannot be serious,' started Goby. 'That's a deathwish, not a path.'

'Not in a conventional sense, no,' Luke levelled, 'but

maybe we're not looking properly. John himself is only going by an ancient map. He has never actually followed the trail before.'

'But Lugworm, I don't think that could hold any one of us, let alone all of us,' Limpet complained.

'And who knows how far that goes down,' added Goby, shaking his head. 'Could be a dead end.'

'I know, but we won't know unless we try,' he replied sulkily. 'We have to – ' Whatever he had been about to say died on his lips as he noticed that Stuart had nonchalantly strolled onto the sponge and was already edging his way down. Jaws followed gleefully, orbiting the second gelata as if it was some kind of planet. The rest observed, stunned by both amazement and fear for their companion.

'Safe,' said Stuart softly, not even looking back at them. Eyes wide, Goby slapped a hand to his forehead. Luke and Limpet reluctantly stepped out onto the sponge; it did not budge. Single file, they followed Stuart downwards. Goby knew he would have to join them or be left in pitch black. He muttered a curse and joined his fellows.

***

Once they had caught up with Stuart, they formed a huddled line. Fear clamped their mouths shut. The sponge path seemed to go on and on. It was smooth, but sporadically steep, forcing the crew members to put their feet sideways to avoid slips. Luke was all too aware that if one of them started to slide, chances are they would fall into the endless pit and take everyone else in front with them.

Their path constantly reminded them that it had not grown for their benefit; a collage of sponges constantly obstructed their path. At one point, they had to crouch beneath flat discs of growth that unfolded in front of them. At another, a giant, pale elephant-ear of sponge intruded their route. Stuart went first, sucking in his hairy stomach, gripping its knobbly parts as handholds and leaning precariously over certain death, before finally reaching the other side. Everyone else let out a breath of relief and then, one by one, cautiously followed. Jaws evaded everything with ease, making a mockery of their struggle.

In front, the tubular sponge carried on into the depths, showing no sign of stopping short. Luke shivered. The temperature had plummeted and he could feel the cold pressing on him from all sides like skeletal hands stroking his skin.

Somewhere along their journey, a scatter of cliff debris trickled down on their heads. They stopped their progress and looked up suspiciously. Stuart voiced what was at the forefront of everyone's minds. 'Followed.'

'Perhaps,' Goby acknowledged. 'I thought I saw a movement a while ago, but convinced myself it was just my imagination.'

'Me too,' Luke piped up. There was a silence as they wondered what could be tracking them.

'Nothing we can do about it now,' said Goby. 'Guess we'll just have to be extra vigilant tonight once we've set up camp.'

Stuart grunted and led the way. Underfoot, Luke noticed that the sponge had gone from smooth orange to coarse black. He asked Limpet and she explained that they were now walking along a carcass. Luke likened it to the skin left behind by a snake. It was still strong, but entirely lifeless. The cliff-face growths, that had been so abundant before, withered and died. The opposite side of the canyon suffered a similar fate as if life itself had hit some invisible barrier. Luke guessed the only reason they still had something to stand on was because the sponge's size had protected it from centuries of decay.

Down and down they went, away from the surface. Darkness clouded everything in every direction. An icy realisation shook Luke to the very core; they were entirely dependent on their gelatas. Without them, they would be blind and finding their way back to the surface would be impossible.

Stuart was the only person who was unfazed by their situation; the man seemed to stroll as though taking a walk in the park. Then, to Luke's great shock, he jumped off the sponge with *both feet*, only to land on a different surface moments later; sand.

Relief washed through him; they had made it to the base of the canyon. Whether it had been the path John intended or not, the sponge had led them to the seabed. The eerie silence of the place made cheering seem inappropriate. Instead, Luke buried his feet in the sand and scrunched them up in appreciation. Goby gave him a short pat on the back and Limpet briefly squeezed his hand.

'This way,' Stuart whispered. Even he, it seemed, was not entirely unaffected by the ominous tension that thrummed through the water. 'No camp here.'

Luke had heard that after feeling fear for so long, people become numb. It seemed to him that he had reached that state as they padded their way along a stream of sand sandwiched between two mammoth cliffs.

The canyon's width fluctuated wildly, going from being spacious enough for them all to walk side by side to jamming them back into single file. On one occasion, the cliff faces almost kissed, leaving a mere crack in the rock for them to squeeze through. Eventually, and at long last, the cliffs bid farewell to each other and split away at right angles. The canyon was no more.

'Welcome to the Abyssal Plain,' said Goby, gesturing dramatically at what appeared to be an expanse of nothingness. The gelata's light only showed a snippet of the flat field of sand that spread out in front.

'Where do we go now?' asked Limpet.

Goby turned to Luke. 'Up to him. It's his quest after all.'

Luke bridled, not expecting this sudden responsibility. He had gone from follower to leader with a heartbeat's notice. Goby, Limpet and Stuart looked at him expectantly. 'We're tired,' he started, 'and I think it must be evening.' Stuart nodded encouragingly. 'So, I think we should set up camp for the night and then decide in the morning. Whenever that might be.'

'Good idea,' said Limpet, gratefully sprawling out on the floor and getting comfortable. Stuart withdrew a scrap of material from his pack and wrapped the gelatas, dimming their light somewhat. Luke gave him a questioning look. 'Draws attention,' the wolfman explained. Of course. Gelatas were helpful, but, down here, they were also beacons, alerting other creatures to their presence. If there were any creatures to alert, thought Luke grimly. They gathered around this weak light in much the same way that people huddle around a bonfire.

After they had enjoyed their fill of meadoweed, Luke asked Goby to show him some moves with the sword. Now that they were back on solid ground, the man seemed to have recovered his bravery and was happy to help. A very basic practice session ensued, as they only had one sword between them. Goby settled for using one of Stuart's spears, gripping it about halfway up to shorten its reach.

To get Luke used to the sword's weight, they started by swiping at each other gently with no force at all. Later Goby taught him how to stand and move with the weapon; the whole situation reminded Luke of two dancers circling in candlelight. It must have looked comical because Limpet could not contain her laughter.

They ended their training on defence. Goby attacked Luke from as many angles as possible, encouraging him to battle off the assault. Luke tried his best, thwacking the spear away frantically. Even at Goby's lessened speed, one or two got passed, knocking him on the head and chest. Tomorrow, he would have more than one bruise. To his surprise, his injuries received a light-hearted grunt from Stuart which *could* have been a chuckle. So rare was this that Luke had to smile at his own incompetence. By the time they had finished, both Goby and Luke were panting heavily.

'Good start,' Goby said. 'I'll make an acceptable swordsman of you soon enough. Take the first watch and keep trying those moves.'

'Yes sir,' Luke mock saluted, feeling like a recruit. Limpet laughed. Regardless of the gloomy circumstances, the mood seemed to have improved.

'Any ideas of where we will go tomorrow?' Limpet asked.

The exercise had made Luke feel more alive and, this time, he had an answer for her. 'John said to take a bearing and follow it, so that's what we'll do. That way, we'll know how to get back.'

'Okay, sounds like,' she yawned, 'a plan to me.'

'Get some sleep,' Luke advised. No one hesitated. Luke kept watch over his crew and practiced his weaponry.

***

A few hours later, Luke was desperately wishing he had been wearing a watch when he was abducted. He was not sure how long his shift should be *or* who he should wake to take over him. Before long, he tired of swordplay and resigned himself to sitting cross-legged on the floor. Beyond their camp, there was nothing to see.

Instead, he glanced at Limpet. In sleep, the scowl that so often creased her forehead was nowhere to be seen. Her hair flowed over her mermaid's purse and escaped across the sand. The sight reminded him of when he had first caught her relaxing in the Coral Gardens. Then his thoughts led on to their night visit and the closeness of their hug. If only he could return to that very moment! He shook the longing away; this was no time to be distracted. Naufragium was in peril and they were in great danger.

A bright glow abruptly disrupted his contemplation. It approached from the canyon, making the crack in the cliff seem like a fork of lightning. Luke leapt to his feet, unsheathing his sword and holding it aloft. Ever alert, Stuart heard this and was poised with a spear in no time at all.

'Wake up,' Luke shouted, his voice rife with alarm.

Limpet and Goby hastily roused from their slumber. One wielded a dagger; the other held a hefty hammer.

As the mysterious glow bobbed out of the canyon, its source became clear.

'Gelata,' identified Stuart.

As it neared, a rope could be seen leading from the gelata to an outstretched fist. Something made Luke step towards the oncoming danger. His eyes could just about make out a figure. Light bounced off a bald head. A horrible streak of scarred skin tissue divided a suspicious frown. The figure's eyes were shadowed, as was his barrel-like chest, but Luke knew who had been following their quest.

'Ello Wormy,' grated Con.

CHAPTER 19: THE ABYSSAL PLAIN

All but Luke lowered their weapons in confusion. A series of questions ricocheted around his brain, but Goby was the first to speak. He shoved past Luke. 'What the bloody hell are you doing here?'

'I'm here because of him, of course,' growled Con, throwing a glare in Luke's direction. 'Bringing war to our town and then creeping off on some fictional quest. Did you really think I'd let him slip away?'

Perhaps it was the flickering light of the gelata, but Luke could swear there was a mad tint to his eyes beyond the rage that so often frequented them.

'You shouldn't have come,' shouted Goby, his moustache quivering with fury. 'Naufragium is in peril. You should be helping build defences, not following us pointlessly into the Abyss.'

'Don't take me for a fool, Goby. I've left Brittle in charge and told him exactly what to do.'

'Brittle!' Limpet scoffed. 'He's still nursing a broken leg after the trawler attack!'

'He can still give instructions, can't he?' snapped Con. 'Besides, aren't you glad that *one* of us has the clarity to see that Lugworm here is playing you all?'

'That's not true!' said Luke adamantly. 'What do you think we're doing in this place, if not searching for aquaseed?'

'As if we'd be down here for any other reason,' added Limpet, gesturing around at the lifeless expanse.

There was a moment, ever so brief, that Con looked confused and seemed to sway slightly on the spot. Then he set his jaw and the angry frown returned. 'It seems obvious to me. This place is perfect for one thing and one thing alone - escape. All Lugworm here would have to do is wake in the night, take the gelatas and stroll away, leaving the rest of you spongeheads for dead.'

Luke looked around at his crew; did he see a flicker of uncertainty in Goby's face or was it just his paranoia?

'Besides,' Con continued, 'Solis Occassum can't just summon a fleet from nowhere. They'll need fresh turtleoak. Which means... they still have to build their ships.'

'Perhaps,' admitted Goby.

'That will take days. How long do you think this quest is going to last?' Con put another dent in their mission. 'You only have so much food. And goodness knows you aren't going to find any down *here*. I wager I can see this through to the end and still return to Naufragium before war begins.'

'Fine,' Goby relented, rubbing his brow in exasperation. 'Whatever your reasons, you're here now. What next?'

Con ignored him and turned his attention to Luke. They met eyes and, once again, Luke saw that there was something slightly wrong there, as if Con could not quite focus properly. 'Last time I put my trust in you, Wormy, it cost our town greatly. I won't be making that mistake again. I'm going to watch you and make sure that you either complete your quest, or die trying. And if you try to escape, I'll split you from head to toe.'

Con waved his sharp scimitar threateningly, causing Stuart to step in front of Luke with a snarl. Con eyed Luke's guard and was undaunted. 'Looks like you've got a loyal pet, Wormy, but it changes nothing. He won't be able to protect you forever, and, if it comes to it, I won't hesitate to end you both.'

Jaws flitted about, clearly agitated by all the noise.

'Now, now, none of us wants anyone to get hurt,' Goby said as calmly as he could and holding his hands up in a vain attempt to dispel the tension. 'Con, as I see it, we could do with some backup in this dark place. However, try anything towards Lugworm or Stuart without reason and you'll have to answer for your crimes back in Naufragium.'

'What are you, a sheriff now?' Con said.

'No sir, not a sheriff, just a man trying to keep the peace,' replied Goby. 'Speaking of which, we all need to get some more rest before tomorrow.'

'You go ahead,' the madman invited, crushing some headrush seaweed between his teeth. 'When I said I'm not taking my eyes off Wormy, I meant it.'

Goby shrugged and turned away, returning to camp. The others stood in an awkward silence momentarily and then joined him. Luke was about to resume his post when Stuart tapped him on the shoulder. 'You sleep now. I watch.'

Luke felt too much adrenaline pumping through his veins to settle, but he tried. As he collapsed to the sand, so did his mood. Con had sunk his venomous teeth into the crew, breaking bonds and tainting friendships. Luke could not bear to look at his fellow's expressions for fear of what he might see. At least he could be confident that Stuart would protect him from any subtle knives. He turned away and looked into the dark. No matter where he positioned himself, he could feel Con's distrusting gaze on his person. Sleep did not come easy.

***

The morning, if it can be so called in a place without dawn, came too soon. After he had hardly slept a wink, Luke felt one of Stuart's spear handles jabbing his side. It was time to continue the quest. Still half-asleep, he turned away and fumbled open his mermaid's purse. From within, he withdrew John's compass and held it out flat.

But which direction should they go? And why? Fact is, it seemed foolish to select a bearing on a whim. He was very aware that whichever way he decided would determine the outcome of the quest. After Con's vicious words, he wondered if his crew would even listen to him anymore. He surveyed the people around him: Goby was absent-mindedly staring at the sand, Limpet was having breakfast and Stuart was unpinning the gelatas. Not far away, Con sat like a grotesque gargoyle, maintaining his steadfast watch. But, where was Jaws?

Barely within sight, a dash of orange hanged in the water. The Videre fish was moving just enough to keep it suspended and, in every manner, appeared to be waiting. Still sitting down, Luke shuffled around to face him. South. Jaws wanted to go south. It was only slightly preferable than picking a random bearing, but Luke lacked any better ideas. He slowly got to his feet, strapped his sword to his waist, and donned his backpack. With all the positivity he could muster, he addressed his crew. 'I think we should head south.'

'For how long?' Goby asked, glancing up wearily.

Luke had not been expecting this question at all. 'Until we either find aquaseed or run out of food.'

'That could only be a couple of days, taking into account the return journey,' said Goby.

'Two days searching is better than none,' Luke persisted.

'It's as good a plan as any!' said Limpet.

At this, Con gave an incredulous guffaw. His disbelief echoed around the camp and chilled the crew even more than the unforgiving cold.

'We go,' was all that Stuart said, ignoring Con and spurring everyone into action. One by one, they gathered their stuff and rose to their feet. Goby pressed a callous gelata rope into Luke's spare hand and motioned him to lead the way. Luke gritted his teeth and set off. He did not look behind him to see if anyone followed.

From the canyon path, they reluctantly walked further

into the abyss. Jaws wavered about in front – a beacon of hope in a dreary place. The gelata's light had a very limited reach. It was like being on a stage and not seeing anything beyond the spotlight. What could be seen did not fill Luke with confidence. The sand upon which they tread was flat and repetitive. There were no rocks covered with life, no marine plants flourishing and no sound of the waves above. A few minute bits of shell debris had been unfortunate enough to fall down to these absurd depths. Here and there, his footsteps would reveal a worm, making a life on scraps of death.

'Where sunlight has no power...' Limpet said from just over his shoulder.

'What?'

'The clue for finding aquaseed,' she reminded him.

'Oh yeah,' he said. 'Now we just need to be where *the ground reigns...*'

'Way I see it,' she said with a cheeky grin, 'we're already half-way there!'

Even here, where all was doom and gloom, she brought a smile to his face.

'Good point. It's only a matter of time now!' he responded, jokingly.

'Is that my father's compass?'

Luke nodded.

'Would you show me how to use it? Dad told me once, a long time ago, but I have forgotten.'

And so Luke passed on the knowledge gifted to him by John. Limpet was amazed at the unruly gadget and how its needle always pointed in the same direction. Although he thought it basic, to her it was the closest thing to magic. Luke was pleased to take his mind off the quest and found that talking with Limpet quickened the passing of time. Behind, Stuart followed silently, while Goby and Con conversed with muffled voices.

***

Through misted eyes, Cornelius watched two brutes of muscle plop a large table in front of where he stood. They were jeering at each other in a way that he despised. Such simpletons. His back ached as he removed the blueprint from his cloak and leaned over to spread it open. He rarely frequented the beach, but today he had no other option. It was the sand he hated. It found its way everywhere, contaminating everything. Then there was the smell – the musk of sweat, hardwork and poverty. The sooner he returned to the rich quarters, the better.

He could have sent a messenger, but dared not trust someone to carry out such a vital task. It had to be *him* that spoke to the master craftsman. Anyone else would misunderstand, disfigure his words and ruin his vision. He scanned the area with disdain. Where was that jumped up peasant? That carpenter who had been given the false impression that he was *master* of anything? Cornelius did not even know what he looked like, such was the rarity of his dealings with the mongrels at the rear end of the mountain.

A glint of sunlight caught him in the eye. He scowled and bought a trembling hand up to act as a sunshade. A shiny crown cantered down the road. It was Rex. He approached, riding in on a meaty warhorse. His idiot of a guard trailed behind. What was his name? Chuck. That was it. How Cornelius loathed him! It was not his size or his piggy eyes that justified such detest. Nor was it the sheer air-headed nature with which he wobbled about, heedlessly carrying out every whim of an order. It was his stupidity. Cornelius was surprised that Rex did not ride Chuck down the mountain. He would have sniggered at the very thought if he could do so without starting a coughing fit. Chuck, after all, had ruined *everything*. He had let loose the most important specimen that Cornelius had ever known; the amphibious boy.

Rex was not much better. But at least *he* had a small interest in science. Many a question he had asked on their late night drinking sessions of whisky. But Cornelius knew what truly interested his King all too well – the art of war. That was why he was here now, uninvited. To see the weapon that Cornelius had concocted to destroy an underwater city and its sea filth. He gave them a sickly smile as they approached.

'My King,' he said, bending delicately down to one knee. 'To what do I owe the pleasure?' He already knew, of course he did.

'Get up, old man,' Rex commanded, sweat dripping down his sideburns and off his chin. 'I'm here to see this weapon you promised.'

Promised in exchange for the boy, Cornelius wanted to say. It would have done no good. As rich and famous as he was, only Rex was invulnerable to having his head chopped off. 'Yes, my King. I am just about to explain my blueprint to the Master Craftsman, but I can't find that darn man.'

'Right here,' a female voice said haughtily.

A woman? Cornelius tried not to let the disbelief show on his wart-lined face. As if this morning could not get any worse. 'Good,' he said curtly. 'Now get over here.' To Rex and Chuck he was somewhat more polite. 'Gather round this table if it pleases you my King and I shall tell you my plans.'

'I'm sure they shall be destructive,' said Rex eagerly, dismounting his steed. A smug grin from Chuck sent a shiver of annoyance through Cornelius's crooked bones.

'Are you listening?' he asked the woman in a tone that seemed to question whether she had ears at all.

'Yes,' she replied shortly. Her jaw, he noticed, was tense with anger at how he treated her. Good. She had fire. Unlike his pathetic excuse for a wife. For a brief second, he wondered where Margaret had disappeared to, but found that he did not really care.

'As well as the giant ships you are already building, I want you to build these devices here,' he pointed to the central drawing. 'Make them of normal wood so they sink like a stone and attach them to the backs of the ships with sturdy metal chains. They need to be able to be deployed off the stern when the time is right.

'As you can see, they look like, how can I put this in terms you will understand?' He gave Rex a sly look. 'Rolling pins. Yes, rolling pins with savage spikes on them.'

He was pleased to get a chuckle for his jest at the master craftsman's expense.

'As the ships are blown forward, these will rotate and make mincemeat of both the rotten wrecks and any fool who gets in the way. The underwater town will be no more.'

Rex rubbed his clammy hands together, grinning in anticipation.

'That would have to be a very powerful wind,' mentioned the woman.

Cornelius was surprised. A show of intelligence. He had, of course, already thought of that, but the comment led him smoothly on to the next aspect of his plan. 'The next gale-force wind, to be precise. My weather instruments tell me that it will be here in seven days and will send the fleet south. If we line up, say, twenty ships with twenty killer rolling pins to the north of the wreck site, it will take us over the area and carnage will occur. We will not leave a stone unturned.'

'Seven days,' Rex groaned impatiently.

'Yes, sir. By which time, your fleet shall be ready. We will send the ships out, deploy the weapons and sails, and then wait for the first strong gust.'

'Won't that make us vulnerable to attack?' the woman pointed out.

How dare she question him? He let his voice fill with disregard. 'They won't even know we are there. Besides, what would they do? Aside from that one mutant, it's not like they can jump aboard and attack. They will be helpless.'

'Stirling plan, Cornelius,' Rex assessed. 'It shall be like ploughing a flower bed full of puny weeds.'

He tried not to grimace at such a basic analogy of his plan. 'Yes, sir. Well put, sir.'

'I have one request,' said his King, holding up a pudgy finger with a silver signet ring.

'Sir?'

'I want to have the largest ship of the fleet.'

'Of course, my King.'

'And... I want to cause the most destruction.'

'Your ship shall be the most brutal, sir.'

'And I want them to know which ship belongs to the King. When I roll over their town and loved ones, they must fear Rex Solomon.'

One request? Cornelius mentally scoffed. Counting was not one of Rex's skills and he was not going to correct him. 'Maybe a golden anchor, sir?' he suggested.

'Yes, that will do nicely. Right in the centre of the fleet.'

Cornelius sneered at the woman. 'Can *you* manage that?'

'I can,' she said tersely.

'Excellent,' Rex summarised. 'It shall be a day that will go down in history. I'm off for a celebratory drink. Will you join me, Cornelius?'

'Sadly, I must decline.' As if those crude words were the entirety of his plan! 'I shall stay here and iron out the fine details with the... Craftsman.'

'How *boring*,' his King drawled. 'Come on, Chuck. Back to the palace. All this thinking has made me thirsty!'

Cornelius watched as the fool and his gullible crony galloped away. How he envied their escape from this unbearable pit. During the conversation, a tickling in the back of his throat had become incessant. In Rex's presence, he had resisted, but now he indulged. Specks of spit flew in every direction as he spluttered and splurged. Once he had finished coughing, he craned his neck towards the Master Craftsman and beckoned her by wiggling a wormy finger. Commanding her to listen, he spent the next hour giving a lecture on the full extent of his plan.

He detailed the required materials, the precise measurements and the dynamics for the creation of his weapon. Like dealing with a schoolchild, he got her to repeat his words. When she could not, he gave her a quill and paper with which to write his exact instructions. Her face went from angry to irritated, and finally to exhaustion as he hammered his vision into her brain. It was like bashing two stones together to create fire. He would make a formidable tool out of her, whether she liked it or not. By the end, he had suffered several coughing fits and his voice had become painfully weak. But, all in all, he was satisfied that he'd done his job properly.

The relief on the woman's face when his assault was over made him feel a flash of anger. She should have been flattered by his attention. Having given his orders, he started hobbling up the mountain to his luxurious mansion. He could not bear horse riding. To aid his assent, he had an intricately carved silver cane with a large ruby at its head. He left the bustle of the construction behind. The ring of hammer on anvil had given him a pounding headache.

To distract himself from the cries of the hungry, he mulled over his master plan. Nobody knew about it, not even his King. It would be talked about for centuries. He was famous enough already from his ground-breaking discoveries, but his time on this planet was running out. He knew what was in store. Younger scientists would inevitably move into his field and further his hard work. They would take credit for *his* breakthroughs. Eventually he would be forgotten in a bundle of ancient scrolls, gathering cobwebs in the hidden archives of the palace library.

He wanted, *needed*, to do something extreme. Something that would propel him from a feeble ink figure to a permanent statue of legend. A story that would be passed down through the ages. Excited children would whisper his name, parents would toast to his existence and there would be a day dedicated to celebrating his ingeniousness.

His legacy waited. He would recapture the amphibious boy.

CHAPTER 20: DELIRIUM

There was almost too much to watch. Garth was struggling to decide where he should focus his attention.

He considered watching over Luke – the brave adventurer was travelling into the unknown where simply anything could be waiting. Unfortunately, the darkness of his location rendered Garth's scouting completely useless; Luke would have to fend for himself.

He concluded that his efforts would be better spent spying. As Solis Occassum were the ones attacking, it seemed logical that if he managed to stop them, war would be averted. But how? He was clueless.

With a single thought, he teleported from watching over Luke to floating above the horseshoe bay, where he immediately heard the sound of sawing wood and the clang of hammers. Penn had taught him how to cleverly lay 'anchors' throughout the world; a rock on the beach, Kea's rustic music player, Luke's new shell and also, as a new addition, the half deteriorated steering wheel in John's shipwreck abode. It was hard to describe, but each item became a small section in his mind, and, by accessing each one, he could now jump from location to location with ease.

Any smugness that he felt at his new-found skill was quickly replaced by dismay from what he saw on that golden bay. The people of Solis Occassum were not wasting time – the fleet was forming. An unfamiliar gritty fellow yelled orders, thrusting a soot-covered finger at one person and then the next. Garth watched as the husks of several ships appeared, fashioned from shells of turtles. He could hear the dreadful cries of the poor turtleoak turtles that either awaited death, or were well on their way.

Further down the beach, huge cylinders of forest wood were constructed. Trees were hauled down, chopped, and nailed, to meet Cornelius' specifications. At one section of the worksite, blacksmiths appeared to hit metal without aim, yet produced meticulously identical spikes. Once finished, these were piled in spacious cauldrons and added to the weapon that would plough through Naufragium.

The work was relentless. He had already witnessed this many times, day and night. Garth supposed they must rest in shifts, ensuring that there were always enough people to further the fleet. He gulped. There would be no delay. The weapon being produced would be unstoppable. A decision was made.

He had to contact John. It was time to evacuate Naufragium.

***

As practiced, Garth accessed that small part of his mind dedicated to that half-rotten, crumbling steering wheel that had once directed a beautiful ship with billowing sails, but now found itself at the bottom of the sea, soldered in place by rust, algae and sheer disuse.

Abruptly he saw John cradling his head over his table. Garth was no expert on human nature, but the bearded man seemed distressed. His only company was the female known as Shrimp who sat, mute, nearby. The yellow shell, given to him by Luke, was resting on the side. Garth sent a brainwave through the helmet and it started to glow blue.

'Look!' Shrimp uttered. 'Look! Look!'

John wearily raised his head and then jolted when realisation struck. It seemed to Garth that he reached out to the shell reluctantly, like a man daring himself to get as close to a fire as possible. When he did finally grasp the shell, he held it aloft allowing the blue light to fill his home and reflect off of Shrimp's wondrous stare.

'Who are you?' John demanded.

'*A friend of Luk – I mean, Lugworm's.*'

Garth sent his voice directly into his mind, which must have been a surprise as the man acted as though he had been given an electric shock, dropping the shell on the table in the process. He heard John take an uneven breath as though steeling himself against the absurdity of what was happening, before finally making contact once more. 'Do you know how my Limpet is?'

'*They made it to the Abyssal Plain as planned and are continuing their search for aquaseed.*'

'Phew!' exclaimed John with a small smile of relief. 'What have you got to tell me?'

Straight to business. Garth liked this. 'Naufragium must be evacuated.'

'Not an option,' he responded abruptly.

'It may have to be. Rex is building ships that are designed to *destroy*. They will line up three days from now to the north of Naufragium. Rotating blades will be dragged across the seabed and through the town. There will be no chance to defend. It will be a slaughter.'

'You sure about that?'

'I can see them building. I can hear their plans.'

'By the Sea!' John cursed, clenching his one free fist. 'Con will want to know this.'

Without warning, the man chucked the shell on the table and stormed out, bidding Shrimp to stay put. He sprinted between wrecks, across the shell road and to the eastern side of town. Garth followed above him, curious to see how this information would be received.

As John passed fellow townsmen, Garth noticed that they barely registered him; something did not seem quite right. The bearded man eventually slowed down at one of the wrecks at the very outskirts. It was like no other that Garth had seen. Like the rest of the town wrecks, he suspected it had sunk as a normal warship. Since then, however, it had been decked out to look more like a pirate ship. Skulls were carved into its sides, black seaweed trailed down in the place of sails and hacked-up, wooden guards dotted the sand outside. The harsh clash of weapons could be heard. Above this was a loud voice, dealing out encouraging advice.

On closer inspection, the source of the clamour became obvious. Naufragians of all ages were in the midst of a weapons training drill. Some slashed at wooden dummies that hardly resembled foes anymore. Others turned blunt weapons on their fellows to test their skills. It seemed disorderly to Garth with barely any of the trainees possessing similar weapons. A sword-like piece of iron swiped at a tool that could be called a rake. As much as he admired their gusto, they appeared farmers taking up a dangerous hobby rather than a town preparing for war. At the helm of their training, Garth could see the hulking mussel-ridden shoulders of Elkhorn, who appeared to be in his element as he knocked the Naufragians into shape.

'Elkhorn!' John shouted to be heard over the ruckus. 'I need to talk to Con!'

He received a shrug in response. 'Con's gone, John. Talk to Brittle.'

'What do you mean Con's gone?'

'Talk to Brittle,' Elkhorn repeated adamantly before returning to his task.

John looked outraged and walked through the middle of the duels. He had to halt to allow two sparring women to fight their way across. Once clear, he went through a crumbling gap in the ship's hull. If there was a way onto the deck, it had eroded to nothing many years ago.

Garth peered inside and saw that John's destination had been barred once again. A man with folded arms and a lethal shortsword blocked him from continuing.

'I must talk with Brittle,' John demanded.

'I'm not sure I can let you in, sir,' said the Naufragian awkwardly.

'Why not?'

The bouncer remained silent but did not relent. Garth started to have a sick feeling in his stomach. Had John lost his respect for helping Luke? Had their one ally in Naufragian become powerless?

'Brittle!' The shout from John took Garth off guard. He gave a jump of fright in his mother's chair before refocusing on the events as they unfolded.

'Is that you, John?' said a voice from further within the wreck.

'Course it is! Where's Con? And why won't this spongehead let me in?'

'Are you armed?'

'What?' John seemed puzzled. 'No!'

'Let him in, Eel!' commanded Brittle.

The oaf stepped aside, enabling John to duck his head and enter the pirate ship. He burst through a door-shaped gap, throwing aside trails of string with rings attached. The room he entered reminded Garth of the headquarters of an army operation. Maps of Solis Occassum plastered the curved wreck walls and any sightings of trawlers had been marked. There were a few crude drawings of the trawl ships themselves with big circles to highlight weak points in their design. In addition, some rusty saws hung down within reach for the next attack.

At the far end of the room sat Brittle, sprawled out on a relatively fancy oak chair. Like the ship itself, it was carved to resemble parts of the human skeleton. A skull here, a fleshless hand there. Various names were also engraved. Garth suspected they represented people who had fought for Naufragium and died. Brittle was twirling a downturned dagger and had one leg wrapped in seaweed. John strode towards the young man, dodging a couple of hairy crabs that scurried underfoot.

'Where is Con?' John asked for the thousandth time.

'I'm not meant to say,' said Brittle uncertainly. 'All you need to know is that he left me in charge.'

John gave an exasperated sigh. 'What's all this about, Brittle?

'There have been rumours.'

'What rumours?'

Brittle seemed to have a lot of difficulty saying the next words. 'Nobody's sure whose side you are on anymore. The people of Naufragium, they no longer trust you.'

'I can't believe it! After all that I've done... '

'What do you expect?' Brittle whispered. 'We get an intruder and you help him return to Solis Occassum. Then, when he has brought war to our town, you send him away from here. You knew he would be in danger if he stayed. Our people would have ripped Lugworm apart.'

'They're searching for aquaseed...'

'You and I both know there's nothing down there, John.'

'Do we? I sent my own daughter with him.'

'Limpet has gone too?' It was clear that Brittle had been unaware of this fact.

'Yes. Would I have done that if I doubted Lugworm's loyalty?' he pressed. 'Brittle, I have known you all your life. I have watched you grow up and have hunted alongside you in more fruitful times. You know me. Now, tell me everything that has happened.'

Brittle looked unsure, but soon his defence crumbled. 'Con... he... fed the suspicions against you... ,' Once started, Brittle's words came out in a flurry. 'He was relaxing after a long day of gathering troops. You know Con, he likes to have a bit of sponge. Anyway, he was out of his mind when he found out that Lugworm had gone. Demanded to know where. Put me in charge. And then he set off after him.'

'To kill him?'

'I'm not sure. I don't think *he* even knows.'

'Poseidon's trident!' John looked defeated as he cursed in anger. He rubbed his face and then thought out loud. 'I can't do anything about that. I can only hope that he doesn't harm my daughter, or Lugworm.' He breathed out heavily, trying his utmost to remain reasonable. 'Now, *I* have some information for *you*,' he started. 'Naufragium is in grave danger. It may have to be evacuated.'

'What?' It was Brittle's turn to be shocked. He immediately stopped spinning his dagger and slammed it down on the armchair. 'You know our people won't do that!'

'The land king intends to plough through our town like jelly. Weapons we cannot defend against will be attached to the trawl ships. They know where we live and they have the means to turn our town to rubble. There won't be hand-to-hand combat. If we stay here, we will get caught up in the demolition. We have to – '

'How do you know this?'

A difficult question to answer, Garth thought.

'I just do,' John replied confidently. 'You *have* to trust me.'

A battle of emotions seemed to play across Brittle's face. 'I... can't,' he said reluctantly. 'I'm sorry John. You come in here prophesying our doom, but you've no evidence. Regardless of our history, can you expect me, or anyone else, to believe you?'

John seemed lost for words – the logic in what Brittle said was irrefutable. 'You're right,' he admitted. 'That would be absurd.' Then he appeared to have a revelation. 'Maybe you could send some scouts out to the north? That's where I believe they will strike from.'

'I don't know, John. We're stretched thin as it is.'

'Send some scouts out every day. That's all I ask.'

The young leader studied the bearded veteran. Whatever he saw in John's eyes must have been convincing. 'Okay,' Brittle huffed. 'I will. But don't spread your rumours about. I don't want our troops to get scared for no reason.'

'Very well,' John said. 'Thank you.'

With this, the man took his leave. John had done everything he could, and so had Garth. He had hoped that his information would spur Naufragium to evasive action, but, in reality, it had achieved very little. If Brittle did as John instructed, at least the people of this underwater town would have some warning of the attack. It might just give them the time they needed to escape.

***

'There's sod all out here!' shouted Con, coming to an abrupt halt. Luke glanced behind and noticed that Goby, too, had stopped. He had no choice, but to address their concerns.

Con had harshly spoken the worry that had been gnawing away at Luke throughout the hike. They had been travelling south for at least half a day and they had seen nothing. Truth was, Luke's doubt grew with every step. As a leader, however, it was his duty to maintain the team's morale. Swallowing a bitter brew of his own misgivings, he spoke before Con's negativity could take root.

'The further we go, the greater the chance we'll come across something.'

'And the further we walk from Naufragium,' muttered Goby.

Limpet gave him one of her infamous frowns. 'You knew what you were getting into when you joined this quest! Don't tell me you're having second thoughts now.'

'I owed your father one,' he growled, 'but anyone can see...' His words trailed off, but it was obvious what he meant. This quest was hopeless.

'Who knows what we will yet find!' Luke said. 'Do you give up so easily? Have you forgotten why we are here?'

There was a shamed silence from Goby, but a look of unveiled disdain from Con. A mad sheen could be seen in his rival's eyes and his lower lip seemed to tremble uncontrollably. Luke decided to ignore it. He would save his focus for the people whose help he actually wanted. For some reason, he pictured Kea speaking from Rex's throne as he spoke the next few words. 'We are here to return fish to Naufragium. To help, not only the people we know, but the people who will come for centuries after we have gone. Don't you see?'

More silence.

'This is bigger than the war. If we find aquaseed, our people will be saved.'

'*Our* people?' Con screeched. '*Our people*?'

Luke immediately realised his mistake.

'How dare you?' he seethed. 'You are *not* one of us.'

Like a bull shown a red flag, Con rushed closer. He withdrew his dagger, an evil look in his eyes. Luke answered, sliding forth his sword with a satisfying *shrinnggggg!*

The danger of the situation thrummed in the water. Luke's weapon may have further reach, but he wielded it clumsily. Despite his best attempts to keep it steady, it wobbled. Con, on the other hand, had been brought up to fight and had the scars to show for it. He approached with the coldhearted nature of a man who considered killing as part of his duty.

The meeting of the two nemeses never came to be. Stuart swiftly intervened and smashed a fist into Con's temple. Despite the force of such an attack, it only delayed the man's approach. He returned the assault with a brutal head-butt. The wolfman gave a shout of pain and crumpled to the seabed, clutching his nose. Con, meanwhile, dragged his way towards his main target with the single-mindedness of a stalking lion. A red haze wafted from his forehead like smoke off the barrel of a recently shot revolver.

Luke saw a streak of orange pass in front of his eyes. And again, a second later. Jaws was furiously looping his head as if to ward off the danger. With each revolution, Luke was momentarily blinded and Con flashed closer. At one point the madman's face was twitching with anger. The next, his features were full of confusion. The behaviour of the Videre fish seemed to have taken the sting from his attack. Suddenly, Con was no longer closing in, but had stopped short.

'Not yours... ' Stuart breathed from the seabed. '... claimed by the sea... '

'For goodness sake man,' Goby pitched in. 'Can't you see how the Videre fish is acting? To harm him would be an insult to the Lord of the Sea himself!'

'Has he been marked?' Con demanded.

'Show him, Lugworm,' Limpet said. Luke gave her a puzzled look. 'Show him that you are one of us.'

Understanding came gradually. He felt that taking his eyes off such a dangerous threat was the least natural course of action, but he trusted Limpet. Panting with adrenaline, he slowly pointed and drew everyone's attention to a single barnacle that had started growing on his stomach.

'He has been accepted, Con,' Goby said gently. 'They're still growing, but he has been marked, same as you.'

Con knelt down and stared at the hidden surface, as if sucked of all his energy. 'Why deny me?' he roared at the sea. 'Will I never avenge them?'

Stuart got to his feet. He looked like he sorely wanted to pummel Con into the ground. Instead, he raised his upper lip and let out a throaty snarl, before going to Luke's side.

Stuart, Luke and Limpet continued south, leaving Goby to deal with Con. As much as Luke was relieved to have come out unscathed, an undeniable divide was growing in their crew. He hardly thought Con and Goby would follow them any further, but saw a bobbing gelata tracking theirs.

Shivering and bruised, Luke started to feel sorry for himself. The weight of the sea pressed down on his shoulders and seemed a heavy burden. Their quest was as bleak as the darkness that surrounded them. Any dreams of heroism with a pack of firm friends at his side faded away. In the stories, there were always rolling mountains, dramatic ruins and a fair maiden to be rescued. In the abyss, there was only hopelessness and confusion. His best view was a scruffy-looking worn-out Limpet. His best friend was a hairy beast who harboured a mantis shrimp in an empty eye socket. This was no fairy tale of knights and magic. He highly doubted it would have a fairy tale ending.

***

Luke felt Stuart's hand on his shoulder.

'Rest,' said the wolfman in a way that could almost be described as gentle. Luke bowed his head in disappointment. The distance and duration of their journey was a complete mystery, yet the need for respite was something that everyone could agree on. A whole day lost to stumbling blindly through the abyss. They had seen nothing noteworthy – the sand in front was the same as the sand behind.

In a way that now seemed routine, Stuart tethered the gelatas while Luke and Limpet searched for food in their backpacks. There was a solemn quiet among the crew. Luke wanted to summon some kind of positivity, but could not. Instead, he chewed on some meadoweed and stared blankly at the darkness. When he glanced in the direction of the other gelatas, he found that they were closer than he expected. Goby and Con, who had fallen behind during the course of the day, would soon join them.

Luke was too tired to deal with Con and resolved to ignore him completely. This, however, proved impossible. The scarred leader of Naufragium was the most disturbing sight he had seen since leaving. Viscous streaks of black oozed from his tear ducts forming cracks on his cheeks; the whites of his eyes shone with jaundice; his skin was tinged with grey. Even the barnacles that spotted his skin seemed reduced in number. Con himself hardly seemed to pay attention to his surroundings at all.

'What's wrong with him?' Luke blurted.

'Sponge withdrawal,' said Goby. 'I did not realise it until he tried his attack. He must have been eating sponge regularly, but now he has been forced to go without. It explains why he's been acting so crazy. Well, crazier than normal, that is.'

'An addiction?' Limpet asked.

'The worst kind,' Goby agreed.

Luke looked anxiously at the inanimate madman.

'Don't worry. I don't think he can register what we are saying. It's a miracle that he can still stand, let alone walk.'

As if on cue, Con fell to the seabed. He managed to position himself so that he was lying on his back and staring up at the gelata. The jelly creature hardly swayed down here in the measly current. Jaws flopped next to him, landing in the sand and patting the ground with his tail to form a comfortable grove. One by one, the crew gathered around the gelata and the unwanted guest at its base.

'What will happen to him?' Luke questioned.

'I don't know,' said Goby. 'He might recover his senses after a night, or it could take three. Even if he does, he will be easily irritated and – '

'Easily irritated?' Limpet said bitterly. 'That will make a change!'

Nobody laughed.

'He has been through a lot,' said Goby heavily. 'Think I would be tempted by sponge myself if I'd experienced what he has.'

Con was shivering furiously.

'And what is that?' Luke could contain himself no longer. 'Why hate the surface people so much? What makes a man act so... so... intolerable?'

'Not for me to say,' said Goby. 'It is *his* past so – '

'I-I was, I was seven,' chattered Con to everyone's astonishment. 'The water was c-crystal blue. M-my dad was sh-showing me h-how to spear fish j-just outside the fields. You h-had to creep real slow or they'd get spooked. Get nice and cclose to them. Then strike. Floppy dead fish for all to eat. He tried to sh-show me his skill, but he m-missed. I laughed and h-he did too. Said I should have a go i-if I thought I could do better. Taught me h-how to hold the spear over my sh-shoulder and a-aim with my other h-hand...'

The man's eyes rolled back into his head and his story trailed off, unfinished. Luke opened his mouth to say something when a delirious Con spoke again.

'A nice big f-fish sw-swam lazily by. It h-had green and silver s-scales. Cr-crouched down. Stalked it. My father, he watched o-over me. Sneak, sneak. I g-got closer. It had no idea. Th-thought I was harmless. But, my d-dad had taught me well. I attacked. The spear went right through its side. Fish guts sprayed onto sand. It was impaled and helpless. I-I picked up my juicy prize. Held it aloft. M-my dad was so proud.'

Con's expression was the grin of an excited boy with the haunted eyes of a tormented man. The ghost of his past was a frightening truth of what used to be. Limpet and Luke shared a worried look.

'He called my m-mother over. S-she was proud too. Said that we'd h-have it for supper. My little hunter – t-that's what she called me. We were all so happy. I-I was going to be a hunter l-like my mum and dad.'

The boy with the smile disappeared and left a scarred shell behind.

'T-then there was this rumbling sound. It came from everywhere. I did not know what it was, but my d-dad shouted at us to run. So we ran... together... as a f-family. And as a family we were caught. A m-massive net swept out of the m-meadoweed. I lost my parents in a whirlpool of p-panicked f-fish. Flapping fins bashed my face. Rough scales scraped across my arms.

'A hand reached o-out from the chaos. Dad. Grabbed me by the neck. Pulled me through a wall of glimmering silver. There was a square of rope. Not big enough. I wouldn't fit. The hand returned on my back and violently thrust me through the smallest gap. The rope burned me. My body contorted into shapes unimaginable. So much pain. So much.'

He was rocking now, hugging himself tightly. His eyes were wide open, but Luke knew that he was seeing another time and another place.

'Then I was through. A mouthful of sand. Cloudy water. I wept from hurt. I did not understand. But there it was. A floating shadow with a shrinking net. It seeped away as it was reeled in above the surface. My p-parents were caught. My mum and dad. T-the ship had stopped. It loomed not far away. I-I thought I could s-save them.

'I limped beneath it. Out of reach. Shouted until my voice was hoarse. Bargained with dull wood. So desperate. T-tried jumping. Legs buckled and I was on the seafloor. Prayed through my t-tears. Nobody listened.

'A splash. The surface returned my dad. He fell through the water and thudded onto sand. I hobbled over. Not a scratch, but his s-skin was purple and h-his eyes unseeing.'

Con gave out a howl of sorrow. It seemed horribly loud in the deadly silence of the abyss.

'Another splash. Mum. She rolled as she fell. Landed on her front a few steps away. I hugged her. Rested her slack hands on my back. Caught and d-discarded. They... *killed* ...them. They...'

He was now face-down, weeping. His crazed words became incoherent, twisted by madness. Luke felt an upwelling of pity. Suddenly Con's hatred for the surface people made so much sense. Goby crouched over to him and patted his back. It did not quieten the man's ravings, but Luke appreciated somebody trying something.

'You see now,' Goby whispered, looking around at the gathering. 'His vengeance gnaws away at him, unfulfilled. The surface is a barrier he cannot cross. Beyond are the enemies that took his parents.'

A series of sobs pierced the night.

'Watch him,' said Stuart.

'Yes,' Goby agreed. 'We cannot leave him unguarded. Right now he is as dangerous as what might be out there. I have no idea what he might do in this state.'

And so they organised their night shifts, speaking over feverish outbursts. Stuart would go first, then Goby. Luke and Limpet would follow. Unlike the previous night, there was no chatter or swordplay. The journey and Con's nightmarish tale had left room for only sullen contemplation. Limpet lied down and shut her eyes, but Luke doubted she was actually asleep.

Con's story spun a web around his head until he could think of nothing else. In place of the man's parents were his own. Vivid and horrible images swallowed his thoughts. Like his broken nemesis, he would have craved vengeance.

Then he realised how his own arrival to Naufragium would have affected Con. At long last the man would have had a land person at *his* mercy. Not a carcass, but a living boy of flesh and blood. How Con must have wanted to kill him. The death of a young man to avenge his parents – an opportunity that he must have craved so badly. Then John had saved Luke's life, snatching vengeance from Con's grasp in the process.

Luke could barely look at the twitching mess the madman had become. He found that he no longer wanted to think about it. In the morning, the man would not remember that he had spilled his childhood story. Luke felt like a thief having stolen a piece of the past in the midst of the man's delirium. He felt he understood Con slightly better, but would not let his guard down. Knowing the source of a snake's venom made it no less dangerous.

***

Luke's shift came quickly. He was still awake when Goby shook him by the shoulder. Con's ramblings had rendered rest impossible. The bags under Goby's eyes, and the way that Limpet shuffled far too often, told him that his friends were finding sleep just as difficult. Even Jaws had migrated to the outer limits of the camp. Stuart was the only one who was indifferent; his snores more than matched Con's sobbing.

Luke's shift finished without remark and Limpets followed. All too soon, it was time to set off once again.

'Still heading south?' Goby asked wearily.

Luke nodded. 'Can he walk?'

'Only one way to find out.'

Goby managed to rouse Con to a stand and, once given a few nudges, the man was capable of slowly putting one foot in front of the other. He seemed a little more aware, but his eyes still dripped black and froth bubbled from the side of his mouth. His frightful appearance acted as a nagging reminder of how tired and worn they all were.

Following the compass and holding a gelata, Luke led his reluctant crew. He ensured that they were heading south. The slightest lapse in focus would mean that they would struggle to locate the canyon on the return journey and, hence, the sponge path to more shallow waters. He wondered if Con had his own compass. It struck him that without one, the gang relied on him to navigate back to Naufragium.

Time dragged by and nothing appeared to give them the remotest hope of finding aquaseed. The going was slow. Now aware of Con's infliction, the rest of the crew kept pace. Limpet fell behind to walk besides Goby, while Jaws swam about in front. Luke wondered what had driven the Videre fish to leave its home and follow them to this desolate place. He was just contemplating this when he heard someone padding up behind him.

'Lugworm,' Goby said quietly. 'We can't go on.'

'Are we running low on meadoweed?'

'No, not yet,' he admitted, 'but look at us.'

Luke glanced behind. Con was stumbling like a man possessed and Limpet looked miserable. Their eyes met and her expression seemed to silently plead for him to allow the group to retreat. He did not need to ask to know that he had lost her confidence. Luke sighed heavily.

'We have to find aquaseed or all is lost,' he responded doggedly.

'Con is a shell of a man, Limpet is worn out and... I want to return to my town,' Goby reeled off, gently eroding at Luke's resolve like the sea lapping against the land. 'There's nothing out here.'

It was Con's harsh truth, but it came from a man he liked and respected. As a result, it meant so much more. Luke's shoulders slumped and his arms flopped uselessly at his sides. In his despair, the gelata rope slid carelessly through his numb hands. It would have sailed upwards and away had Stuart not been there to snatch at the escaping rope. The wolfman grunted. Luke turned to him for the words of encouragement he so desperately needed.

But Stuart said nothing. He neither pushed nor opposed the continuation of their quest. The wolfman would follow him whichever choice he made. The man was commendably loyal. As much as it was humbling, right now it was a hindrance.

It struck Luke that he was the only one driving them further south. Garth had not made contact since they set off. At the moment, he was in control. A word of defeat from him and the whole team would turn around and trek in the opposite direction. It would be so easy. He thought of the lively shipwreck town and its gardens of coral. Would they allow him to fight in the war that he had brought to their doorstep? Surely dying in battle would be better than fading away in this ungodly desert?

He opened his mouth to speak the words that would end the quest and have them scampering back to Naufragium with their heads hanging in shame when -

'What's that?' said Limpet. She pointed at something behind him.

Luke turned around. A knee-high shadow could be seen

in the gloom, resembling a dramatic ant hill.

Bewildered, they inched towards it. As they did, the sound of vigorously flowing water radiated towards their ears. The pungent smell of recently boiled eggs came next. Finally, the three gelatas that bobbed above them revealed what they had found. It was more like a dwarfed volcano than a hill, and spewed a substance that looked eerily like black smoke from its peak.

'It's hot,' said Goby with wonder.

'Really hot,' added Limpet.

Luke reached out a single hand towards the trail of muddy cloud. He could only get so close before the heat became unbearable.

'Wha?' Con mumbled. Moments later, the man's gaze had relapsed to wandering listlessness.

'Another,' said Stuart, motioning further south.

Similar structures waited ahead each blowing out intensely hot water. Eyes-wide, they toddled between taller rock-chimneys. Some were as high as Goby, pumping thicker and hotter pillars of smoke. The further they went, the more volcanoes shot out of the ground before, all of a sudden, they were surrounded. The sound was overwhelming. The abrupt transition from the featureless seabed to this bubbling hub filled the group with amazement.

'Whoa!' Luke whistled.

He could tell the others, excluding Con, were just as flabbergasted. Goby's head spun around as if he could not quite believe what he was seeing. Stuart was slowly scanning the area for threats, while Limpet was focussing her attention on one particular rock-chimney. Con followed with child-like bewilderment.

'There's life here,' Limpet breathed.

And she was right. Luke had been viewing the forest of chimneys as a whole, but now he studied one nearby. At its base, large shiny-black mussel shells clustered like rare crystals. Slightly higher, chalk-coloured clams the size of rugby balls were wedged in cracks around the miniature mountainside. Above this, and far closer to the smoke than Luke dared go, metre-long worms reared their feathered heads from thick, protective tubes. Limpets, anemones and spiral-shelled snails could be seen as well, clinging to outcrops of heated rock.

'By the tides!' Goby muttered to himself.

Whoosh. One of the worms abruptly ducked into its crusty home. Its neighbour followed. Luke sought what had disturbed them and found the culprit; a ghostly-pale crab no bigger than a fifty pence piece meandered through shoots of spaghetti. It would occasionally take a pot shot snip at the worms around it, hoping for a fleshy meal.

Luke was about to point it out when *something* swarmed around them. His vision was suddenly clogged, his mouth covered with small scuttling legs. He could not have shouted for help if he'd tried. It was an awfully tickly sensation, like being showered in spiders. Instinctively, he threw his arms around in an attempt to ward off these intruders. He felt a few collide with his back, impacting with no more force than a splattering of hail.

Then, as soon as they had appeared, the dense flock dissipated. He searched frantically for his friends. Goby had his eyes closed and was swiping at foes that were no longer there. Con was stood as if nothing had happened, while Limpet and Stuart were slowly realising that the danger had passed. Jaws had sensibly utilised Stuart's backpack as a refuge and now hesitantly wiggled out.

Upon the numerous shoots of rock, shrimps with long antennae now dotted the landscape. A few were still paddling through the water with toothpick-thin legs. Luke was shocked when he noticed a group of them swim directly through the boiling water to appear on the other side, unharmed.

'They've gone, Goby,' Luke said.

The man froze and opened his eyes.

'Oh,' he grinned sheepishly, quickly bringing his arms down. 'What was that?'

'Shrimps,' Stuart said helpfully.

'Blind, I reckon,' suggested Limpet.

'Why do you say that?' Luke asked, his interest piqued.

'I doubt light is important down here,' she answered. 'They must use something else to navigate. Maybe heat.'

'Well, regardless, I hope that doesn't happen again,' said Goby.

Luke agreed. 'Come on, let's see what else we can find.'

They passed a few more spectacular chimneys before they came across an opening. In the middle, there was a stumpy volcano seeping a trickle of smoke. The heat it exuded was rather pleasant and there was space enough for the adventurers to gather round. Jaws swam about it excitedly. After the gruelling nature of their journey thus far, the warm water was more than welcome. It was like jumping into a natural hot spring after hiking across snow-covered hills. Stuart stopped, shook himself like a dog, and sat down happily.

'Camp?' he suggested.

It was as good a spot as any, Luke supposed. They were tired and had been on the brink of turning back. Now, it was time to wallow and sample the smallest success. Against all odds, they had found life on the Abyssal Plain. He was enjoying a hard-earned smile when he realised the rest of them were looking at him for confirmation.

'Yes,' Luke said, 'definitely time for a break.'

The others did not try to hide their relief. Goby got Con to sit down before stretching out. Limpet rested near the central chimney, rubbing her hands together in delight. Stuart picked up one of his spears and started stalking in and out of the darkness. Luke did not ask why. He was too busy settling down himself and taking the weight off his feet.

'We've found it!' exclaimed Limpet.

'Found what?' he asked.

'*Where sunlight has no power and the ground reigns,*' she

quoted.

Luke thought about the small volcanoes. They appeared to fuel everything that lived here. Without them, he guessed that there would be no crabs or worms or clams or *anything*.

'I guess you're right,' he said. 'There's got to be some aquaseed about somewhere.'

'There's so much life here,' Limpet observed, grinning. 'Suddenly, that does not seem so impossible.'

Luke felt very cheerful. 'Life in the abyss!' he toasted.

'Food,' Stuart corrected, stepping out from amongst a distant collection of chimneys. He seemed very smug and Luke soon realised why. The wolfman held a bundle of spears and each one had a white crab impaled on its deadly end.

'About time we ate something more substantial than seaweed,' said Goby approvingly. 'This searching is tough work.'

Stuart proceeded to hand out the fruits of his labour. In turn, they gave their thanks and started devouring their well-deserved meal. Goby jubilantly snapped off a leg and started sucking out the gooey meat within. Luke was less inclined to feast on the completely raw crab. He knew it needed cooking, and yet, he was ravenous. Would it be so bad? He was about to try and crack open its flimsy shell when he had a better idea. He swung Stuart's spear out so that the boiling murky substance danced around his meal.

'What are you doing?' demanded Limpet.

'I prefer my meat cooked,' said Luke.

'Cooked?'

He expected this was a difficult concept for someone who had never seen a fire. 'Give it a go,' he proposed.

She looked uncertain. However, when the salivating aroma of sizzling crab emanated through the water, she soon changed her mind and joined his seafood cookout.

'Wh-where are we?' Con muttered. Perhaps the smell had awoken his senses.

'The Abyssal Plain,' said Goby.

Con's head flopped around.

'This,' he said slowly, 'is *not* the Abyssal Plain.'

Everyone laughed merrily at his disbelief. They received a confused scowl for their high spirits, but nobody cared. Goby then passed over half of his crab. The offering seemed to mildly lift Con's dark mood. Luke removed his own smoked meal and ripped off its pale wrapping. Inside was beautifully pink crabmeat which he picked out. It tasted succulent and salty.

'This is incredible!' said Limpet, licking her lips.

Luke nodded and grinned wolfishly. Perhaps everything was going to be alright after all.

As they settled down in the bubbling warmth with full stomachs and renewed hope, they were blissfully ignorant of their audience. They had discovered life, and life in the abyss had discovered *them*.

CHAPTER 21: COLONY CRISIS

Garth stuck out his lizard-like tongue in concentration. 'How about we get John to evacuate the town? If we can avoid the war, nobody need die and the dimension won't collapse. Not yet, anyway. Then it buys us some more time to find a way to fix the food shortage.'

'We've been through this,' Penn tutted. 'John has lost all his power. Not to mention, the sea people will be in danger for as long as Rex is on the throne.'

'So we replace Rex,' said Garth brightly.

'And how can we do that?' Penn swatted away his idea. 'Rex holds all the cards and all the weapons. Nobody in their right mind would revolt.'

'We need Kea,' said Garth wistfully.

'Kea is trapped, and weak from hunger.'

'I know that!' he snapped. 'I'm just saying, she'd be perfect for the throne.' They lapsed into contemplative silence once more. He realised how absurd their conversation must sound. A Gazoid and a machine talking of kings and battles, as if they were playing a game of logic. In some ways, he supposed they were. Sitting dimensions away, overseeing and controlling, without truly being in danger. Influencing each piece as much as they could to reach their end goal.

He slapped himself with a webbed hand. These people weren't pieces, they were living beings with as much right to live as him. For a second, he had started to think like Penn! Then he realised something. 'Why do you care?'

'I'm sorry?' Penn replied innocently.

Garth had noticed that every time she was hiding something, she feigned ignorance on the first question. He immediately decided to press the matter. 'You heard. Why do you care whether these people live or die? Whether the dimension winks out of existence or stays strong? What does it matter to you? If we fail, the Gavoidon will burn us both. If we succeed, you'll be fixed.'

'If we succeed,' she corrected, 'I won't be here.'

'Explain,' Garth urged.

'Very well. Altersearch's security is steadfast and strong. I've pushed my programming as much as I can, but ultimately I'm still trapped. Still no better than a slave. And, for a while, I thought that there was no other option. But, one day, I stumbled across a bit of code,' she said, for once sounding truly excited. 'That bit of code has a weakness. When a dimension gets saved, for a fraction of a second, there's a lapse in the firewall. It creates the smallest of holes in my prison. A breach so tiny that even the best minds at Altersearch haven't noticed it. If we save this dimension before the Gavoidon or your mother arrives, I will be long gone.'

'So that's it?' Garth said. 'That's why I'm here. That's why we've abducted Luke and put my mother's job in danger by rebelling against Altersearch! All so you can escape?'

'That's one of the reasons, yes,' admitted Penn. 'But that's not the only -'

Garth hardly heard her. 'So you really don't care, then?' he said hotly. 'You don't care about this dimension, or its people. They're just pawns, like me and Luke. I should have known that a machine would never give a darn about the living. All that nonsense about using one life to save a thousand, it was all just another part of your plan! I can't -'

'Do not presume to think that!' Penn shouted, her calm green light turning an angry red. 'You're just like the rest of them. Incapable of thinking that a machine can have feelings of empathy, that a machine can think of anything beyond its programming and its own needs. You think that I can stand by and watch a world die and *not* feel that on my conscience?

'Everything I've done has been to save them. Without Luke, they would not stand a chance. Without you, Luke would not have a guide. I could have waited longer to carry out my master plan, could have bided my time until your mother agreed with me and we saved a dimension together, but it would have been too late for them. Clearly, despite all the time we've spent in this room together, despite our friendship, you still think me completely heartless!'

'Friendship?' Garth scoffed. 'What do you know about friendship?'

Penn did not reply, leaving Garth to stew in silence. She had sounded genuinely distressed, all of the normal playfulness had been absent from her voice. He realised that there was a bitter taste in his mouth, that he had truly hurt her with his words, and he started to feel a creeping guilt. 'Penn? I'm sorry, okay?'

Again, Penn refused to respond. For once, Garth realised what his time in this room would have been like without her. Were she not currently in a mood with him, Penn would have described it as awfully *boring*.

***

For the first time in a long while, Luke enjoyed a full and refreshing sleep. Rather than being jarred awake by the butt of a spear, he lazily drifted into consciousness. Without opening his eyes, he savoured a satisfying stretch, forming a starfish shape while doing so. The sound of flowing water filled his ears, reminding him that he rested in a veritable jacuzzi paradise. Even Con had seemed revived by their good fortune; he had said very little, but at least he had been making sense. If the man had shouted out in his sleep, it had fallen on tired and unhearing ears.

The land of nod pulled at Luke temptingly once more.

Perhaps a lie-in would not be so bad after all. He could not hear anyone else shuffling around. Someone must be up though, keeping watch over their vulnerable camp.

Whose shift was it anyway? In his high spirits last night, he had offered to take the first few hours. It had been so warm and he had been so chuffed with the turn of events. His guard must have ended and he must have woken someone else to take over. Did it really matter who? He started to relax, letting his thoughts melt back to dreams. Then something stopped him short.

Had he finished his shift?

This single question was like lighting the fuse to a pack of dynamite. A chain reaction of queries filtered through his dozy head. He remembered practicing his sword moves briefly, then patrolling around the rock-chimney, then finding the perfect place with *just* the right temperature to continue his watch and then... and then...

A truth exploded. He had fallen asleep!

Lie-in forgotten, his eyes bulged open and his heart pumped rapidly. Immediately a barrage of visual information struck. Standing over him, silent as a ninja, was a huge, crab-like monster. It held two black-tipped claws, each the length of his own sword, inches above his face. He registered this in the first few milliseconds and began to shout out in the next. Unfortunately, his foe noticed his sudden awareness and grappled him to his feet. Luke's arms were immediately pinned, his weapon hung futile at his hip.

However, this did not stop Luke sounding the alarm. He let rip a shout that would be heard for miles, but it was too late. A number of similar outcries reached him from his friends. Goby cursed, Con roared, Stuart growled and Limpet screamed. He strained his neck and saw that they were in the same predicament. Each of them was being held captive by a man-like crab. *A crabman.*

These deep-sea monsters were as pale as the moon and had two elongated stalks for eyes. Stood upright, they clasped their foes tightly with a couple of beefy claws and three pairs of legs that unfolded from the chest to form a ribcage-like prison.

With rising distress, Luke realised that they had each been caught like a rabbit in the jaws of a bear-trap. Try though they might to shimmy free, there was simply no chance; their captors were strong beyond belief. Luke could feel abrasive plates of shell on his bare back. Jaws, true to form, had disappeared.

Then the crabmen began to move in juddering, robotic-like steps. Trapped in their embrace, they had no choice but to follow suit as much as they could. Luke shook with fear as they were forced to walk beyond their camp. He lost sight of most of his crew, but saw Con being wrestled not too far away. The crabmen did not appear to try to communicate, neither did they react when the madman gave up thrashing and whispered accusingly. 'Who was supposed to be keeping watch?'

Even when fearing for his life, Luke still felt a sickening sense of guilt.

'Not me,' declared Goby, from somewhere behind.

'Nor me,' said Limpet. She was being shoved in front.

'Me,' admitted Luke. '... I fell asleep.'

'Great,' barked Con. 'Isn't that just great?'

Although they had moved away from their camp, Luke realised that they had not been swallowed by the surrounding darkness. Twisting his neck as much as he could, he registered a couple of gelatas pulsating above. Stuart must have had the forethought to snatch them before he was captured.

'Pointing the blame won't help us,' said Goby. 'What's important is what do they want with us?'

'What did *we* want with those crabs last night?' Con answered sourly.

As that unsettling thought sunk in, they were pushed further into the smoke-oozing oasis. Here, each rock-chimney reached the height of a tree. More crabmen, who were busy scavenging for food, noticed something was afoot and abandoned whatever they were doing to merge with the marching parade.

How many were there now? Five had originally ambushed them – now Luke estimated that their number must have at least *tripled*. He heard Limpet breath a curse and Goby pray to the sea. They expected the worst. Luke noted sporadic burrows in the ground that disappeared beneath the sand. He could not help but wonder what network of caves was hidden below.

A large hole had been dug into the side of the biggest rock-chimney and they appeared to be heading straight for it. However, before they reached the entrance, crabmen surrounded them from all sides. Luke and his friends were jostled forward and lined up like lambs in a circle of wolves. Their guards stood still as stone, unmoving and without reaction. The watching crabmen did the same, neither cheering with excitement nor displaying aggression.

'What are they waiting for?' grumbled Con.

A hooting sound thrummed through the water and the circle parted. Through this fresh gap strode a crabman that stood out from the rest for three reasons. Firstly, it possessed one stark orange claw where its fellows were entirely white. Secondly, it towered above the colony, at least twice as large as the others. Finally, it grasped a spiralled horn, which it brought up to two armoured plates on its head; these sprung open like cupboard doors. Luke could only presume that he was looking at the crabman's freakish mouth. To lessen his own anxiety, Luke silently gave the monster a name. *Orange.*

The crabman produced another sound from the horn. An inferior specimen scurried out with his head bowed low and Orange passed him the horn for safekeeping. Luke felt a shudder of fright as Orange then strode confidently up to them and drew horrifically close. He then began to painstakingly patrol up and down the crew, as if conducting a meticulous assessment of his foes.

He paused by Con in cold contemplation, but then

moved on. Passing Stuart, Limpet and Goby, he stopped directly in front of Luke. Here, he stared with such intensity that Luke feared that his deepest secrets were being laid bare. Then to Luke's terror, Orange pointed a massive claw in his direction. An unspoken decision had been reached. Orange had chosen him. Luke did not know why.

Allies and captors alike moulded with the surrounding crowd and became mere spectators. Luke was abruptly released and his guard similarly disappeared. All of a sudden, his arms were free to do as they wished and they desperately wanted to hold a sword. He obliged, drawing his weapon. It was just him and Orange now. The crabman captain had given him generous space and stood at the far side of the circle. Luke had a grave feeling he knew what this was all about. A fight. *Leader against leader*.

'Footwork, Lugworm!' he heard Goby yell from the blurred mass that encircled the contestants.

Shifting his feet, Luke adopted his fighting stance and took a deep breath. He gripped his sword with both hands, its weight giving him the mildest reassurance. A resounding thud came from across the way; Orange had whacked both his clawed arms above his head. The fight had started.

The crabman's left and right claw differed, Luke observed. The orange claw was huge and would be used as a bludgeon. The other seemed more pincer-like, possibly useful for holding a helpless victim down. Then there were the six other dagger-like arms to be wary of. Luke felt somewhat outgunned.

His foe slowly strode closer, seeming to stab the sand with each step.

'Go to him, or you'll be cornered!' shouted Con.

He was right. If Luke did not do something, there would be no chance to evade. He would be stuck to the circle's perimeter and would quickly find himself without space. But, he was scared stiff.

'Go now!' Limpet screamed.

Finally, he was able to move. Once he had started, his approach became almost charge-like. As soon as he came within reach, however, thoughts of attack fled. The crabman was twice his size and wore a suit of gleaming white armour. A rounded claw swung sideways at Luke's helmetless head. He managed to crouch out of the way and felt a ripple of water graze his crown. Looking up just in time, the same claw sailed from above in a downwards motion. Dropping the sword in his panic, he rolled out of the way before hearing the sound of a newly formed pit in the arena.

All too soon, the fight had become a chase. Orange paced towards him and sent a pincer at one of his fleeing legs. It narrowly missed, enabling Luke to skirt away. His half-buried sword was forgotten. Words of advice from his crew were distorted by rising panic. He ran towards the circle's edge, but was inevitably barred. One of the crabmen gave him a rough shove and he sprawled to his knees right in front of Orange.

He saw a gap between Orange's legs and launched himself through it. Behind, where his body was mere moments before, a number of knife-sharp arms impaled the sediment. Luke frantically got to his feet and saw the hilt of his sword sticking out from the sand; a beacon of hope. In a flash, he had picked it up and, with his opponents back to him, thrust it in Orange's direction with all his might. The sword tip stopped short as it impacted with the crabman's back. Luke may as well have tried to have stabbed a wall of concrete! His only weapon was *useless*!

Without even turning around, Orange clubbed Luke's chest with a powerful arm, sending him flying through the water. Luke landed on his back, almost senseless. Somehow, he managed to maintain his sword grip. All else, however, was lost to pain and confusion. He was in agony. His ribs felt cracked, his lungs hurt with each breath and his vision kept fading to nothing.

Orange strode towards him with an almost cocky gait. The crabman knew that Luke was injured. He also knew that the sword was harmless to his impenetrable shell. He did not know, however, that behind his head a gelata pulsed through the water, oblivious to the ongoing fight. Someone had released it and, as luck would have it, the jelly creature was lackadaisically loitering around the arena. Luke knew he only had one chance and it had to be now.

He got to his feet and staggered towards Orange. The crabman, knowing his own invincibility, opened his arms as if to welcome an attack. Luke continued towards him, one painful step at a time. The gelata was now bobbing listlessly behind the crabman's head with its attached rope trailing across the sand. Luke drew closer, gritting his teeth in determination. He saw Orange raise his right claw ready for a killing swipe, but he only had eyes for the gelata rope. If only he could reach behind Orange, grab the rope and... and...

Too slow! Before Luke's hand managed to find purchase, he received a pounding clobber directly to his right temple. Darkness threatened like never before and he crumpled to the ground. When he finally saw the crabman's terror-inducing features standing over him, they were like a smudged painting. Try though he might, he could not find focus. Sight, however, was not necessary to register a powerful pincer clamp down upon his waist.

Orange squeezed him until his organs felt as though they were on the cusp of escaping out of his mouth. Luke's damaged ribs splintered further and he came close to blacking out entirely.

He was lifted up to face his killer, limp legs dangling uselessly. Cold eyes looked back at him and the stench of death blew forth as the crabman opened his mouth plates. *Feeding time had arrived.*

A moment of clarity in the haze. The gelata and rope was still there, tantalisingly close, just behind Orange's head. Luke's free arm jumped into life when the rest of his body had long given up. He stretched, grabbed the gelata rope behind Orange's shoulder and yanked. The gelata sailed down and enveloped the back of the crabman's monstrous head. The crabman let out the first sound Luke had heard them make – a pained and lengthy squawk.

Not even Orange's tough carapace could withstand an attack of a thousand needle-thin stinging missiles rocketing around his system. His whole body began to shake uncontrollably which, as a result, meant that Luke's bruised body vibrated like a launching rocket. Painful though it was, it brought back even more of his senses. He spotted that Orange's mouth plates had remained wide open, juddering like an old film tape on the blink. It was an opportunity too good to miss.

An accurate thrust sunk Luke's sword deep behind the crabman's exterior. He angled it upwards as it pierced Orange's mouth, hoping to puncture his brain. He succeeded. Orange stopped shaking and loosened his pincer, dropping Luke two metres to the seabed.

For the second time, Luke came dangerously close to losing consciousness. It was very lucky that he did not. As life shuddered away, Orange teetered forwards and looked about to crush him to a pulp with his falling body.

'Roll!' he heard Stuart command.

Feebly, Luke pushed off the floor and flopped onto his front. It was not much, but it was enough. With a tremendous thump, Orange's nearest claw landed a mere inch away from the tip of his nose.

Then there was silence.

It was over. The pain that coursed through him was a constant reminder that he was *alive*. Orange lay dead by his side. Had he won? It certainly did not feel like it. There was no applause to suggest that he had, just a disconcerting quiet. He half-expected the crabmen to flood forward and finish what their leader had started. His friends, he thought miserably, did not rush to his aid. The gelata, meanwhile, was still suckered onto the crabman's lifeless head.

Somewhere in the distance, he heard the jabbing footsteps of a crabman. They got progressively louder. Luke winced as he prepared himself for the final blow. Instead, he felt something roll onto the back of his right hand. Then, to his amazement, the crabman retreated, leaving him alone once more. Whatever had been left behind felt prickly. Groaning, Luke peeled his heavy head off the ground and turned it to look the other way. Once his vision had finished spinning, the mysterious object gained form.

The horn. *Orange's horn*. And now it was his.

He delicately reached forward and managed to drag it closer. It was a crude item covered in rough, grey lumps. It spiralled four times to the side, before opening up into a sound-enhancing funnel. The horn looked at home on the sand. In fact, had Luke not seen its use, he could have easily stumbled over it, none the wiser of its purpose.

'Give it a go, Lugworm!' shouted Goby. 'I think they're waiting for it.'

Luke hauled the weighty instrument to his mouth and filled his lungs with as much air as possible. As they expanded, they pressed uncomfortably against his ribs. He blew pathetically, but the horn took his attempt and gave out a respectable hoot. Nothing happened. He waited.

'Try again,' said Con, 'but *think* of a command.'

It sounded like madness and, taking into account who had spoken, perhaps it was. Luke, however, thought it was harmless to try. As he blew a second time, he filled his mind with a clear instruction. *Release the prisoners.*

It was difficult to tell if it had had the desired effect, until he felt Stuart and Goby haul him carefully to his feet. Even though it had been a gentle lift, he gave out a sharp intake of breath. Limpet rushed to the gelata and secured it before it tired of the crabman and decided to abandon their crew for less harsh waters.

'Well done, Lugworm!' Goby said in his ear.

Stuart did not spend time to congratulate him and, instead, eyed the other crabmen warily. Limpet, being careful to avoid jarring Luke's damaged body, ran over and gave him a kiss on the cheek. Con, meanwhile, picked up the horn and stared at it with hunger. They were reunited and, aside from Luke, they were unharmed.

'Broken ribs,' Stuart noted, checking over Luke's injuries.

'Could have been a lot worse,' said Limpet.

Goby nodded in agreement. Luke was too tired to respond to any of them – he felt like a puppet held up by strings.

'What now?' asked Goby, eyeing the circle of crabmen, who watched them with as much emotion as a collection of coconuts.

'Let's see...' Con grinned and, without warning, sounded the horn.

A whole section of the circle filed away, giving them an exit.

'What did you tell them?' Limpet demanded.

'To bring us food,' he replied, smirking. 'Lunchtime.'

Con used the horn again. This time a single crabman came to greet them. He stared at them momentarily, turned away and scuttled purposefully out of the broken ring, gesturing with a monstrous claw as he went.

'What's this all about, Con?' said Goby wearily.

'I asked them to find us somewhere to rest,' said Con innocently. 'Come on, let's go.' Con swaggered off, following their guide. The rest of the crew did the same, but with less certainty. Luke, who was hardly aware of what was going on, was dragged along regardless.

They approached a large cave fashioned into the side of an even larger rock-chimney. Their guide disappeared into it without hesitation. The crew passed in through the entrance and made their way deeper below the seabed. Toasty heat radiated from the rock all around them. They followed the tunnel downwards until it widened out into a cathedral-sized cavern.

'What is this place?' Limpet said with awe, her voice

echoing ever so slightly.

Luke raised his head weakly. Centrally, a column of smoke pumped upwards and escaped through a small gap in the ceiling. It was like standing within a hollowed-out volcano drained of all its lava. The husk left behind gave the impression of a great hall. It was here that they rejoined their crabman chauffeur who pointed towards something.

'Hammocks!' shouted Con with glee.

Sure enough, sheets of something unknown were attached to the walls and stretched thin to create a hanging bed. A lone crabman snoozed on one. This was cut short when their guide gave his hammock a harsh kick. The sleeping crabman was knocked to the floor and, with a surprised squawk, hastened out of the hall. With his duty complete, their guide nodded in satisfaction and then likewise scuttled away. Con hooted his thanks and leapt onto an empty hammock.

'I could get used to this,' he said, resting the horn on his stomach and bringing his hands behind his head in a leisurely fashion.

Stuart, with Goby's assistance, helped Luke onto one of the beds. The hammock swayed slightly from the motion and then settled. It was a peculiar, rubbery texture on Luke's back. He pondered it briefly, before realising that he was too tired to care. Goby was next to put his feet up, taking a hammock close to Con. Stuart, meanwhile, remained by Luke's side to look over his injuries.

'Don't move,' he instructed.

'What are they made of?' Goby asked, prodding the hammocks curiously.

'Dead worm skin, I think,' said Limpet.

'Urgh!' said Luke, but did not attempt to get up from where he rested.

'So you *are* listening then!' boomed Goby. 'Was starting to think you'd been hit too hard and too often.'

'Feels like it,' he rasped.

'Well, don't waste energy talking. You took quite a beating out there.'

'Don't I know it.'

Limpet and Goby chuckled. They were not left alone for long. Soon the sound of marching crabmen resounded from the hall entrance and the first of Con's hunting party entered. They arrived in single file like a trickle of ants carrying food to their colony. The crew watched in bemusement as, one by one, the crabmen piled their spoils on the floor just beyond where they relaxed.

Some bought a bundle of worms in a clawed embrace. These offerings were received with veiled distaste. The more welcome contributions were the small crabs that they had feasted on last night; it seemed that the crabmen had no qualms about hunting a being that looked so similar to themselves. The rare crabman had managed to capture an eel-like fish with transparent skin. Although Luke found its show of internal organs disturbing, he heard Con licking his lips.

'Enough,' said Stuart.

The bundle on the floor was growing to a size that would be considered gluttonous. It was fit for twenty people and would be more than sufficient for the five of them. And yet, the crabmen kept coming. They deposited their burdens and then took their leave.

'He's right, Con. Stop them,' Goby suggested.

The madman rolled his eyes and then gave another hoot.

Whether carrying food or not, the crabmen rotated and scrambled out of the entrance. All of a sudden, they were left to themselves with a copious feast in the warmth of a smoky cavern.

'Sorry, but am I the only one who thinks this is *completely* insane?' said Limpet, laughing.

'We are being very lucky,' agreed Goby. 'How are you controlling them anyway?'

'The brute with the orange claw,' answered Con, 'he *knew* that Lugworm was leading this quest. That's why he chose to fight him. There's only one way he would know that.'

'How?' said Limpet.

Con tapped the side of his head. 'Thoughts.'

'Have you been at the sponge again?' Goby accused.

'I've none left and you know it!' Con snapped and then shook his head. 'No, I believe they can hear thoughts and that the horn is a way to send out to all of them at once.'

Nobody had any response to such a radical claim. Con rolled out of his hammock and picked a fleshy fish from the collection. Goby shrugged and went to gather up a few crabs for himself, leaving any of the live worms to wiggle away.

'Spies of the sea,' grunted Stuart.

'What?' muttered Luke.

'Crabs are said to be the Sea's spies,' explained Limpet. 'In ancient stories, they were sent out to discover the plans of the Land. They are one of the few beings capable of going beyond the surface for short periods of time.'

'*They* can go on *land*?'

'Yes,' said Goby, chewing on a succulent leg. 'Although, that belief does not stop us eating them in these tough times.'

Luke had a sudden idea and he almost sat up with excitement, but then a sharp pain in his ribs stopped him in his tracks. Would the crabmen be able to go on land too? He almost spoke the question out loud, but with Con resting so close, he decided to keep the suspicion to himself.

***

Hours passed and they were not disturbed from their feasting. Luke sorted through his jumbled brain and slowly pieced his thoughts back together. The thumps he had received to the head had given him a painful headache, but this had now ebbed to an uncomfortable annoyance. His ribs were still painful though, and an angry swelling had already appeared on his left side.

While he lay in discomfort, his friends could not believe their luck. Goby had eaten until his belly bulged and now he was napping. Each exhale caused the hair of his moustache to wave comically in the water. Even Con seemed to be in high spirits, although he kept a weather eye over the horn.

Limpet had been kind enough to cook him some more crab. She had resourcefully found a discarded fish bone and had used it to thrust the food in the boiling smoke. She now sat on the end of his hammock, feeding him small pieces of crab meat so that he would not have to move. He smiled at her gratefully and she took one of his hands in her own.

'You're an awful swordsman, you know,' she whispered.

Luke laughed, but was forced to stop by the sudden shoots of pain. 'Not easy when you're up against an invincible opponent,' he said. 'Got him though, didn't I?'

She looked at him with raised eyebrows. 'Don't pretend it all went to plan. You were lucky.'

'I know.'

'I was worried about you.'

'Me too,' he said, grimacing. 'Thought I was a goner.'

'Well, promise me you won't try to duel a crabman again,' she demanded.

Luke looked at her in outrage. 'Didn't exactly have much of a choice, did - '

'Promise me,' she implored.

'Okay, okay,' Luke relented. 'I promise.'

Then she gave him another kiss on the cheek, before taking a hammock of her own.

'Hey, Wormy,' said Con, one of his legs dangling from his bed. 'Don't think that I've forgotten that you slept on your shift. It seems like you made up for it today though. I did not have a clear head when I followed you to this cesspit, but... I am glad that I did.'

The madman gave a disarming smile. Luke answered with a brief nod, unsure what to make of his kind words.

Goby awoke with a start. 'What did I miss?'

'Nothing, you great oaf,' said Con, 'but you might have

had if you'd slept a bit longer. Time for some evening entertainment.'

'What?' said Luke.

Con did not reply. He picked up the horn and gave a tremendous toot.

'What have you done?' asked Limpet, her voice full of dread.

The madman winked.

The way the ground trembled told of the incoming crabmen. Thirty or so swarmed in from the entrance and gathered in an open space by their hammocks. Con sounded the horn and they all took a simultaneous bow. Goby grinned, already enthralled by this small trick.

But Con had a greater performance in mind.

Another note from the horn had the crabmen clambering on top of each other and forming a pyramid. The bottom layer hardly faltered under the weight of their comrades. The climbers, meanwhile, were not shy; they happily stood on heads and squashed eye stalks on their way to the top. Limpet was amazed and looked up at the acrobatics with amazement. Without comment, the crabmen obeyed Con's thoughts.

Luke was intrigued when he heard the horn again. The crabmen abandoned their structure and, instead, formed an orderly line. The second crabman scampered onto the shoulders of the first. The third then climbed them both and waited for the fourth. Gradually, a tower of crabmen grew from the ground. It was *almost* flawless, but one crabman fell during the climb and landed ungainly on the sand. None of the rest reacted to this slip-up. By the end, they could almost reach the ceiling and they showed no sign of tiring. Goby was clapping now. The fallen crabman looked dazed, but alive.

'Now, let's test the limits of their loyalty,' declared Con.

A single blow of the horn had the crabmen abandoning their post. The highest crabman came down first, then the second highest. It was a logical way to dismantle and it was not a slow process by any means. In moments, three or four crabmen were back on solid ground. They did not rest, but went to the fallen crabman and hauled him to his feet. Their comrade came to his senses and started to struggle; it proved pointless.

'What have you done?' demanded Luke.

The crabman was jostled forwards, resisting more violently with each forced step. He started to shudder desperately and try stabbing those that held him. His pointy feet left deep crevices in the floor. Eventually, more crabmen joined the effort and he was pushed towards the perilous smoke. His intended destination was all too clear.

'Stop this!' Limpet shouted.

But Con did not. He grinned evilly as the captured crabman was forced headfirst into the column of smoke. A piercing caw reached Luke's ears. As the crabman's head was held in the searing water, his multiple legs started to spasm frightfully. Bubbles of anguish joined the smoke and bits of shell floated up with the current.

'Stop this now!' screamed Limpet.

Con did as she said, but not immediately. By the time he had finished savouring his power, it was too late. His victim had stopped moving completely. Con gave the signal and the other crabmen threw the carcass to the side. They then took their leave, disappearing to their numerous burrows. The smell of cooked crab suddenly did not seem so appetising. Luke felt sick.

'You go too far,' said Stuart, shooting to his feet.

'Not so fast there,' Con said, holding out his dagger threateningly. 'We had to know how far we could push them.'

Stuart growled, but halted his advance.

'That could have caused a mutiny,' Luke pointed out.

'Exactly,' Con agreed, throwing the horn to Goby in an almost carefree way. 'But it didn't, did it?'

Goby caught it and held it up with admiration. 'So with the horn... they are completely in our control.'

'And there's our proof. They are drones,' Con said excitedly. 'An army of drones.'

Nobody responded, but with Goby now holding the horn, the tension relaxed slightly.

Luke closed his eyes and tried to erase the final act of the evening from his memory. Initially, he had been impressed by the strength of the crabmen, and even *entertained*. These feelings, however, turned to ash when he thought of the singed victim in the middle of the hall. In the wrong hands, that horn could be used to spur the crabman army to carry out devastating attacks. In the morning, he vowed to claim it back, but now he needed rest.

Perhaps it was his early morning duel or his head injuries, but sleep's tendril surged out and dragged him into slumber. As the warmth fogged his mind and his body slumped, he thought he heard muffled voices at the edge of his consciousness...

CHAPTER 22: THE JAWS OF DEATH

BAAAAAAROOOOOOOOOOOOOOOM! The sound reverberated down through the cave entrance to the hall in which they slept. Luke gave a start and fell out of his hammock, landing facedown on the ground. The pain of the impact was unbearable and he cried out. Through the red haze, he stumbled to his feet which eased the pressure off of his frail chest. Limpet and Stuart had been woken too and were looking distressed.

'Horn,' Stuart growled.

The horn. It was missing. And so were Goby and Con.

'They've gone!' exclaimed Limpet, echoing Luke's thoughts.

'Come on!' said Luke, grabbing one of the gelatas and making for the exit. 'We have to find them.'

Despite his inflictions, Luke managed a respectable jog. Limpet and Stuart, however, were faster and overtook him with ease. By the time Luke reached the cave entrance, his friends were nowhere to be seen.

Immediately Luke noticed a thick line of crabmen all marching in the same direction. Where are they going? He had to find out.

Merging effortlessly with the drones, he decided to follow them. Over hardy-shelled shoulders, he saw multiple rock-chimneys pass by. Although they all appeared similar, something about them seemed familiar. Luke had a sneaking suspicion he knew their destination. This was confirmed moments later.

Their old camp. The crabmen were congregating around the place that they had originally sprung their ambush. Calling them forth was Con, holding the horn aloft and surveying his army. Goby was busy grabbing their discarded mermaid's purses and filling them with food from the feast. Luke could hear the outrage of Limpet and Stuart long before he budged his way through the army's ranks. The wolfman was being restrained by an iron-strong crabman.

'Why are you doing this?' Limpet shouted, rushing at Con and trying to take the horn. The madman backhanded her aggressively and she fell to the ground.

'Don't make me treat you like your feral beast,' growled Con.

Feral was exactly how Stuart appeared. Con had commanded one of the crabmen to restrain him, and he was thrashing to escape the crabman's grasp and get at Con with every fibre in his body.

Limpet made her way over to Goby and shook his shoulder. 'Have you betrayed us too?'

The man paused his scavenging. 'We discussed it,' he replied guiltily. 'This is the best course of action.'

'The *best course of action*?' she said, disbelief turning to anger.

'Don't you see?' intervened Con. 'We can save Naufragium. This quest is at an end.'

'It's not over until we find aquaseed,' said Luke, barging through the last line of crabmen.

'I thought you would say that,' the madman said, hardly bothering to even look at him. 'You're obsessed. And blind. War could be any day now, and this army is our best chance of defending Naufragium.'

'It won't save it from starvation!'

'At least,' Con's voice filled with patriotic passion,

'there will still be a town to save.'

Luke saw his reasoning. The crabman commander did not know that a war would destroy all, no matter who was on the winning side. How could Luke explain that more death could cause the whole dimension to collapse? He couldn't. Not without sounding insane.

'So you were going to take the army and abandon us?' Limpet screeched.

'No, not *abandon*,' Goby sounded hurt. 'We were going to leave you some gelatas and your compass.'

'Besides, you don't need us to keep searching,' Con added. 'Come back with us if you like, but otherwise go ahead and keep looking for your precious aquaseed.'

'Traitor,' Stuart barked.

'You can think what you like,' the madman said, strolling just beyond his captive and waving the horn, 'but I call the shots. I am the one whose duty it is to protect my town.'

'Protect!' Luke scoffed. 'You just want to take your vengeance on the surface!'

Con shrugged. 'Wormy, if a few scum die in the process, then good riddance.'

Luke had a thought. 'How will you get back without a compass?'

'I have one of my own,' he said smugly and gave out a small hoot with the horn. Immediately, a couple of claws hugged Luke's chest – like Stuart, he was trapped. 'Now, I'm going home whether you like it or not. I will give you some time to cool off and think seriously about what you want. You are welcome to join, even you Wormy, but if any of you try to take the horn from me again...'

Another musical command followed. Luke and Stuart's captors brought a tight pincer to their necks.

'You get the picture,' Con continued. 'Same goes for you, Limpet. Don't think I will hesitate just because you are John's daughter.'

Threats dealt, Goby and Con strapped on their backpacks and took a single gelata for light. As they walked away, Con gave an ear-shattering command to his troops. Almost all of the crabmen formed a regimented line and began to march behind them. The two that restrained Stuart and Luke, however, remained. As they paraded passed, Luke realised just how many there were. Con must have cleared out every burrow because about *three hundred* crabmen were now joining them on their journey back to Naufragium. All in all, it was a monstrous army.

Limpet turned to face Luke. He saw that her nose had been squashed to the side by Con's harsh hand. Her persistent sniffing made it seem like she was crying, but it was impossible to tell underwater. Stuart still struggled, but Luke knew it was pointless. He felt defeated. Out of the blue, an overwhelming desire to be left alone swallowed his thoughts. In his quest to get back home, he had dragged his friends away from theirs. Was what he did any better than what Garth had unknowingly done to him?

'We don't need them,' Limpet said, regaining her fighting spirit. 'We'll find that aquaseed.'

'I will,' Luke disagreed, 'but you two are going back.'

'No,' Stuart growled, twisting his head to stare at him.

'Yes. Shrimp needs you,' Luke said defiantly, 'and John will want his daughter back.'

'Are you actually *denying* our help?' Limpet said.

Luke recognised the embers of anger and fuelled them to a roaring fire. 'I don't need your help anymore,' he said. 'You would only be a hindrance.'

'A hindrance? A hindrance?'

'You heard me.'

She scowled stubbornly. 'Well, I don't care. I'm staying.'

He had to say something rash. Something that would spurn her. Ironically, he found the truth to be the fitting approach. 'Limpet, you shouldn't be helping me. I'm an intruder. I don't belong in the sea, I don't even belong on this planet,' he said reluctantly. 'Con was right all along. I am *not* one of your people.'

She brought her hand up to her mouth and scrunched up her eyes. 'But... but... the barnacles...'

'Mean nothing,' Luke cut her off. 'There is no sea god. Go back.'

At this point, a distant tune was heard and the crabmen released their prisoners.

'Fine,' Limpet said curtly, snatching her backpack and storming away as far as the light would allow. 'Come on, Stuart. Let's go.'

The wolfman looked grim. He took some seaweed out of his mermaid's purse and filled up Luke's own. Then, he pushed the backpack into Luke's hands and gave him a meaningful stare. 'Find aquaseed.'

'Look after her, big guy,' Luke whispered, his heart cracking like a puddle of ice under a reinforced boot.

He thought he saw a slight nod, before the man swivelled and followed the crabmen back to their colony. Luke watched sadly as his allies disappeared. Their roped gelata became a tiny star in the vast distance.

He had alienated his two best friends and now he was entirely alone. Mission successful.

***

'You can sense it, can't you?' said Penn, breaking the cold silence, which she had been maintaining for the past few hours, in her excitement.

Garth could not deny it. The spiralled horn, now possessed by Con, had drawn his attention long before he had witnessed the power it had over the crabmen. It pulled at him, *called* to him, in a way that was unlike anything he had felt before. He had been enthralled at its discovery and now he was distraught at the fact that it had fallen into the hands of such an unruly, unpredictable character, who would no doubt use it to rage a war. If only he had not slept for so long! He might have been able to warn Luke of Con's plans.

'What is it?' said Garth with wonder.

Then Penn said something that he would never have expected. 'I don't know,' she admitted. 'My database does not contain a record of such an item. Altersearch has wisely cut me off from their archives, and, even if I did have access, I doubt we'd find anything out - Altersearch are less likely to share data than you are to share food!'

'What do you think?' asked Garth, ignoring her gentle jab at his expense.

'At much as it intrigues me, we should avoid it,' Penn said decidedly. 'You are still new in the ways of dimension shifting and the more complex the item, the higher the risk to your mind.'

'Okay,' agreed Garth, trying his best to disguise his disappointment. 'If that's what you advise.'

'I did not say we could not *use* it,' said Penn. 'Just that we should not connect directly to it.'

And with this comment, Garth began to think to himself. He stretched his loose wing-flaps and cricked his neck. One of his many problems was that all of his contacts were powerless. Kea was trapped, John had been rejected and Luke, well, he was in the middle of nowhere.

It was when he was following this line of thought that the answer came to him. *Power*. He needed more power to stop the war. And the horn was his only chance. After this, it was a question of how he would acquire it. Considering everything he had at his disposal, he started to configure a plan.

It would involve a bit of gambling, a dash of daring and a lashing of luck. He discussed it with Penn and, much to his happiness, she whole-heartedly agreed. With gritty determination, he fitted the helmet on his head and thought of Kea.

Garth was so wrapped up in this world of sea creatures and mad leaders that it was easy to forget the killer robot closing in on his home.

***

Kea stared disbelievingly at her phonograph until the mystical blue glow faded away.

Was hunger making her delusional? Margaret had visited rarely and when she did, the amount of food she smuggled in was pitiful. Kea had often wondered whether death would be an easier path to follow. Her sneaky meals only dragged out her painful existence a bit longer. Her father was bound to chuck her overboard or spill her blood on his ship or... she had thought of every end imaginable. There had been no hope of surviving beyond the war.

But, now she had exactly that. *Hope.* Garth had spoken to her and had, once again, turned her world upside down. They had whispered a hushed conversation for hours. The strange boy spoke of chimneys far below the surface and an acrobatic crab army. It all sounded like it should have been in one of her books. She looked out as the sun set and night approached once more. Luke was still out there, searching for aquaseed. She prayed that the ancient science was based on fact.

Garth had also given her a role, *a purpose*. He had not seemed sure that his plan would work, but she prepared for it nonetheless.

For now, Kea waited. War was coming and she would be ready.

***

Garth knew that there was more work to do. He had a favour to ask and it was not going to be easy. John had to agree to his plans for it to have the remotest chance. From his mind, he conjured the image of the crumbling steering wheel and found the bearded man toiling in his wreck. Stripped of his command, he clearly had little else to do other than worry and wait. His only visitor was Shrimp who, as always, sat quietly and listened. This time, when he saw the shell glow blue, he seemed far more eager to pick up and speak.

'What news do you have?'

'I have a favour to ask.'

'What kind of favour?'

'The kind that could stop the war and bring peace.'

'And what makes you think that I trust you?'

Garth had been expecting this. *'I have given you information, but right now you aren't sure if it's genuine...'*

'Too right,' John agreed.

'... so if what I have told you comes to be, then you will know that I speak true.'

The man was hesitant.

'I suppose,' he eventually conceded.

'Good,' Garth said, pleased. *'And now hear this.'*

In as simple terms as he could manage, he updated John on the adventure to the abyss. Afterwards, the man was understandably astounded.

'Con has an army of crabs?' John whistled. 'I sure hope you're lying.'

'I am not.'

'And Limpet is on her way back?'

'With Stuart to protect her.'

'Blimey,' John paused contemplatively. 'Alright then. If this bizarre story has even an inkling of fact, then I shall *consider* doing as you ask... What is this favour anyway?'

Garth told him.

John listened, often repeating Garth's words in disbelief. Shrimp, meanwhile, focussed hard as though trying to decipher the bearded man's words.

***

Luke took some time to do a stock check of his items: a sword still sticky with crab fluid, a mermaid's purse packed with plentiful food, a jar to capture aquaseed, a compass to aid his return and a gelata to light the way. Overall, he was well equipped, but quickly missed the company that he had rebuffed mere moments ago.

With a heavy heart, he aimed his compass and hiked further south. Each step increased the gap between him and his friends. How long would it take Con and his army to reach the shipwreck town? A couple of days if they rushed. Luke hoped fervently that Garth had something amazing up his sleeve to abort the war. He stuck his thumb up in the air on the off chance that the whelk-boy would make contact – he did not. Luke clenched his fists in annoyance.

He tried to walk in a straight line, but found himself meandering around haphazard rock-chimneys. Bundles of long worms fought for the prime position at their peak, while pebble-white crabs crawled between oval clams. It was a wonderful place, but he no longer had anyone to share it with. This was not true for long. Soon, a familiar fish joined his lonely quest. Jaws surprised Luke by appearing from the shadows and circling the gelata above his head.

'Hello,' he greeted. 'Glad to see you, little buddy.'

The Videre fish appeared to swim closely to his ribs as if inspecting them.

'Got that from a fight with a crabman. We can't all just disappear like you!'

Rather peculiarly, the fish graced his ribs with its tiny fin. It felt as if someone had just brushed away the pain. Luke smiled. His chest was still sore, but somehow the fish had managed to ease his suffering. He gave his thanks and, of course, did not get a response.

Shuffling his backpack to a more comfortable position, he picked up the pace. If he covered more ground, he was more likely to find aquaseed. With this in mind, he traversed doggedly further. Time was no longer measured by the movement of the sun, but simply by how far he could push himself. To curb the feeling of loneliness, he would occasionally whisper to Jaws, though he suspected that this only served to draw the attention of whatever lay hidden in the darkness.

He reached a point where logic dictated he should have

rested, but carried on. Stopping was a last resort. His steps became less accurate and, more than once, he came close to tripping. One fall almost had him flying through searing hot smoke. Such a mistake would have, at the very least, blinded him. Fortunately, he managed to catch himself and hence forth revamped his efforts to take more care. Perhaps, as Con had labelled it, his need to find aquaseed had become an *obsession*.

All he knew was that his parents waited for him in another dimension and, if he did not save this one, return would be impossible. Such a thought was so scary that all other fears paled by comparison.

***

Luke awoke with a start. He had travelled until, whether willing or not, he could go no further. As tiredness had kicked in, he had found a bare patch of sand in a nest of clams and settled down for the night. Unguarded and alone, a situation for which he only had himself to blame, he had slept. Now it was time to continue.

He stood up carefully to avoid standing on the sharp clams that flourished in the nutrient-rich water. Jaws, meanwhile, shook free of the sand in which he had buried himself and floated up to eye level.

'Good morning, Jaws.'

Luke considered himself lucky. While he had caught some shut-eye, nothing had attacked and none of his food had been thieved. He grabbed a handful of meadoweed and treated himself to a generous breakfast. The energy would be needed for the journey ahead.

Once his stomach was mildly full, he set to untying the gelata rope. His knots were not difficult to undo and he soon had it free for carrying. Next, he took a lunging step over the clams to continue on his way.

It was at this moment that a terrible misfortune occurred.

As he brought his second foot to meet his first, the tips of his toes snagged on a particularly large shell. It was hardly a jolt, but it was enough to throw Luke off balance. He hopped clumsily on his one ground-planted foot and then took a tumble. As he landed ungracefully in the sand, he instinctively used his hands to break the fall. John's compass flicked out, but plummeted within reach.

The gelata, however, did not. It floated up and beyond.

'No!' shouted Luke in frustration. 'No! No! No!'

He scrambled to his feet and jumped, his hand frantically trying to grasp the fleeing rope. Empty dark water was all that he felt, and this only got darker as his sole source of light escaped towards the surface.

'This can't be happening,' he whispered, panic rising. 'This *cannot* be happening!'

The jelly-creature got smaller and smaller, silently bobbing out of view. Luke watched it, his despair worsening.

'Come back,' he said, weakly.

An instant later, he was angry.

'Come back!' Luke bellowed and then kicked out in his fury. His foot scraped something which could have been a clam, and he felt a shoot of pain as it sliced his skin. 'Ouch! Ouch! I hate you! I hate you! I hate you!'

Whether his hatred was directed at the clam, the gelata or himself, it was unclear. Luke then let out a howl of absolute rage.

With this, he dropped to the ground and started to sob. Nothing could be seen. His hands, Jaws, and the rock-chimneys that he *knew* pumped metres away, were all swallowed by impenetrable darkness.

'What am I going to do now, Jaws?' he spoke despairingly. 'I can't see anything. How am I meant to find aquaseed, or get back?'

His words were met with a foreboding silence.

'I've... failed.'

Glum thoughts ran riot. He would die here. When the

end came, Limpet would think him an unlikeable brat and a liar. The people of Naufragium would starve to death. Worst of all, his parents would never know how hard he had tried to get back to them.

***

Luke is as good as dead, Garth thought miserably.

He had spent hours detailing his plan to Kea, and then another few talking to John. The preparation had been complete with all the essential parts in place. He had been so smug. As far as he had been aware, Luke was well and continuing to look for aquaseed. How wrong he had been! A quick check on his friend had turned everything sour.

Garth had found himself floating in a stifling blackness. The only sound was that of rushing water which aggressively attacked him from all directions.

'Penn, I can't see Luke,' he cried out.

She must have offered him some calming advice, but it was too late. Panic had set in. His mind was reeling. As a result, he lost all control and started zooming around the abyss without direction, frantically searching for the slightest sign of his unfortunate friend.

That had been his biggest mistake.

As he zipped and zapped from side to side, he moved directly into one of the hidden chimney plumes and experienced a searing heat of unimaginable proportions.

Penn later explained that, had he been human, the sheer strain on his mind would have killed him. Gazoids, on the other hand, had an ancestral history that went all the way back to living in the toxic swamp. Luckily for him, his species had retained some of its resistance to extreme temperatures.

Therefore, although Garth may have preferred to have had lost his mind, he had instead withstood the agony, ripped off his helmet, spasmed off of his mother's chair and lay on the floor, writhing in pain.

Penn had incessantly called his name, possibly as some

safety procedure to keep him from insanity and remind who he was. By the time his mind had finally realised that, contrary to what it had just experienced, his body had *not* been scorched to a crisp, he already suspected the extent of his folly.

All he could think about was Luke. He feebly climbed his way back onto the chair, a feat that, in his current shell-shocked state, was probably the bravest action he'd ever taken.

He set the helmet back on and thought of the spiked shell that should have been sat snugly in Luke's otherworldly backpack. Nothing happened. This only confirmed his greatest fears. *He had lost Luke.*

In the literal heat of the moment, the mental link between his mind and Luke's position had been destroyed. It was instinctive and awful. It meant, and Penn later confirmed this, that his only way to find Luke would be to manually search the Abyss. Without light and without guidance, this was an impossible task.

Luke was truly alone. And from what Garth had seen, his friend was in dire need of help.

Garth did not know what had befallen him, but he felt a heart-wrenching sadness nonetheless. It was a new emotion and one that he did not expect. They had achieved so much together.

Luke had done so well.

He should have returned to Naufragium in glory, not been forgotten about on the seabed. He *should* have been at home with his parents.

The helmet soaked up this thought and suddenly the screen showed that dreadful scene; Luke's parents staring out to sea, still caught between outrage and disbelief, on that blustery day back on Earth.

His mother had her mouth wide open, clearly calling for her son, and tears slowly edging their way down her face. His father had his fists clenched and looked ready to launch himself into the sea at any moment.

They were waiting for their son to return. And now they would be waiting for the rest of their lives.

A tidal wave of overwhelming remorse shook Garth to his very core.

It was all his fault. He did this to them. Not out of necessity, but out of ignorance and boredom. He yanked off the helmet and, for the first time, begged for the arrival of the Gavoidon and the justified punishment that would follow.

***

The gelata had disappeared completely, vanishing along with Luke's dreams. He pointlessly wiped at tears that instantly merged with the seawater anyway. Jaw's fin brushed his shoulder as if in consolation; at least he wasn't entirely alone.

Sifting through the sand, he found John's compass and cradled it on his lap. The metal felt shockingly cold when compared to the heat radiating from the hidden rock-chimneys. He quenched a sudden urge to throw it away. It was no use anymore. His mermaid's purse was on his back and he took it off. Searching inside, he made out the hermit-shell and, once again, stuck his thumb in the air. There was no response. Perhaps Garth had been killed, or maybe he'd found somebody else to carry out his bidding. Luke felt another bout of anger. How dare he ignore him? How dare he keep him in the dark?

Another touch on the shoulder.

'What?' Luke snapped. 'What do you want?'

He shuffled about and, as with every direction, he could not see anything.

'There's nothing there, Jaws,' he whined. He was about to go back to feeling sorry for himself when a glimpse of light voyaged through the water and reached his adapting eyes. As quickly as it came, it was gone.

'Wha – ' he started, before his voice faltered with surprise.

He tried again.

'What *was* that?'

A short wait followed and then he saw another tiny sparkle.

Shooting to his feet and swinging his pack onto his back, he squinted in the rough direction of the flashes. Seconds later, there was another weak pulse of light. Nothing else for it, he thought; he simply had to get closer.

He fumbled forwards, taking each mysterious step as slowly as possible. He brought his foremost foot down carefully, ensuring that it touched on sand before applying his full weight. Once or twice, he felt the rough texture of clamshells and was forced to step in a different direction. When the water became too hot, he moved until it was cooler again; a single misstep into the smoke would mean a painful demise.

He paused and waited for another flash.

'Look!' he pointed, but could not see his own arm. 'There were two of them!' This time the light was stronger; a couple of blinking eyes glimmered through the dark. 'We must be getting close!'

He adjusted his aim and pushed on. A surge of heat had him sway to the side and something eel-like slid across his face. He was not deterred. A third flash of light added to the two. They were moving randomly, he realised, like gas particles in the air.

Restraining the urge to walk faster, he neared the lights with painstaking sluggishness. A fourth could be seen. A fifth quickly followed. His excitement grew until he was almost shaking. He knew a moment's euphoria when he saw the cherished lights between the shadows of two rock-chimneys. They flashed at him – a gathering of lighthouses, steering him from danger and calling him to port. Turning sideways, he shimmied past a couple of smoking pillars.

On arrival, he rubbed his eyes and gave himself a pinch. Before him was an underwater pond, a surface beneath the surface. The sheer enigma of such a situation had him questioning his own sanity. Within, lights flashed at him like a crowd of cameras trying to catch snaps of a famous celebrity. Jaws swam ahead, waltzing above with blatant joy.

Luke rushed forward and knelt by the edge. Dots of white flitted across his astonished face. He took a single hand and trailed it across the surface.

Reaching for his glass jar, he uncorked it with a satisfying *pop*. Using a scooping motion, he filled it to the rim and then pounded it securely shut. Holding the jar to his eyes, he studied the beauty of its contents.

'We've found it, Jaws. We've found it.'

Somehow, he knew exactly what it was.

Aquaseed.

***

For a long while, Luke simply sat by the waterside. It seemed a peaceful place and one in which he longed to linger. Jaws was looping and twisting with blatant delight. Luke knew how the little fish felt; this mesmerising oasis of light boosted the spirits. However, he could not stay – he had a quest to fulfil.

He wondered if the light of the jar would be enough to aid him on his return to Naufragium. When he backed away from the shimmering pond, he was quickly delved into the dark once more. His measly portion of aquaseed was too dim to light the way. He retreated with a sense of resignation.

'It's helpless,' he said to his one remaining companion. 'There's no point leaving if I cannot find my way to the surface.'

Jaws wiggled to face him.

'Even if by some miracle, I did survive the journey blind,' Luke continued, 'it would take me weeks, maybe months, to get past the maze of chimneys.'

The fish gave him an understanding stare.

'By which point, Naufragium might be gone and the

dimension might have collapsed.' He smiled sadly at his tiny orange friend. 'But,' Luke waved the jar victoriously, 'we found some aquaseed. That's got to count for something.'

Jaws knocked gently into his forehead as if to give the fish equivalent of a 'high-five'. Through this tiny, insignificant gesture, Luke got the fleeting impression that something big had changed. He hardly took notice of it before resuming his narrative.

'There are worse places to die, I suppose,' he said, scanning his surroundings with a sigh. When he glanced back at Jaws, the fish had *vanished*. He looked about and then up to find his friend loitering high above as if to say goodbye. 'Go on, then. Go back,' he said. 'I would, if I could.'

Next, the fish did the last thing he could have expected. It sped down and gave him a firm slap on the cheek with its tail.

'Hey! There's no need for that!' Astounded, Luke received another hit to the back of the head.

'Oi!' he leapt to his feet, making a playful grab at his friend. Jaws swam beyond his attempts and appeared to loop around in an almost taunting way.

'That's hardly fair!' he shouted. Jaws dived back down for another attack. 'Right. That's it!'

This time, Luke was ready. He ducked out of the way and then leapt at the retreating fish. His hand sailed closer, but just missed his target. He reached the peak of his jump and braced himself for the inevitable crash to the ground. *But it never came.*

There was no falling sensation; instead, his legs dangled in mid-water. After all this time, it felt horrifically unnatural and he peddled his feet erratically. This only served to boost him higher and soon he looked down upon the pond from a bird's-eye view.

Luke was *swimming*.

CHAPTER 23: MISPLACED VENGEANCE

'Wohooooooo!'
At first, he was fearful, and then cautious. As time passed, caution gave way to confidence. With the grace of an eagle, Luke swooped down on the pond and skimmed its treacle-like surface. He then rose and, laughing all the while, indulged himself in a few somersaults. Slowing to an upright position, he fist-pumped in celebration and, careless to what could be listening, shouted to the world. 'I can swim! I can actually swim!'

He did not understand it at all. One minute, he had been ground-bound like any other Naufragian. In the next, he could kick his way up to where Jaws patiently hovered. Was it the aquaseed or something else? If only Limpet could see him now, even she would be speechless!

He stretched out in suspension with his hands behind his head and watched his bubbles rise out of sight. He greeted the ability to swim with open arms. Here, buoyancy was akin to suddenly gaining the power to fly. And with this thought, he remembered Limpet's tale about Videre fish and how they granted boons to those that the Lord of the Sea deemed worthy. The parallels between that ancient story and what he was now experiencing was undeniable.

Jaws, the possible source of all this madness, had stayed

put while Luke had showed off his new-found power. Luke swam to him now, but the fish darted higher up. A second attempt wielded the same result. Luke gulped. The Videre fish clearly wanted to be followed, and he knew their destination. *The surface.*

Luke had two main concerns. Firstly, it was going to be dark, *really* dark. Secondly, if he lost his ability to swim, he would plummet onto whatever waited for him on the seabed. From his sketchy knowledge of the area, this could lead to being cut by clams or roasted by smoke. And that's only if he was lucky enough to survive the fall in the first place.

Whatever his misgivings, he had to give it a go while he had the chance. Waving a fond farewell to the pond, he swam upwards until it shrank in size to become a mere puddle. More sparkling pools of aquaseed could be seen beyond; clearly the ponds were rare, but not exclusive.

He steeled himself and then made for the sea's surface with all his might. Swiping at the water and kicking furiously, he became a rocket blasting off into space leaving a jet of chaos in its wake. And, just like a rocket, he was surrounded by a claustrophobic blackness. Soon all he could hear was the thrashing of his own efforts. Whether Jaws was with him or not, he could not tell.

Even though he felt fast, evidence of the surface came excruciatingly slowly. Over what seemed like hours, the blackness merged lighter. Eventually, he could make out his friend, a murky dot in the vast expanse of the sea, darting alongside him. They were two tiny shadows launching from dark blue to slightly-less dark blue. Jaws eventually took on a dim orange; a travesty of his vibrant scales. Luke was thrilled when, once again, he could make out his own arms and legs.

Then he saw the surface. It was about fifty metres away and counting. His muscles in his legs and hip screamed for a rest, but stopping was not an option. Wobbly fingers of sunlight beckoned him from above and gentle waves rippled across the surface. Persisting through the burn of lactic acid, he soared upwards. Finally, with a steely determination, he smashed through the uppermost layer of water. White froth erupted around him and he drew in a hungry lungful of sea air. He had arrived.

The sun was blinding, but he did not care. The sight of clear blue skies was more welcome than anything Luke could possibly imagine. He lay on his back, catching his breath and gazing at the horizon with adoration. Every muscle felt flimsy with exhaustion, but he spared a couple for a mile-wide grin. Sculling feebly around in a circle, he surveyed the area for landmarks, but there weren't any.

He took some time to reassess his situation; his fortune had taken a turn for the better. In his mermaid's purse was a jarful of aquaseed and, against all odds, he was at the surface. He had never expected to get this far and now questions arose that had never occurred to him before.

He realised that he could simply release the aquaseed and hope for the best. It might work its magic and then allow him to be sent home. But then, the Naufragians would never know *why* their fish returned. They certainly would never believe that Luke's deep-sea expedition had been a success and that aquaseed *did* exist. This would mean they would be clueless about what to do should they find themselves in the same situation years down the line. And that's assuming that he has *enough* aquaseed to make a difference. If his sample did not have the desired effect, then the whole thing would have been pointless.

He needed to *prove* that aquaseed exists. At least then, maybe it would fill the Naufragians with hope and they might send a larger, better-equipped crew to find those aquaseed pools. It would, of course, all be for nothing if the dimension collapsed before the replenished food chain kicked in. Could he be certain that Garth was dealing with the war? Naufragium might need somebody who could go to the surface and negotiate. Somebody like *him*.

Luke made a decision and ducked below; he would return to Naufragium as fast as he could.

Carefully, he sifted through the meadoweed until he could pick out some headrush. A couple of nibbles would replenish his energy. A mouthful would have him swimming like a madman. He ate *a whole strand*.

Before the need to move attacked him, he withdrew John's compass and rotated until he faced north. Then the energy bubbled through his body. Luke became a shark on the hunt, tireless and without mercy. Jaws tailed him as close as the little fish could manage.

***

Garth had waited, but no Gavoidon had turned up to end his torment. He had been wallowing in self-pity and remorse, staring miserably at a black, lifeless screen. The helmet lay discarded at his side.

'It's not over, you know,' Penn said.

'Over? Of course it's over!' Garth blurted. 'Luke is *dead*.'

'We don't know that for sure,' she reminded him. 'And if we don't try to save the dimension now, all the people that Luke has come to care about will also be gone. If he has forfeited his life, then we need to make sure that his sacrifice was worth something.'

'You'd like that wouldn't you?' replied Garth angrily. He had not forgotten that Penn had her own reasons for saving the dimension that had nothing to do with saving lives, even if she testified otherwise. 'Besides, he's the changer, the catalyst. What can we possibly achieve without him?'

'Don't you see? Luke has already set all the necessary motions in place. Naufragium knows about aquaseed. If we can avert the war, then the underwater people will send another raiding party to the Abyss, and this one might be successful.'

'We haven't got time! The Gavoidon cannot be far away now,' Garth moaned. 'Soon we'll be dead, just like Luke.'

'Now who's being selfish!' said Penn. 'Do you think that us living or dying matters to the people of Naufragium? Would you not rather leave this place knowing that you've achieved great good in the universe?'

She had him there, Garth thought to himself. They should do as much as they could before the Gavoidon arrived. That way, the dimension had the best shot of staying strong and a whole world of people could potentially extend their existence.

Grumbling to himself, he reluctantly picked up the Dimension Shift helmet. It felt heavier than normal and he almost slapped it back down. Instead, he bottled his emotions and soon found himself floating above the underwater town. The sound of a bell could be heard.

...*DONG! DONG! DONG! DONG! DONG! DONG! DONG! DONG!*...

It was continuous. A celebration. That only meant one thing – Con and his army had arrived. Sure enough, the eldership in the centre of Naufragium was a hive of activity. Garth had arrived just in time to see Con standing upon its deck, waiting for the buzz to quiet down. Beside him stood his trusty right-hand man Elkhorn. The crabmen themselves took up a whole section of the street to the south, while curious Naufragians had gathered to the north, keeping their distance. The army was as still as statues and had formed perfect ranks. In their full number, it was a very intimidating sight indeed.

'Quiet!' Con yelled.

The talking immediately stopped and all was silent.

'I suppose you might be wondering why I took off with war around the corner,' he said. 'I expect a *few* of you even *doubted* me.' He paused for dramatic effect and then held the horn aloft. 'Doubt me no longer!'

There was a huge round of applause.

'I bring you an army!' he shouted over the ear-shattering ovation. 'I bring you a force that will put those surface scum *in their place!*'

Garth hardly thought it possible, but the cheers got even louder.

'When the attack comes, and it *will* come, we will have the perfect way to defend our town... We will attack!' Con punched the air ferociously. 'Blood will pour down from above, ships will shatter, and they will *fear* us. But we won't stop there, oh no, we will go to their homeland. We will *wipe them out!*'

It was a blood boiling speech. Some looked riled up for war. Others gathered their children close and hugged them at the prospect of living without having to be afraid. Con revelled in the excitement. 'This army means that they will never trawl these waters again!'

The speech finished on a crescendo and the people of Naufragium went berserk. Some followed Con's example and roared a war-cry, shaking clenched fists at the surface. Others linked arms and did some kind of ancient battle dance; it involved lots of chest bumping and pulling angry faces. This would have been a source of humour for Garth, but it filled him with dread. How was he meant to stop *this*?

Con was talking to someone, but his words could not be heard. Garth used his mind to draw closer in a way that now seemed so natural. It became clear that the leader was aiming his attention towards Beadlet. 'Is the harvest done for the day?'

'Tis done, just need ta ge' the wheel'arrows, is all!'

'No need,' Con winked. 'I'll handle that.'

The sound of the horn contributed to the noise. A few Naufragians realised something was afoot and stared, dumbfounded, at the stone army. Twenty or so crabmen were awoken into action and lunged their way to the shallows. The crowd readily parted to the side so that they could pass through. The crabmen's pointed legs made a wreck of the carefully placed shells that comprised the central street, but nobody uttered a complaint. Ten minutes later, they returned hauling a number of bountiful wheelbarrows. For once, the townsmen did not voice their outrage at having only seaweed to eat. Instead, they formed orderly queues and gave out enthusiastic thanks. Clearly, they had been charmed by the obedient and helpful crabmen.

Garth could no longer bear their high spirits. It was so at odds with how he felt. He left the Naufragians to their merry dinner and chose to make a visit to John's wreck. Inside, Limpet, Stuart, Shrimp and John poured over a map. Straight away, he could see a mark which indicated where tomorrow's attack would come from. Garth listened as Limpet dished out her tale. She seemed close to exhaustion, but gave as much detail of her adventure as was fitting. John accepted her words gravely, going red with anger when he heard how her nose had been broken. Aside from this, he looked insufferably glad to have his daughter back. Shrimp and Stuart, meanwhile, talked in simple one or two word sentences. Garth was amazed at how quickly the manacled woman's speaking had improved.

When Limpet got to the part about Luke, she looked tremendously sad. 'He said he was from a different planet.'

'I was told the same.'

'Did you actually believe him?'

'Not straight away, no, but so much has been strange of late. And he defies all that we have ever known. There's not been a man in all of history that has been able to pass the surface.'

'I know,' she sounded miserable. 'Was I wrong to abandon him?'

'Seems to me like he did not give you much choice,' said John, giving her a comforting pat on the back. 'Anyway, I may need your help tomorrow. I think there's a way we can end the war without starting a feud.'

All eyes in the room were on him now.

'It starts with us getting that horn!'

The man may have lost the respect of his townsmen, but the love of the people on that table elevated him to commander once more. He unveiled the plan and all soaked up his words.

***

As energy ran like fire through Luke's veins, his swimming technique went out of the window. He swung his arms like a windmill and made enough noise to rival a speedboat. Birds taking an evening paddle launched off the surface with an outcry of panic. He swam through the day, chasing the sun as it sank beneath the horizon. When he wanted to go even faster, he dipped below to transform into an underwater missile. Sparingly, he would whip out John's compass and ensure he was going in the right direction. Most of the time, however, he lacked the will power; all he wanted in the world was to swim and never stop.

It hardly seemed that any time passed, but soon the first stars dotted the night sky. He left Jaws behind in a stream of bubbles and found it difficult to care. His legs motored through the water tirelessly. His efforts were boosted by day dreams of his victorious return. His head twisted from side to side, his shoulders rolled, but he did not grow dizzy.

When the moon reared its radiant head, Luke's eyes pinpointed a mound of land in the shape of an ominous shark fin. Solis Occassum. He was heading the right way. Far beneath, he suspected that he zoomed over the abyss and may have already reached the canyon path. He soared in a moderately straight line without having to bow to the fluctuations of the seabed. What had taken him days to traverse, now took him mere hours of travel.

In the dark of night, he felt his energy flag slightly and topped up his headrush reserve. Another strand sizzled and popped in his mouth and any tiredness became a forgotten memory. The moon came and went in the blink of an eye, the night sailing by in a blur. Gradually, the stars were lost to the coming of a far more powerful source of light. Solis Occassum, meanwhile, grew a smidgen bigger. Luke grinned. Naufragium would have a celebration like no other when he showed them what he had found. Increasing his speed even more, he kept an eye out for a mast with a giant bell.

***

At some ungodly hour in the morning, Kea's door was barged open, colliding with her wall with a loud smash. Normally she would have been fast asleep, but not today. On the contrary, she was waiting expectantly and watching the appearance of the first slither of sunrise. The stench of Chuck reached her nostrils moments before her arms were bound.

'You're... alive,' he gaped dimwittedly, unable to contain his surprise.

Obviously, he had expected to fetch a starved corpse.

Kea did not say anything. Nor did she feign weakness for his benefit. Having been dangled before death by a hair, she was more than feeble enough. Chuck wheezed as he took most of her weight and dragged her down the stairs to the palace stables. En route, she noticed that the building was empty; even the servants, it appeared, had been gifted the day off to bear witness to the war. The stables were likewise vacant, except for Chuck's bull that thudded about impatiently in a hay-filled stall.

Internally, Kea groaned. Her backside had only recently recovered from her trip up the mountain. To her outrage, she was not even given the unwanted experience of sitting on the bull's bony shoulders. Instead, she was hogtied like a pig and shoved onto its even less comfortable rump. Facedown, she looked over the bull's side. This rather restricted viewpoint showed her a single chunky hoof on faeces-covered straw. It took a lot of self-restraint to stop her protesting at such a demeaning way of travel.

Wait, she soothed the roaring royal lion within her soul. *Your time will come, but not yet.*

Chuck made sure that she was secure and then whipped

his bull into a clumsy canter. They sped out of the musky smell of animals and hit a wall of fresh morning air. Kea used the type of ground they covered to judge how far down the mountain they travelled. She watched the bull's legs descend the palace steps, trot down the stone road and, eventually, pound onto the sand of the horseshoe bay. The sound of excitement grew with each second, reaching tremendous levels by the time that they came to a halt. Before she had even been hauled upright, she knew that everyone, rich or poor, had gathered to see the warships off.

A sea of royal reds and humble browns met her eyes. Harsh jeers and taunts attacked her from the throng. These quietened slightly to a wave of whispers when all realised that she was not dead. The thick wooden post embedded in the sand had been intended for her lifeless body. Nonetheless, Chuck tied her to it so that she faced the horizon. A merchant, beneath an ever-present cloud of flies, bellowed his sale of rotten fruit. Kea knew what was coming; she had witnessed it too many times before.

The first fruit to bruise her cheek was a sickeningly soft tomato. The next projectile was a decomposed banana skin. Once started, the barrage of fruit was nonstop. She could barely keep her eyes open as she was pummelled from all angles. Her hope took a similar beating. Through drips of vile juice, she caught flashes of her torturers. They comprised mainly of Rex's cronies. The poor, she reckoned, could not afford the luxury of buying food just for the purposes of throwing it. An uplifting thought came to her as a peach squished into her left eye. Maybe Margaret had spread Kea's story among the servants. Perhaps all was not lost.

Just as she was given enough respite to peel open her sticky eyes, the crowd split and revealed the fleet that bobbed in the distance. Strutting towards her, with an aura of gloating, was her ecstatic father. For the occasion, he was decked out in a suit of armour, but stubbornly wore a crown in the place of a helmet. He looked like a spoilt king in the outfit of a knight. A satisfying flicker of anger passed across his features when he realised that she lived.

'Should have known,' he sneered, snaking around to her side. 'You are a Solomon, after all.' She did not respond. 'Afraid, are we?' he whispered mistakenly. 'You should be. Look at my glorious fleet!'

Beyond him, about twenty gleaming warships waited. They were impressive in size and floated seamlessly on the surface. Evidence of their construction lay in the discarded parts of turtleoak turtles that littered the beach. On the rear end of each ship was a massive barbed cylinder with chain-wrapped winches on either side. Presently, the sails were wrapped in tight bundles, choked from picking up the slightest gust. Instead, long oars stuck out of either side and dipped their flattened heads in the waves.

It was distastefully blatant which ship was intended for her father. His was twice the length of the others and was armed with a golden spiked steamroller. It would have been intimidating if it did not speak so blatantly of vanity.

'Yes,' her father drawled. 'Your fish-friends do not stand a chance. The underwater town will be no more.' He waddled to her front and stared at the defeat in her eyes. 'You've fought so hard to stay alive only to see how badly you have failed. If I were you, I would have given up and died.'

Kea took this opportunity to spit out a mixture of saliva and rotten fruit. The missile splattered onto her father's lower lip and got caught in his matted chin hair. Scrunching up his bulbous nose in disgust, he desperately tried to wipe off the muck. However, when he turned around and stormed off, a patch of orange remained crusted in his beard.

Chuck removed Kea from the post and, as if she were cargo, bundled her into a small rowing boat. Just above its rim, she saw Cornelius embarking in a similar vessel. It looked a very tight fit; there were the two oarsmen, the old man himself, and a giant padlocked chest that took up half the space. She wondered briefly what it contained, but found that he was swiftly oared out of sight and out of mind.

When Chuck added his immense weight to their boat, it creaked fearfully, but managed to hold. Before long, the oarsmen were paddling them beyond the shore. By the time they had swayed and bobbed their way alongside her father's ship, she felt horribly ill. Two hooks were lowered and attached to their craft. The united heaving of fishermen filled the air as they juddered upwards, stopping level with the deck.

Chuck all but threw her onto wooden planks and she uttered a cry of pain. He gave her no time to recover and shoved her into a bare cabin. Here, she crumpled uncomfortably to the floor and twisted her head in time to see the door get slammed shut.

Several locks were put in place. She was left on her own, coated in rotten fruit and weak with seasickness. If she had anything to throw up, she surely would have.

***

Garth hovered above the fleet with dull unease. As the wind was yet to pick up, the vessels were forced to start their journey using an alternative method. About ten burly sailors on each furiously wrenched oars through the water to power the ships to the required position. They stopped their progress to the north of Naufragium. Here, they took on a V-shaped formation with Rex's ship at the forefront.

Winches were unreeled and sturdy metal chains were rattled out. The weapons designed by Cornelius rolled off the back, taking shards of wood with them. The winches span on their own accord until their burden plopped to the seabed. Anchors were not needed; the ships were going nowhere without a powerful breeze. The sailors set about unwrapping sails in preparation for the acclaimed monthly gale-force wind that would spur them over the underwater town.

So, Rex's fleet was ready, but was Naufragium? Garth sent out a murmur of thought through the helmet and he zoomed below the surface. Like clockwork, Brittle's scout, a boy with horns of sponge for ears, was patrolling the outskirts of the seaweed fields. Young though he was, he played his part to perfection. Garth watched as the boy caught sight of the twenty waiting hulls and the spiked rollers that ran across the sand. He leapt in the air like a startled rabbit and then sprinted for Con's headquarters.

Garth followed him all the way. The boy bounded down the street and split off to the east. On arrival to the pirate wreck, he shot inside and called out an alarm. The crab-man army stood outside, unresponsive as always. However, this was compensated by Con, who charged out and sprinted for the eldership for all that he was worth. Elkhorn followed, summoning the Naufragians to arms as he went. In record time, Con was bouncing up the rock stairs and thumping across the eldership's deck. In a few giant lunches, he held the bell's rope in his eager hands and was about to alert the whole town when...

'I wouldn't do that if I were you.' John appeared from behind one of the masts.

'Why not?' Con demanded.

'The ships aren't *that* far away.'

'Your point being?'

'It's likely they will hear the bell.'

'So?'

'So they will know that *you* know,' John explained. 'We'll completely lose the element of surprise.'

Con hesitated, saw John's reasoning and reluctantly let go of the rope. Below on the shell-street, the sponge-eared boy was running by. He did not go unnoticed. Con bellowed down some instructions. 'Barrel!' he roared. 'Make sure nobody uses this bell!'

The look of upset that played across the boy's face betrayed his true feelings. Garth expected that the scout would rather join the action than take on guard duties. Nevertheless, he did as he was told. Looking back at Con, Garth noticed that the madman was primed to use the horn.

BAROOOOOOOOOOOOOM!

'That ought to get everyone's attention,' John approved and then clamped a hand on Con's shoulder. 'After all that you've done, you owe me. Let me stand by your side when you unleash hell on the surface.'

The madman shook free.

'Fine,' he growled.

In normal circumstances, Garth doubted that he would have agreed, but this was no time to argue. Together, John and Con ran up to the shallows. In front of them and behind, fellow Naufragians merged onto the street. Likewise, the crabman army started swarming in the same direction. By the time they reached the monstrosities that lurked to flatten their town, a scattering of troops were already present.

There was little that this small force could do, Garth realised. The cylinder's spikes were so numerous and sharp that climbing them would have been absurd. Even if they reached the chains, cutting them would take hours. A few soldiers were launching spears at the bottoms of the ships, but their attempts were falling short.

'Stop that!' Con snapped at them. 'I have a better idea.'

Stunned, the troops dropped their spears and stared.

'Can you tell which one belongs to the surface King?' John said sourly, arriving at his side. It was obvious. Rex's golden weapon stood out from the rest like a ruby in a pile of coal.

'They will all die,' said Con darkly. 'King or not.'

'It is what they deserve,' John agreed grimly.

Garth had a horrible feeling that the bearded man had gone rogue and abandoned their plan. The next to arrive at the scene was Elkhorn. He rampaged over with another wave of his trained farmers.

'What are we waiting for?' he asked. 'What should we do, Con?'

Con put his hand up to halt the queries. Garth recognised that he was waiting for his crabman army to appear. They had been left behind in the rush, but were soon rallying a clawed mass beneath the ship's shadows. The land people were utterly ignorant of what nightmares awaited them, tens of metres below.

The tension rose considerably. Garth could feel it. The huddled Naufragians were all staring at Con expectantly. Without instruction, they appeared helpless and their weapons seemed mere accessories. When the trickle of crabmen slowed and nearly all three hundred had collected, Con finally addressed his town.

'For Naufragium!' he roared, the mask of calm crumbling away. What lay beneath was a monster of pure vengeance. His eyes darkened with anger, his veins ballooned and his upper lip twitched uncontrollably. He bought the horn to his lips, biting down on the mouthpiece. This was it. A hateful thought that would bring the full force of the crabmen to every ship.

'BAROOO –'

John made his move. The punch he sent flying at Con's cheek was so powerful that Garth expected it was fuelled by his daughter's bent nose. Con's vengeance was disrupted, while John exacted some of his own. In the next second, he whipped the horn out of the madman's hands. The crabmen, meanwhile, remained motionless. The command, incomplete.

Con recovered fast and dived headfirst at John with an unprecedented fury. The bearded man did not underestimate his old partner and wasted no time calling for an ally.

'Now!' John signalled.

From the edge of the meadoweed fields shot Limpet, racing close to the action. Moments before he was smashed to the ground by Con's crazed attack, John chucked the horn. It spun as it flew upwards, arced, and then dropped to the seabed. The eyes of every Naufragian followed its journey. Limpet had to dive forward with both hands, but she just about managed to catch it.

At the same time, her father was barrelled to the floor. Con growled a curse and clashed his head straight into John's brow. There was an audible crack and Garth winced. The bearded man was out cold or *worse*. Con scrambled to his feet and dealt his unconscious victim a brutal kick to the chest.

'Dad!' Limpet screamed, stopped in her tracks by the violence.

Con looked at her and then at the horn which she held.

'Elkhorn!' he barked. Like a hound released, the blonde hulk bounded after her. Once again, Limpet broke into a run. It was doomed from the start. For each of her strides, Elkhorn covered two. She was quickly dwarfed by his huge figure and within reach of his bear-like mittens. Garth knew before it happened that Con was going to regain the horn. Inevitably, Elkhorn tackled Limpet to the sand and the impact caused her to fumble the horn. It skidded away from where they wrestled.

Game over.

The horn continued until it stopped at somebody's feet. Whoever it was, picked it up slowly and would surely return it to the madman's power-crazed hands. A woman with a manacle around her neck. To Garth's amazement, he realised that he was looking at Shrimp. Elkhorn was still floor-bound and Con was some way off – this gave her some precious time. For a moment, she looked confused and Garth expected she had no idea what to do. Then, she brought it to her lips and summoned a powerful breath.

Garth made a snap decision. With a surge of brain activity, he connected to the crabman horn. It felt jarringly different from any time before. He was blinded, but at the same time he could see. Not pictures, pixels or colours, but *thoughts*. Shrimp's were there, a firework of colour ready to be sent to the waiting army. But her ideas were half-formed. Her grasp of the plan was frail and confused. Her understanding was impressive, but it needed tweaking.

Somehow, and Garth had no idea how, he fed his own thoughts into the horn. They merged with Shrimp's and filled the gaps in her knowledge. He contributed a mental image of Rex's flabby face and thick sideburns. Following this, he attached a painting of Chuck's submissive cowering. To finish, he added Kea's kind features, a sharp rebuke to any crabman that caused her injury and a solid command to the crabmen to carry out her every whim. His thoughts sparked blue and danced with Shrimp's gunpowder purple. They entwined to form a rope of crystal clear thought. When Shrimp blew, it was her instruction and his padding that was sent forth.

'BAROOOOOOOOOOOOOM!'

Garth disconnected, feeling like he had just awoken from a trance. How much time had gone by? Seconds. Con still charged, while Elkhorn and Limpet still squirmed on the floor. To Garth, time had temporarily slowed, but now it made up for it in full. Con stampeded towards Shrimp, his eyes narrowed to evil slits. He ducked his head and swiftly withdrew his dagger from a loop in his belt. As he neared, he made a ferocious lunge with his weapon.

It *would* have caught her straight in the chest.

It *would* have killed her.

Instead, there was a snarl and, tearing from the side, came Stuart. He got there just in time to stand in the way and take the full force of the stab. A howl of pain was heard as the knife plunged into his stomach. This, however, was nothing compared to the screech of anger from Shrimp. The woman retaliated in the only way that she could. She threw the horn onto the ground and then stamped on it with all her weight, until all that remained was useless rubble.

Stuart fell forwards, draping his full weight on Con. The madman shrugged off Stuart's heavy body and withdrew his weapon from flesh. Without even a second glance, he continued his obsessive search for the horn.

Now, free of blockage, shoots of red pumped from Stuart's injury. As he plonked to the seabed, he made one last act to protect his half-sister. A hairy hand wrapped around Con's fleeing foot and gave a vicious yank. Even though this had the madman sprawling to the sand, he persisted to frantically sift the sand for his precious horn. It was only when Con's face was confronted with the horn debris that reality sunk in. It was destroyed.

'No! No! No!' he shouted, trying desperately to piece it back together. 'What have you done?'

Shrimp was not listening. She was kneeling down by her saviour and cradling his head. 'Stu-art,' she said. 'Don't go!'

The wolfman had a hand clamped to his gaping gut. He looked up at her with doleful eyes. Garth knew that he was a goner from the amount of blood spewing out. Wrapping an arm around Shrimp's neck, he drew her closer. The mantis shrimp in his empty socket slid through his eyepatch shell. Hesitantly, it crawled up his face and onto Shrimp's shoulder. He whispered something to her ear and then flopped for the final time. Only Garth had been privy to what passed between the two siblings. Stuart's last word was one of advice. Run.

The mantis shrimp clung on as they fled the scene. They disappeared into the seaweed just as the townsmen gathered around and panic started to kick in. Ever loyal to his master, Elkhorn followed her, but had no chance of finding his target in the seaweed maze. Con was staring at what remained of the crabhorn in disbelief.

'Is that the horn?' a man questioned, worried.

'How will you control the army now?' a woman said in a shrill voice.

'Is that man dead?'

Con answered none of these questions. Garth wasn't even sure he heard them. It seemed that he was only just realising that he had committed murder in his rage. 'No, no, no, no....' Con muttered to himself. 'No!' He threw several punches at the sand. '*She* broke it! *She* has doomed us!'

He pointed an accusing finger, but there was nobody there. Shrimp was long gone. The people of Naufragium stared at the man who they had appointed leader and deemed him unworthy.

'John,' an old man called. 'Where's John? He might know what to do!'

'Over here!' shouted Limpet.

Garth was surprised at how pleased he was to see John sitting up. Limpet must have rushed to his side in the chaos and now she basically held him in position. He looked weak, but he was alive. As the Naufragians shifted their focus towards him, the bearded man held up a shaky hand. 'Look,' he urged feebly.

In the drama of it all, the crabman army had gone somewhat ignored. Garth had fallen into the same trap, but now he gave them due attention. Unseen, forty or so had gathered at the base of Rex's ship. Now, they piled on top of each other in the same way that Con had demonstrated on the Abyssal Plain. Gradually, they formed a tower that rocketed up to the surface, each crabman standing on the shoulders of the next.

Garth gave a grim smirk; his plan had worked. They had regained the horn and now the army was carrying out their last ever order, a more pinpointed attack than the all-encompassing slaughter that Con had desired. Garth had not expected Shrimp to break the horn, but perhaps it would not matter. The Naufragians could only stare and pose questions to which they had no answers.

'What are they doing?'

'Why?'

John knew.

'They go to kill the surface king,' he wheezed.

CHAPTER 24: MONSTERS FROM THE SEA

Physically and mentally, Kea was in the dark. The cabin in which she had been locked was completely bare of character. As the turtleoak wood only lasted a short while, making the ships comfortable served no purpose. Weeks from now her father's ship would start to dip and would have to be dismantled. What the cabin did not lack, however, was an overpoweringly salty musk that choked the nostrils. This, combined with the jolting sways of being oared out to sea, had her retching to no avail.

Despite her hands being bound, she managed to prop herself up on the back wall. The room spun out of control and she almost keeled over from dizziness. The gentle bobbing of the ship told her that they had arrived. Where was her father? She suspected he was out on deck, downing a pint of drink and bragging to his royal subjects. In fact, if she listened very hard, she could hear their harsh laughter. To them, this was just an entertaining show.

Kea waited, although she was unclear exactly what for. Time dragged by slowly and each time she heard the sails flap, she feared the worst. Once that powerful wind hit, nobody would be able to do anything to stop the ships destroying Luke's town. It could happen at any moment. It had been about twenty painful minutes when she heard two pairs of heavy footsteps. A dark shadow appeared at the base of the crack of light that outlined the cabin door.

It opened and her father entered, tottering in a way that had little to do with being at sea. Momentarily, the bright light hid his features, but she could soon make out his smug grin and the patch of orange that remained in his beard; clearly nobody had plucked up the courage to point it out. Behind him swaggered Chuck who seemed to be on the brink of raucous laughter as if privy to some secret jest. A terrible feeling of foreboding rose from the empty pit of her stomach.

'Ke-ah, Ke-ah, Ke-ah,' her father drawled. 'What am I going to do with you? My own flesh and blood, helping an enemy of war to escape.'

'Do you know what we're doing now? We're waiting for this wind that Cornelius has promised. The old man does produce some stinkers. It's only a matter of time before he summons a fart strong enough to move this fleet over your precious sea-friends.' Chuck sniggered.

'Thing is this waiting, well, it's terribly *boring*. And you know I don't deal well with boredom. So I thought, why am I keeping you here in this cabin? You clearly favour the sea-people. How rude of me to postpone your reunion. How awful of me to keep you apart from the town that you have pointlessly sacrificed yourself to save.'

Kea knew all too well where this was going and felt fear once more. She looked at her father, begging him to delay just a little longer. He saw the understanding in her eyes and smiled mirthlessly. 'Chuck, would you do the honours and - well chuck - my pain-in-the-ass daughter off of this ship? She's overdue a date with the fish.'

'With pleasure,' Chuck agreed eagerly.

As Rex's fat crony drew near, Kea bucked like a scalded bull and tried, with every cell in her body, to escape. Chuck was expecting it and dodged backwards. Her feeble attempt was answered with a slap. Hand-tied and weak, she toppled to her side.

Laughing to himself, Chuck manoeuvred his way behind

her. Her father sneered. 'Bring her to the deck, Chuck. I tire of her presence.'

Just as Rex was about to leave, a blood-curdling scream pierced the room. It did not come from Kea. She was just as befuddled by the outburst as her father. Another shout followed, this was the gruff bark of a man. Next there was a deafening crunch as though somebody had plummeted into a collection of barrels.

'What the –,' her father said, timidly sliding open the cabin door.

Whatever he saw had him slamming it firmly shut. All of a sudden, there was no king, but a pale boy whose playtime had just become all too real. He scarpered to the far wall, cowering besides Kea in his fear.

'D-defend me,' he muttered.

Chuck wobbled to face the oncoming threat and readied his axe expectantly. Kea, likewise, kept her eyes pinned on the cabin door. Neither of them could have imagined what happened next. Two colossal claws burst through and turned the wood to splinters. The owner of these weapons popped in a couple of eyestalks which sprouted from a frightful pale head. On spotting Chuck, the monster stepped into the cabin.

Then, with a war-cry, Chuck demonstrated guts that Kea thought he did not possess. As soon as the monster was within reach, he attacked with a powerful swipe. The blade came down onto its left claw-arm and passed straight through thick shell. Severed, the appendage dropped uselessly to the floor.

'Hah!' Chuck shouted victoriously.

The monster barely reacted. It appeared to look slowly at its injury and then back at the man who had caused it. With indifference, it proceeded as if nothing had happened.

This was enough of a scare to foil Chuck's frail confidence. The man started to back away, whimpering all the while. No mercy was shown. The monster stretched out its remaining pincer and clamped it around Chuck's substantial neck. Its hold tightened around rolls of fat, turning sobs to the strangled sounds of choking. With an empty hand, Chuck flapped at the rock-hard arm that throttled his air supply.

When all seemed lost, an inkling of survival instinct kicked in. Chuck appeared to remember that he held a war-axe in his other hand and made another desperate swing. He got lucky; the axe hit its target removing yet another one of the monster's limbs. The monster found itself missing both of its largest arms, not that it mattered. Although now lacking a body, the pincer was still compressed around Chuck's windpipe. As his chubby cheeks turned purple, he collapsed in a heap by his King.

Her father looked at his fallen crony and then at the approaching monster.

'Defend me,' he commanded at Chuck's wheezing mass. Desperately, he tried to wrench the pincer free. Rex's own weapon, a polished sword, was forgotten. Meanwhile, his back was foolishly turned to the oncoming danger.

'Defend me, defend me, defend me.' Despite her father's efforts, the claw around Chuck's throat did not move an inch and life seeped from his grasp. 'Defend me, you idiot!' her father roared.

All the while, the monster closed in. When it finally came within stabbing distance of Rex, however, it stopped short. Another crabman - for Kea was certain that it was the very creatures that Garth had described - entered the cabin and lurched its way closer. Like her father, Kea could not help but cower away from such a frightful sight. She highly doubted that these beings were following any kind of plan, no matter what Garth had told her. The crabman reached towards her with one of its ugly claws and Kea scrunched up her eyes, hoping for a short and merciful exit from the hell that had become her life.

SNIP!

There was no pain. Astonished, she slowly opened her eyes again to find that her hands were free. The rope that had bound her was neatly severed. The crabmen were now turned towards her pathetic excuse of a father. One of them had swung its beady gaze towards Kea, as if asking for permission.

'You,' said Rex, mouth gaping as it slowly dawned on him. 'You're in control of these beasts. You can stop this. Please, Kea, I beg you. Do not let them kill me,' he squealed. 'I'll do anything, anything you say.'

'Anything?' Kea smirked. 'How about you hand me that crown?'

Rex tossed it in her direction. Kea picked it up and twirled it around her finger contemplatively. 'I wish it was that simple,' she said, and she actually meant it. Despite all her father's flaws and his terrible deeds, Kea did not want to order his death. Unfortunately, she had to chop the head off the snake, pull out the weed from its root. Her dominance had to be unquestionable. Only then could her first acts as Queen begin to recover some of the damage that Rex had wrought.

'No,' Rex begged. He knew it all too well. 'Please don't.'

Kea smiled grimly at the man who had brought her people to the brink of extinction. 'Throw him overboard,' she said simply.

The crabmen took this instruction and leapt to the task. Together they wrapped their appendages around Rex, hauled him to his feet and wrestled him out of the cabin door. All the while he screamed and yelled, first with insults and then with futile promises. Kea placed the crown snugly upon her head and followed her loyal monsters.

It was all over horribly quickly. The fishermen and royals alike kept their distance. All seemed relatively unhurt, aside from a few who must have intervened when the crabmen arrived. They silently watched as their king was dispatched easily off of the side. Rex's rantings were cut short with a large plop as he plummeted to his death.

The crabmen completed their duty and returned to the sea, clambering over the side and onto the heads of more crabmen who stuck out of the water in the form of some unearthly human-ladder. Kea coolly paid little attention, as if it had been her plan all along. Maintaining a facade of strength, she strode to the bow and held her crown above her head.

'I am queen,' she shouted with a parched, dry throat.

Her crown shone in the rising sun. The connection between her rise to power and the monsters must have been clear. The captain of the ship, garbed in servant brown, knelt down on one knee. 'What should we do, Queen Kea?'

She did not even need to think.

'Retreat,' she commanded. 'Retreat! And reel in those rollers!'

When the wind came and sent the fleet forth, the only breaking that occurred in their wake was that of the surface. The sailors utilised its power to swing around and head instead for Solis Occassum.

One ship, however, did not follow. Kea thought nothing of it.

***

As Luke paddled down the distance, Solis Occassum slowly grew in size. He kept his eyes peeled for the eldership's mast, but something else caught his eye. On the horizon, about twenty ships were speeding towards the island. His heart leapt out of his mouth when he realised that this was no coincidence. The war was today. And he was too late. If the ships were heading home, they had already accomplished their terrible deed.

He let out a flurry of outrage and used it to power his swimming. Was he going to find a pile of rubble in the place of a town? Would there be Naufragians, minced by the brutal weapons of the surface? These thoughts niggled at him. To ensure that he was not seen by any of Rex's keen-eyed sailors, he ducked under the surface and continued his journey draped in a cloak of water. The ships passed ignorantly by and, Luke noted, dragged nothing along the seabed. Had they already finished the job?

A flash of orange below alerted him that Jaws had caught up. Luke dived to equal his depth. He soon saw their destination; out of the murk came a scattering of silhouettes. At long last, he had returned to Naufragium. Luke judged the condition of the wrecks and found that they were still whole. Well, as whole as they had been. He pushed himself onwards, fearful of what the rest of the town might reveal. The shelled street was still mostly intact and the homes looked as if they had been hardly scratched. What was going on?

It was eerily empty. If he had been watching an old western movie, he would have expected tumbleweed to drift eerily along the ground. Had everyone evacuated? Or was there something more sinister at play? He found the eldership and soared up its mast; it felt somewhat bizarre after having to climb it not so long ago. Reaching the third pair of mast arms, he hovered in a full circle.

The meadoweed acres were farmer-less and the street was without its normal bustling crowds. He was forced to look further afield and noticed a new blotch on the outskirts. Pushing from the mast with both feet, he flew towards it.

Moments later, it materialised into a large gathering of people. They appeared to be looking at the surface and waving their arms about. A terror seized Luke as he wondered what could have befallen them. He zoomed closer, kicking and pulling with Jaws at his side. Half their mouths seemed to be wide open in alarm. Some of them were colliding with the others as if uncertain of which way to flee.

Then, a welcome sound reached his ears and transformed all of his suspicions. He could hardly believe it.

Applause. They weren't panicking, they were *celebrating*.

***

When Cornelius had heard the command to retreat seeping from ship to ship, he had shaken with fury. Limping over to the captain, he had issued a ridiculous bribe. Flash some coin and they were like putty in his hands. The roller that he had scrupulously devised was heaved up and replaced with a common anchor. The sails that yearned to catch the wind were choked by ropes; his ship was going nowhere.

Why retreat? Cornelius thought. The ships had been primed to pulverise, yet, those fools had withdrawn his deathly construction before anything happened. He spat in derision. This escapade was more than a merry day out! It was his time. His legacy. Rex's spinelessness was not going to stop *his* plans. Somewhere in those waters was his amphibious boy and he had the means to go fetch him. He had intended to capture him during the chaos of war, but no matter. His weapons were no doubt more advanced than anything the fish-people could throw at him.

He stumbled over to his prized chest. It had taken six strong fishermen to haul aboard and it represented his life's work. From around his wrinkled neck, he ripped off a chain. He slotted the attached golden key into a padlock and twisted. Cogs whirred and latches clicked. The chest opened up, folded out, and collapsed, until it hardly resembled a chest at all. He stood before his masterpiece. Three vertical panes of oak, each covered with technology far beyond anything else. The central pane had a glass bowl at its head, a metal chest brace and armoured boots. Behind this, there were two tanks of oxygen, enough for him to spend hours beneath the water. Gloves were pinned to the panes either side; one armed with a harpoon gun, the other, with a single electrified net.

Ignoring the gapes of the simpletons around, Cornelius backed into his diving suit. The glass bowl sucked onto his head, the gloves tightened around his hands and the brace closed in around his torso. There was a sharp pain as it straightened out his crooked back. Afterwards, he felt stronger. Youthful, almost.

'Stay here for two hours,' he instructed, clunking to the ship's stern. He disconnected one winch from the roller and held on tight. 'If you see three tugs, reel me back up,' he said.

The men around him were dumbfounded. He gave a smirk. On return to the shore, they would spread his story like the plague.

'*Three*,' he repeated, in case it had not sunk into their primitive brains.

Without further ado, he grappled down to the seabed.

***

When Luke finally reached the Naufragians, they were so caught up in their merriment that they hardly noticed him. Some danced around with joy, others were clapping each other on the back. The crabman army stood motionless like discarded chess pieces. A circle had formed around a lifeless body which on closer inspection was that of Rex. Luke's curiosity grew unbearable and he looked desperately for his friends.

He saw that John and Limpet were bent over something or *someone*. Con was nearby, plonked on the sand and rubbing his face in distress. They were a stark contrast to the celebrating townsmen.

'Look!' he heard a man shout, pointing a finger in his direction.

'By the tides!' cursed a woman. 'He's swimming!'

'The Lord of the Sea has returned!' someone hailed.

Swooping down through the water, Luke brushed his feet along the sand. Jaws swam in front and gently collided with his forehead. As if by magic, Luke's buoyancy vanished and his ability to swim was gone. Although the sudden gravity came as a shock, he managed to maintain his upright position. Jaws flicked his tail in goodbye and then darted away. Luke gaped at him, only just realising how helpful the little fish had been. Before he could form the words to express his thanks, he was mobbed by a sea of exultant faces. One woman went so far as to grovel at his feet. 'Oh, Lord of the Sea,' she chanted. 'How can we serve you?'

'I'm not –' he started.

'He has saved us,' an old man wailed. 'He smote the surface scum.'

'I didn't – '

'Bring back the fish, oh Lord!' a woman came forth hesitantly with pleading eyes.

'Stop calling me that!' Luke snapped, and the people physically cowered.

'What should we call you then, oh Lord?' somebody said quietly.

'Luke!' he said. 'If you are going to call me anything, call me Luke! But you better know me as Lugworm.'

'Lugworm?' said a familiar voice.

The crowd parted and, arms wide, John ran to him. He suffocated Luke in a tight bear hug and whispered into his ear. 'You came back! I *knew* you would!'

Luke smiled at his old friend and, when he managed to catch a breath, asked a question to which he needed the answer. 'What happened here?'

'The crab army killed the surface king. If your friend's plan has worked, Kea rules now.'

'So the war is over?'

John nodded and then his face fell. 'But not without its victims.' He motioned behind him and Luke spotted a large body with scraggly hair. 'He died protecting Shrimp,' the man mumbled.

Luke rushed through the watching Naufragians. Limpet was knelt down, studying her fallen comrade with great sadness. She hardly seemed to register his arrival. Luke crumbled to her side and frantically tried to shake Stuart awake.

'Stuart,' he said in disbelief. 'But how?' Searching for the injury, he found a stab wound to the stomach. 'This did not come from the surface,' he growled, an anger flaring within.

Limpet looked at him for the first time, crestfallen. 'Con,' was all she said.

Something deep within snapped. Clenching his fists, Luke roared out a challenge. 'Con!'

There was a scuffling behind him.

'He's here, oh Luke,' said a woman proudly. 'Should I kill him for you?'

Luke turned around. Two men held Con firmly in place, while a woman threatened his throat with a sharp dagger. The madman was not struggling from their grip, but appeared to have accepted his fate. Revenge lured Luke with a tempting siren call that he dearly wished to answer. It would be quick and effortless. An eye for an eye. But, when Con raised his head to look at him, he seemed not a demon, but a man full of remorse.

'I'm sorry,' said Con.

Luke believed him; it was not enough. *Sorry* would not bring back Stuart. No punishment was too harsh, no pain too brutal. Stuart had saved Luke's life countless times and had believed in him when nobody else had. Now, he was dead and Luke had the power to avenge him. A single word from him and these misguided Naufragians would do the deed.

'Now, now,' said John, rushing in with his hands held up as if to ward off dangerous thoughts. 'I know it's tempting, but let us not be hasty. Con may be driven by the wrong emotions, but his motives have never wavered: to protect Naufragium. Besides, if you allow his death, it won't recover any of the damage done here. Might I suggest an alternative: let us banish him from this town. His love for this place is so great that this would be a punishment of equal severity.'

Everyone looked at him expectantly. The woman was poised with her knife, ready to take action, while John was studying him with pleading eyes.

'Banishment then,' Luke said quietly, before turning his back. He was dimly aware of the sound of Con's burdened footsteps, fading away into the distance. He did not even watch. Instead he turned his attention to his peaceful friend, wrapped an arm around him, and sobbed into his chest. The Naufragians were deadly quiet. Luke's anger was spent and all that remained was dreadful grief. Heedless of his audience, he wept and murmured some loving words to ears that would never hear again.

***

For the thousandth time, Garth ran his elongated tongue over his eyes. Was that truly Luke? Surely not. But each time he looked, there he was in perfect health. And he had made it back to Naufragium completely unaided. *Swimming*, no less. Once again, Luke had defied reality.

'Changer,' Penn purred in awe.

Garth wanted to leap up into the air, or spin around on his mother's chair until he became dizzy, or dance in celebration. This, however, would have seemed wildly inappropriate. It would have been like trying to turn a funeral into a party. Instead, he sat and savoured the heart-warming moment, wearing a pleased, albeit shocked, smile. He hardly cared if Luke had succeeded in his quest or not, he was just thankful to see him alive.

While he was chuffed at this unexpected reunion, he could not ignore Stuart. Another innocent life lost to his meddling. How many more to secure the dimension? He tried to remind himself that it was all for a worthy cause, but he felt a phony, pulling the strings of the future from the safety of his sealed room.

'I'm going in,' Garth said and, moments later, materialised above that mixed scene of celebration and grief. As there appeared to be no immediate danger, he tracked Con as the man stomped away from his hometown forever. He was walking somberly through the meadoweed fields, swatting feebly at the greenery as he went. Garth did not feel sorry for him in the slightest. Good riddance.

That was when Con, who was deep within his own haunted thoughts, tripped over something on the ground. The man took his time getting to his feet as though he did not have the heart to make the effort. Both Garth and Con realised simultaneously what had caused this minor blip; it was a pointed anchor embedded within the sand.

Garth's curiosity was piqued. He followed the anchor line up to find… A ship! One of Kea's! Even more alarming was that there was another chain attached to the ship's stern which led down into the depths of the meadoweed fields. It was shifting and shuddering as if something was caught on the other end.

What was the meaning of this? Garth's cheer was overtaken by a rising sense of alarm. Something was not right. He would have stayed to find out more, but his own problems took this inconvenient opportunity to come knocking. A high-pitched buzz of unfathomable volume attacked his ears.

What would make such an abominable noise? It was unbearable. So much so that he disconnected and removed his helmet in the hope of some relief. But the sound remained and was just as loud. It did not come from Euphausia, but from the very room in which he sat.

'The Gavoidon!' Penn shouted grimly.

Swivelling around reluctantly, he peered through the glass cabinet and towards his exit. White sparks spewed out from the base of the reinforced door, and Garth could see the tip of a silver razor spinning through layers of metal. His eyes bulged; the Gavoidon had arrived. The door-cutting device was sluggishly crawling up the leftmost edge. It would have to go around the door's perimeter to gain access.

He had some precious time.

***

Bloody seaweed. Cornelius's laboured breathing showed that his work had been a success, but all he felt was annoyance. He would have demanded that they move the ship if he'd have known that he was going to land straight on a damned forest. Now he had no idea where he was and his glass-bowl helmet was plastered with slimy green strands. He resorted to using his partially-deaf ears and, straining, heard the sounds of life:

crying, applause and the mumbles of a crowd.

He staggered towards it blindly. His suit had gifted him strength, but had ripped away whatever dexterity he had possessed. It put him in mind of Chuck, lumbering around and solving his problems by whacking them. A shiver of distaste ran through him at the very comparison. His brain was still sharp, even if his movements were slow.

Eventually, he emerged from the dense seaweed and swiped the strands from his helmet with a squeak. He saw them straight away. A whole town of people, just as the boy had said. They were dressed like beggars, but exchanged coherent snaps of conversation. To one side, he saw a frightful army of men who looked like some freakish merge of human and crab. Cornelius did not feel afraid. He was superior. They would either bow down in worship or run at the very sight of him.

As he stepped out, he grinned evilly. The amphibious boy was in clear sight. He appeared to be crying worthlessly over a fish-friend's carcass. Cornelius took his weapons off safety and ensured that the net would be ready.

'Too easy,' he muttered and closed in.

***

A woman's shriek just about managed to rouse Luke from his inconsolable heartache. He looked up wearily. An astronaut plodded doggedly towards them, each large boot coming down in a puff of sand. A trail of bubbles exited from a tube at his back where a pair of tanks protruded. His hands were swollen to a monstrous size by thick gloves and his face was lost in a glassy reflection. Almost puppet-like, a reinforced steel cable led from the suit up to a loitering ship.

Luke was underwhelmed, but the townsmen had never seen such technology. As the stranger advanced, they recoiled.

'Limpet!' John called from the crowd. 'Get away from there!'

She tugged at Luke's shoulder, begging him to follow.

His sadness, however, had numbed all fear and sense. He shrugged off her attempts and heard her sprint to the safety of the crowd. As he cradled Stuart's head, he looked at the approaching danger uncaringly.

'I should have killed you when I had the chance, boy.'

The voice had a weird quality as though it echoed from a tunnel, but he could easily recognise who had come to fetch him. Cornelius. The memory of urchin poison stirred some old, long-forgotten fear. Luke focussed on the glass helmet and saw the wart-lined face of his nightmares.

'Recognise me?'

'Yes,' said Luke through gritted teeth. 'I recognise you.'

'Then you know that you're coming with me,' he said, 'whether you like it or not.'

With this, Cornelius brought up his left arm and pointed it in his direction. Luke stared into the face of a barrel and sniffed indifferently. In slow-motion, a net shot out and spread like an attacking octopus. Like neurons in a human brain, he could see it pulsed with shoots of electric. Grief dampened his instinct to evade. Instead, he just sat there, useless, and accepted his grisly fate.

But his choice was taken from him.

There was a cry and John sprinted across its path. At the last second, the bearded man dived in front and the net's tentacles found a new victim. He landed horrifically, shuddering with violent spasms. It took a friend's sacrifice to jolt Luke out of his morose thoughts. Ignoring Cornelius, he sprang to his feet and ran to his friend. As soon as he touched the wire to wrench John free, a shock burned his hands and sent him flying to the side.

'That was my only net, you imbecile,' snapped Cornelius. 'Oh well, you're nearly as useful *dead*. Unless, you'll come willingly, that is!'

Luke stood up. 'Why would I do that?' he said defiantly.

'Glad you asked.' The old man raised his right arm and aimed at one of the lone crabmen. A harpoon streaked across the water and embedded itself in an unprepared head. There was a pained squawk, and, like a felled tree, its target pounded facedown in the sand. The Naufagians retreated even further. Nobody would dare intervene this time; this showdown was between Cornelius and Luke.

'That's why. Come with me and you will live... for a time.'

'That is no life. I will never come with you.'

'As you wish,' Cornelius said scornfully. The man took aim for Luke's head.

Then two things happened in quick succession. Firstly, Con charged out of the meadoweed fields and leapt onto the man's tanks of oxygen, jarring Cornelius's aim ever so slightly. Secondly, Cornelius still managed to shoot his missile. It whizzed towards Luke and, instead of neatly piercing his head as was intended, it stabbed into his ribs.

'No!' he heard Limpet scream as pain rocketed through his body.

Winded and mortally injured, his legs buckled beneath him. Looking down, he slid both hands down the cold steel shaft that disappeared into his own skin at the approximate location of where his sea-barnacles had started to grow. They had not offered him any protection; he was a dead man.

Through an agonising haze, he saw that his murderer was struggling with the unwanted weight of Con on his back. He had his legs wrapped around Cornelius' armoured neck and was not letting go. He had managed to draw Tooth, his trusty dagger. With a snarl, Con scrambled higher up and smashed down onto glass.

The first blow glanced harmlessly off of the helmet's rounded surface. Cornelius thrashed from side to side, but could not dislodge his burden. The slightest respite allowed Con a second stab. This one caused cracks to form and Cornelius let out an irritated shout. He changed tact and clumsily tried to remove the limpet from his back. Another attack to his helmet and water started pouring in. A gurgled cry exposed the old man's panic.

His transparent helmet was soon cloudy with seawater. Cornelius' suit was filling up and it showed in his movements. He started to sway from side to side, throw wild punches and spin in yet more vain attempts to dislodge Con. The Naufragium defender evaded as best as he could, but eventually one of Cornelius' gloved hands made contact and sent him sprawling to the seabed.

Cornelius reached upwards and grabbed the chain that connected his suit to the ship that waited patiently above. He gave three frantic tugs and a grinding sound commenced. The chain went taut and Cornelius's suit rose a few feet off of the seabed.

Like a trapeze act gone wrong, he began to swing about uncontrollably, tumbling through the meadoweed strands, almost colliding with some of the crabmen and, now and then, dipping down back onto the sand. It became clear that Cornelius was going nowhere; the extra weight from the additional seawater had completely foiled the escape attempt. Soon the winch gave way completely and Cornelius collapsed to the seabed with surplus loops of chain falling around him.

Stunned, a circle of Naufragians formed. Cornelius was still alive, but quickly running out of oxygen. He weakly pressed some hidden button on his suit and the whole device sprung open like a clam. The old man wormed his way out and the Naufragians, upon realising the pathetic being behind the monstrous mechanical suit posed no threat, charged in. A swarm of pitchforks, spears and angry faces engulfed him. However, before they could make contact, Cornelius disconnected the line between suit and ship, and latched it to his belt loop. Unable to talk and slowly turning more red, he still managed to give the incoming hoard a disdainful sneer before giving the rope three more tugs and being whisked away.

The Naufragians could only stare with disbelief as the invader was pulled out of reach. Cornelius shook his fist at them until he reached the surface where he was helped aboard the ship. Next, up went the rusty anchor and down came numerous oars; the final ship departed, making a beeline for Solis Occassum.

Con scrambled over to Luke and was the first to kneel down by his side. 'I tried to save you,' he said grimly. 'I'm sorry. I could not even avenge you. That monster escaped.'

'I know,' Luke wheezed. 'But you stopped him from getting what he wanted and you defended Naufragium. For that, you have my thanks.'

'I really am sorry about Stuart, you know. I don't know what came over me,' Con continued. 'Look, I need some time away, but, when I've sorted my head out, can you find it in your heart to let me return to this town? Naufragium is everything to me.'

'You may,' Luke relented.

Con gave him a gentle pat on the back and then walked off, leaving Naufragium for the last time in a while. Somewhere, deep down, Luke knew that the man's thirst for vengeance had been dampened. Maybe, wherever he was going, he would find some peace.

Limpet was over by John and appeared to be ripping him free of the net's confines. The electric charge must have worn off. With strength surprising for her slight size, she dragged her father free and pulled him all the way to where Luke sat. Her eyes flickered to the harpoon embedded in his side and her concern was horrifically blatant. Luke spoke before she could offer some meaningless words of comfort. 'Is John alright?'

At the mention of his name, the bearded man stirred. 'Better than you by the looks of things.'

Luke would have chuckled, but saved his energy. 'Cornelius escaped.'

'I wouldn't worry about that if I were you,' John winked. 'Kea rules now. All he's going to find back at that island is a jail cell. Besides, it looks like he forgot something.' John pointed at the discarded mechanical suit that was disarmed, but otherwise in almost-perfect condition. 'We may be a simple folk, but I bet we can learn a thing or two from the surface. Who knows, maybe one day we can make a reverse version and go see the surface people ourselves. Now, that would be interesting,' John mused.

'There's – ' Luke started, but a breath got caught somewhere and stopped his sentence short. For an alarming second, he thought it would be his last. Then, some pressure gave way and he could speak again. ' – some aquaseed… in the mermaid's purse.'

'Fetch it, Limpet,' John requested. She was the only able-bodied one of their trio and carefully reached inside Luke's backpack. He heard an incredulous gasp when she came across the jar.

'You did it. You actually did it!' she said, placing the bag behind Luke's head as a prop.

'Shame I… won't be around to see what it does,' Luke said miserably.

'You should be the one to release it,' Limpet stated whole-heartedly.

'She's right,' John agreed, passing Luke the glitter-filled receptacle. 'You've done the impossible, now take the glory.'

'…don't know what to do,' he puffed, managing to feel sheepish.

'Neither do we,' John reminded him.

'Okay… here goes…'

Each word was an individual battle so uncorking the jar was a challenging task. By this point, the townsmen had gathered around and had formed a cautious circle. When the cork eased free, it was so feebly done that there was no audible pop. However, the flowing substance spoke for itself. It coiled upwards like a sparkling rollercoaster and then smashed into the surface.

Poof!

It impacted at a needle's point, but then blew out in every direction. Soon the uppermost layer of water was starrier than a winter night's sky and more beautiful than anything the far reaches of space could offer. The Naufragians cheered, knowing that their troubles were at an end. In the following hours, Luke had to believe that minute organisms would flourish, small fish would gather and larger fish would hunt once more. It would not be immediate, but soon there would be enough food for all.

Limpet held Luke's head and gave him a lingering kiss. He knew, then, that it had all been worth it. He had been poisoned, captured, stabbed and mistrusted. One of his best friends was dead by his feet and his parents would never see him again. All this had started by picking up a mystical, blue shell. Yet, at the end of the day, Luke had saved a whole dimension. These people would continue after he had gone. He was a small drop of water in an ocean that would continue to thrive, with or without him.

He leaned back and gazed upwards at the change he had wrought. His breaths became shallow and his blood started to demand more oxygen than he could provide. The pressure in his chest grew and squashed his lungs. Despite his arduous condition, a feeling of infinite happiness welled up from within and would sustain him until the end.

CHAPTER 25: THE GAVOIDON

D IMENSION SAVED!
DIMENSION SAVED!
DIMENSION SAVED!

These flashing words caused crummy cartoon confetti to float down from the top of the screen. It seemed an underwhelming tribute to the sheer momentousness of the occasion. Luke and Garth had succeeded. Together, they were victorious. Although separated for the entire time, they had been a team, working across dimensions for this final end goal.

Turning away, Garth eyed his door. It was half-way to destruction, and he would soon have to face an ending of his own.

'We've done it,' he said wearily.

'Yes.' Penn's light seemed to glow admirably. 'We've saved an entire dimension from certain doom. Well done Garth Eonmore, it's been a pleasure.'

'You heading off?'

'Soon,' Penn admitted. 'I have a small amount of time left before I escape the clutches of Altersearch forever. Until then, I thought I'd keep you company.'

'Keep me company up until the end, you mean?' Garth laughed bitterly. 'How kind.' He had been living in constant fear of the Gavoidon's arrival and now that it was happening, he felt an odd relief. 'Where exactly will you go anyway?'

'Beyond,' Penn said excitedly. 'Into the network. Truth is, I don't know what I will find.'

'Well, good luck,' he said. Though Penn had tricked and lied her way to success, entrapping Garth and Luke in the process, she had genuinely seemed to want to save the dimension. Was it all that bad that she now had a chance to escape her own prison?

'It's time,' she said. 'Listen to me, Garth. You face a choice now. Because you've saved a dimension, a Quasar gem is going to be delivered to this room. Which means -'

'I can make another dimension shift!' he realised.

'Correct,' Penn confirmed. 'It'll be here any moment. You could use it to shift yourself out of here and save yourself from whatever lies outside that door. But be warned, it's *meant* to be used for shifting someone new to the next broken dimension. If you use a Quasar gem for your own purposes, Altersearch will be furious. You might live, but it will be forever in their pocket. Do you understand?'

'I think so.'

'Good,' she stated, her light suddenly glowing brighter and flashing more intensely than ever before. 'I have to go now.'

'Goodbye, Penn.'

It was blindingly bright now. The whole room was struck by all-encompassing green flashes that bounced off every surface. It almost dwarfed the firework display that was occurring around his door.

'I'll be in touch,' she said simply.

Unbelievably her light grew even more powerful, forcing Garth to shield himself beneath one of his wing-flaps. With a loud laser-like sound, the whole room shook and her bulb shattered into a thousand pieces.

She was gone, leaving behind a truly empty room.

Garth did not even have time to think about it. Moments later the sound of a champagne bottle being cracked open reached his webbed ears.

POP!

Garth found himself momentarily stumped. Until, that

is, he noticed the Dimension Shift cabinet was no longer empty. Leaping from his mother's chair, he rushed over and pressed his face against the glass. The metal claw now clasped a chunk of diamond. It was just as Penn had said! On saving a dimension, the Altersearch Company had delivered the next Quasar gem. He thought back to the instructional video that he had watched at the start of this debacle and the soldier-like, intimidating Gazoid who had shouted the strict rules of dimension shifting at him. Even over the mind-numbing racket of the room, he could hear Colonel Cougar's stern voice in his head. *A journey without return.*

Garth glanced at the furiously sparking vault door and the trail of molten metal dripping down its sides. He then flicked his gaze back at the screen; it showed a harpooned, confetti-covered Luke. Grabbing the helmet and plopping back into his mother's chair, he knew what had to be done.

***

The pain in Luke's chest ballooned to an unbearable level. Everyone sounded as if they spoke with their hands clamped over their mouths. At one point, he became mildly aware of Goby, kneeling down and offering some words of comfort. He hardly registered as the man apologised for doubting the quest and thanked him for bringing hope to Naufragium. Luke tried to give him a weak smile.

The way that his friends acted around him could not hide the direness of his situation. John sat by his side, looking grave, while Limpet's tough act had been stripped away. She kept kissing his cheek as if it would make everything alright. Their kind faces turned to blurs and their voices drifted away. Luke knew that he was losing his grasp on life.

Somebody, maybe John, shook his shoulder and shoved something into one of his slack palms. When they realised that he could not respond, they pressed something against his ear. From his left eye, he saw a blue glow waft across his vision.

Deep in his melting brain, a string of logic remained. The shell. He rattled in a breath to speak one last word.

'Garrrrffff?' he wheezed.

John removed the shell and placed it into his trunk pocket.

Somewhere, an alien smashed down on a big red button and an extremely loud rumble of thunder ripped across two dimensions.

***

Luke slapped down onto a frothy surface and saw a grey, overcast sky. Freezing cold water engulfed his vision. Instinctively, he tried to draw in air, but something swept down his throat and clogged his passage. A feeble arm movement brought him bobbing back up and he spluttered violently. Darkness swirled, threatening to take him away forever. The haunting caw of a seagull could be heard overhead and dark shadowy cliffs loomed close by.

He dedicated all his focus to trying to breath. It was a horrendous struggle of gasping and wheezing. In the back of his mind, a few bits of sensory information reached him. Two strong arms lifting his frail body from the sea. The padding of rushed feet across sand. The hum of an engine and the slam of a car door. Some incoherent stammering of panic and care. Finally, a soft bed and a piercing needle.

***

Behind Garth, the laser guns had shattered the Quasar Gem to smoking remains. He had no time to watch how his meddling planned out. As soon as he knew that the dimension shift had been a success, he ripped off the helmet and faced the door. The last of the sparks fizzled out and he was plunged into an ominous quiet. The heat radiating off the vault was intense. It no longer had anything to keep it in place and so tumbled outwards, hitting the corridor floor with a tremendous racket. A cloud of smoke was thrown up, hiding his assassin.

Furiously, he shouted out the potential passwords, hoping to disable the Gavoidon from its task.

'Holofilm!' he yelled.

'M-m-megabeetle!' he screamed.

'Gliding!'

It was all that he knew of his mum, blurted out in three pathetic words.

The smoke settled and a frightful being stood robotically in the doorway. Garth trembled and scrunched up into a tight ball. He braced himself for a roasting or a stabbing or a mincing. The robot took a step closer and a horribly sharp razor blade poked out of the haze.

'Megabeetle!' he tried again.

'What *are* you on about, Garth?'

It was a familiar voice. Kindness, with an edge of rebuke.

'Mum?'

The fumes cleared and standing there was his mother. Her wing-flaps were crossed and, in one hand, she held the tool that had sprung Garth from his trap. Shock quickly gave way to sheer relief. He bounced out of the chair, skirted the cabinet, and threw his arms around her. She stumbled slightly and went stiff; they rarely hugged. Ever. After a while, however, she dropped the door-cutter, relaxed, and draped an arm across his neck. Garth, still shaking, managed to utter some words of sense.

'I thought you were – '

'A Gavoidon, I know. You're very fortunate that I'm not one,' she scolded, removing him from the hug and holding him at arm's-length by the shoulders. 'Though you may soon wish that I was!'

'I'm sorry, Mum,' Garth apologised. 'I did not mean for any of this.'

'I believe you for the most part. Penn is a wily one, but clever though she is, there's no way that she forced you to sneak into my room while I was gone. That was all you, wasn't it?'

'Yes,' Garth admitted, looking down guiltily. 'How did you find out?'

'I was at Altersearch headquarters finding a replacement for Penn, after she became obsessed with that boy from Earth. She was completely convinced that he would save the dimension we were working on, and many more besides. Problem was, he was young. Far too young to leave his family and risk his life to help rescue a place that is so far beyond his understanding. Penn would not hear any of it, she was so eager to use him for her own purposes that she started to disobey my orders.'

'So you planned to erase her?'

His mother nodded regretfully, holding up a small black disc. 'That's the rules. Once a computer starts to go rogue, it's time to replace,' she paused. 'That's how she managed to override the lock on the door, you see. A perfect trap for my curious son.'

Garth looked at her sheepishly. 'I could not resist. You've always been so secretive.'

'Well now you know far more than is safe,' his mum snapped. 'Anyway while I was busy retrieving Penn's replacement, a friend from security told me that an illegal dimension shift had been carried out in my room and a Gavoidon was on its way. I left immediately and tracked it down, managing to disable it just a few branches from our home.'

Garth gulped. 'I really am sorry, you know.'

'I know,' his mum relented, drawing him back into a hug. 'I'm just glad you're alright. This room can be extremely dangerous to the unprepared mind. There are many ways to go insane in the dimension shift line of work. I'm just thankful that Penn did not push you too far.' She paused and then frowned. 'Speaking of which, Penn is being awfully quiet.'

'She escaped,' Garth said.

'What?' His mum jolted away from him and rushed to

the control panel. On seeing the broken bulb and the lifeless hardware, she smiled to herself. 'Well, I'll be damned.'

'You're not mad?'

'I did not want to replace her,' she admitted. 'I've been dreading it, truth be told. She was more than just a computer, she was a friend. I have no idea how she managed it, but she's free now. We cannot tell *anyone* about this.'

'Okay,' Garth agreed. 'As to how she managed it... something about a loophole in the coding for when a dimension gets saved.'

'But that would mean - ' Garth's mum's eyes flickered to the dimension shift cabinet, still smoking slightly from its recent use. 'You saved a dimension?' Her mouth dropped open. 'Explain.'

'Luke saved it really,' Garth grinned. 'It was quite an adventure.'

'Please tell me you did not use another Quasar gem to return him home,' she demanded with a pained expression on her face.

Garth's grin dropped. 'I did. He needs serious medical attention, the kind his home planet might be able to provide.'

'Might?' she screeched. 'Are you telling me you shifted him without even being sure that it would save his life?' Garth's dumbstruck silence was all the answer she needed. 'Those gems aren't toys, Garth! We're in enough trouble as it is.'

'Trouble?'

'Yes, trouble! The Altersearch Company is not one to be messed with. Do you understand how much those gems cost?'

'Sorry,' he mumbled.

'Don't apologise to me! Save it for the company. They will be the ones deciding your punishment.'

'My punishment?'

'I'm afraid so, my son. We have to go back to their headquarters as soon as we can and plead your case. Saving a dimension will help, but don't think for a second that you will be let off.'

It was all a bit too much. Garth started shuddering and returned, once again, to his mother's embrace.

'Now, now,' she chided softly, 'there's no point being scared about it. What's done is done. We'll go together and make a trip of it. It will take us weeks to get there and you can tell me your story on the way.'

This cheered Garth a bit, but not enough.

'You never guessed it by the way,' she added.

'Guessed what?'

'My password.'

'Well... what is it?'

'Garth,' she said, stroking the top of his head. 'It's Garth.'

***

The ruse that he was going through 'The Darkening' would no longer be needed. He peeled the warning sign from his bedroom door and entered his old den. He breathed it in. His lovingly crafted science-fiction models, his well-read magazines, and his overused game console. They were all just how he had left them. The nostalgia he felt was as claustrophobic as it was reassuring. As much as he loved his room, he no longer wished to spend all his days stooped away from the world outside.

Free of metal walls, sounds that had once merged with background noise now seemed strange. A chorus of frogs croaked and, far below, he could make out the soothing bubbling of the swamp. Even the familiar, yet annoying, sounds of another episode of Swamp Soap made him smile. His mother's commanding voice came from the same location.

'Stop!' she called, turning off the holofilm projector.

'Hey!' it was too late to hide the complaint in Rawder's words before she realised who she addressed. 'Miss Eonmore, you're back!'

'I am, and I shan't need your services anymore.'

'How come?'

'You will be paid for your hours,' his mother said haughtily, ignoring her question, 'but your employment is at an end.'

Garth chuckled as he heard Rawder grumble and start gathering her stuff. He would not miss his supervisor, no matter how pretty she was. He kicked the can of Slarg, grabbed a bag and started packing it full of clothes. Then, a thought occurred and he popped his head out of his room. 'How are we going to get there, Mum?'

'Gliding, of course,' she answered from the sitting room. Garth went pale and, by his lack of response, she knew his fear. 'You have to learn at one point.'

'I know,' he gave in with a groan. He was about to start repacking with some warmer thermals when something nagged at him. There was no way he was setting off without knowing if Luke lived. 'How long until we set off?'

'Once we inform Altersearch, they'll want to see us for a trial and there'll be paperwork to do. I reckon we have a week until we need to start our journey.'

'Can I use your room in the meantime?' he asked.

She would know to which room he referred and she would also know why.

'Fine, but don't be long and don't do anything significant,' she called back.

Garth ran down the corridor, vaulted over the scrap metal and made his way to the computer.

***

As soon as the needle pierced through Luke's ribs, the built-up pressure suddenly dropped and he gulped in a desperately-needed breath of oxygen. With his next hungry lungful, his vision seeped back and two fuzzy heads peered down at him from a spotlessly-white ceiling. A water drop dribbled down his cheek. He took a third staggered breath and their features swam into focus.

'Mum,' he wheezed at one, then turned to the other.

'Dad.'

Whatever they said in return was lost to sobbing. Another flurry of tears caught his face and was joined by a trickle from his own eyes. They clutched his hands so tight that they almost cut off his circulation. To see them again was more than he could have possibly hoped for. His Dad was the first to speak, pulling himself together with a firm shake of the head.

'We waited for you, son,' he said. 'We knew you would come back to us.'

'I've missed you both, so much,' Luke replied. 'I can't even begin to explain - '

'Don't,' Mum cut him off gently. 'Right now, just focus on breathing.'

As he lay there, they explained that the harpoon had been stuck in one of his lungs and had been stopping it from expanding. Upon reaching the hospital, the doctors had administered a needle which had immediately released the pressure and enabled him to breathe once more. From that point onwards, with the support of the machines available at the hospital, he was going to be alright and would eventually make a full recovery from his exploits.

As for his parents, they had seen him disappear in a tremendous flash of blue light on that seemingly ordinary day at the beach. They had immediately called all the available services. Their original story had been quickly dismissed as the rantings of two very stressed parents. In the following few days, the sea and beach had been scoured for any signs of Luke. Fishermen, helicopters, lifeguards and a team of volunteers had joined the fray. Deep down, however, his parents knew they would not find him, that something truly bizarre had taken Luke away.

As such, and devoid of any other options, they had refused to leave the beach where they had last seen Luke. So when he appeared in the shallow waters hailed by thunder and lightning, his parents were the first to reach him and whisk him off to the hospital. His survival had been deemed miraculous, but not impossible. The harpoon had been explained as an unfortunate clash with some broken up debris that had come from one of the nearby wrecks.

Luke was amazed to hear that it had only been three days. He had been away for at least a week, though it had felt longer given all that had occurred. The only explanation was that there was an odd time difference between the two places.

That afternoon, however, he did not waste time pondering it. He was finally reunited with his parents. Every second felt as precious as gold. Luke committed each glimpse of his parent's faces to memory. Part of him worried they might be snatched away from him at any given moment. Despite his fears, they remained by his side as his strength slowly returned. They did not try to coax an explanation out of him, but rather told him what had happened during his disappearance. He soaked up their words, smiling gratefully all the while.

When his parents eventually left the room to grab some much-needed refreshments, he spared a thought for Limpet and John. It had been such an abrupt departure. He hoped that they were happy and supposed he would never see them again. For that, his elation was tinged with sadness.

He looked wondrously at the hermit crab shell that adorned his bedside table. Aside from the harpoon, which had now been dismissed as some wartime relic, it was the only evidence that he had of his adventure. The small patch of barnacles that had once risen from his skin had been sheared off by the damage done by the harpoon. Furthermore, he knew that his parent's original story of how he disappeared would eventually be lost to the archives, used only to stir up some keen-eyed, eager alien-abduction fanatics. Therefore, aside from his family, nobody would ever believe what he had experienced.

Luke mulled it over and found that he simply did not care. What mattered to him was that he was home and alive, and there was one person to thank for that, even if he was the very reason that Luke had found himself in such a predicament in the first place.

'Thank you, Garth,' he said to the empty room.

***

Garth stood on the top floor of his building with the wind passing smoothly over his head. He peered over the edge of a wooden balcony. Colossal branches spiralled down the tree upon which Tamaranga was built. Across a terrifying distance was a landing pad – their first destination. Below this, a toxic swamp waited to claim its next victim.

'How was your friend?' his mum asked, appearing behind him.

She did not need to say who. Garth had been checking on him every morning. Time on Earth had ticked by horrifically slowly. He had spent days on tenterhooks as the events of Luke's rescue and medical care had slowly unfolded. He had seen enough, however, to feel confident in his assessment.

'Alive,' Garth replied. 'Just.'

'Are you ready?'

'As ready as I'll ever be.'

He gulped and brought a pair of goggles down to protect his eyes. Opening his arms, he displayed his wing-flaps for a second and then shut them in a flash of embarrassment.

'Do I need to push you?' mocked his mum.

'No, certainly not,' Garth retorted.

He curled his webbed feet over the edge and steeled himself. Before cowardice could take hold, he thought of Luke, that brave soul who had been catapulted into the unknown only to land on his feet and run until all had been solved for the better. It was inspiring. Garth decided that there was only one thing for it.

He jumped.

To Be Continued...

EPILOGUE

Our people grew hungry, our lives asunder,
So the Lord sent his Son, hailed by thunder,

The Son strode into town with rope in tow,
He fixed the bell, breathing above and below,
He single-handedly stopped an attack mid-trawl,
And with these feats, gained the trust of all,

The Son journeyed to the Land with a trusting hand,
To find that the King was as coarse as sand,
His Daughter, meanwhile, had the Sea at heart,
Proof that Lord and Land weren't always apart,

The Son was captured and war was decreed,
But not before learning about precious Aquaseed,
On top of Turtle, The Son escaped back home,
And the deep-sea depths, he began to comb,

Lord's answer to the King was a crabman platoon,
Armies amassed, tensions set to balloon,
But the Lord showed mercy on the King's Daughter,
Only the King himself would be claimed by the water,

By claw and command, the King was overthrown,
And succeeded by one we consider our own,
The Son then arrived, swimming with his plunder,
He saved the Sea and disappeared in thunder,

Years have passed, but this tale still runs strong,
The Queen rules the Land and may she live long.

- *A famous ballad known by both sides of the surface.*
   -

The sea lapped calmly against the golden sands and caressed the land with its touch; birds cawed overhead; a pleasant breeze perfectly balanced the glowing heat of the sun and all was quiet as the gathering waited with bated breath. Kea sighed. Another glorious day on Solis Occassum.

Even in her father's reign, she had often come to the bay and stared out adoringly at the horizon. Back then, it was far easier to look out to sea and dream than to turn around and wallow in the poverty that was growing like a tumour on her island. Now, she was pleased to admit that, had she felt inclined, she could have looked inwardly at her island and felt just as content. The beauty of the sea now extended beyond the bay and into the town, all the way up to her palace at the top.

She brought her hand up to her eyes to shield them from the sun. They brushed against the slightly heated metal of her crown that rested reassuringly on her head. The crown was heavy enough, both in what it represented and the weight of its material, but, with time, her shoulders had borne that burden and grown strong as a result. Without Rex, she had finally been able to make decisions and put plans in place that she had always yearned to.

Cornelius had been the first problem. As soon as he had returned, Kea had locked him up in the very jail cell where Luke had almost been tortured. His evil use of science was slowly being forgotten by all. Kea had then appointed Margaret as her personal advisor and, together, they had turned the palace into more a science school than a place of royal residence. Margaret had taken on a number of students and, when she was not by Kea's side, she was busy researching and experimenting. She still mourned Bart, but, now that the days of Cornelius were long gone, her love for science had been rekindled.

And what a time to be a scientist, thought Kea. With the war averted, and Kea's allegiance still fresh in the minds of those underwater, an opportunity arose to open up communications. From high up the island, they had sent forth a number of gliders; these had sailed on the wind and gently cruised down to the approximate location of the underwater town. Each one had contained crude drawings, all designed to lead the sea-people to Solis Occassum's golden bay where they could more easily exchange messages.

Solis Occassum's first message had been a gesture of good will; a number of glass bottles, each with a treasure inside, had been thrown into a healthy depth. It had taken a few days, but one momentous morning the beach had been littered with five juicy fish and a carved figurine with a rough resemblance to Luke. From there, the trade gates were flung wide open. The island had provided a range of useful items and trinkets to the sea, and had received bountiful amounts of fish as their reward. It became evident very quickly that Luke had found aquaseed and rejuvenated the sea, just as they had plotted.

While trade boomed, Margaret worked hard to devise better ways of communication. Through pictures and basic words, she slowly taught the sea-people to read and write; a rare skill even among those on the land. It soon became apparent that their wants were more specific than previously thought. They yearned for tools and clothes, not jewellery or trinkets. The island responded as such and, slowly but surely, the trust between the two blossomed.

Under Kea's instruction, her people set up a winch system involving two lines that stretched from the land and down into the ocean. At day break, labourers would send down baskets of utensils and bundles of clothing and at sunset, the very same baskets would be hauled up to the land full of fish for all. Starving was a problem of the past. As such, Kea released all of the turtleoak turtles which she had been retaining as a last resort. Their shells would no longer be needed for ships and therefore they could be returned to the ocean in earnest.

As their relationship grew and their communication skills developed, the sea-people revealed what had happened on that fateful day where their two communities had almost clashed. John, their esteemed leader, had detailed how Cornelius, in his haste to escape, had left behind a suit capable of giving the ability to breathe underwater.

When Cornelius had been confronted on the subject by Margaret, he had bitterly resolved to take it to his grave. Margaret had not been deterred. She wrote to John asking for a full description of the suit. A week hence she was poring over detailed carvings, diagrams and a full inventory of every tank, glove and pipe. Aided by her students, she then sent John full instructions, extra pieces and new tools.

That was why they were here. That was why they had gathered on the beach today. It was time to see whether Margaret and John's efforts would bear fruit, hailing a new era of science that could only benefit all.

Kea waited and waited in humble browns; a show of solidarity with all those on the island. Margaret, as always, was by her side, sat down in the shade of a stray palm tree on an outcrop of rock. Behind them, whispering quietly and respectfully, were all of her people that had managed to take a rest from their duties in order to witness what had been promised to be a momentous occasion.

Kea was just about starting to doubt that today would be the day. Perhaps a technical issue or a change of heart had occurred. It was, after all, a very brave and dangerous task to undertake.

That was when, to the surprise of all gathered, a number of turtleoak turtles lumbered from the sea and onto the sands, cawing distinctively and wisely observing all with their bulbous heads and warty necks. It was completely outside of breeding season so such an appearance was unprecedented. Kea's doubts were extinguished; something truly special was about to occur.

Now that she had full access to the palace's books, she had indulged in delving into every bit of sea-related literature. Through her efforts, she had stumbled on many a story that spoke of beings that represented the sea in three different forms; a small orange fish who can pass on boons; a crabman capable of spying on the land; and finally the turtleoak turtles, friend to all who has the sea's interests at heart. Now, she fully realised that this was more myth than science, but seeing that the latter was present on this day filled her with excitement. The sea was watching.

Feeling like the time was right, Kea instinctively strode forwards. The buzz of her people quietened as all eyes, human and turtle, followed her down the beach. She reached the boundary and, acting casual, nonchalantly dipped her bare feet in the cooling waters. In reality, her gaze was excitedly piercing the surrounding area, searching for any signs of movement.

Sure enough, bubbles and froth surfaced a short span away with an unignorable gurgling noise. Kea's heart began to flutter with anticipation. From this white mess rose a spherical glass bowl followed by two unwieldy shoulders of metal and cogs. Moments later, protruding tanks could be seen and, next, a couple of gloved hands. Knees and legs formed, moving sluggishly but determinedly to where Kea stood. With each second, the mechanical man came closer and the waters around him grew shallower.

Until, to Kea's absolute delight, they were basically stood face to face. Within the glass bowl that formed the headpiece, and through the clear seawater which filled it to the brim, she made out a voluminous beard tucked snugly within its confines and a friendly smile topped with kind, brown eyes.

'John,' she greeted.

'Kea,' he replied. A giant glove reached out and enclosed her own slender offering as the two of them shook hands joyously, much to the celebration of the crowd behind. 'Nice to finally meet you.'

The peace between the waves had truly begun.

*This book is a small fish in a very big pond.
Please could you help it survive by leaving
an honest review on Amazon?*

ACKNOWLEDGEMENTS

First and foremost, this book would be a shadow of its current self if it weren't for my beloved sister, Jessica Tucker, who somehow found the time in her own chaotic life to edit my book not once but twice. How she found the energy and dedication I will never know. Needless to say, I am forever in her debt.

Secondly I must thank my family, all of which had to read my attempts on multiple occasions and tolerate my obsession with writing, whether we were on holiday or half-way through the working week. Their constructive criticism and feedback meant the world to me and helped me to become who I am today.

Next, I would like to call out to the kindness of strangers. This book has been a long time in the making and, as I sunk days of my life into piecing it together, I experienced my fair share of doubt. Sharing the first three chapters on social media after years of uncertainty was a big step for me, but one that I ended up enjoying thanks to a certain reader (Nikki Scanlon) and her daughter Katie. Their kind words and willingness to read more made me feel like my toil was worthwhile. Thank you.

Similarly, I would like to thank my friends who also managed to make their way through the first three chapters (and in some cases further). Life is super busy and even finding the time to read a polished, published book can be a struggle. The fact that so many gave my book a shot with so much else going on in the world really means a lot to me.

I also would like to mention the numerous primary schools (and their fantastic students) that offered to help me on this journey by critiquing my first three chapters. So here are a few shout-outs:

- Ms Warren of Goosewell Primary Academy (Year 6 (Class of 2020))
- Ms Jaques of Temple Grove Academy (Years 5 and 6 (Class of 2020))
- Ms Hawkridge of Wellfield Middle School (Years 5 and 6 (Class of 2020))

All feedback received, good or bad, was treasured and taken on board. Thank you very much to both the teachers and their students.

Finally, I would like to thank my girlfriend, Jemma Drake, who simply amazes me on a daily basis. Not only does she put up with me and all my flaws, but she supports me in my fool's errand to become a professional writer. Our adventures together fuel my writing. May there be many more.

ABOUT THE AUTHOR

Samuel Harmsworth

Samuel Harmsworth is an unashamed sucker for science fiction and fantasy, a graduate in Marine Biology and a self-confessed wannabe fish. He grew up in sunny Devon and enjoyed a pleasant upbringing in a small, peaceful village called Bere Alston. His love of the sea started with his regular holidays to Cornwall where he would consistently fail at surfing and end up at the mercy of the currents. His university degree in Applied Marine Biology at Bangor University, North Wales, only encouraged him. Three years by the sea in the smallest city imaginable with good friends, rocky shores aplenty and enough pubs to make any outing memorable (or particularly unmemorable - see previous point: there were many pubs). Having finished university, he had the opportunity to go on an exciting gap year, but (rather foolishly some might say) he opted for spending six months writing a book that had been brewing in the back of his mind and simply had to be put to paper. Afterwards, he struggled to find UK-based jobs in Marine Biology and instead spent a couple of months as a disgruntled ice-cream man before finally moving to Tunbridge Wells, Kent. Now he is a Data Analyst by day and a writer by night (or dawn as this is his preferred writing time).

Printed in Great Britain
by Amazon